Praise for
CHILD OF LIGHT

"A fresh world, a new voice, but the same high quality Brooks always delivers. You'll be glad you joined the expedition."
—Robin Hobb, *New York Times* bestselling author of *Assassin's Fate*.

"*Child of Light* is enchantingly feral. Precise in his prose, clever in his worldbuilding, Brooks stretches new muscles to explore a young woman's quest for identity. The pace is rapid as a river, but this one twists hard and runs deep."
—Pierce Brown, #1 *New York Times* bestselling author

"With *Child of Light*, Terry Brooks continues to enchant both long-time fans and generations of new readers."
—Peter V. Brett, *New York Times*
bestselling author of *The Desert Prince*

"With a unique setting that is a heady dystopic blend of mysticism and the future, *Child of Light* is an otherworldly adventure from the fertile mind of one of the most beloved storytellers of our generation."
—Wesley Chu, #1 *New York Times*
bestselling author of The War Arts Saga

"Terry Brooks unleashed is a wonderful thing. In *Child of Light*, he's teasing us with a world that is both fairy tale and deadly serious, and keeping us off-guard the entire time, unsure of how to take . . . anyone and anything. It's not really a "mystery," but it is, and even with the startling reveals, there's so much more left to explore and discover. I want to go back to Viridian Deep and know that I will."
—R. A. Salvatore, author of The Legend of Drizzt series
and the Demon Wars Saga

"Brooks's first fantasy since retiring the long-running Shannara series offers an enticing new mystery while delivering enough familiar elements—in both tone and worldbuilding—to make his fans feel right at home. . . . Auris is a tough but enchanting protagonist, and the page-turning mystery of her magical origins form the novel's heart. Brooks's fans will be thrilled to have a new series to savor."
—*Publishers Weekly*

BY TERRY BROOKS

SHANNARA

SHANNARA

First King of Shannara
The Sword of Shannara
The Elfstones of Shannara
The Wishsong of Shannara

THE HERITAGE OF SHANNARA

The Scions of Shannara
The Druid of Shannara
The Elf Queen of Shannara
The Talismans of Shannara

THE VOYAGE OF THE JERLE SHANNARA

Ilse Witch
Antrax
Morgawr

HIGH DRUID OF SHANNARA

Jarka Ruus
Tanequil
Straken

THE DARK LEGACY OF SHANNARA

Wards of Faerie
Bloodfire Quest
Witch Wraith

THE DEFENDERS OF SHANNARA

The High Druid's Blade
The Darkling Child
The Sorcerer's Daughter

THE FALL OF SHANNARA

The Black Elfstone
The Skaar Invasion
The Stiehl Assassin
The Last Druid

PRE-SHANNARA

GENESIS OF SHANNARA

Armageddon's Children
The Elves of Cintra
The Gypsy Morph

LEGENDS OF SHANNARA

Bearers of the Black Stuff
The Measure of the Magic
The World of Shannara

THE MAGIC KINGDOM OF LANDOVER

Magic Kingdom for Sale—Sold!
The Black Unicorn
Wizard at Large
The Tangle Box
Witches' Brew
A Princess of Landover

THE WORD AND THE VOID

Running with the Demon
A Knight of the Word
Angel Fire East

VIRIDIAN DEEP

Child of Light
Daughter of Darkness

*Sometimes the Magic Works:
Lessons from a Writing Life*

CHILD
OF
LIGHT

CHILD
OF
LIGHT

TERRY BROOKS

NEW YORK

2022 Del Rey Trade Paperback Edition

Copyright © 2021 by Terry Brooks
Excerpt from *Daughter of Darkness* by Terry Brooks
copyright © 2022 by Terry Brooks

Published in the United States by Del Rey, an imprint of Random House,
a division of Penguin Random House LLC, New York.

DEL REY and the CIRCLE colophon are registered trademarks of
Penguin Random House LLC.

Originally published in hardcover in the United States by Del Rey, an imprint of
Random House, a division of Penguin Random House LLC, in 2021.

This book contains an excerpt from the forthcoming book
Daughter of Darkness by Terry Brooks. This excerpt has been set for this edition
only and may not reflect the final content of the forthcoming edition.

ISBN 978-0-593-35740-8
Ebook ISBN 978-0-593-35739-2

Printed in the United States of America on acid-free paper

randomhousebooks.com

4 6 8 9 7 5

Book design by Edwin Vazquez

FOR JUDINE

MY NORTH STAR

CHILD
OF
LIGHT

ONE

WE BREAK OUT AT MIDNIGHT, JUST AS WE AGREED. LIKE ghosts risen from our graves to reclaim the lives that were stolen from us, we flee.

We are quick and we are fast, one following the other, staying in order the way Tommy has taught us, pretending it's just a drill, knowing it isn't. No one speaks, no one whispers; no one makes any sound they can avoid. There are no mistakes because there can be no mistakes. Others who have tried to escape this facility before have all made at least one mistake. And all are dead.

Courage, I tell myself. I am desperate to get free. We all are. *Don't think. Just go!*

There are fifteen of us—too many for what we are attempting. But once someone is in, it is impossible to decide later that they are out—unless of course you are willing to kill them to keep them from talking. I couldn't do that. None of us could. We're just kids. Ordinary kids in other circumstances; something else now. But still, just kids, not killers. Not yet, anyway. None of us has killed anyone—except maybe JoJo. He says he has, but we can't be sure about what he has or hasn't done. He's big on talk, but you can usually tell when someone is padding the truth, making himself appear to be something he isn't. We all thought that was what he was doing.

But still we wonder.

We started out as a group of eight: Tommy, Malik, Barris and Breck, Wince, JoJo, Khoury, and me. That would have been enough if together we possessed the skills and knowledge that are needed. But we need more to make this escape happen, as we find out quickly enough once we begin to talk our way through the plan. So we are forced to bring in other kids. It is easy enough to choose the ones we are looking for. All we have to do is keep our eyes and ears open until we discover the handful we need. There are only about 330 of us in the camp. I don't know if other camps exist.

Still, I assume there must be more. Given this one's purpose, there pretty much have to be. It's simple mathematics. Our captors number in the hundreds. We call them Goblins—though in truth we have no idea who or what they really are, save not Human. Piggish faces, warped and twisted limbs, bodies much larger than those of Humans, skin hanging loose in gray mottled folds, voices that communicate as often with grunts and snorts as with words. They are despicable creatures that transcend our worst nightmares. The kids in the prison are here to serve them. We are brought here from all over and raised in captivity. Our lives are predetermined. Someone is needed to maintain and operate the hydroponic farms and weapons factories. But the Goblins require something else from us in payment for their services as our jailers. Goblins are carnivores and require fresh meat, so prisoners offer a ready source of both food *and* labor.

Our fates as prisoners are fixed. From the moment we arrive, all of us must work to maintain or repair the prison and grounds or be eaten. The disabled, weak, and injured kids are dispatched early. Those who remain healthy and able-bodied are allowed to grow until they are deemed adults and then sent to the reproductive pens, the work farms, and the factories. Unless, as sometimes happens, overpopulation of the prison requires a culling. Then the healthy are eaten, too. Our numbers are never allowed to fluctuate far. If too many die, new kids take their place. Where do the Goblins find them? Where did they find any of us? How are we chosen? No one knows. I don't know what I am doing here, and this seems to be true for the others as well.

The one common denominator we all share is that no one seems to miss us. Some of us are orphans. Others had families—gone now? I wonder if it is the same in the other camps, the ones we never see. Is it different for them? I don't know; I have no way of knowing. I just hope it isn't something worse.

All of us are between the ages of ten and twenty. Adults and little kids are kept elsewhere; we don't know where. Kids like us are designated as worker bees until we are determined to be old enough for transport to the reproductive pens. There we are paired off and forced to make babies. Once you spend enough time in the pens to renew the population, you are shipped out to work the farms and factories. If you are unable to reproduce or work, you are retired. That's what it is called—*retired*. A euphemism for *executed*. Put down because you no longer serve any useful purpose. Disposed of because, if you can't work and you can't reproduce, you are just taking up space. Sometimes they keep you for other reasons—but not often and not for long. And not for pets. Goblins don't have pets. Just those monstrous things they call Ronks, and those are used primarily for hunting. You can imagine what sort of hunting, right?

I am nineteen years of age, as best as I can tell, but the Goblins don't know it. I look very young for my age. Luck of the draw. Because in another year, maybe less, they'll quit caring how I look. They will send me to the pens anyway. I have already made myself a promise. I won't make babies for them. I will die first.

The fifteen of us trying to break free have agreed about what is going to happen. There are only two possibilities. *All of us will get out or none of us will.* If it is the latter, there is no point in wondering about our future. If it's the former, we will be hunted like animals—because, like I say, that is how the Goblins see us.

We go out of our cellblock in two groups—one of seven, one of eight—using lockpicks fashioned during the weeks of planning, opening all the doors we can to allow others to do what they want so long as they understand they are not to follow us. Some try anyway because they see it as their only chance, but JoJo discourages them as only JoJo can. What happens to them after that, I don't know. I can't stop to think about it because when you are on the run you don't have time to think about anything but what's going to happen if you are caught.

Once clear of the cells we take out the night guards who patrol the walkways—a process carried out by Tommy and Malik using makeshift knives one of our group has fashioned from stolen pieces of shop metal. Their efforts are quick and silent, and the blood on their clothes marks a rite of passage. We race down the stairs to the cellars and through the storage areas. The Goblins don't see us; they don't hear us. Guards standing watch outside the doors of the compounds have no idea yet what is happening inside. Why would they even think about it? You don't think much about your animals once they are safely penned in for the night. You just lock them in and come back for them in the morning. Escape? To what end? Even if we get out, where will we go? We will be missed quickly enough during the morning count; we will be hunted down and brought back. Most will be made an example of. I have seen what that means; they assemble everyone to watch. It isn't something you are likely to forget. It takes a long time to die when you are systematically dismembered. It serves as a useful deterrent to further escape attempts.

Except that sometimes even that isn't enough. When survival means you live in a cage and are reduced to the life of an imprisoned animal, a chance at freedom is worth any risk.

The tunnel we crawl through is actually an old drainage pipe. It is only used during the flooding periods, and we aren't in one now. Finding the pipe was a rare piece of luck. At first we figured we'd have to climb over or tunnel under the prison walls, using rope ladders for the former or endless digging for the latter. But Wince found the opening to the pipe by accident one day while mopping the cellar floors. It lay behind an iron lid fastened to the stone block wall, but he could tell the lid was meant to open and close and he figured out how to do it. Next time he was sent down he carried lockpicks concealed in the soles of his shoes. It took him only minutes to release the seal on the lid. Once he got that far he wriggled his way inside (being every bit as supple and stretchy as a desert cat) and found a hatch that opened into the pipe. Not long after that, he was moved from mopping floors to organizing store-rooms, but he still risked everything to slip away and unseal the hatch, crawl inside, and follow it both ways, discovering that one direction took you to what appeared to be a very deep spill pit and the other to beyond the walls and a way out onto the wastelands.

It was Tommy who decided this is how we would escape. A grate seals the far end, but that is hardly enough to stop us if we can make a substance that will melt and break the lock. A big problem without access to chemical corrosives, but then Khoury surprised me by saying she could provide what we needed from the dissolvent she works with in the labs. What was left was to figure out when we would go and how we would survive once we were outside the walls. How big are the wastelands? How many miles would we have to walk to cross them? We were all either born in prison or brought here from other places, and we don't know where anything is. But Tommy found a way onto the roof one day on the pretense of checking for damage after a storm, and his report was deeply troubling. There is nothing but open ground and scrub brush for as far as the eye can see.

No one knows for sure what is out there. How are we supposed to stay alive knowing so little?

But Tommy had an answer for this just as he did for everything. He is the son of survivalists after all, and he knows how to stay alive in any environment. He knows where to find food and water. He knows how to hunt and camp and hide so we can't be found—how to create a false trail and conceal his tracks. You can't learn how to do all that unless you've done it, and he has. Unlike the rest save for me, he lived free until he was in his teens, when a Goblin patrol caught his family in the open and took them prisoner. Tommy was brought here. He doesn't know what happened to his parents—he never saw them again—but Tommy is a survivor; we all know that. We designated him as our leader because he is our best chance for staying alive.

Tommy chose me first for his escape plan because I know something of the larger world—although not as much as I pretend—and because I have made it clear that I am determined not to be left behind. We are attracted to each other, and we share confidences. Together—to the extent such things are possible behind prison walls—we make a good team.

Others were added to our little team as time passed. Carefully added. We are a diverse group, united by a common goal but fully aware of the risk we are running.

Girls and boys are housed together in indiscriminate fashion save for one rule: Opposite sexes are never allowed to share the same cell. Reproduction is tightly controlled, and forbidden altogether where we are. Tommy's cellmate is Malik; mine is Khoury—which is one of the reasons she ended up coming with us. But twin sisters are housed on one side of JoJo's cell, and he got to know them pretty well. It was his suggestion we bring them along. Barris and Breck are twins, even though they don't look very much alike. Breck is a chameleon, Barris unchanging. Breck knows how to make things out of scraps and leavings others would never think to bother with. She can fashion clothes, boots, gloves, and hats to protect against the sun, because exposure poses a definite risk if you are caught out in it for too long. Barris is wise and centered and a good source of advice. She always knows what needs to be asked and answered, and someone like that can do a lot of good when you are on the run.

Malik is big and strong, and there was never any question about including him. He is able to lift and haul like a machine. Nothing seems to be beyond him. Incongruously, he is one of the more docile and obedient of us. He is quiet most of the time, seldom chooses to speak—just sits there listening. He latched on to Tommy early, follows him about like a pet dog, and does whatever Tommy asks of him. This can prove to be a problem if Tommy isn't smart about the influence he wields over Malik, but he is careful never to abuse it. After all, it is important to have someone who possesses that size and strength on your side. Still, if Malik ever switches his allegiance or decides Tommy has betrayed him in some way, there will be problems.

We crawl through the drainage pipe in single file, Tommy in the lead, Khoury right behind so she can use the substance she has stolen from the camp labs to break down the metal of the locks and allow us to get out once we reach the grate. We go in single file, same as before, no talking, and no sounds at all. We crawl in darkness, eyes as adjusted to the black as they can be, everyone keeping their heads down. It seems to take much longer to reach the grate than is actually possible, and the feeling of being trapped is pervasive. But no one loses heart or breaks down. Everyone stays in control.

On reaching the drain cover, Khoury moves to the forefront and uncaps the melting substance and pours it on the locks. Steam, a hissing sound, and a sharp, pungent stench ensue. It takes three applications, but finally the locks fall apart and the grate comes free. Malik is there to grab it so it doesn't make any sound when it starts to tumble away, gripping it with both hands as he leans out to lower it into the scrub-choked ditch outside. He goes out after it, then reaches back to help the other kids climb down the steep, slippery sides of the ditch.

In moments we are all in the clear. We stand as a group at the bottom of the ditch and say our goodbyes. Our core group of eight will go one way. The second group of add-ons will go the other. There is no particular reason for the choices of direction. But Tommy's thinking is that we will stand a better chance if we split up and reduce our numbers. Common sense. It is easier to track larger groups. Once we are far enough away from the prison, we will all split up again. If we are lucky, most of us will make it out. We will have our chances, each one of us. But I know it won't be enough. Because each of us fully believes that he or she will survive, while common sense says that some of us won't.

I go with Tommy, Malik, JoJo, Barris and Breck, Wince, and Khoury. We go left; the others go right. None of us has the slightest idea in what direction we are traveling or what lies ahead. It doesn't matter, so long as it takes us as far away from the prison as possible before we have to surface onto the flats. The night is cloudless, and moon- and starlight brighten the terrain. Once we crawl out of the ditch we will be exposed. It is bad enough that we will be tracked by the Ronks; worse still if natural light reveals us clearly enough that the Goblins' long-range weapons can bring us down. The Goblins have carriers, too. They will use them to try to find us quickly, crisscrossing the flats until they stumble over us. Luck will prove valuable, if fickle. But foot pursuit using the Ronks doesn't require luck, only patience.

A sudden terrible thought presses in on me, driving straight past my determination. *This is suicidal.* I don't want to think it, but I do. It is a wicked whisper inside my head, a dark promise that foretells my future with sly certainty. I have been fooling myself into thinking escape is possible. It is not. I am going to die.

As if in response to this invasive conviction, everything goes to hell a minute later. Shouts rise up from the other direction—from the direction in which the other group went—sharp and clear, deep-throated and guttural. Goblins. Screams follow and weapons fire reverberates. Spitfires: the nickname given to the long-barreled automatic weapons used by the Goblins, spewing projectiles in sustained or single bursts. There are growls and snarls from the Ronks, and the screams increase. Frantic activity. Desperate pleas rise out of the madness. Our friends, begging. A few final, awful sounds of dying and then silence once more.

They are all gone. All seven of them, caught and killed. I know it is so. I know it as surely as I know we will be next.

Tommy scrambles out of the ditch and looks around. Sees something and beckons us out. We follow him up in a mad rush. Distant vehicle lights shine in the darkness, revealing movement: Ronks. Impossible to mistake them for anything else—hunched shoulders, burly and shaggy bodies, all of them tearing at the remains of our friends. They are a long way off, but it feels like they are already on top of us. The others in my group start out, but I cannot move.

"Auris!" Tommy grabs my arm and drags me away.

Forget them. They're gone.

Does he speak the words or do I think them instead? Doesn't matter, does it? It is what it is.

We run. I'm not sure toward what, if anything, but I do know why. Escape requires movement, and we are moving fast and hard. Ahead there is a building, low and squat. Tommy heads for it, and we follow. Is there safety to be found? Does Tommy know something we don't? Did he know this building was here and is that why he insists on running toward it?

Tommy, the survivalist, trying to keep us alive. I have to believe that.

I glance back once. The lights of the pursuing vehicles are moving, swinging about in our direction. Coming for us.

We reach the building and find a pair of wide doors opening into it. They are heavily locked. Khoury uses her substance once more, but there isn't all that much left. The metal sizzles and steams, but the lock holds. Malik shoves forward abruptly, seizes the locks in both hands, and yanks hard while twisting—once, twice. The lock separates and the door opens.

We rush inside. Black as darkest night, but light from the moon and stars illuminates four vehicles, all of them similar to the ones coming for us. We clamber into the closest—all but Tommy, who is doing something under the hood. Then he is aboard and in the driver's seat and we are off, bursting out of the building with a surge of power, tires spinning and then gaining traction, racing wildly across the flats.

"Which way?" he yells, as confused by the dark, featureless look of the landscape as the rest of us.

No one answers, because no one knows what to say. Except . . .

maybe I do. I have the oddest feeling that I know just which way we should go. Maybe I am crazy but my certainty tugs hard at me.

"That way!" I shout suddenly. And maybe Tommy is crazy, too, because he follows my lead without hesitation, swinging the vehicle in the direction I am pointing.

Behind us, we find three vehicles giving pursuit, Goblins in each, their spitfires flashing. Hunkered down for protection, we hear the sound of multiple charges pinging off the armored shell of our sturdy machine. We have no weapons save for a few handmade knives. But JoJo rummages around inside a footlocker in the rear of the vehicle's interior and yanks out a pair of long-barreled spitfires. He grins in wild abandon as he flings open a top hatch and rises up to fire at our pursuers. I can't see the results, can't determine the consequences. JoJo drops back down.

We hit a series of rough spots that throw us all over. Another barrage of weapons fire strikes our vehicle, bouncing off the armor and flying away into nowhere. Except for one that doesn't. That one penetrates through a crack in a vent behind the driver, flying about like a guided missile gone rogue. It stops only after it slams into the back of Tommy's head.

Just like that, he is dead.

The shock freezes us all in place, until JoJo screams, "Grab the steering!"

Tommy is slumped over the controls. Malik lifts him away, settling him onto his lap and clasping his friend's lifeless body like a parent would a child, whispering to him. JoJo vaults over the seats and takes Tommy's place. He fumbles about for a few precious moments that cost us speed and distance from our pursuers, and then figures it out. Our vehicle lurches forward with a fresh surge of power, widening our lead anew. I am already thinking about what we have lost. Without Tommy, we have no survivalist knowledge, no steady voice of command, and no leadership to guide us.

Suddenly I am incensed. At fate for depriving us so pointlessly, at the Goblins for being the animals they are, at life in general for its quixotic nature, and mostly at myself for just sitting there. I snatch up the spitfire that JoJo has abandoned and poke my head through the hatch. My hair flies out in a dark stream as I sight down the barrel and start firing in sharp bursts. Whatever sort of ammunition we are using, it is deadly. The spitfire's charges streak in fiery lines to their target—the front windshield of the closest pursuer—and the driver's head explodes. The vehicle veers away, tumbles end-over-end, and bursts into flames.

One down, two to go.

I am newly confident now, emboldened, the bloodlust rushing through me red-hot as I take aim at the tires of the second Goblin vehicle, thinking to take it out as well. How did I learn to shoot like this? I don't remember ever having used a weapon that wasn't a blade, but the spitfire feels oddly natural, familiar. Instinctively I know that if I hold down on the trigger, the spitfire will release six short bursts—which is what happened with the first vehicle. If I press and release, it will send a single rocket with six times the punch. I test my instincts by taking aim at the tires and pressing once on the trigger. A rocket streaks out, but the tires hold. I try again. Still nothing. Bullets fly all around me and I duck down. The tires are tougher. I will have to go back to attacking the windshield.

No one tries to take my place in the top hatch. All of them are cheering me on, surprised and grateful that I know how to use the weapon. Flush with excitement, I rise up and open fire once more—this time with a quick release aimed at the windshield. The charge strikes with such force that the glass explodes into fragments. I keep firing. The vehicle catches fire, veers away, and is gone.

More cheers and shouts of appreciation and encouragement. I duck down again, grinning madly. I have a purpose now. I have a use. I have a way to vent my rage. I am elated enough to think we are going to escape after all, that we will get out of this mess and find help.

We are flying across the flats, JoJo doing the best he can to keep us away from the deep ruts and cracks in the hardpan that can slow us down, his face intense. Everything is happening so quickly, but it feels just the opposite; time is all but stopped and we are frozen in place. I check the spitfire, unsure of its load, then cast it aside and take up the other one. A moment to take a deep breath, and I prepare to lift myself back through the hatch for another go at the last pursuer.

But suddenly JoJo looks in the side mirror and grunts in fury. "Something happening back there! Hold on!"

I poke my head and shoulders out of the hatch for a quick look, spitfire extended. Our pursuer is almost on top of us, a fiery charge exploding out of a port above its heavy front bumper. The charge slams into our carrier's rear end and everything goes up in fire and smoke and screams. The entire back shield disappears, and I am thrown halfway out of the hatch and onto the roof.

An instant later the Goblins hit us with a second charge, and our vehicle shudders, lurches, hits a crevice or rut or rough patch, and takes flight. When it comes down again, it is listing heavily and I am flying through the air. Somehow I manage to hold on to the spitfire when the carrier and I part ways—when I am separated from the others entirely—clutching it as if it might give me wings so I can fly to safety. I pinwheel through the air, everything a jumble, then land with a shock so severe I am sure I have broken every bone in my body.

I slide into blackness and everything disappears.

TWO

WHEN I REGAIN CONSCIOUSNESS, THE SUN IS SHINING DOWN on me.

Okay, I'm alive. I've at least got that much working for me. But the memory of last night's events is sharp-edged and raw, and being alive doesn't begin to ease the pain.

I lie where I am for a moment, reliving it all. Commandeering an armored vehicle and trying to outrun the Goblins who came after us. Tommy dying instantaneously, a fluke, killed by an errant charge from a spitfire. Taking out two of three vehicles closing in on us, then being struck by cannon fire from the third at close range. *Two out of three wasn't enough.* JoJo losing control. The carrier veering away and launching skyward amid shouts and screams— amid chaos. And then becoming separated from the others, thrown out of the hatch and into the air. Coming down hard. And then nothing.

I cannot understand why I am alive. I cannot begin to understand why every bone in my body isn't broken. But however I fell, it clearly wasn't enough to damage me seriously. I ache everywhere, but a quick exploration of my torso and limbs reveals no evidence of lasting damage. Bumps, scrapes, and bruises—nothing more. Everything seems intact.

Still, why aren't I dead? Wouldn't the Goblins have come back to find and finish me? Or did they crash, too?

I lever myself into a sitting position and look around. I am lying in a swale with scrub brush growing all around me. I wonder how far I was thrown. From where I sit, I cannot see anything but the sides of the swale and the blue of the sky. At night I might have been entirely hidden. At a guess, I imagine the last vehicle's occupants were less than eager to do much more than a cursory search before returning home. No one could have survived being flung away like I was. Surely the impact would have killed me outright.

Yet here I am.

I don't want to, but I have to go look for the others. For our crashed vehicle and their lifeless bodies. Better I find them than don't, I think. If I don't, I'll know they have been taken back to be disposed of—piece by piece, before an audience. No one should have to face that.

Slowly, I climb to my feet and stand looking around. I cannot see anything from where I stand. I force my angry, aching body to perform basic movements it would just as soon avoid. My joints and muscles scream angrily in protest as I climb out of the swale and look around. My vision is suspect, the glare of the sun working hard to make me blind, but the wastelands seem a vast unchanging expanse of scrub, hardpan, and sand. My clothes are ripped and torn, bloodied and stained. My boots are still on my feet, but I have no hat or gloves or pack; all were left inside the vehicle.

Then I see what is left of it, crumpled hood buried in the earth, two tires shot out, the rear end in the air, the whole vehicle resting nose-down at a forty-five-degree angle. A body lies close by. Tommy, I decide, recognizing his clothes. I don't see anyone else, so I have to go closer. I do so reluctantly, wishing it wasn't necessary—not wanting to see what I know is waiting there.

Coming up on the crumpled vehicle, I see that the entire rear end has been blown out by that last charge—the one that sent it careening off wildly and me flying. Torn, jagged pieces of metal look like the teeth of some terrible animal. Vast splotches of blood, dried in the sun, coat what remains of the shell. I see body parts, detached from the body, caught in those metal teeth. I walk around and take a quick look. Can't tell who they belong to, but from their size and shape I can tell they are female. Barris and Breck were sitting in back.

I walk to the front and stoop to be sure the body on the ground belongs to Tommy. It does. I look through the driver's-side window. JoJo lies slumped over the controls. The force of the crash has shattered his face and left him pinned on the steering column. I turn away quickly, trying not to retch and failing. I complete a circuit of the wreck and then make another. No sign of the other three—Malik, Khoury, or Wince.

I can't leave it at that; can't stand the thought. I have to widen my search and make sure they were taken. I start a fresh round of circling that takes me in a widening spiral away from the vehicle and into the surrounding wastelands. I take time enough to be sure I miss nothing—all the while wanting to just walk away and accept the inevitable. They are dead—all my friends, all those I escaped with—hunted down and destroyed. How I escaped cannot be explained, save by declaring it a miracle.

Then, abruptly, I find Wince. He is lying behind a patch of scrub well off to one side, farther away from the vehicle than I was. There is blood all over his midsection and on the ground around him, and at once I think him dead. But when I kneel to make certain, I find a pulse and then his eyes open and he stares at me. "Wince," I whisper.

He smiles faintly and nods. "Auris. I . . ."

He coughs and cannot continue. I bend close to check his wounds, which are many. But the worst is where the blood leaks from a mass of torn flesh in his stomach. "Easy, Wince," I caution. I know he is dying. He cannot survive this wound, even if he could survive the others.

"Stay with . . . me?" he whispers.

"Yes. Are all the others . . . ?"

"I think. I . . . crawled away . . . after crash. Goblins didn't bother looking. There was . . ."

He coughs blood and grimaces. "We never . . . had . . ."

He goes still. He is dead. That he managed to survive the night in this condition is nothing short of astonishing. His wounds were fatal, yet he hung on. I close his eyes, hating everything, wishing I could have done something. Knowing I couldn't. The Goblins must have taken Malik and Khoury back with them to be executed. I close my eyes against the picture this conjures and climb to my feet, leaving Wince where he lies.

I have to get out of here. I have to start walking. The longer I stay, the greater the chance that I will be present if the Goblins decide to return. I can't risk that. I am too beat up. I would be taken like Malik and Khoury and dismembered.

I walk back to the crash and search the vehicle for my pack. I strap it on, fit my hat to my head to keep the sun off, grab every bit of food and water I can find and jam them in a second pack, then step away. Should I take a weapon? I look for one but cannot find either spitfire. They were all we had. I am reduced to relying on my long knife and my wits. Scant protection against almost everything. Nevertheless, they will have to do.

Gear in hand, I set out on foot across the wastelands, heading away in the direction that still continues to tug at me, even now—away from the Goblins, away from death at their hands.

I do not look back.

I begin to cry shortly after—for my dead friends and our lost opportunity, for the unfairness of a world that has taken them, and for my inability to change any of it. Why Humans are hunted and imprisoned is obvious—we are there to provide labor and sustenance for the Goblins. But how did this come about in the first place? How did we Humans come to be so disdained and marginalized that subjugating us like cattle became our future?

I walk until I quit thinking about any of it and the tears evaporate from my face, and then I walk some more. I have a long way to go to reach anything at all. I expected this, but the reality is daunting. I walk all day, stopping only to eat a bit of food and drink a little water. By nightfall nothing has changed. I am beginning to wonder if it ever will—even if only enough to give me some encouragement to keep going.

I am still following my crazy compulsion to move in this direction, but what if I am wrong? What if the Goblins come after me once again, or if they just stumble on me while in pursuit of something or someone else? There won't be any hiding from them out here in the daylight. There won't be any chance of being overlooked, as I was last night. The consequences are carved on the stone surface of my heart, and I cannot pretend they aren't.

My thoughts wander. Poor Tommy. I liked him so much. He was smart and quick-witted. For him to have been killed so suddenly, so randomly, still shocks me. Losing JoJo and Wince and Barris and Breck feels no less soul deadening. And probably Khoury and Malik, too, by now. All dead. And all for nothing. Escape was our only chance, and we all believed it possible. We were wrong. We were fools.

By the close of the third day, I am exhausted and depressed. I will die out here soon. How can I survive in the heat, making this endless trek? I am so alone. Not a rabbit or a burrow creature to be seen. Not even a bird, save rarely. This place is a graveyard waiting to add me to its number. I lie bundled in my jacket, in the clothes Barris salvaged and remade from scraps Wince found, and I stare at the sky. The boots were stolen from the Goblin supply room—cut down and modified to fit our smaller feet. Mine are already starting to come apart at the seams, loosening from the heat and stress.

But it is my mind that worries me most. I am beginning to lose the ability to focus. I am having hallucinations, imagining things that aren't there. I have a fever and nothing with which to treat it. I close my eyes and catalog what I know about myself in an effort to ward off what I fear is coming.

My full name is Auris Afton Grieg. I am nineteen, or close to it.

I have no brothers and sisters. My parents are lost to me—probably dead. I have long dark hair, and my skin is a soft olive color. I am strong for someone so small. I stand only six inches over five feet, but I can work hard all day. I am stubborn and determined. I am told I have a nice laugh and a good singing voice. I am slender and athletic; my parents used to hike me into the mountains when there were still mountains. And still parents—because I know I had them once, even if I can't recall them.

I don't remember where I came from—names, places, locations, anything. I have no idea where in the larger world I used to live or in how many different places. I remember houses and trees and parks and buildings. I remember towns. I went to school, but I don't remember anything about it.

A few things I can recall. I know I was deeply loved by my mother and father, and I have a strong sense of that love enfolding me as I grew. I remember hearing about the Goblins without ever actually seeing one; they were rumors, phantoms, creatures used to frighten children who were disobedient. Not that my parents ever used such threats. Friends told me; I had friends before, though I recall nothing specific about them.

The larger world in which I grew? A blank. Any history of its peoples and its governments? Nothing.

There are dreams sometimes—harsh, bitter, ugly dreams of what I think is my life from before my imprisonment, moments when terrible things happened to me—but I can never remember the particulars. They refuse to linger beyond slumber . . . save one. That one will not be banished, even though I wish it would. In the dream, dark figures surround my parents—faceless ghosts that reach for them, hands grasping. My mother screams. My father shouts in fury. Someone is bleeding. But their attackers persist. Their intentions are clear: My parents will die. I never see it happen, but I know it is inevitable. Why this one persists when all the others are as ephemeral as my memories, I cannot say.

On the nights this dream comes, I wake drenched in sweat, shaking and wishing so hard I could stop.

In the beginning of my imprisonment I talked about the dream with Tommy, but Tommy thought you could dismiss such things by simply willing them away. Once I knew that, I quit mentioning it. His memories were strong and sure; he could not identify with my lack. He liked to think of me as strong and certain, and I liked thinking of myself that way as well. It was best, I decided, to keep my fears and uncertainties to myself. So I had learned to do just that, even though it left me feeling very alone. I was different from the others, and I knew it. I was one of them, yet not.

And now with Tommy and the others gone, there is no one left to talk to anyway.

But I am a survivor. I survived what killed all my friends. I will not let it kill me.

AFTER ANOTHER WEEK OF MY FORCED MARCH, I AM NO LONGER SURE that anything I remember or have forgotten matters. I can barely walk; my entire body is a mass of aches and failing joints. My clothes are in shreds and my boots are falling apart—by now bound together by strips of my clothing torn into rags. I am forced to rest more often. My food and water are dangerously low. It has stayed hot the entire time, and the sun's heat is slowly draining my life away. I am not sure how much longer I can go on.

And still the wastelands stretch away, an endless expanse that disappears into the horizon as if dropping off the end of the world. Where are all the people and cities and forests and mountains I remember? Have they all disappeared in some sort of cataclysmic event? Are these empty flats all that remain? Worse, have I perhaps been mistaken in choosing to walk in this direction?

The dream about my parents returns twice—the same dream, the same sense of the inevitable, the same lingering horror when I wake. The distant past, I tell myself. A lost part of my life, a nightmare that no longer has any real relevance. Yet it persists.

On the night of the eleventh day since I began walking, a different dream comes to me. I dream of a place so wonderful and so real that it almost shocks me awake. There is a huge lake stretching out in front of me, calm and deep blue and so clear you can see the fish swimming within its depths. I am not standing on its shores yet, but walking toward them eagerly, anticipating how wonderful it will feel to bathe in their waters. But even though I walk as fast as I can, I do not get any closer. I just walk in place; something holds me back from my destination.

I realize then what it is. I do not deserve to reach those welcoming waters. My friends are all dead while I am alive. I should be with them in the netherworld. I should be as dead as they are. All my attention has been focused on myself, and that is selfish and unforgivable. What am I thinking? I am not supposed to be alive. I am supposed to be with my friends.

The sound of engines cuts through the silence then, coming from behind me. I try to turn to look, but I cannot seem to do so. I am frozen in place, a statue. It doesn't matter, though. I know what is back there and why. I know that my fate has already been decided. I scream in spite of my decision to accept my lot because I cannot help myself. I am terrified of what will become of me. I have no courage now, no self-confidence or determination. I am filled with terror.

I scream once more as the vehicles roar to a stop behind me and . . .

And I wake, alone and shaking.

This dream, unlike all the others save the one about my parents, I remember clearly upon waking.

I am now twelve days into my journey and pretty much played out. I cannot imagine how I will go on another day after this—or perhaps even to the end of this one. I plod along in a defeated, dejected slouch, all my concentration focused on putting one foot in front of the other. The sun blazes down with increasing weight, the heat intense and my resistance thin. Now and then I glance up hopefully, but there is no help to be found. I keep thinking I must reach something, sooner or later. I must at least see a change in the endless desolation of the terrain.

And then I do. I look up, and there on the horizon is a shimmer of blue. I blink in disbelief, knowing it is a mirage, a false promise. But no; I have found a lake—a lake so huge it seems to stretch from horizon to horizon. Right away, I think of my dream. This is the lake from my dream! I cannot believe it. Did I really dream something before it happened? Am I fated to become a seer of the future? But this makes no sense. I have no abilities of that sort; I never have.

I stop where I am and close my eyes, letting my other senses experience what my sight has already revealed. I can smell the water. I can smell weeds and grasses and damp all mixed together. I can hear the sound of waves lapping gently against the shores. I can hear seabirds. I am crying again, broken by joy and gratitude. I will not die alone in the desert; I will live after all. I lick out with my parched tongue, but I am not yet close enough to taste what lies ahead.

So I open my eyes and begin to walk once more. I go slowly because I cannot go any faster. I am drained of strength and riddled with pain. But still I go on, forcing myself, determined anew to reach the goal I have struggled to reach for almost two weeks. My footsteps drag and I stumble constantly, but I keep on my feet and do not allow myself to fall. This is a miracle; there is no other word for it. A miracle. And I will not let go of it no matter what.

I am smiling now, infused with the promise of salvation. I can see the line of the lake (ocean?) more clearly now—the blue of the water abutting the tans and browns of the shoreline. I can see birds flying overhead, tracing graceful white lines against the pale-blue sky. Then I see something more—something outlined in vague strokes against the backdrop of the water. Is it moving? I cannot tell, even when I squint. It is taking shape, but slowly, emerging gradually from the shimmer of the heat.

And then, from behind me, the sound of an engine becomes audible. I feel my blood turn cold and my hopes sink. The dream showed me something else, too, didn't it? It showed me pursued by my captors. In the dream I could not manage to look around. Here

I must. I turn and see the vehicle speeding across the flats, clouds of dust and dirt rising from behind it. There is no question of its intent. It is coming directly for me.

I cannot believe this is happening and I am devastated anew. I try to run, but my legs cannot manage it. I have no strength left for sudden bursts of speed, no matter the urgency. I am shackled by my debilitated condition, and I can do no more than continue to lurch ahead. Head down, body straining, I stumble on without looking back again—even when I hear the roar of the engine rising with its approach. I will not go back. I will not be taken. I will die first. My knife is out and in my hand. A quick cut across my throat and my suffering is over. I do not know if I have the nerve, but I am certain of my desperation.

The Goblins are almost on top of me when I hear a change in the sound of the engine. It lessens abruptly—an indication that it is slowing. Do they think to run me down on foot rather than with their carrier? Do they want me alive that badly? I stumble on, unable to think what else to do. A quick glance over my shoulder reveals that the vehicle has stopped and the Goblins are looking out at me.

But no. Not at me. *Past* me! At something else, something that is up ahead. Something that has given them pause.

I slow my shuffle and follow their gaze.

At first I cannot decide what I am looking at. My vision is already poor—my eyes dust-clouded and my concentration erratic. So I stop altogether and squint. A figure stands there, not a hundred yards away, still as stone, looking out at me and at the vehicle and the Goblins. I squint some more.

Behind me, I hear the engine fire up anew, and I look back quickly. The Goblins are turning around and leaving. They have given up the chase. I am free once more.

I look back at the figure ahead. It is a tall, slender young man. He holds what appears to be a spear in one hand, upright and steady, butt resting against the ground.

A young man, out here alone.

He begins to walk toward me, his approach slow and steady, his spear carried out to one side.

I revise my thinking.

Not a young man.

Not even Human.

THREE

I STAND MY GROUND AS MY RESCUER CONTINUES TO APPROACH. Since he has just saved me from the Goblins, it seems irrational to turn and flee just because he doesn't look like I do. My determination to stand fast is further bolstered by the fact that I am barely able to stand upright, let alone attempt any sort of flight. Sometimes you have to settle for doing what you can as opposed to what you think you should.

Besides, I am admittedly curious to find out something about this strange . . . Words fail me as I try to put a name to him. Him? How can I know even that much?

I can't, but it is my impression, and I decide to go with it.

Proportionately, he appears to be cast in the Human mold, but his skin is decidedly and unmistakably green—the coloration shading from sage to pine, like sunlight passing through a leafy glade. His hair is black, held back from his face by a leather band tied about his forehead, so that it streams loose and long down past his shoulders. Nothing odd about that—until I notice that his hair sprouts tiny leaves and shoots of deep forest green, as if he is in the process of budding out like a plant or tree. His eyebrows are dark like his hair, but have the look of moss. Hair similar to that on his head runs all up and down the undersides of his bare arms in narrow rows. His eyes are very large—luminous, bright amber—and his nose is narrow and slightly hooked. His mouth is a straight line, his lips almost invisible. And when he offers a quick smile, I see sharp pointed teeth.

He wears clothing more patchwork than uniform in its look, and all of it badly worn. His long, slender feet are bare, and they each appear to have more than five toes—a momentary impression—but I do not want to be caught staring and so cannot be sure. He never stops looking at me as he slows and stops, still several feet away. Perhaps, I think, he is afraid he might scare me and is cautious about offering greetings.

I am wrong, I realize an instant later. My green rescuer is taking this time to look me over. I am emboldened enough then to do the same with him.

A few long moments pass while we just look at each other.

"Thank you for saving me," I say finally.

He gives me a nod. "You are a Human."

I am a bit put off by this. "Yes, and you are not."

"I am Fae."

"And I'm Auris."

More staring. "That isn't my name," he corrects. "Fae is what I am. I am one of the Faerie Folk."

Now I am just plain embarrassed. I nod stupidly. "I didn't understand. I don't know any Faerie Folk."

This sounds equally stupid, but I press on. "How do you know what I am?"

He regards me the way a naturalist might an intriguing bug. "I have encountered Humans before."

"Where? Here? Outside the Goblin prisons?"

"Yes. Their clothing told me that was where they had come from, but they all died soon after I found them."

I don't want to know how or why. I don't want to hear anything more about it. "What happened just now?" I ask, still confused about why my pursuers turned back. "Those Goblins just looked at you and gave up the chase. Why would they do that?"

He considers. "They are afraid of me. I would have stopped them."

"How would you have managed that? They have weapons. They are killers."

"They know me. And they know I have this."

He holds out the length of wood he is carrying—which is not a spear at all, but an intricately carved staff marked by black and gray striations with splashes of red all through it. When I bend closer to peer at it, he offers it to me. Hesitantly, I take it from him to examine. I turn it over and over in my hands, marveling at the smooth, warm surface, the rich texture, and the unexpected heaviness.

"Why are they afraid of this?" I ask. "What does it do?"

"It channels my *inish* and uses it to protect me. It is a very powerful magic, and they know better than to risk testing it further."

He reaches for it and I hand it back. His claims about what this staff can do seem exaggerated; to me, it seems only a beautifully shaped length of wood. Still, I don't press the matter. I am growing comfortable with him, both with being close and with conversing. He does not seem to mean me any harm and has done nothing to frighten me. I don't want to do anything to change that.

"How come you can speak my language?" I ask before I can muzzle myself, my need to know more about him overpowering both caution and manners.

"I speak every language."

"*Every* language? No one does that."

"The Fae do. They have the ability to understand any language spoken to them." He pauses, giving me a closer look. "You really haven't met one of us before? Not even once? Not anywhere?"

I shake my head. "I lived somewhere else, far away. I don't remember where, though I wish I could. I was taken by the Goblins and brought to their prison several years ago. I never met anyone who wasn't Human before that."

"Which prison did you come from? What was it called?"

"I don't know. I can't remember."

"How did you get here, then? You were in the prison? But you left?"

It's cute the way he says it, so perfectly serious. His way of expressing himself is almost quaint. I tell him an abbreviated version of my escape with the other fourteen kids and what befell us. I keep it deliberately short, because I do not wish to dwell on it. And in spite of his reassurances that he has scared the Goblins away, I am dubious. How long before they return with reinforcements? I have no intention of being taken prisoner ever again.

I end with a brief sketch of my journey through the wastelands, coming upon him just when I am at the end of my rope, with my pursuers nipping at my heels. But keeping my story short does not help assuage the pain. Remembering how the lives of my friends were snuffed out so swiftly and violently makes me sick to my stomach, and I wish nothing more than to put the trek across the wastelands into the dustbin along with the rest of my memories. Instead I must focus on what lies ahead, hoping that my future will justify my rescue and that my existence from here forward will improve—though I know this is a way of seeking penance, of a sort, for living when the others did not.

"You have come through so much," he says. "You are a very strong woman, Auris."

Strong? I shake my head dismissively. "No, I'm not. I'm just lucky. Lucky to escape the Goblins, and lucky to find you—just plain lucky all the way around. The others would be here with me if their own luck hadn't deserted them."

"You are too quick to dismiss what you have done. We are not given the power to choose our fate. Fate always decides for us in the end, though we can choose the direction and make the journey. We do as much for ourselves as we can. Sometimes it is enough; sometimes it isn't. But we must try; it is in the nature of our character to always try."

I stare at him, thinking through what he says. Then I run my fingers through my tangled, filthy hair and shrug. "Maybe." I give him a look. "Will you tell me your name?"

A request, not a demand. I sense this is how things are done if you are Fae. He smiles anew. "Harrow."

"A Fae name?"

"A *Forest Sylvan* name. I am one of a particular type of Fae. The Fae are a large population of many different kinds." He pauses. "I can tell you more later, but we should go now."

I feel a little of the tension drain out of me. I am more than ready. "Where are we going?"

"Away from here. Your captors may choose to come back for you, so this is not a good place to linger."

"You live somewhere else?"

He nods and points to the huge body of water behind him. "Across Roughlin Wake. In the forests of Viridian Deep."

I glance at the lake and shake my head. "It looks big enough to be an ocean."

"An ocean might be a bit much for just the two of us to cross. There is an ocean farther south called Blue Forever, but we don't have to worry about crossing that."

He turns and starts away, and I trudge dutifully after him, drawing on some source of energy I did not know I had. I have some reservations about what lies ahead, but none at all about what happens if I do not go with him.

"How did you find me?" I ask as we approach the water. "You said you don't live here."

"I am a Watcher for my people, and this is my territory. This, and some of the country that is my homeland on the other side of the Roughlin. I come here periodically to make certain our enemies do not make incursions beyond the shoreline. If they keep to the interior of the wastelands, we let them be. But sometimes they forget their manners and I have to remind them."

"That seems very dangerous. Why do you do it?"

He looks confused. "It is what I am meant to do."

He offers nothing more, so we walk in silence until we reach the shores of Roughlin Wake. The water is choppy.

"How are we going to cross?" I ask.

"I have a boat."

A boat? I decide I am about to discover if I am susceptible to seasickness. I don't remember ever being on water, but I know what can happen if your stomach betrays you. Already I am experiencing queasiness just from imagining the crossing.

"How far is it to the other side?" Once again, I cannot seem to help myself. "Is it a long way?"

He gives me a quizzical look. "You're worried?"

I nod. "I've never been on water of any kind. Sometimes, heavy motion makes Humans sick. I worry I'm not strong enough for this. I've been walking in the heat for two weeks, and I do not feel like I am ready for any more rough travel."

"I will help you."

A promise spoken with such conviction that I don't say another word. He glances around, giving a lingering look back the way we came, then has me sit down at the shore's edge. He sits cross-legged before me and I adjust myself, mimicking his position. He reaches out for my hands and—after a momentary hesitation—I give them to him. His fingers are long and narrow, his nails a deep emerald. I don't know what texture I expected from his green skin, but it is soft and supple, the same as mine. He holds my fingers loosely, his own moving gently, warmth from his hands extending into mine. A discernible pulse travels up my arms and into my body, and my eyes close in response to the instant sense of relief it offers.

He begins to sing, then. The words are soft and wholly unintelligible. They might not even be words, only sounds—but whatever he is doing, it is restoring strength to my damaged body. I feel myself healing, and my emotions—which have been in a tumult—start to settle and grow calm. The entire time we sit like this, he feeds me his strength—I call it *strength* because I have no other word for it—in order to mend me. I am at peace.

When he is finished, he releases my hands. "You should be much stronger now, and you will not become sick when we make our crossing. All will be well, Auris. I did not rescue you only to lose you again."

It is a simple enough expression of reassurance, and yet I find myself thinking that it means something more. "I am grateful," I say in response, still dazed from his ministrations. "For everything you are doing for me."

When my eyes open again, I find his bright, amber gaze fixed on me, and I shiver in response. "Do you not see what this is? My finding you as I have? This is the way fate works to shape our lives. Everything happens for a reason, though we might not always know what that reason is. I was meant to find you and bring you to safety. My *inish* whispers it is so."

I come down to earth with a jolt. Not only does this sound crazy, but it raises more questions than it answers. What does he think is happening here? And what in the world is *inish*?

But there is no time and this is not the place to pursue the matter because he is already standing at the edge of the lake on a small beach, calling out into the empty expanse of the waters. Overhead, the sky is still clear and now a deeper blue as the sun sinks slowly toward the western horizon, its heat lessened but its intensity still strong. A breeze comes off Roughlin Wake, and its cool touch feels like freedom. I breathe in the pungent lake air, tasting it; it tantalizes me with the promise of new life. I am on my way to something so much better. How can I not be, given where I have been?

Something appears out on the water then—a bit of movement that slowly begins to take shape. The minutes pass, and soon it is revealed: a boat indeed, neither small nor large. It rides the waves smoothly and without effort, coming steadily toward us. There is no one aboard, yet it seems to sail as if crewed. I glance over and see Harrow directing its progress with movements of his arms and hands. I have no idea how he can manage this, but I am entranced.

When the boat is in the shallows, he leads me into the water and out to where it rocks back and forth. Hands about my waist, he lifts me aboard and onto the more forward of two wooden planks that serve as seats. Then a quick leap from the water and he is sitting behind me on the second. I look around appraisingly. The boat is constructed of wooden staves fastened to a curved frame with wooden dowels. A single mast sits fixed to the centerboard. The boat is perhaps twenty feet in length, the prow and stern higher than the sides and curved upward. There are no oars, but there is a tiller fastened to a rudder. A sail is wrapped about the mast, which he loosens and lets flap open into the wind. Then with a quick motion of one hand he brings the boat about, and we are off, cutting across the deep blue of the lake.

It is a joy watching him maneuver this strange craft, even though I have no idea exactly what it is he is doing. His hands direct our progress some of the time, and at other times he simply uses the rudder. He does this almost without thinking, his motions smooth and assured.

We travel without incident until we are so far out that the shoreline behind us disappears and no land is visible. The waves are choppy and sometimes very rough as we progress, but we are never knocked about or in danger. Nor do I get seasick. Whatever Harrow did back on shore must have worked. I travel in complete comfort and with a confidence I did not expect. I glance over at him now and again to watch what he is doing, but it remains mysterious enough that I cannot quite figure it out.

At one point the wind shifts in a way that blows the tangle of my soiled, sweat-soaked hair directly into my face, and I am ashamed of how bad I smell. I wish I had washed myself, if only marginally. But there is no help for it now, and I can do nothing more than promise myself a good bath at the first opportunity.

We sail for perhaps an hour in our little craft, and then I catch Harrow looking off to the north, his expression suddenly intense. When I follow his gaze I spy another craft on the water—one noticeably bigger and heading our way. I look over at my rescuer. "Who is that?"

He shakes his head. "Goblins."

The same Goblins that run the prisons I escaped? Or something else, something entirely different? I want to ask more, but the intensity of his expression suggests it would be best to just let him get on with it. The way he looks at the other boat does not feel reassuring. Watching it come closer, I can see why. It is much larger than ours, and it is marked by a series of huge jagged spikes protruding from its prow. There are two masts from which dark pennants flutter, and what appear to be catapults are mounted both port and starboard. A warship, I think.

"Are the Goblins enemies of the Sylvans?" I ask.

"They are enemies of all the Fae. They live along the northern shores of Roughlin Wake and consider these waters to be theirs. We think otherwise; these waters belong to no one people. Mostly, we are able to avoid the Goblins in our travels back and forth, but not today, it seems. Do not worry. They won't trouble us for long."

I am pleased by the reassurance, but not so sure it is warranted. The enemy craft is bearing down on us with increasing rapidity. The huge black sails catch the winds more successfully than our one small bit of canvas can, propelling the Goblins forward with such speed they will overtake us in minutes.

Will they ram us? If they do, those spikes will tear our little boat to pieces. And if that happens, I am in trouble, because I can't swim. I never learned how. (Though how I know this is something of a mystery.) There is no land in sight. I glance at Harrow, but he is concentrating so hard on maneuvering our craft that I do not want to interrupt him. Hopefully, whatever he is concentrating on will get us safely away.

And then the weather changes dramatically. Gone are the blue skies and sunlight, replaced by clouds and heavy winds. Gone is the sense of peace and calm that has surrounded us the entire time we have been on the water. It has begun to rain. The Goblins are still steering toward us, and their intent is clear. I can see the ramming spikes on the warship's prow, steel-tipped and sharp.

I am suddenly afraid in a way I have not been since fleeing the prisons. I can feel panic creeping through me as I imagine myself thrown into the waters below. I can feel the shock of the cold, and the pull of my sodden clothing dragging me down into the dark—away from the air I breathe, away from any chance of living. I manage to hold myself steady, to stay silent, to still my urge to shake, but only barely.

What can I do to save myself?

What hope do I have if I am flung into the lake?

Then abruptly the waters between the Goblins' boat and ours darken all at once—a darkness that verges on full black. I grip my seat as if somehow it might save me. Ahead of me, Harrow is thrusting his arms in quick motions toward the attacking ship—almost as if it is his intention to hold it or to turn it away.

Then the Goblin ship simply disappears.

I gasp audibly at the suddenness of it. There one moment, and gone entirely the next.

"What . . . ?" I manage in shock, but then go silent again.

Our craft gives a sudden lurch, a burst of speed propelling us forward with enough thrust that I am forced to hang on tightly to keep from being thrown backward. I close my eyes in anticipation of being rammed, but nothing happens.

When I open them seconds later, we are alone on the waters of Roughlin Wake, back in the pale light of the receding sun, which is lowering toward the horizon. Overhead the skies are clear once more, and the world is exactly as it was only minutes earlier.

I turn to look back at him in disbelief. "What just happened?"

"Not as much as you might think. Look over there."

He points. A large black storm cloud is floating across the surface of the lake. Inside, just barely visible within the shifting darkness, is the jagged outline of the Goblin ship, moving off in the wrong direction, the storm cloud clinging to it tenaciously, refusing to be dislodged.

I blink. "You did that?"

"It is mostly an illusion. I created something for them to believe

in and then planted the image in their minds so they could continue to see it until we were safely out of sight." He pauses. "A bit
of Fae magic."

"But I see it, too!"

The Sylvan nods. "So do I. There wasn't time to pick and
choose which of us the magic would impact—only to make it seem
real to all of us. Don't worry; it isn't."

"Well, it seemed real enough!"

Harrow laughs softly as he turns back to face forward, and I am
instantly irritated. Couldn't he have said something? I believed we
were about to be smashed to bits, and all the time we were . . .
what? Not in danger? Not even seeing something real?

More use of *inish*, I think darkly. But then I push back against
my anger and remember that I am alive and well because of this
strange creature. Can I justify being angry with someone who has
just saved my life not once but twice—and who is taking me to
safety?

Probably.

But I compromise with a mix of irritation and gratitude.

FOUR

WE SAIL ON INTO THE DARKNESS, BUT THERE IS SUFFICIENT
illumination from the moon and stars for us to find our
way. I have no trouble at all picking out the cliffs ahead when we
finally near land sometime around midnight. I am so tired by then
I have fallen asleep, and Harrow is forced to wake me so I can
watch our approach. He is right to do so. He could have chosen to
let me sleep, but he senses in that strange way of his when I might
want something. And I do want to see this—our first sighting of
land as we approach our destination.

I sit forward at the prow and watch the landscape assume increasing definition. The mountains are easy to pick out, and when
I ask he tells me they are called the Skyscrape. They appear at first
to be right on the shoreline—I lack sufficient depth perception in
the darkness to tell they are not—but as we continue to draw closer
I realize there are forested hills between the shore and the mountains. It is impossible to tell how far back those mountains are situated or how big the country beyond might be, but Harrow tells me

it will take us another two days to reach his homeland, which lies beyond the Skyscrape in a series of interlocking valleys.

His homeland, he tells me, is called Viridian Deep.

I can see trees now—or at least bits and pieces of some and faint outlines of others. But I see enough to determine the trees are of varied types. There are no trees in the wastelands larger than a Goblin, and none at all anywhere near the prison. I remember trees from my other life—one of the few things I do remember clearly—but some of these trees are massive. Some appear so large I think it must be a trick of the light—an enhancement brought about by nightfall and lack of clear vision. I want to know if they really are as large as they seem. I want to see for myself.

I want to see everything.

But when we beach our craft in a small cove where it cannot be easily seen, Harrow says we will camp close by for the night. It is still two days to Viridian Deep, and we will need our strength. Since I am already badly worn down and have to be woken just to view our landing, I am in no position to argue with him. Nor would I wish to; I am exhausted all over again. Sightseeing will have to wait for daylight and opportunity.

My rescuer leads me inland off the shoreline. When I suggest it might be pleasant to stay on the beach and sleep under the stars and an open sky after being confined so long to a cellblock prison room, he shakes his head.

"It sounds wonderful, and I understand your reason for wanting to do so. And you will one day. But not here and not now. There are creatures living within Roughlin Wake that feed on things lying on or near the shoreline. I think we should try to avoid this."

Again, I can hardly argue. This is not my world. I do not yet know enough to understand the nature and extent of its dangers. I nod and smile in agreement, and we walk on. Harrow has given me boots from the boat to replace my own, which have almost fallen apart. While they are not an exact fit, they are close enough. We travel inland for a short distance before he leads me to an encampment that he tells me he established some years back to provide him with safe haven during his excursions abroad. There is a tree house set within the branches of a broad-leafed behemoth, with a trunk that rises straight up for more than thirty feet before branching. He chose it, he tells me, because it cannot be easily climbed. A rope hangs from one of the high limbs, knotted at regular intervals, and he puts me on his back, arms about his neck, and pulls us up effortlessly.

Once atop the platform, we settle into a lean-to shelter where there are blankets and a strange warming device that helps to chase off the night chill. We do not talk again as we curl up beside each other and close our eyes. I would like to ask more questions about this land and its Fae, but I am too tired to pursue the matter, and Harrow reveals his own disinclination to converse by turning his back as we stretch out. Still, the solidity of his presence at my side warms me—maybe more so than the strange device.

Sleep comes quickly, and on this night it is deep and dreamless.

I do not wake until I sense my companion moving about. By then it is daylight again, and I rise at once. I wish I could bathe—my body and my clothing are sweat-soaked and my hair a tangled mess. When I ask if there might be some chance to do so, he beckons me over to the rope. Before we descend, he reveals a pack I failed to notice earlier, straps it over his shoulders, and takes up his staff. I am strong enough today to lower myself on my own. He leads me into the trees to where a small pond of crystal-clear water is sheltered in a grove of conifers. How long has it been, if ever, since I have seen something as welcoming as this? He deposits the pack on the ground and promises he will stay close and keep watch so that I may wash without being disturbed.

I do not ask if what he will be watching might include me because I cannot find a reason to care. I barely wait for him to disappear before opening the pack to find hard soap and a towel, and a clean shirt. I am astonished he can manage to scrounge up such items, given the limited purpose and primitive nature of his camp. I strip off my clothing and climb into the pond, finding the waters unexpectedly warm. I would like to luxuriate in their soothing comfort forever, but I know we must start walking soon.

So I bathe myself and then wash out my pants and set them in a patch of sun and just soak for a time. When I sense I am pushing my luck, I dry off. I have no underthings and apparently neither does he—hardly a surprise. Dressing quickly in damp pants, I find the tunic a reasonable fit—as much so as the boots he gave me last night. I call for Harrow, and he comes out to find me ready. He gives me a quick once-over (it is only then I find myself blushing, wondering what he has seen) before he leads me back to the camp.

We eat a spare breakfast of some odd but tasty fruit and hunks of hard bread and cheese he retrieves from his lean-to. How they can be edible after sitting out here in the wilds for who-knows-how-long is a mystery, but I am famished and do not question what I am given. I find the food and the accompaniment of cold water more than adequate.

"Two days to reach where you live?" I ask at one point. "To this place you call Viridian Deep?"

He nods. "It is the ancient homeland of the Fae, who have lived there for thousands of years. Our population is well over one million, and there are more than twenty varieties of Fae living in the valleys of the Deep and the highlands surrounding them. The Sylvans are the dominant type, but there are many Sprites and Nyiads, too. My mother and father are both Forest Sylvans."

"I am surprised I have never heard of any of this before—not of Viridian Deep or the Fae." Although I guess you could argue that since I can't remember much of my past life, that's not too surprising. I might have heard something of both once and forgotten. "I wish my memory were better."

"What is wrong with your memory?" he asks.

"I lost it."

"How?"

I shrug. "I'm not sure. But I wish I could do something to get it back."

He chews thoughtfully. "Maybe you can. There are ways."

"Are you saying . . . ?"

He makes a dismissive gesture as he interrupts. "That's for later. But understand, most Humans have not even heard of the Fae, though we have been here for thousands of years. They know nothing of Sprites or Sylvans, or even of Goblins and the prisons they operate. Government officials in the Ministry keep us a secret. *Those* are the Humans we fear."

This is news to me. So there *is* a functional Human society, unaware of the prisons in which I and my friends were kept? And what of this Ministry? What is that all about? I instantly want to know more, but Harrow is already continuing.

"The rest do not believe we are real. Faerie-kind is thought to be the province of legend and story—not a reality with which they should concern themselves. And we prefer it that way."

I frown. "But you would think that some Humans would have found their way here by now. After thousands of years, how could your existence remain a secret?"

"When we reach home, I will explain."

"I would like that," I say encouragingly.

He doesn't respond, so I ask the question that has been burning inside me since he first mentioned it. "You said something about government officials in the Ministry. Does this mean that there is still a Human government? That there are still free Humans?"

He looks at me strangely. "Of course. Did you not know that?"

"I don't know much about anything outside the prisons," I confess. "But what of the Goblin prisons? How does the Human government let their own people be imprisoned?"

He looks at me almost sadly. "Let them? It's the Ministry that *runs* the prisons. The Goblins just administer them."

I am shocked into silence. Humans imprisoning fellow Humans? But why? I am not sure I want to ask this . . . or even know the answer.

"What will you do with me after we reach Viridian Deep?" I ask instead. "I am not one of the Fae, and I should probably try to find my way back to my real home."

He hesitates. "You will go where fate says you must, and I will see to it that you get there safely."

I give him a long, appraising look. What isn't he telling me? "Why are you doing all this? Don't think me rude, please—I am deeply grateful. I cannot say it often enough. You saved my life. You gave me back my freedom. But you risk so much, and you do so for a stranger."

His brow furrows. "There is a saying among the Fae. If you save someone's life, that life becomes your responsibility. I believe that. I think we are all responsible for the lives of others—even beyond what the old saying requires."

"I don't know if I believe that," I admit.

"I think you do; you just haven't had to test your belief. If our situations were reversed, you would take responsibility for my life, wouldn't you? Of course you would. Perhaps in the days ahead, while you rest and grow strong again, you will come to understand this better. Life with the Fae will offer you a different perspective. It will provide new opportunities and new experiences."

Life with the Fae? He talks as if I am staying here, as if it is settled.

I shake my head doubtfully. "Again, I am grateful. But I am still not sure why you are doing all this. I am nothing special to you."

He nods. "Nor I to you, save what chance has made us both to each other. Consider our relationship, Auris. We are newfound friends. We come from different worlds and backgrounds, yet we have shared an experience that transcends such differences. It impacts me as much as it does you, even if it might not seem that way. In time, I think you will come to understand this."

He rises and says it is time to start out, so we do. Leaving Roughlin Wake and the camp behind, we set out for the interior of this new land, walking through woods and over hills, into and out of valleys and across streams. The day is warm and welcoming, and I feel reborn into the world. Birdsong fills the forest air, and small animals scurry to and fro. I find myself smiling just at the thought of being alive and well and free. I find myself crying, too, now and then—crying at the thought of my friends, lost to me forever, cry-ing for those still trapped in the Goblin prisons, and crying for my parents who are likely forever gone. My emotions are a jumbled mess, and I cannot seem to persuade them to settle.

Harrow must notice; how could he not? But he says nothing and lets me indulge whatever my emotions demand of me. Now and then he explains something about the land and what lives on it, digressing into treatises about certain kinds of trees and forest life, about the weather and its vicissitudes, about sources of water and food, and about other minutiae he thinks I should be aware of. I listen dutifully—sometimes with half an ear, sometimes intently. I study him surreptitiously, still getting used to his arresting look; I am less distracted by it now than I was at first. His rare smile is becoming a welcome sight. I no longer find his pointed teeth off-putting. His lean form, long arms, and easy stride give him a catlike grace. His eyes miss nothing, and he draws my attention to every-thing he thinks I should see.

But it's those amber eyes that I cannot stop admiring. I have never seen eyes like his. It is more than their size or color, which in and of themselves would be enough to draw anyone's attention. It is their exceptional warmth. When Harrow looks at me, I am con-sumed by the intensity of it. I am made to feel as if nothing in the world is more important to him than I am. I know this is ridiculous and without foundation, but his eyes make me feel that way and I revel in the feeling. I want him to look at me like that forever. Those eyes make me feel good about myself in a way nothing ever has.

Stop it, I whisper in my head and force myself to look away. But before long, I am looking back at him again—gazing into those eyes.

We walk all day, and by nightfall are past the lowland forests and foothills and close to the edge of the mountains. We stop at their base for the night, again in a camp he has previously estab-lished, this time an alcove in the rocks that opens to the east. He builds a fire to keep us warm, clearly not concerned about alerting anyone to our presence. He hunts down and kills a rabbit and roasts it over the flames, and I have never tasted anything so good. He offers me a skin filled with wine, and I drink it without questioning its possible effect. It makes me grow sleepy, but I want to talk some more and press on to ask questions I have been pondering all day.

"How did you become a Watcher? Are others in your family Watchers, too?"

"Only me and my sister. You have to have an affinity for it. You have to be comfortable with yourself. And you have to cherish the solitary life it requires. It's not often you spend time with others—and not at all while on patrol. There is a rootless quality to your existence—a sense of distance, homelessness, and separation—that you have to accept and master. There are many who could not manage such a life, but I am lucky. I have always wanted to live this way."

"It sounds lonely. I don't know if I could do it."

He spares me a quick smile. "I don't recommend it. In addition to everything else, you need to have a talent for mastering significant forms of magic if you want to survive."

"But you were born with magic, weren't you?"

"I was. But much of it is acquired and has to be learned. Magic is a large and complex skill set, and you have to devote time to mastering it."

I think this through, trying to imagine how it would feel to be able to use magic. I could protect myself. I could protect others. I could have used magic back there in the prison to help us all stay alive. But would I feel even worse than I do now if I'd had the use of magic and still failed to save anyone? Is it better not to have it at all than to have too little?

I want to ask him this, but at the same time I don't. Just speaking the words will hurt, considering possibilities that no longer matter.

"Tell me something about *inish*," I suggest instead. "You've mentioned it several times now. How does it work?"

He furrows his brow and looks down. "It is not easy to explain.

You have your body and then you have your inner self, the part of you that is physical and the part that is . . . I suppose you would say spiritual. The part that no one can see—even you—but that you can always feel. It moves you, speaks to you, debates with you. It is your inner self—the self that decides what you think and what you believe and how you see the larger world. Does that make sense to you?"

I nod. "Of course. Humans would call it your soul."

"Mostly, *inish* determines who and what you are, though it can also govern your physical self and cause you to act in certain ways. Most people know it is there and that it affects them, but they have no idea there are ways to control it and to access the power it possesses. If you wish to use magic, you must learn this. Your *inish* will bring to life any strength you want to control and channel its use. But doing this is difficult. You have to be born with an ability to access and control your *inish*. Among the Fae, most are capable of this to some degree—mostly in small but useful ways—but not many can apply it in the ways that I can. That requires something more."

"What?"

He thinks for a moment. "Strength beyond the physical. Strength of will, determination, and intent—you have to use all three to bring things that can't be otherwise seen into existence. Magic is invisible until applied. It is hidden within you. To bring it alive requires mastery, so that you can shape it as you want."

"So to create an illusion of a storm cloud and to cause it to surround and blind a Goblin ship, you have to imagine it into being? Is that how it works?"

"Something like that. I can try to show you sometime how to reach into your inner self and bring a bit of magic to life. At least I think I can. I am not sure how it might work with you, but would you like to try?"

I am not at all sure about what this might require, but I nod anyway. To have magic would be incredible. "Can we do it right now?"

He smiles and shakes his head. "So impatient, Auris. No, I think it had better wait. It requires your full attention and works best when you are settled. We can see about your *inish* potential in Viridian Deep."

So we drop the subject, and I am left to consider how channeling your *inish* might work and to imagine the sort of control you must possess in order to make the magic happen. I consider myself strong-minded and determined—I do not think I would still be alive otherwise—but I sense that using magic demands something further. I cannot put a name to it, but I know it is there, waiting for me to decide what it is.

I am looking forward to discovering more. And I am anxious to learn it with Harrow as my teacher.

Oddly, I am no longer thinking of trying to go home. Instead my thoughts are fixed on spending more time in this new country. With the Fae—but with Harrow, in particular. With my rescuer and safe haven. We have bonded over the past two days, through our shared experience and my deep sense of gratitude. How could I feel otherwise? But even more important, we have become friends. I presume a bit here, but I do believe it is so. And I cannot help wondering if maybe it isn't something more. I find something wonderful in the warmth of his amber eyes and the fleeting charm of his rare grins. I find myself wondering what it would feel like to touch that strange leafy hair. Would the leaves be bristly or soft? But then I also wonder if I should even be considering such a thing. He is an alien creature—a Faerie. I know nothing about the Fae and very little about him in particular. I know what he did for me, but I also suspect he would have done the same for anyone. He is built that way; he has that kind of heart.

As I settle down for sleep, I realize how foolish I am being, and how deeply deluded I am about these fantasies I am entertaining. I understand, in a rational way, why I should let go of all this and just keep myself to myself.

Yet I don't want to. After so long in a cage, I thought I wanted nothing more than to feel free. But now I think that is not enough.

I want to belong somewhere, too—and will do whatever it takes to make that happen.

Even if the end result causes me pain. If nothing else, the pain will make me feel more alive than I have in years.

Our sleep is undisturbed, and the next morning, we reach a forest that stretches like a wall across the land—so thick with closely packed conifers, it is impossible to see more than a few yards ahead. The path becomes harder, yet Harrow does not seem bothered. He simply pushes his way through the shaggy boughs and calls for me to follow. Overhead, the limbs from even larger trees begin to blot out much of the sky and sunlight. I must pay closer attention to stay with him, to keep up and not let him out of my sight. If I were to lose him in this morass, I might not even know which way he went. Concentration of this sort quickly gives me a headache, and pushing past endless clusters of needled boughs, coupled with a constant avoidance of the exposed tree roots seeking to trip me up, forces me to stay tightly focused.

"How much longer?" I ask finally, breathing hard as I watch his back while he continues to forge ahead, seemingly tireless.

"A bit," he answers, his voice muffled. "Do you need to rest?"

I do, but I refuse to admit it. I want to be strong in the way he is, not showing any sort of weakness. It is enough that he has saved me twice already and brought me this far. I do not care to demonstrate that I require even more from him.

We have gone a considerable distance when he abruptly stops and holds up his hand. He freezes as he does so, and I do the same, listening. Wind blows through the upper branches, rustling their needles, but I hear nothing else. We wait, still frozen, me watching him as he searches the forest for whatever has disturbed him.

"Wait here," he whispers, glancing back at me. "Do not move from this spot."

And then he is gone, fading into the trees. I will be helplessly lost if he does not return. I trust him to come back and do not think for one instant he will do anything less.

But still . . .

The minutes pass with agonizing slowness. I cannot tell how long I wait but it seems like forever. There is no sign of Harrow or of anything else. I listen intently and glance about now and then, just in case. What would I do, I wonder, if something threatened me? I can run, but it will be futile; I have no chance of escaping any creature that is familiar with these woods. And I was told to stay where I am, wasn't I? Isn't Harrow counting on that in order to find me again?

But blind trust is a fickle lady, and she can turn on you in a second. Hands come around my face and cover my mouth, sealing away the cry of shock I emit. The hands are cold and webbed—that much I can tell before the gag goes into my mouth.

I struggle in vain, overpowered by who or whatever has hold of me. In the next instant I am picked up like a sack of feed and carted off into the trees.

FIVE

I AM CARRIED FOR SOME DISTANCE, STRUGGLING THE WHOLE time, trying to break free but unable to find the leverage to do so. Many hands hold me fast, several pairs on either side. They belong to a strange collection of small Fae. I don't have to guess at this. Even though my mouth is gagged, I am not blindfolded. Their distinctive features tell me right away what they are. As to their particular variety, I can only guess. These creatures have webbed hands, along with angular faces that sport thick crests of spiky black hair running from their foreheads to their necks. Their eyes and noses are narrow slits that look as if they could entirely seal off their vision and smell when closed. They have no visible ears, but what they do have—what I notice right away—are gills on their necks.

Didn't Harrow say something about Water Sprites? Perhaps that's what these are. But aren't they supposed to be friendly?

They talk among themselves the whole time they carry me, but their words are unintelligible. After a time, I realize they are not speaking in any language I have heard before. Much of what they are saying comes across as grunts and other odd sounds that do not approximate words. I try to make sense of them at first, but eventually I give up. It just sounds like gibberish.

We reach an unexpected clearing in the forest and they lower me to the ground, keeping me pinned in place as they gather around for a closer look. They are studying me. More words or sounds or whatever all those other noises are meant to be are exchanged—along with curious glances—and then one leans close and removes the gag.

"What are you doing?" I demand of him. A boy, I decide, gills or not. "You have to take me back. Right now!"

"Ah," the boy says with a surprised look. "You are Human."

So like Harrow, they can understand and speak other languages. "And you are an idiot! What do you think you are going to do with me? Cook me up for dinner?"

They all find this idea immensely funny, save for one. A girl, I decide, recognizable for her body shape and the look of her hair, which is feathered and fluffed out. "We're going to do what we want!" she declares.

I start to offer a retort and then stop myself. Realization dawns as I study them further. These are children! Maybe some of them are in their teens, but none of them is fully grown. This is some sort of game! These kids are playing with me.

"Can I sit up?" I ask the boy who talked to me first.

He nods. "Just don't try to run away."

I lever myself into a sitting position. "You shouldn't have done that. If you had just come up to me and asked, I would have been happy to talk to you."

"You were with a Watcher—whichever one it was. And a Watcher's not about to stop for us. Besides, taking you away from him was fun."

"Fun for the moment, maybe. But he will come looking for me."

The boy shrugs. "Let him. What are you doing with a Watcher anyway? Where did you come from?"

"The prisons on the other side of Roughlin Wake. I escaped and had gotten as far as the eastern shore when he found me. He brought me here."

"Are you a girl?" one of them asks abruptly.

"You can't tell?"

"Not with your clothes on. Take them off."

"I will not!"

"Why? We've never seen a naked Human before."

They look genuinely curious—not that this changes anything. "If I asked you to strip, how would you feel about that?" I snap angrily.

It was the wrong thing to say. In mere seconds, they are all standing naked in front of me, waiting expectantly. Apparently they are used to shedding their clothes. Six boys and two girls; it isn't so difficult to tell which is which. Their bodies are different in some ways, but not so different from those of Human kids.

"Now you," the leader orders.

I shoot him a dark look and leap to my feet, hands curling into fists. "Not a chance. Put your clothes back on, and we can talk."

Understand—I am not embarrassed to be naked. In the prison, our jailers stripped us of our clothes plenty of times—not because they wanted to ogle us but because they wanted to make sure we weren't hiding any weapons. Being studied as if I were a specimen in a scientific experiment is nothing new to me.

On the other hand, I don't like people telling me what to do. And now that I am free, I am not about to put up with anything I find offensive.

Still, they look so forlorn that I relent. Partially.

"I'm a girl. Trust me. You can look at me all you want, but my clothes stay on."

A few exchange looks, some shrugs, and a scattering of grins, and they are crowding close. A few fingers poke at me, touching my hair, my neck, and my arms. I stand my ground, meeting their curious gazes.

"Look!" says one. "No scales or fins. No gills, either. She's not a water creature. I don't think she can even swim."

Which is true, of course, but it's starting to feel personal.

"She's kind of white," yet another whispers. "She looks a bit like a dead fish."

"What should we do with her?" asks another.

No one seems to know. Apparently getting a closer look was as far ahead as any of them had planned.

"All right, that's enough," I say—and my tone of voice must carry enough of a threat, because they all back away. "Are you going to take me back to where you found me?" I ask the leader.

"I don't know," he replies. "Maybe you ought to come back to the tri-pad with us and let the others have a look. Most have never seen a Human before."

I shake my head. "I am not an exhibit. You've had a chance to examine me, but Harrow will be looking for me. He won't be happy when he finds me gone."

The response is immediate. Murmurs of "Harrow?" are repeated in urgent voices. Everyone suddenly looks very worried.

"Hurry up, everyone, get dressed," the leader orders. "We have to take her back!"

He is already pulling on his own clothes, and the others are doing the same. I stand there in confusion, staring. Once they are all dressed, the leader seizes my arm, trying to hurry me along. I yank free of his grip and push him down. "Don't grab me like that!"

He leaps to his feet and starts for me, but a voice stops him in his tracks. "What is happening here? Zedlin, look at me."

We all turn toward the voice. Harrow stands at the edge of the clearing, tall and lean and sharp-eyed as he looks from one to the other. The leader is stammering out an answer. "We didn't know," he said. "We just wanted to talk to her." He shrugs, gesturing point-lessly. "We don't get to see Humans very often."

"So, youngling, in order to talk to her you brought her away from where I left her. And then?"

One of the boys starts to cry, and I realize suddenly how young they all are. Sometimes it is hard to tell with Humans, and it is the same with the Fae. But a couple are scared out of their wits—that much is clear. Even Zedlin seems frightened.

"It was my fault," I announce suddenly, surprising myself. "They came across me, and I asked them who they were and what they were doing. Then we came over here—where there was space to visit—so we could talk. I should have stayed where you left me, but I was curious."

Harrow nods. "You have to be careful about giving in to curiosity." He is speaking to all of us now. "Sometimes it can get you into a whole river of trouble. But you all seem happy enough, so let's leave it there. Auris, we have to go on."

With a quick wave to the youngsters—all of whom look immensely relieved to be spared whatever they are afraid Harrow might do to them if I told the truth—I follow the Forest Sylvan back into the trees.

"Goodbye, Auris," I hear Zedlin call after me, and a chorus of voices join in.

I smile in spite of myself.

AFTER WE HAVE WALKED FOR A TIME, I ASK, "ARE THOSE KIDS WATER Sprites?"

Harrow gives me a look. "You didn't get around to exchanging *that* piece of information? It's kind of an odd thing to overlook when you meet someone for the first time. Do you want to tell me what really happened?"

I shrug. "They were curious about me. Like they said, they apparently don't see many Humans. No harm was intended."

Though I hoped I was done with being treated like an exotic specimen by anyone.

"Isn't this Sylvan country?" I ask, anxious to change the subject.

"This is the boundary country between the Sylvan and Sprite homelands—a sort of border where both can be found." He pauses. "I hope Zedlin and those others haven't done something you don't want to talk about, Auris."

They have and I don't, but I also understand they weren't trying to humiliate me. They were playing a game so they could learn something about Humans that they didn't know—which is quite a lot, I expect. How we actually look is an obvious source of curiosity. They just failed to understand the effect it would have on me. It felt a bit too much like being in prison again.

"Zedlin seems to know you," I say.

"He wants to be a Watcher. The Sprites have Watchers, too. The difference is that they patrol their waterways as well as their lands because they live on both. Zedlin hasn't gotten much encouragement from the Sprites, who believe him too small and impulsive, but I made the unfortunate mistake of showing interest in his goal a while back, so now he thinks of me as his mentor. Sadly, I find myself teaching him as much about proper behavior as I do about his intended future. I'm not sure, but I don't think he has any parents. Just those kids he runs with. They might all be orphans."

I think about the boy. It is hard to tell much about anyone after only one meeting, but if Harrow is correct I suddenly feel a certain kinship with this boy. I wonder if I will see him again.

We pass out of the trees as the day approaches sunset and stand on the edge of a precipice that overlooks a vast, sprawling forest divided by ridgelines and peaks. The forest is so large it covers hundreds of thousands of acres. The ridgelines are not connected but have the look of walls, formed by nature to divide the forests into separate chambers. Some are made up primarily of conifers that are thickly clustered and uniform in their look; some are deciduous, with trees that range from towering giants to slender saplings. Some are an emerald green in color, vibrant and luminous, and some pale by comparison, nearly lime. The height of their trunks and spread of their boughs seem to play a significant part in where they have taken root, but they tend to grow in recognizable clusters, the seedlings of the dominant overpowering those with less presence.

It is the tallest trees that draw my eye. Even from where I stand on the cliff edge, I can tell that the largest of these are well over three hundred feet high. I imagine climbing one and building a nest. I imagine how it would feel to sit that far above the earth.

Then, as I continue to scan across the interlocking valleys and their diverse forests, I realize something. There *are* buildings nestled among the trees—some with their foundations set upon the ground so that only their roofs are clearly visible, but many more raised up into the branches themselves, built either into or against the trunks or set upon platforms fastened within the limbs.

"Our home city," Harrow says quietly, guessing from my reaction what I am looking at. "We are Sylvans, and the forests are where we live. We make good use of everything. Some of us reside within the limbs, some shelter beneath them, and others still burrow down within the roots. You will see."

He leads me down a steep pathway that begins not far from where we stand—one that curls back and forth, snakelike, as it winds its way slowly but steadily to the forest floor. Once there, we enter the first and largest of the three valleys. Here, deciduous trees rule, giants and dwarfs together, all of them providing shelter and succor to their Fae inhabitants. The Watcher leads me along pathways worn from usage that bring us into clusters of ground dwellings and small shops, all scattered here and there as they bracket larger roadways. The Forest Sylvan people are everywhere, all with characteristics similar to Harrow's—all distinctive and recognizable for what they are. Many pause in what they are doing or where they are going to gaze at me, but I understand their reaction and keep my gaze directed straight ahead. A few wave or call out to Harrow, who responds politely but keeps moving.

Then, in my curiosity to see more, I look up into the trees and spy the vast network of homes situated aloft. All are connected to elevated walkways by ramps, bridges, and stairs—a cleverly designed travel system within the upper levels of the branches, a puzzle-work of tree lanes for those living and working well above the forest floor. This looks to be a very different world. The sizes and shapes of the elevated homes and buildings vary greatly—most smaller and more ornate, intricately painted jewels within the verdant green of the upper boughs, but some are huge. Some appear to have rooms that are open to the sky. Some appear to be suspended by chains or ropes.

Although it is almost full dark, the city is still draped in shadows cast by the setting sun. But lights are beginning to come on everywhere. It seems to happen all at once, and the effect is astonishing. It is as if thousands of candles have been lit all over—at ground level and in treetops both. There are no flames, however, and I understand why the Fae would not want to use fire in a forest, no matter how well managed. These flameless lamps give off a different sort of light—one that is softer and more diffuse. There is a magical quality to their steadfastness and colors, and it gives the city a dreamlike appearance.

I cannot help myself. I stop where I am and just stare at everything around me. "This is so wonderful," I whisper.

Harrow hears. "Viridian is that. The ancient homeland of the Forest Sylvan since . . . well, forever. Does it feel like you could live here?"

I stare at him in shock. Is he suggesting I might be able to do so? I cannot make myself ask the question: *Do you mean it?* "I would live here in a hot minute!"

He smiles. "There is still much more to see, and more days in which to see it. You are to be our guest, Auris. This is your home as long as you wish it. In time, you will decide if this is where you want to stay."

As we walk on, I tingle with excitement. At every turn there is something new to discover. A garden of hanging plants secured to a trellis is raised high up into the trees and lit all about with tiny lights, revealing a latticework of narrow walkways for their tenders. Carriages pulled by creatures I might have read about as a child but did not believe could exist pass silently and gracefully through the dark—some down the broader avenues, others in the air, flying. Taverns and canopied food stalls cradled by huge limbs are suspended overhead and offer food at tables that are covered by broad awnings strung with colored lights. Small Fae children no bigger than a minute hang on vines and ropes a few feet off the ground, swinging back and forth, squealing with delight, their mothers keeping close watch as they visit with one another.

So much to marvel at. So very much.

"How can you stand to leave here?" I ask him impulsively. "How can you be away on your duties as Watcher knowing what you are leaving behind?"

"It is precisely *because* I love what I am leaving that I am able to do so. I go for the very express purpose of keeping it all safe and protected. I go to make sure that any threat is blunted before it even gets close."

He shakes his head. "Seeing it like this—alive and glowing and beautiful—you would think there could be nothing that would ever dare to disturb such a place. But the Fae have enemies. The Goblins would seize it and destroy it for no better reason than to make us homeless. We have been ancestral enemies for untold eons, and there is a deep bitterness ingrained in both our peoples. Goblins hate the Fae and everything we stand for. They covet what we have in Viridian Deep and wish it to be theirs. It is in their nature to be warlike; it is in ours to seek peace. The two are not compatible. There are other creatures possessed of this same mind-set—other types of Fae. They, too, would see us destroyed. But they live far enough away that any invasion has always seemed too risky. So we mostly are tasked with keeping the Goblins at bay."

"It sounds like what the Goblins felt about Humans where I was imprisoned."

He pauses and gives me a funny look. Then he points to a nearby bench. "Come sit with me for a moment."

I do. The bench is handcrafted from a type of wood I have never seen, shaped and polished and kept gleaming through constant care; you can tell. He looks at me quizzically, lowers his head in momentary thought, then speaks. "How did you settle on using the name Goblins for your captors?"

"Other kids used the name like a slur, so I ended up doing so, too. Why are you asking?"

"Your captors are one and the same as our ancient enemies. There is only one type of Goblin, and it is they who run the prisons in the wastelands."

"Are you sure?" I shake my head. "I thought it was just a name."

"It is not. Goblins are a type of Fae. I have done battle with them while a Watcher. I have chased them off the shores of Rough-lin Wake. I have gotten to know them all too well. There is no doubt. Your Goblins and mine are the same."

I shake my head in confusion. "So why are they helping Humans to imprison other Humans?"

But he holds up his hand to silence me. "I'll explain more later. I have to tell you something else first."

The way he says it warns me I am in for some sort of harsh revelation. But I suspect I cannot hide from it, so I simply nod for him to continue.

He looks at me strangely, and his look is one of both sadness and joy. Not knowing the context, I am unable to tell which of these emotions is dominant, or if he feels them in equal measure. His expression is confusing.

"Did your mother and father ever tell you anything about your name? Did either one explain why you were given that name?"

I shake my head. "I don't remember anything about it. I think they made it up. I didn't like it at first, but I kind of do now. It's unusual."

He bites at his lip—a telling reaction. "Auris is a Fae name."

I stare anew. "That must be a coincidence."

"A rather big coincidence, if that's what it is. It means 'child of light' in our language."

"But I don't look like the Fae. I look like what I am—a Human."

"A mixed partnering of Fae and Human—although uncommon—usually results in a child who shows traits of both peoples. But over the centuries there have been exceptions—instances where a child looks entirely like one or the other. Admittedly, it is exceedingly rare, but it is also possible."

I try to remember what my parents looked like, but I cannot remember their faces—or much of anything about them. Not anymore. All that has been lost. I think they were Human—am pretty sure, even with my memories so vague—but nothing is certain.

He meets my confused gaze. "You say that Viridian feels like it could be your new home. You say you love it enough you could live here. I think there is a good reason for that."

He takes a deep breath. "I think Viridian Deep is *already* your home, and you are simply returning to it. I think you are one of us."

SIX

I THINK THIS IS ALREADY YOUR HOME.

A revelation that would have shocked anyone, but I am stunned by the possibility it might actually be true. Harrow seems to believe it, and I do not think he would speak the words if he didn't. He has to know how enchanted I am by Viridian Deep, how very wonderful I find the prospect that I might belong here.

But he knows as well that I am deeply conflicted. How could what he tells me be true? I do not come from here; I come from another place entirely. I remember too much of how it looked and felt—even if I have lost the specifics of my time there. I may not remember my mother and father well enough to picture them, but at the same time I am certain both of them are Human and not Fae.

I point this out to Harrow and demand that he explain why he thinks this. I don't look like the Fae; I don't know anything about them that he hasn't told or shown me. I don't have even the faintest recollection of this city.

"I am telling you what I believe," he answers. "I know it is a shock to hear this, but I have been considering it ever since we met and you told me your name, a Fae name—though there are other factors at work here, as well. I think we should leave it for tonight, though. You've had a hard journey to reach this place. It is late, and you should eat something before you sleep. Over dinner, I will try to explain more."

He rises from the bench and takes me farther into the city, where we eat at one of the treetop venues beneath a lighted canopy. The Fae look at me with obvious interest, but I keep my eyes on Harrow. For all the ways in which he looks very different than I do, I find him attractive—in the way you might an exotic flower: the lines that define his features, the sweeps and curves of his lean body, his arresting crest of spiky hair and its strange mix of tiny leaves. Once again I feel the urge to touch it—to discover what it feels like. To have leaves growing on you seems weird in the abstract. But in the actual—at least where he is concerned—it is somehow right.

This leads me to consider what it might mean to discover that what he believes about my parents is true—that one is Human and one Fae. Such a strange possibility to imagine, I can barely make myself believe it. I have never thought of myself as anything but Human. But if he is right, I will have to start thinking of myself in an entirely new way. I do not know if such a thing is possible when I possess no distinguishing Fae features. How can I see myself as one of the Fae when there is no demonstrable evidence of it? How can I accept that they are my people, too?

Harrow interrupts my thoughts. "The mystery of your personal history is yours to resolve, Auris," he begins, "but perhaps I can help you by explaining a little about the Fae and their connection to the Human world. I've already told you that the connection is tenuous. Our existence is not common knowledge to the Humans, but there *are* some who know we are here. They know this not because they have come into our world, but because the Goblins have. After all, the Goblins are Fae, too. Until recently, this didn't matter, but now it does. An alliance has been formed between Goblins and Humans. It came about in part because the Human

Ministry wanted to find a way into Viridian Deep to exploit our magic, and because the Goblins became greedy to acquire the newly developed Human technology that might help them overcome our Sylvan magic. The alliance was made between a small group of officials from within the Ministry and the Goblins who inhabit the wastelands and the northern mountains above Roughlin Wake. How they found each other and managed to arrive at this agreement is unknown, but the Ministry agreed to build a series of prisons within the wastelands, put the Goblins in charge, and provided them with weapons and armored vehicles. In addition, they arranged for a steady supply of children from the Human population. Whomever they sent to the prisons would be kept there until they died. The Goblins could work them, breed them, or eat them as they chose. The unspoken understanding was that the prisoners would all be children. In addition, the Goblins could poach any stray children to add to those the Ministry supplied so long as they did not reveal themselves to the general population. As you know, once they had these children locked away, they might do with them as they wished."

I stare at him in shock. "Why would Humans agree to this? Why would they be willing give up their own children to be eaten?"

"These children were not their own," Harrow replies. "These were the children of parents who had died or abandoned them. Most were orphans and strays, children who had no protection. None of them knew why they were in the prisons."

I am sickened by the thought that a nation and a people I had considered my own would do such a thing. Is this what happened to me? I had always assumed I was taken by force and without Human knowledge, but I will have to start looking at my imprisonment differently.

"What do the Humans get in return?" I ask. "Have the Goblins provided them with a way into Viridian Deep?"

"No. The Goblins, for all their savagery, are not stupid. They know that if they provide a way into Viridian Deep, their usefulness would end. So they refuse to do that. Instead, they act as spies and hunters for the Ministry. By doing so, they keep a tight hold on their secrets while continuing to gain possession of the weapons and armored vehicles the Humans have developed. Goblins lack the skills and the knowledge to develop such things on their own; they need the Humans to provide both."

I shake my head in disgust. "But you said telling me this might reveal something that would show me more about who I am. How does any of this help?"

Harrow's eyes lock on mine. "You were—as far as you knew— a Human imprisoned by Goblins. But how did that happen? Either your parents chose to give you up or someone took you from them and locked you away. You have to find out which it was and why it was done. You also have to find out if any of this is related to what I think is also true—that you are one of the Fae. You ended up where you did for a reason, and perhaps it has something to do with your Fae identity."

"If I have one. If you are right about me, after all."

Harrow just smiles.

When dinner is finished, he takes me to my new living quarters and bids me good night. I am quartered in a small cottage in an elevated tree compound close by where Harrow lives. He does not elaborate on his own situation; nor do I think it appropriate to ask. I am grateful enough for the bed and lodging. I am drained from two weeks of traveling to reach this haven of peace and safety.

There are clothes in a wardrobe. There is food and drink in a cold locker and pantry. There is a bed and a washroom with a shower and soap. I can sleep as late as I like. He will come to check on me at midday. I thank him and go inside, closing the door behind me. In an act of supreme confidence, I do not lock it. I do not know why at first. I simply tell myself it is because I feel safe enough that I do not see the need. In retrospect, I realize the truth. It is the first time in years that I have not been locked away by jailers, and I do not intend to be a jailer to myself.

I go immediately into the washroom, strip off my clothing, and again bathe myself. I did so in that pool on our journey here, but I still don't feel entirely clean. I take a long shower, using the soap freely, letting my body come back to life. After years in the prison, every shower will forever be an unimaginable luxury. I want to stay under that spray of warm water forever. But eventually fatigue begins to set in, so I exit and dry off. I start for the closet and then change my mind. Instead I walk to a small mirror and stand naked before it, examining myself carefully, looking for any visible evidence that I might be Fae. I find nothing. Not a single hint that I am anything but Human.

By now I am very sleepy. I go to the wardrobe and rummage through it to find sleepwear. Then I fall into bed, feeling grateful again for being given this wonderful chance to rest and recover.

I am asleep in moments.

In my sleep, I dream. My dreams are not of anything recognizable, but they are sweet and cradle me with their softness and their warmth. Figures hover at the edges and now and then suggest they might show themselves, but they never do. Music plays at odd intervals but it is nothing I have ever heard and seems to come from nowhere.

When I wake, sunshine is pouring through the windows of the cottage, bright and welcoming, and I feel as if I am reborn into the world.

I rise, dress, and eat a little fruit and bread from the pantry. There is tea, and I make some. It has an odd taste, but it serves its purpose and gives me comfort. I am reminded that frequently it is the little things that matter. I remember Tommy giving me an orange once while we were in prison. He must have stolen it—a dismembering offense. It was the first fruit I had tasted since I arrived. He passed it to me furtively, cautioned me to eat it out of sight of the Goblins, and smiled. That smile—I do miss it.

I spend a few minutes crying for Tommy. I wish he were here to see this. I wish all of them were.

It is not yet midday, so I go outside and find a small bench next to my cottage door and sit there in the sun watching the Fae come and go around me. They all carry on with their lives, and I am fascinated to watch them do so. I consider the fact that I am in a very different situation than they are. Their lives have been settled and steady for years. Mine is about to start anew. While they already have a life, I still do not.

In a rush, memories of the prison come flooding back, and I have to fight to hold them off. It is not easy; those memories dominate me still. And while they serve no purpose now other than to haunt me, they will always remind me of what it took to stay alive.

I close my eyes and force them away, turning my thoughts instead to a life lived here, in Viridian Deep. I am not entirely successful . . . until I feel something brush against my arm. I open my eyes and find a small Fae child standing next to me—a girl with flowing dark green tresses and fine features. She stares up at me speculatively, waiting to see what I will do. She is clearly unafraid; she is also clearly curious.

"Hello," I say.

"Hello," she replies, in my own language. Apparently Harrow wasn't exaggerating about the facility with which the Fae can master languages—even at a very young age.

"What is your name?" I ask.

"Char."

"What does it mean?"

"Smile." And she gives me one.

I smile back. "I am Auris."

"You don't look like us."

"I'm not. I'm Human. A visitor to Viridian."

"Do you like Harrow?"

This catches me off guard. "Yes, I do. He brought me here."

"He is my brother. I live over there." She points. "But he lives over there." She points vaguely in another direction. "Farther away, with Ronden."

His brother? His sister? Someone closer? I take a deep breath to steady myself. I know so little about Harrow, but apparently I am not letting it stop me from imagining things I shouldn't.

"I have to go now," Char announces cheerfully. "I have to do chores with Ramey."

She turns and scampers off with all the dexterity and quickness of a tree squirrel, and I am left more than a little confused. Harrow mentioned a sister, who was also a Watcher. But who are these others? *Ronden? Ramey?* Does Harrow have other siblings, too? After all, he talked of a mother and father. This is his home, the ancient home of the larger part of the Fae population.

But Ronden, whom he lives with—who is Ronden?

Oddly frustrated, I rise and go back inside and make myself some more tea. I carry the cup back outside and sit down on the bench again. I wait to see if Char will come back again. She does not. Nor does anyone else. I sit quietly and watch the Fae make their way along the tree lanes threading the limbs aloft and following the avenues below. No one speaks to me, but one or two smile.

Harrow appears seemingly out of nowhere, joining me on the bench. "Did you sleep well?" he asks without preamble, and I nod. "Eat something?" I nod again. "Find everything you needed?"

Now I am laughing. "Yes, yes. You can stop quizzing me about my comforts. After years in a Goblin prison, how could I complain about anything? I am very happy. I love my cottage; it has everything I need. I already want to live here forever!"

This last declaration is impulsive, and I immediately wish I hadn't made it. He is giving me a look, so I redden and move quickly to change the subject. "I met your little sister, Char. She came over to say hello."

"She would. She didn't wake you, did she?"

"No. I was sitting right here drinking tea. She only stayed a minute."

"A word of warning. She will be back."

"I would love that." I make a quick decision. I brush back stray locks of my freshly washed hair and say, as casually as I can manage,

"She told me where she lives, right over there." I point. "But she was quick to explain that you don't live there. You live the other way." Again I point. "With Ronden."

I try not to emphasize the name—not to sound as if I am fishing for information. Although, of course, I am.

My efforts fail. He simply nods. "Yes. Ronden is also a Watcher."

He offers no further information, and though deeply irritated with myself for caring, I push the matter aside. "Can we talk more about what you told me last night?"

He nods. "Let me take you somewhere first. I want to show you a little more of the city."

We rise and descend from the elevated tree lanes via a series of narrow, winding wooden steps. On reaching the ground, Harrow leads me through a network of dozens of homes and shops, turning down more avenues than I could possibly remember were I to go back on my own. I am made acutely aware of how much I depend on him while I am housed inside the city. Eventually, should I be invited to remain and decide to do so, I might learn to find my way around. But it will take awhile.

We walk a long time, and soon the buildings grow sparser and the forest begins to close about us. Roads disappear and pathways take their place, winding and intersecting with no indication of what they are for. But Harrow knows his way well enough that there is never any hesitation. I ask him questions about the trees I am seeing, and he answers. He is patient with an inexperienced girl who wants to know everything. But finally I decide maybe he has had enough and go silent.

He lets me remain that way without comment, although on the narrower pathways where we must walk in single file he looks back regularly to make sure I am still there.

Finally, we reach an arched trellis formed of woven vines blooming with a mix of purple and scarlet flowers. The impact amid all the green is startling. Harrow smiles with pleasure when he sees the look on my face as I take in the dazzling vibrancy of the blooms and smell their sweet scents. We pass through the arch and head down via a pathway hemmed in on all sides by hemlocks grown so closely together that they form a solid wall of interlocking boughs. We walk on another few yards to a second archway constructed exactly like the first, and I find myself in a vast, sprawling shade garden filled with streams of sunlight and color from flowering plants and bushes of every conceivable hue, all of it warded by the trunks and boughs of massive conifers that encircle the perimeter. Ahead, a broad, winding pathway leads down to a lake and a clear blue waterfall.

I gasp in genuine shock. It is the most beautiful sight I have ever seen, an entirely different fairyland than the city that surrounds it—this one all aglow with colors and scents, the waterfall a soft rippling against a steady chitter of birdsong. We walk straight to it—I think I would have done so even if Harrow hadn't led the way—and stand at the lake's edge as I admire this new wonder. The waterfall doesn't so much tumble and splash as simply roll over layers of rock, giving it the look of a veil, shimmering as it reflects the sunlight.

"This is Promise Falls," Harrow tells me, his voice gone very quiet. "It is named for the promises Fae women and men offer to each other when they agree to partner. Such a promise is sacred, and once made it is never broken."

I cannot speak. I can barely nod. Why has he brought me here? I flash on Char's mention of Ronden, and I wonder if this place is where he once brought her. I experience a sinking feeling in the pit of my stomach and tears spring unbidden to my eyes. I am instantly angry with myself. Why am I thinking this way? For all I know, Ronden could be his brother. I almost ask, but it feels wrong to push.

Instead, I brush away the tears with a casual gesture and say, "It is very beautiful here."

"Let's sit while we talk," he suggests and moves toward one of several benches positioned off to either side to allow for viewing the falls. I follow wordlessly, blocking away all thoughts of partnering and sacred promises and Ronden.

We sit, and at last he turns his gaze on me. I have everything under control by now and smile back as he begins to speak. "Aside from what I have already told you about why I think you are Fae, there is one thing more I need to tell you. Some of the Fae are blessed—or sometimes, I think, cursed—with the ability to sense things about others. I am one of those. If I am in another's presence, I often recognize something about them—even when they don't know it themselves. It was this way with you. That you were able to escape and survive to reach me under horrific circumstances was the first clear indicator. It told me that something was bringing you here—something strong enough to transcend all obstacles. Your name suggested what it was. Your story about your lost life and your parents confirmed it. There is enough, when you put it all together, that I think we must try something to reveal the story of your lost years."

He pauses, his eyes staring into mine. "Would you like to do this? Would you want to know what you might have forgotten, or would you rather leave things as they are?"

Right away I know I am not sure—about any of what he has just said. Is he saying he can tell me something about my life without even knowing me? If he can, do I want to hear about it? Maybe the past is best left where it is. What will it do to me to discover things about myself I don't want to know—or had deliberately managed to forget? There are too many variables to think this is a good idea.

Yet I cannot help wondering. Learning about my life seems important, revealing chunks of time and information that will potentially fill in huge gaps in my understanding of myself. Perhaps I *should* find out and make the best of it. Am I really better off keeping myself ignorant when I have a chance to learn?

"I know this is difficult," Harrow says when I have not responded. "It would be difficult for anyone, but much harder for you. You have lost everything and find yourself in a strange place, and now you are being told that a forgotten part of your life can be revealed to you if you make the choice to allow it."

What should I do? What would anyone in this situation do? I look for a way to delay giving an answer. I need more information.

"How would this happen?" I ask. "How will you discover the truth about me if I don't know it?"

"I can't, if you really don't know. But many times you know more than you think, and there are ways to bring that out of you—to cause you to remember. The Fae have magic users who are able to do this. We call them Seers. What they do to help doesn't hurt; it doesn't even happen while you are awake. You will be in a trance, but you will be told what you revealed when you wake, if the memory leaves you once more."

I think about it for a minute. "What if I don't want to know? Can I control what I reveal and hide the bad things?"

He sighs. "No. Either the Seers or I would have to make that decision for you. You would have to trust us to choose what to reveal and what to hold back."

I trust Harrow implicitly. If I tell him not to reveal anything he believes I might not want to hear, then he will do so.

"Would you do that for me if I asked? Would you ask the Seers to trust you to make this decision?"

He hesitates. "If you wished. I feel strongly that you need to know your origins, assuming they can be determined. We all need to know as much as we can about ourselves. It helps us to understand who we are—and sometimes what more we are meant to be."

I don't know that I agree. Sometimes, I think we know too much about ourselves already. It might even be true that our memories act as a filter, softening those things we are uncomfortable with, or ashamed of, or reluctant to reveal. We might forget—or fail to remember—because we cannot live with such knowledge.

I stand. "Can we walk the gardens some more?"

He nods and rises with me. Together we begin a lengthy circuit of the pathways, enjoying the flowers and trees and small streams that make these gardens such a fantasy. I begin to notice small children playing in grassy areas—some with parents and caregivers, some with older children. They look happy and carefree, and I wonder if I was like that when I was little. I wasn't taken until I was in my teens, so there was an entire childhood before that—a child-

hood about which I remember next to nothing. Though what fragments of memory I do have suggest it was not spent here.

There are other Fae having picnics. I ask Harrow what the Fae
call them, and he shrugs. For the Fae, these are just small relax-
ations from your day's regular schedule, he says, but there seems to
be no specific word. I don't remember having picnics myself—
certainly not in the prison, but also not before then. Yet I remember
the word. I must have heard it somewhere, known it from another
time, experienced it in the same way these Fae children are.

I explain this to Harrow, who says, "Then that is what you and
I shall call them from now on."

"My loss of memory has always bothered me," I say impulsively.
"In the prisons, I had to pretend I knew something so I wouldn't
seem too odd. But the truth is I remember almost nothing—just
hints that I might have known or experienced something, even if I
cannot remember any of the specifics. It's as if I have no past at all."

He doesn't respond for a long time. Then he says, very quietly,
"Then we must be sure you have a future."

After we finish our tour, we walk back to the cottage and sit
outside on the bench once more. I am already tired, and I did not
think I would be after doing so little. But I am apparently not yet
fully recovered. I wonder suddenly if I ever will be.

"Are you unwell?" Harrow asks suddenly.

I shake my head. Suddenly, everything overwhelms me, buries
me in hopeless despair, rolls past all my defenses and leaves me
exposed and vulnerable. I am adrift in a world in which I do not
belong. I am struggling to make sense of my life, which is so clearly
in tatters. There is no past save the horror of the prisons, and no
future that cannot be yanked away in a heartbeat. And the person
I have come to depend on lives—and perhaps is partnered with—
Ronden.

The tears that have threatened since Promise Falls suddenly
break free.

"What is going to become of me?" I blurt out before I can stop
myself.

He reaches over and takes my hands in his—an unexpected response. "I've already promised that you can stay here as long as you wish. Do not think for a minute that we would ever send you away."

"But if I don't let you discover the truth about me? Or if I do, and it is something terrible?"

"It will change nothing. You are not here to be judged. You are not obligated to us in any way."

I nod, head lowered, desperate to stop the tears. Otherwise, he will think that crying is all I do. I am not that girl. I was never that girl. I was as hard and sharp as nails in that prison, and I have not lost that protective edge. I haven't.

"I don't know what is wrong with me," I lie as I feel him squeeze my hands reassuringly. "I am what Humans call a hot mess. I am fighting myself in order to be the self I know I am." I look up again. "Thank you for helping me."

Surely my imaginings about Ronden are mistaken. How can anything that feels this true be so wrong?

Footsteps draw our attention, and a young woman approaches from the direction of Harrow's lodgings. "Dear One," she greets him, and I feel a stab of fear. "Is everything all right?"

She is very pretty, with long emerald hair lush with tiny leaves, and depthless sea-green eyes that capture and hold—a willowy creature fine-featured and lithe in movement and gait. She comes up to him, bends down and kisses him lightly at the corner of his mouth. "Is this Auris?"

He releases my hands. "It is. Auris, this is Ronden."

So, not his brother, then. I feel a stab of anguish.

Ronden shifts and bends down to kiss me, too. I manage not to recoil or to do more than reach up and touch her arm as her hand lands on my shoulder—a response of affection to the one she is of- fering. But I think I might sink into the wood of the decking on which I am now trapped. Of course she is beautiful and friendly. How could Harrow ever align himself with anyone else? I am sud- denly, foolishly devastated. But what did I expect from him that I should be so affected? Had he ever been anything but kind? Had he ever once indicated he might want something more from me?

Me. A nineteen-year-old girl with no future, an uncertain past, and looks that clearly designate me as a Human.

"I hope you are finding a way to heal, Auris," Ronden says with a smile. "You have suffered a great deal, but you will heal here and be welcome by all of Harrow's family. You must come to dinner tomorrow."

"Not tomorrow," Harrow interrupts quickly. "That's when the Sylvan High Council meets."

"Then the day after." She gives him a look. "When you return, straighten things up a bit, will you? I am off for training and will see you at dinner. Or whenever you get back."

She turns and walks off, and we both watch her go. She is like a bit of soft light and shimmer as she disappears down the tree lane.

My mouth is dry and my emotions twisted and adrift. I don't know what to do or say.

And then suddenly, I do. "I want to know, Harrow," I tell him. "I want to know everything. The whole truth about my past. I want to uncover everything I have forgotten."

He gives me a steady look. "Are you certain?"

Am I? Certain enough, I think. For all the parts of my life I can remember, I have had only myself to rely on. But how can I continue to do so unless I know who I truly am? Right now, I am no more than a house built of sand. A single wave could wash me away. I need a firmer foundation. I need the truth. "Yes."

"Then we will begin your search tomorrow."

seven

MIDDAY ARRIVES, AND WITH IT NEWS. I HAVE BEEN ASKED to appear before the Sylvan High Council so that I might tell my story and explain my unexpected appearance in Viridian.

I pass an anxious afternoon with Harrow on the bench outside my cottage discussing what I might expect. What he reveals is troubling. Apparently, the High Council is less likely to be welcoming than Harrow had led me to believe with all his talk about making Viridian Deep my new home. Humans are not welcome here, and word has gotten around. I notice that Harrow seems oddly reticent as he briefs me, as if there might be something he is hiding.

"What is it you are not telling me?" I ask at last.

He looks uneasy, but seems on the verge of opening up when Char arrives quite unexpectedly, bearing food and drink. Since we are fully visible from her home, I assume her mother must have decided to take matters in hand. I am wrong. It is Char who has assembled and prepared this meal, and whom I begin to realize is apparently gifted in a significant number of ways.

When I express my surprise, she gives me a look.

"Children," she advises me solemnly, "are taught most basic life skills early. I have been cooking meals for my family for the past year. I am good at it. I have my own recipe book. I made it myself."

The food is delicious. Chicken cooked in a clay pot, a vegetable medley, potatoes steamed in cream and herbs, and biscuits. How she manages all this I cannot imagine, but I am suitably impressed and I tell her so. She beams with pride.

"You are going to be my new best friend," she whispers in my ear after she kisses me on the cheek. "We will be just like sisters."

I smile uncertainly. This assumes a lot. Will I be here long enough for that? Will I be allowed to stay? "I would love to be your sister," I reply.

"You will come live with me. You can share my bedroom."

Harrow laughs and shakes his head. "Wait until she sees what your room looks like, little mouse. Unless, of course, you have decided to finally clean it in my absence?"

Char gives him a look. "My room is just fine. Everything is where I want it to be. I just happen to like collecting stuff. Auris won't mind, will you?"

I cock my head at her. "I don't know about that. I guess it depends more on what your mother thinks than what I do."

"She will think exactly like me!" the little girl insists.

When we have finished eating, the industrious Char gathers up the plates and utensils, gives her brother a smug look, and marches off.

"She really did prepare the meal," Harrow says quietly, watching her walk off. "She wouldn't say so if she hadn't. She's proud of her skills. And she is very eager to show them off. She's still very young, but she has already shown herself to be very determined. If she sets her mind to something, it is done."

"Takes after you," I point out.

"Maybe." He sighs. "But you are right that I've been holding something back about tonight. About the High Council. About my family, too. Something I haven't mentioned yet that you need to know. But it is difficult for me to discuss it."

I smile uncertainly. This sounds faintly ominous. "Please tell me."

He flashes me a hint of an encouraging smile. "Very well. There are currently five sitting members on the council. Four are respected members of the community—Mastras Andustick, Elkinstow, and Pahl, and Mistra Coslyn—who have been serving three year terms over the past ten years." He pauses—almost as if uncertain how to continue. But continue he does. "The last member is Ancrow, chair of the High Council, and she will serve for the duration of her life or until her voluntary retirement. She has served now for more than twenty years. How she feels about you will have a large impact on how our request is handled."

Harrow's amber eyes find mine and hold me prisoner. "She is also my mother."

I don't like the way he speaks her name. There is an edge to the way he says it, and I realize that this is the first time he has spoken of her. I think back and recall that at some point he made mention of parents and a family, but he never told me anything specific about them.

"Your mother sits on the High Council? She must be considered important in the community," I say. Then I ask, "Shouldn't this be helpful?"

He smiles and glances away, breaking the spell he is casting on me. "It should, but it might not. She is deeply revered, but deeply flawed as well. She loves me, I think, but she loves Viridian Deep and the Sylvan nation more. She has a deep streak of nationalism, and she does not think Sylvans should intermingle in any meaningful way with the other Fae peoples. And especially not with Humans."

"But you brought me here. You saved my life. Won't that count for something?"

"Again, it should . . . but it might not. Her first inclination is likely to want you gone. An outsider, an outlander, an alien creature. We will have to convince her otherwise. I will speak on your behalf and ask that you be allowed to remain with us while we discover if what my instincts tell me about you is true—that you are in some way both Fae and Sylvan. It will require you to be strong when she questions you, but you must also be respectful."

I think about my situation as a guest of the Fae. I think about how much I like it here. The thought of being cast out is terrifying. But being terrified serves no purpose. What matters now is being strong and being careful.

"Understand," he continues, "the other four members will have a say in the matter and they are not so beholden to her as I am. They will voice what they think and not be intimidated. But she is frequently the one who determines the outcome."

I nod and smile. "I understand. I will do my best. Perhaps it won't be as bad as you fear. Perhaps she will like me enough to want me to stay."

"Perhaps," he agrees.

But the way he says it is not reassuring.

THE HIGH COUNCIL CHAMBERS ARE ELEVATED MID-CITY AMONG A series of other government buildings—some constructed on the grounds surrounding, some on platforms adjoining our destination. We go alone to the meeting, Harrow and I, which he only now advises me was called for the special purpose of hearing my story and deciding my fate as a guest in Viridian. I will not be asked to leave until I am fully recovered, but I already realize something else—something that Harrow has chosen not to admit directly.

If I lack a blood connection to the Forest Sylvan nation, I will be asked to leave eventually . . . if his mother has her way.

"She has good reason for feeling this way," Harrow explains as we walk to the meeting.

The evening is pleasantly cool and the lights of the city wink to life all around us, tiny fireflies of brightness in the forest deep. Overhead, stars fill a cloudless sky and a crescent moon is visible in the south quadrant. The people of the city move about us, coming and going from work or dinner or visits, all engaged in their own lives and caring nothing for mine. I wonder how it would feel if I were one of them. I wonder if it would change me in ways I don't suspect—if my thoughts or beliefs or hopes or fears would be different than they are now. I imagine they would, but mostly I wonder if I will get the chance to find out.

I am very afraid I will not—and I work hard to tamp down that fear with a determination and confidence I do not truly feel.

"There have been wars over the years with other peoples," Harrow continues. "I suppose there have always been wars and always will be. Some of them were with the Fae nations, and some with other nations entirely. In the course of those wars the Forest Sylvans have always prevailed—in part because of our numbers and our love for our homeland, and in part because of our magic and our fighting skills. The Goblins remain our worst enemies—the ones most determined to put an end to our way of life. Our efforts at peaceful coexistence have failed. It doesn't help that they hunt us so brutally. And they do hunt us—constantly. I think, by now, they no longer even know why the desire to see us destroyed is so ingrained in their national psyche. We have warred with them for centuries, but we have always prevailed in the end. Yet there has been a cost."

His tone of voice changes. "My father was a part of that cost."

I see the anguish on his face. "What are you saying? That your father was . . ."

I can't finish the sentence, so Harrow does it for me. "Killed in an attack. But while it was Goblins who carried out the attack, it was Humans who organized and led it. A joint effort to break down a defensive line we had formed to keep them from getting too near Viridian."

"The result of the alliance between Humans and Goblins you told me about last night." I make it a statement of fact.

Harrow nods. "My father was a Watcher like me. He was on a patrol with some others—including my mother—when they were surrounded and captured. The Goblins hung most of the party from trees at the edge of Viridian Deep, my father among them, and left them as an object lesson. My mother watched it happen. She was taken prisoner, but escaped later."

"Oh, my God, Harrow!"

He nods. "My father's death nearly destroyed her, and it did kill something inside her. She became a much harder and less tolerant person after that. She knew of the alliance between Goblins and Humans. She knew of the part the Humans had played. She always hated the Goblins anyway, but now she hates the Humans even more. They have no real place in our wars and in our world. They are unwelcome intruders. She sees all Humans this way, and while she can be pleasant enough when she chooses, what she thinks in her private thoughts is another matter entirely."

"But I have nothing to do with any of this! I didn't even know about it. She would hate a young woman just because she is Human?"

Harrow shrugs. "I guess we are going to find out."

We follow the tree lanes farther until we arrive at a grove of trees so tall it seems as if their upper branches scrape against the sky. At an even higher elevation than where I stand, a series of broad platforms interlock to provide support for a gathering of perhaps half a dozen very large buildings formed of polished wood and large glass windows that clearly provide wide-ranging views over all of Viridian Deep. Some of the buildings are constructed of a series of cantilevered stories stacked one on top of the other. One is very tall and narrow with windows placed regularly all up and down the sides. Another is low and broad and rounded—as if to provide a gathering place when calling together the entire populace is required.

But it is the array of colors that draws my attention. A variety of blues and greens, reds and yellows, and a vibrant shade of deep purple create a rainbow throughout the complex. The colors have been purposely arranged so that each band arcs across the sides of the buildings, spilling from one to the next to suggest a rainbow that never ends. It is an astonishing effect.

"Wow," I say softly.

Harrow doesn't know the word, but he recognizes the amazement in my voice. "This is Forum Prime, our collection of public houses." He points to the low-roofed, rounded building. "The High Council meets here tonight."

"Kind of large for seven people, isn't it? Or are there more who will be there?" I suddenly panic. "It isn't open to everyone, is it? I don't have to tell my story to everyone, do I?"

He shakes his head. "Just to the High Council. That building has more than the central chambers for meetings. We will be in a smaller side room."

We walk toward it along a broad pathway that is clearly meant to be an entry walk for large numbers of Sylvans, and as we do lights flash all along its length, providing a greeting. The lights are a soft blue in color and wink on and off slowly. They seem to be saying *Welcome* but they might also be saying *Beware*. I choose to go with the former.

When we reach a broad entryway, Harrow touches an indistinguishable part of one of two double doors, causing it to swing open. We walk through into a broad antechamber that peels off in both directions. What I see ahead of me, through a set of partially open doors, is a huge gathering space—a stage ringed on three sides by thousands upon thousands of chairs set on gradually elevated levels of risers. But without pausing, Harrow leads me to the left through a series of corridors and further doorways until we finally enter the meeting room of the Viridian High Council.

I recognize his mother at once. Her gaze fixes on me immediately.

I have never met Ancrow and have never heard her described, but it makes no difference. There are two women on the High Council, but I know which one she is immediately. She studies me boldly, and I study her back. I think that whatever else happens, I must not show any sign of weakness. I had decided on this even before I entered the room, but on meeting her gaze I know my instincts were correct. She is stunningly beautiful by any measure, with fine, strong, Sylvan features, a long mane of flowing black hair, and eyes as pale as winter's light. She wears hunting clothes, and gloves cover her hands. She has the appearance of a very strong, very determined woman, and I think if I appear in any way vulnerable, she will eat me alive.

"Eminences," Harrow says, and gives the five a small bow.

I do the same, trying to appear not awkward but merely courteous. I have no idea if I carry it off.

We move to stand before the table behind which the five sit. Oddly enough Ancrow sits at one end rather than in the middle, which is where I would expect the chair of the High Council to be. I think she does this purposefully—perhaps to indicate she considers herself nothing special compared with the other four, or perhaps to throw off those who do not know her station. I face them calmly, eyes shifting from one face to another, giving them a chance to get a good look at me and judge me accordingly.

"Permission to speak?" Harrow asks.

"You may speak, Watcher," says his mother.

Her voice is low and rough. Her tone is neutral. Harrow might be anybody. She gives no indication that she will extend her son special consideration.

Harrow goes on to address the council at length, detailing the events that led to finding me, saving me from the Goblins, and bringing me back to Viridian—exhausted, injured, and famished. He concludes with a single telling sentence:

"I have reason to believe that Auris is a Sylvan."

There are looks of astonishment all around from the council members. His mother is the first to speak. "You know the rules of our community, Watcher. No Humans are to be allowed within our boundaries. Yet you deliberately bring us this one and claim she is a Sylvan? Perhaps you have failed to look at her?"

"With all due respect, Mother, my belief goes deeper than what appears on the surface. My senses—my instincts—tell me she is one of us. And before you make a comment about my instincts being unreliable, let me remind you—all of you—that my instincts are what allow me to serve as a Watcher. My instincts are what keep me alive. They guide me; they protect me. They have never failed me, and it would be strange to think they are failing me now."

"You have overstepped," another member suggests.

"I have done what I would hope any of us would do as Sylvan people, Mastra Elkinstow. I have brought a desperate escapee from the Goblin prisons to a place of safety. Leaving her to be recaptured by her jailers or to die from exposure or starvation is unthinkable. If she is one of us, she deserves to be brought home. But even if she isn't, it would be cruel to leave her on her own."

His mother is shaking her head in disagreement, her face stern, her lips compressed into a tight line. "This is a huge transgression, Harrow. This girl is not one of us. She is an imposter."

Harrow actually laughs. "Half dead and with Goblins on her heels, she fights her way to the coast and allows me to find her—all without knowing I am even there in the first place—so she can work her way into our good graces? All the while fooling me into believing she is a Sylvan when she looks exactly like a Human? What a ridiculous suggestion, Mother. A child could come up with something better if deceit was intended."

"What is it you are asking for?" a third member—a woman with an expressive face and a calm, relaxed demeanor—asks quietly. "And can we all try to be civil while we are conducting this inquiry? We are all friends and compatriots—and some are family. Let us remember to honor our bonds."

Harrow pauses and looks at me. "Before I tell you what I want, Mistra Coslyn, I think you should hear a little of what Auris remembers of her life and her trials in getting this far. Would you grant her permission to speak?"

"Of course. Auris, please tell us something about your life—what you remember from before the prisons, during your captivity, and since meeting up with Harrow."

So I do, taking my time, trying not to miss anything I think is important. I admit I remember almost nothing of my childhood, that the whole of my life before being imprisoned is a blank. I admit I remember nothing of how the Goblins took me or of the fates of my parents. I tell them briefly about my five years of imprisonment before escaping with my friends, and how I watched them all die before finally being saved by Harrow.

No one interrupts with questions or objections. Ancrow watches me with hard eyes and a stone face. She will never believe me. She will never accept that I could be what Harrow thinks I am while looking like I do. To her, I am some freak of nature, or a very good liar.

"I want to make something clear," I finish, fighting down my doubts and fears about what is to become of me. "I have never believed I was anything but a Human, but I have been forced to accept that it is possible my own people gave me to the Goblins. I found my way to Harrow, and he saved my life. He told me that he thought I might be a Sylvan—but I am as shocked as you that this could be so. I do want to stay here; I freely admit it. I have lost everything else in my life, and I don't even know where my home is, should I be told to leave. So I will do whatever is required of me should I be allowed to stay."

I stop talking and take a step back, meeting Ancrow's dismissive look with a firmly determined one of my own. I may lose out on my efforts to remain, but I will not be intimidated. I have not survived the prisons and my flight, the deaths of my friends and the horrors of the wastelands, to be laid low now by a mother's doubts.

"Staying in Viridian is impossible," Ancrow says quite deliberately, making it clear she thinks I am lying or pretending or maybe even mad—but certainly making it clear there will be no consideration given to my plea.

"Watcher," says Mistra Coslyn who, in speaking earlier, evidenced a calmer, more reasonable attitude, "tell us now what you are seeking. What is it you think you can do to help Auris?"

"I would take her to one of the Seers for a reading of her life. A Seer will be able to retrieve memories that have been lost and perhaps could uncover something of her future. I would ask your permission to discover if my instincts about Auris are deceiving me, or if they reveal a fundamental truth about who and what she is."

"Any use of the Seers is restricted to Sylvans," Ancrow points out at once. "No Human is allowed to seek their wisdom."

"The High Council can extend approval," Harrow counters. "Why are you arguing against this, Mother? After what she has endured tonight, Auris is entitled to vindication. As am I."

"*Is* she entitled to it?" Ancrow wheels on the councilwoman who has sought to discover Harrow's wishes. "I think we have heard enough, Coslyn. I vote to deny this sacred privilege to this outsider Human."

Coslyn shakes her head slowly. "I think Harrow is right. If there is a way to discover the truth, we should take it. I vote to allow it."

Mistra Coslyn and Ancrow are sitting at opposite ends of the table, and the three who sit between them put their heads together for just a moment before parting again and facing us. Only one speaks—an older man with a wizened face and bright-emerald eyes. He has about him the gravitas of an elder statesman.

"I am Mastra Pahl, young lady." He smiles. "You have weathered a lot to reach us, and it seems your journey needs a final destination. We would be remiss if we did not do what we could to help provide this. The remaining members of this council believe that Harrow offers the best solution. His request is allowed, and you will be provided a Seer and a time to meet. Go with the forest gods and carry with you our best wishes."

Ancrow rises at once. "It seems I am being overruled! Very well. I will allow this if for no better reason than to indulge my foolish son. But you have been warned. You will regret taking this action when I am proved right about her."

She gives the other members of the High Council a scathing look, which she then shares with her son, and without bothering even to glance my way storms from the room.

Harrow and I offer our thanks to those members who remain and, after being provided with the name of a Seer who will meet with us on the morrow and the time and place of that meeting, we are dismissed.

As we leave the room, Harrow says softly, "She will get over it."

He speaks of his mother. He speaks as a son who loves his mother enough to believe she will come to her senses. But I think maybe she won't.

HARROW WALKS ME BACK TO MY COTTAGE and tells me he will come for me tomorrow. Our meeting with the Seer will take place at midday, so he will arrive by midmorning. He asks me if I am all right, and I assure him I am. After all, I got what I wanted—what I had determined I needed: a chance to discover the truth about my past and my heritage. And by doing so, maybe an opportunity to stay in Viridian Deep.

I close the door and ignite a smokeless lamp, turn toward my little bedroom, and practically jump out of my skin.

Ancrow sits on a settee in the tiny living area, staring at me.

"You frightened me," I tell her with more than a little bite to my words.

"Fair enough. You frightened me, too. In fact, you still do. But I am not one who stays scared and does nothing." She stands and faces me. "I want you to know that it is my intention to find out what you are really doing here. I know what you are, no matter what Harrow might think. I intend to expose you, and I don't care what it takes. No Human will ever be part of this family or this city. I will never allow it. If you think tonight's vote of approval is any guarantee, then you are mistaken."

"Maybe you are the one who is mistaken," I counter, holding my ground. Ancrow towers over me—tall, stern, and vaguely menacing, trying to intimidate me. She succeeds. But I will not give in to her by showing it. I will not reveal any sort of weakness. "What if the Seer says I do have Sylvan blood? What if Harrow's instincts are right?"

"They aren't and you don't. And you will be told as much tomorrow. Having then wasted significant amounts of time and effort on nothing, you will be sent away and told to stay away. I advise you to pay close attention when that happens."

She brushes past me and goes out the door. But Harrow is standing just outside and blocks her way. "Harrow! How did you—"

"Instincts, Mother." He cuts her off. "The ones you think have lied to me about Auris. Rather more reliable than you would like to admit, wouldn't you say?"

Then he steps aside and lets her pass. Her smile is cold. She nods to no one in particular and walks toward her home without looking back. Harrow and I follow her progress without saying anything until she is indoors and out of sight, then we look at each other.

"You could have interceded earlier," I suggest.

He smiles. "It took me a moment to realize she was there. By then she was already expressing her misguided opinions, so I thought I would let her get it out of her system since you can clearly hold your own. You certainly don't seem easily intimidated."

I make a rude noise. "Well, you are mistaken. Your mother is pretty scary."

"So it's been said. Are you all right? Can I leave you alone, or do you need me to stay?"

I almost plead with him to stay, but then think better of it. "I will be fine. Good night."

Before I can change my mind, I go inside and close the door firmly behind me. I wonder as I drift off to sleep later if such an offer will ever come again.

EIGHT

I SLEEP—MUCH BETTER THAN I THOUGHT I WOULD GIVEN THE stress of not knowing what is to become of me and the memory of having been confronted so rudely by Harrow's mother. Maybe it is because I am safe and free for the first time in years, and that feeling settles me even in spite of the other uncertainties. In any case, I wake rested and ready for the new day and my encounter with the Seer, who will try to determine if I have memories of my past that are repressed or simply forgotten.

As I wash and dress, my sense of comfort and well-being lessens as the reality of my situation slowly sinks in. I am here at the sufferance of the Fae, but of Harrow in particular. If he was less important to the community, if his mother was not chair of the High Council, if there was not a chance that I might be one of the Fae (in some mysterious way I cannot begin to imagine), I might well be thrown out into the wide world with no clue where to go next. I can take nothing for granted in this situation. I must live as best I can with the knowledge that everything is ephemeral and subject to change. I will never go back to the Goblin prisons, but I cannot be sure that anywhere else I could go will offer me the escape I was seeking when I broke out of that hellish place with my now dead friends.

This realization is sobering enough that I immediately push it aside and turn my thoughts to other considerations.

Right away, I think of Harrow. I am in an odd place where he is concerned. On the one hand he has saved my life, brought me to his home, made me feel a part of his family (his mother excepted), and shown enough interest in me that I've been entertaining possibilities of a life with him that I really have no right to imagine. On the other hand, there is his still-unresolved connection with Ronden. Why would I expect someone who is partnered with a beautiful woman like Ronden to care enough about me to consider me more than a friend? Yes, he rescued me, but that hardly seems reason enough for the sort of attachment I find myself yearning for. While I am not immune to the feelings he stirs in me—the longing and the excitement—I know how little I have to offer while Ronden is in the picture. If I think about how inexperienced I am at loving someone, how little I know about what it truly means, I am left feeling woefully inadequate.

Take a look at yourself, Auris. You are not one of the Fae; you are a Human. What do you know about these people save the little you have seen of them and the little Harrow has revealed? Physically, they are not the same as you. Their lives and habits and behaviors are likely very different. Their history and their influences are unfamiliar. To mistake his interest in you as anything more than casual friendship and a kindness you haven't experienced since you were taken from your parents is the worst kind of self-delusion.

I stand in front of the mirror and study my face. I am attractive enough, pretty even in a teenage sort of way, but I am nothing special. I have no experience with relationships of any kind. I have never had a boyfriend, never been in love, never done more than kiss a boy or two while in the prisons—mostly Tommy and once JoJo. But what I feel for Harrow is something else, something deeper and more complicated. I don't know if he feels even close to the same way about me, but I have no reason to think he does. I have no business *allowing* myself to imagine it.

And depending on what happens today, all possibility of any sort of a relationship with Harrow might be yanked away forever.

It is still early. The first light of day is just breaking through the trees, the sun only now cresting the horizon and lifting into the morning sky. The Fae are walking about along the tree lanes on their way to wherever their day's plans are taking them, moving with a sense of purpose and a destination in mind. I wish I had this to look forward to. I wish I had a home and a job and a sense of purpose. I wish I was settled and surrounded by people I knew and cared about—people who cared about me in turn. I wish I had a real life and not a shadow existence that flickers with an unpleasant suggestion of impermanence. I long for a stability that remains elusive.

When I walk out the door to sit on the bench and take in the new day, Harrow is already there. His remarkable eyes fix on mine, and all the doubts and uncertainties I have been feeling fade. He smiles, and I want to kiss him. It is an irrational, foolish impulse, and I quickly step away from it. I can accept readily enough that it is a bad idea. My uncertainties about the future and about his connection with Ronden linger, but neither makes my wanting fade entirely.

"How are you?" he asks as I sit down next to him.

"Fine." I glance away to keep my mind calm and my voice steady. "A little nervous."

"To be expected. But there is really nothing for you to be nervous about. This experience will not be anything like what you had to go through last night with the High Council and my mother. I am sorry for that."

"It isn't something you need to apologize for. You are not responsible for your mother. She obviously feels threatened by me, and I just have to find a way to prove to her that she needn't worry."

"I went to her this morning and we talked."

The way he says it suggests the talk might not have been all that successful. "I don't imagine that was pleasant if it was about me."

"Not especially. But some things needed to be said, so I said them." He runs his fingers through the dark length of his hair— a nervous gesture I have seen before. Then he shakes his head. "She is so determined not to trust you. She is like this about everything, but especially about anything that has to do with Humans."

"I suppose she has good reason for this. If your father . . ."

I trail off, not sure exactly where I am going with this.

Harrow makes an oddly dismissive gesture. "My father was her one true love, and when she lost him she lost a large part of herself. He died at the hands of Goblins, but as I told you before it was the Humans who ordered his death. We found this out later. I told you he was on patrol with several others and they were ambushed and taken. All of them were tortured and then dismembered. You know what this means?"

I do, from being in the prisons. From watching it done to other prisoners. Dismembering means removing your limbs while you are still alive, then hauling what remains of your body to a site where it can be hung up for viewing and left for the carrion birds to feed on. It is a gruesome, horrible death, and I was forced to witness it more times than I care to remember.

"My mother blames herself. She was there with him when it happened, and she could do nothing to prevent it. Now she carries this guilt for her failure. It is an irrational response to being alive when you feel you should be dead. It is the knowledge that when the most important person in your life needed you, you were not able to help them. I tried to change her way of thinking, but she would have none of it. Eventually she ordered me to stop talking about it."

He looks at me again, and his eyes are so sad I can hardly stand to look back at him. "My mother is much more than she appears. She is a national treasure—a hero of the Fae nation. In her early years—before my father, when she was still a young woman—she was a warrior of great fame. She fought in the Ghoul Wars—a decade-long war between the Fae and the undead. The deciding battle was fought at the base of the Skyscrape Mountains at a place called Rampellion. My mother was the commander of the dragon brigade—an elite unit of Fae dragon riders. They are all gone now—as are most of the dragons—but they were a force to be reckoned with back then, and my mother was said to be invincible in battle. She was so young and at the same time so strong. She believed in herself and her soldiers. When the battle hung in the balance at Rampellion, she rallied her brigade and they flew down into the heart of the Ghoul army. By day's end, the Ghouls had been reduced to little more than bits and pieces, and the Sylvan nation was saved."

Harrow smiles, thinking back. "I've heard this story dozens of times from the old folks. I am told my father fought beside her that day. He saved her life several times when it looked like she might be torn from her mount. I think maybe this is a large part of the reason she ended up partnered with him. She knew she would never find anyone like that again."

"But then she couldn't save him in turn," I say quietly. "No wonder she blames Humans, if they had as much to do with it as you say."

"They ordered his execution," Harrow says quietly. "It was at their command that he was killed."

I shake my head. "I am sorry for your family's loss, but all of this seems so strange. Fae and Ghouls, Sylvans and Sprites, Goblins and dragons . . . these are things I always thought belonged in fairy tales. And even knowing what I do now, I find it hard to believe they actually exist."

"Fairy tales have their origins in reality, Auris. In this world, if not in the one you think you came from. Nothing comes from a void; all things have some connection to truth." He sighs. "But I thought you should know that there is more to my mother than her behavior last night. So much of what she used to be has faded. She isn't the same person anymore."

I wonder if anyone can ever claim to be the same after being subjected to such life-altering events. Aren't you always changing, evolving in response to what you learn and experience? This isn't something you can control; it simply happens and you respond to it as best you can. I know it is true for me. Who and what I was as a child and then during my captivity and now upon gaining my freedom feels like it happened to different people at different times—yet they are all still me.

"Would you like me to tell you a little more about what to expect when we go to see the Seer?" Harrow asks me suddenly.

I would, of course. "Mostly, I just want to know what she will do to me. When she helps me recall something, will I remember it later?"

"I don't know for certain," he answers. "Sometimes memories retrieved this way will stay with you afterward, but not always. No one knows why some memories are retained after recovery and some are immediately forgotten again. Perhaps it is because the things you don't remember are the things you didn't want to remember in the first place."

I am perplexed by this process, but not frightened. Not yet, anyway. "Will I be speaking of these memories? Will you be able to hear me talk about them? Or does only the Seer hear them? Or see them?"

"Let me try to explain the process. I think it will help to hear more about it." Harrow wrinkles his forehead a bit, and I smile at how serious it makes him look. "The Seer will be one of three sisters—all of whom were born with the talent and worked to develop it further over the years. They are the only Seers we have in the whole of the Fae nation, and they are very old, so my mother has understandable concerns about overusing them—not that I think it will be a problem with you. The one chosen to read your mind will place you in a trance. You won't feel anything while the seeing is happening. And it is a seeing, although again it can sometimes be something more. You may choose to speak, but the choice will be your own. You will not be made to do anything you don't want to do. The Seer will be working to find hidden truths and memories. If she finds either, she will attempt a recovery."

I think of this as somewhat invasive and potentially embarrassing, but I also want to know the truth about my parents and my childhood. I want to know why Harrow's Watcher instincts tell him I am a Fae when there is nothing to suggest it. I am grasping at possibilities that might provide me with what I want most out of my newly found freedom and my newly realized life: I want to stay in Viridian Deep. I want to stay close to Harrow.

Even if staying close to Harrow might not mean what I hope. Even if Ronden is more important to him than I am.

Even if all this turns out to be true, staying seems important.

We talk until it is time to go, although we drift away from the Seer and the upcoming session and move on to more mundane subjects centering on life among the Fae. Time spent with Harrow—talking about the Fae or exploring their city—is always intriguing, and I cannot imagine having a better teacher. His knowledge is vast, and his willingness to make it available to me is a gift I value. I am hungry to learn of Viridian; I am eager to feel a part of it even if I am little more than a temporary guest. So much of my life has been spent in a vacuum where nothing beyond my existence as a prisoner of the Goblins mattered. I know so little of the world, and so little of what I do know has any useful purpose. So to now be given insights into a place and a people I did not even suspect existed is welcome, and I am eager to consume as much of it as Harrow is willing to allow me.

Only one topic of conversation seems to be off-limits.

When I ask him about his plans for his own life—thinking rather selfishly about my own half-formed hopes and wondering if he might reveal something further about his relationship with Ronden—he shies away from answering almost instantly.

"My life will always be the one I am leading right now," he says quickly in response to my question, using his hands as if to ward it off. "I am a Watcher, and this requires that I serve my people for as long as I am able. To do anything less would be a betrayal of my calling. That is my future, and nothing else matters."

He says it in a way that clearly means he does not wish to discuss it further. I wonder at this. I cannot help but wonder. He has been so open about everything else—so willing to answer all my questions. For him to be so abrupt and dismissive of this seemingly innocuous inquiry confuses me.

It also brings on a serious bout of despair, because I cannot help but think about Ronden. Beautiful Ronden. Is she in any way responsible for Harrow's strange reticence? Once again, I wish I knew the extent to which they are involved with each other. Have they pledged to each other, as it seems the Fae traditionally do at Promise Falls? Are they on the verge of being or even already settled in as partners? They live together, don't they? They share a cottage and they seem so close to each other already, I cannot help but think this is how things must stand.

I realize that once my suspicions are confirmed I can stop daydreaming and move on with my life. Or at least I can try. I can reorder my thinking so that it does not include gauzy daydreams about Harrow. I can become more grounded. Perhaps that would be for the best.

I am amazed sometimes at how good I am at fooling myself.

NINE

BEAMS OF SUNLIGHT POUR DOWN THROUGH BREAKS IN THE canopy to illuminate randomly chosen tableaus in the world of Viridian Deep. Like spotlights, they focus the eye on small scenes in the life of her people, causing me to smile at the randomness of their selections. As I walk with Harrow to our appointed meeting with the Seer, I cannot help but stare. Here, an old woman sits on a porch bench, knitting a scarf for colder weather; already it stretches out well past her perch, as if to furtively sneak away to freedom. There, a clutch of children engage in a game I do not recognize or understand; it involves a small ball they toss back and forth, a series of rings, and some acrobatic dancing that sometimes leaves them balanced on a single foot. Laughter rings out and shrieks of glee rise up. Everywhere, Sylvan life draws the eye and gladdens the heart simply by how carefree and easy it appears.

I wish I were a part of it. I wish I could feel that way about my life. But while I have been calm and accepting up until now of what awaits when I reach the Seer, I am suddenly frightened. It is as if I have lost my nerve when there is no good reason for it. Before we began walking the tree lanes toward our intended destination—toward an uncovering of my secrets and lost memories—I was prepared for what it would mean and how it might impact me. Now, abruptly, it feels as if I have lost my footing and begun to fall—as if I am sliding into an overwhelming sense of despair. Perhaps it is the inescapability of what I am to learn. Perhaps it is the dark possibility of what I will discover. Whatever the case, I can feel my courage fade.

Harrow sees it in my expression. "Do not worry, Auris," he says quietly.

I don't respond, afraid of what I might say. We descend a winding stairway to the forest floor and turn away from the main thoroughfare to go down a pathway leading into a thick patch of conifers. The path is kept open by a judicious trimming of the branches, yet still it disappears at every turn as it snakes among these ancient trunks. Then the sounds of the city begin to fade, muffled by the trees and fresh bursts of birdsong. A whisper of wind brushes my face, cool and refreshing, and I smile in spite of myself.

"Better," Harrow announces, mistaking my reaction to the birds and the wind for a response to his reassurance. I turn my smile on him, needing to feel the connection, to persuade myself that his presence will shield me from the worst of my fears.

Minimize them if not banish them entirely.

My imagination runs wild with speculation, wondering what I am going to discover about myself. How I will stand up to anything truly devastating or sad—something so heart wrenching I cannot live with the knowledge of it? So terrible I will wish I had never agreed to the experiment? I do not know what this might be, but that may be why I feel afraid. Not knowing what I might learn beforehand is worse than knowing and being able to prepare myself in some small way.

We do not talk again for the duration of our walk, and we arrive as silent companions at a decidedly weird building that resembles nothing so much as a child's drawing. The building is an odd configuration of conjoined single-story cottages situated next to and—in one instance—piled on top of one another. To further en-hance the strangeness of this seemingly hodgepodge construction, a wooden stairway winds upward from the center of the building to disappear into the boughs of six intertwined giant spruce trees. Barely visible through the branches—well over fifty feet off the ground—I can just make out another tiny cottage resting precari-ously in shaggy spruce arms.

I stop abruptly for a better look, and Harrow stops with me. I am charmed by what I see—enough so that for a few moments I forget my fears and doubts and just stare with childlike pleasure. If ever there was a fairy-tale cottage in the forest, this is it. It doesn't look like anything I have ever seen; it doesn't even look like something I could have imagined. It is so unique and so compelling, I immedi-ately want to live there. It is a surprising response, but compellingly real. Here, I know, I can find peace. I can see the world and myself in entirely new ways. I can reimagine everything I have ever thought I knew and arrive at an entirely different understanding.

"Isn't it wonderful?" my companion asks, and all I can do is nod.

We are steps from the front door when I glance up again at the tiny cottage sitting within the spruce limbs and catch sight of someone looking down at me. It is a woman, her shoulders covered with a shawl and her thin, pale-green face age-lined. But my sense of her as an ancient is less influenced by how she looks than by how it feels to be in her presence.

She is studying me with intense concentration, then all of a sudden she smiles and twenty years drop away from her face. I star-tle at the new look she has assumed and try to peer more closely at what I am observing. But just like that—just a snap of the fingers—she turns away and is gone.

"That's Maven," Harrow informs me, taking me by the arm to guide me on. "She is the oldest and the most accomplished of the sisters. Look into her eyes long enough, and you will lose yourself there forever."

We walk up to the door, and Harrow knocks. The door opens instantly, and another elderly lady stands before us, her face pleasant but closed away. Her Sylvan features brighten as she recognizes my companion, however. "Harrow," she greets him and leans in for a kiss on the cheek. "Such a slayer of hearts. And this"—she turns now to me—"must be Auris. Welcome, child."

I do not care to be referred to as a child, but when she leans forward for a kiss, I do not hesitate to give it to her.

"This young lady is Benith," Harrow introduces her. "She was my intended once, but she threw me over for another man."

"Yes, 'tis so," Benith agrees, playing along but at the same time rolling her eyes. "It was the best thing for both of us. Now come in, join us for tea."

Benith turns away and leaves it for us to follow. We do, closing the door behind us. We stand in a cluttered living area with several couches and easy chairs and shelf after shelf of jars and boxes. I assume they are filled with special items from the fact that they are all neatly arranged, and I can see herbs and spices and various sprigs through the glass of the jars. There are labels, but I cannot read them. Rugs, throws, and pillows are scattered all over the seating areas and on the floor. To the back and one side of the room I can see a set of stairs leading up—I assume to the tiny elevated cottage.

Benith is small and displays an unexpected sprightliness as she crosses the room to a tea stand and turns. "You need not take umbrage, Auris, at my use of the word *child* when I speak to you. We three are so old that almost everyone we encounter seems like a child. But make no mistake. We see you as you are."

A pause that allows a change of subject follows. "You are a fan of black currant, are you not?"

Indeed I am, but how does she know? I realize I am getting a taste of what lies ahead, and I am strangely reassured by it. Of the three, I already know two whom I could be happy to have look more closely at my hidden self. I expect it will be the same with the third.

But it is not.

"Well, well," a voice creaks out the words with slow emphasis. "Look what the cat dragged in."

The third sister appears, and she is as different from the other two as they are from each other. She has the look of a crone, and although I think it a pejorative term I cannot find a better word to describe her. Her wizened emerald features make her appear much older than her sisters; she is small and bent and withered like a piece of deadwood. She moves with difficulty as she enters the room—seemingly coming out of nowhere—her head cocked to one side and her grayish hair long and uncombed, the leaves that litter its strands beginning to wither. She seems to have just emerged from her bed, wrapped in a robe and looking heavy-eyed.

Her eyes settle on me almost immediately. "What bit of flotsam have you brought us now, Harrow? Can't find enough to do protecting us from the Goblins without bringing odd-looking strays home? This bit of fluff is the one we are to plumb for what secrets she might be hiding? What's your name, girl?"

I bristle up immediately. She reminds me of Ancrow—all sharp edges and suspicions rolled up in a prickly ball. But I remember my place and my need to stay calm. "Auris," I answer.

"A Sylvan name. How interesting. Harrow, are you serious about this? She is a lovely girl, but she doesn't have a speck of Sylvan in her. What are you seeing that we aren't?"

"Dreena, please," her sister cautions.

"Mind your own tongue, sister," Dreena snaps. "She's full-grown and full-minded. She looks to be made of tougher stuff than most. And if she seeks to find the truth through us, she will need to be. Auris, will you take tea? We have black currant. Isn't that your favorite?"

I am reliving my earlier conversation with Benith, so I repeat my answer. I am beginning to get a sense of things, and it now seems that Dreena might be the top dog. But she lets her sister make the tea, motioning me to take a seat on the couch and then sitting next to me. Harrow sits in one of the chairs, a faint smile on his lips. He is enjoying this—not so much my discomfort as the experience of taking tea with these odd ladies. It is obvious he has done this more than a few times already.

Dreena looks at me askance. "You come from the Goblin prisons. You are an escapee? You had friends who came with you?"

"All killed," I say, deciding she already knows this anyway. "Though I wish it were otherwise."

"Yes. But you were lucky and they weren't. Now then, I am the one who will be looking into your memories. I will be thorough, and I will be as gentle as I can, but you will have to trust me. I am not the sort that people are inclined to trust—especially strangers. But trust me you must. Do you understand?"

I nod. She can see right into me.

"Harrow saved you? Even if he hadn't told me earlier, I would know it from the way you look at him. You like him, don't you?"

This is cutting close to the bone, but I must answer or I will look foolish. "I do. He is my friend."

Dreena smirks. "How nice for you. And well said, if you are trying to be delicate." Her eyes twinkle. "Would you prefer that I move on from this particular discussion?"

"Dreena, just stop!" Benith insists, coming over to hand us our teacups, then continuing to stand in front of her sister with a stubborn look on her up-to-now impassive face. "Let's not dabble in places we don't belong."

Dreena shrugs. "There are no such places, Benith, but very well. Auris, let me explain how this works. We sit here on this couch in perfect comfort, right next to each other. We will finish our tea and soon your eyes will grow heavy. I will sing to you, which will cause you to go into a trance. Then I will have a look at your memories— but mostly at those that I can tell have been suppressed. You may realize this is happening or you may not. You may choose to speak or you may remain silent. When I am done, I will wake you and we will talk about what I have discovered. Do you understand?"

I nod. "I do. But if there are bad or questionable things that I have repressed, I would like them left that way." I hesitate. "Unless they have to do with Harrow's belief that I am somehow Fae."

Dreena cocks her head to one side, and her bushy brows knit. "I have little control over what you will remember, child, and I am not in the business of uncovering harsh truths about people's lives just to be mean. I have enough harsh truths in my own life. What I am looking for is an explanation about why Harrow—normally a mentally well-balanced young Sylvan—is suddenly experiencing a conviction for which there seems to be no rational explanation. That, and that alone, is what I will reveal. Drink your tea."

I sip it for a bit as three pairs of eyes fix on me, and then I drink the remainder down quickly. I am immediately sleepy, my eyes closing of their own volition, my breathing deepening. Strong tea, I think—then remember its purpose. I try to relax as I feel myself slipping away. Someone is singing, in a high clear soprano that soothes and calms me further. I am aware of a stillness in the room, and I want to look for Harrow for reassurance but cannot manage to do so.

Harrow, I think—or do I actually say it aloud?

I sink into darkness.

I AM SITTING ALONE IN A ROOM FILLED WITH SHELVING AND CABINETS, with examining tables and medical supplies and equipment—all of it white and clean and gleaming. I am myself, but not myself. I cannot explain it, but while I feel myself to be one thing, I look like something else altogether. I take time to examine my arms and legs and body to be sure I am not imagining this unexpected change, but there it is. What troubles me is that while I can see the change, I cannot explain it or remember how I looked before. Confusion dominates my thinking, and I cannot dredge up an explanation for what by now is a certainty in my head.

More troubling still, I cannot remember my name or anything about my life.

I am a blank slate.

A door opens off to one side, and a man walks through. He looks to be an ordinary man but he wears a doctor's smock. He comes over to me and bends down to peer into my eyes. "Are you feeling better?" he asks.

Better than what? Was I sick? Is he the doctor treating me?

"I don't know who I am," I blurt out.

His face tightens. "You suffered an injury and lost your memory, but it will return with time and care." He forces a smile. I think it is meant to reassure me, but it fails to do so. "Do you . . . remember anything?"

I think to tell him about how I feel like I am a stranger in my own skin, but decide not to. "I don't," I admit.

"Do you know who I am?"

I shake my head. He looks familiar, but not so much that I can remember a name. "Do you have a name?"

He ignores me. Has something gone wrong with his experiment? Is something wrong with me? "Tell me your name," he orders.

I shake my head again, this time almost giving way to tears. "I can't remember it!"

"Your name is Auris, and this is your home," he whispers, leaning close. He tries on another smile, but it doesn't fit. Instinctively, I mistrust him. When he reaches out to touch my hair, I flinch away. He pulls back immediately. "I know this feels strange, but I will see to it that you are well cared for. It will take time and patience. You should regain your memory soon enough, but in the meantime you will have to rest."

I shake my head uncertainly, feeling adrift and directionless. "I am afraid."

"You don't need to be, Auris. Not of me."

Why don't I believe his assurances that all will be well?

As if reading my mind, he says, "I'm your father."

I WAKE FROM MY TRANCE ALMOST VIOLENTLY, JERKING FORWARD hard. Dreena catches me in her arms and holds me upright. Her wizened green face with its pared-back features frightens me momentarily, but she coos reassuringly. Her hand strokes my hair as she murmurs to me, "There, there, everything is all right, Auris. You've come to no harm."

"But I saw him!" I gasp. "I saw everything. My father, an examining room—me, but not me, I don't . . ."

She moves me away from her to arm's length, her grip firm as she holds me fast, her eyes locked on mine with such intensity I cannot look away.

"Listen to me," she says. "You saw some of what there is to see, but you still hide much. You have a very powerful mind and your secrets are locked fast." She nods to confirm what I am hearing. "It might have felt like you saw everything, but there is more. Some of it has to do with what Harrow instinctively realized about your connection to the Fae."

She turns to stare at him, and I follow her gaze. Harrow wears a determined expression, but it is laced with worry. He nods to me reassuringly; he is still there and will be there until this is over.

"You were right to bring her to us," Benith adds from where she now stands across the room. "You are not who you seem to be, Auris. But Dreena senses what needs doing in order to find out what you are hiding. Am I right, sister?"

Dreena nods. "Call Maven. This will require all three of us."

Benith disappears momentarily, and when she returns tiny Maven is with her, come down from her elevated cottage to join us. She takes one look at me and says, "Oh, my!"

I experience this terrible feeling of having been revealed to be something alien—something so anathema to everyone that, as soon as the sisters' seeing work is completed, I will be dispatched as swiftly as possible to the farthest reaches of this land. I feel it with such certainty I am instantly terrified.

"I want this to stop!" I cry.

Instantly Harrow is kneeling before me, taking my hands in his, letting me look into those mesmerizing eyes. I calm down, but not as quickly and completely as I usually do under his gaze.

"I don't want to know any more," I whisper.

He shakes his head. "Auris, nothing has been revealed that really matters. Nothing that we can explain without looking deeper. You've done so well. Just another few minutes and it will be over."

He shifts closer to me. Our faces are practically touching. "Listen to me. I have never heard of the sisters all acting in concert to uncover something. One is always enough. Whatever is buried inside you, it must be buried deeply. It is also a great credit to you that they are willing to expend the energy. They sense that there is something important hidden in your mind—something important about you and the Fae nation. If they felt otherwise, we would have been sent packing."

I shake my head in denial. "There isn't anything!"

But there is a stricken look to his expression—one I have not seen before—deep and affecting. Harrow needs me to continue. He is pleading with me as much for himself as for me, and to my surprise I do not resent or mistrust it.

He leans closer still, and I feel his breath on my face—an act of unexpected intimacy. I wonder in that moment if he might kiss me, but . . . No. We just stare at each other momentarily, then he mouths three words: *Please. Do this.*

I nod to the sisters, who now begin to gather around me. Benith brings me a second cup of the tea and hands it to me. "Drink it all quickly," she instructs.

Dreena begins to sing once more, my thoughts scatter, and my mind goes still. All three sisters are touching me—one my face, one my shoulders, and one my legs—in a joint laying-on of hands. I am only dimly aware of this, already sliding away into my trance once more, the world about me disappearing.

Harrow remains kneeling before me, still holding my hands in his.

I want him there always.

I STAND IN A DIFFERENT ROOM; THIS ONE LOOKS TO BE A BEDCHAMBER. My father stands before me, his face a mask of concentration and secret thoughts. He gives me a smile and says, "This will only take moments, and it will keep you safe. It will tamp down the impulses that might otherwise cause you to react in stress."

He sounds as if he is instructing me in something, but I can't think what it is. My thoughts remain fuzzy. I stare at him in confusion, and he shakes his head. "Do you understand me, Auris?"

I nod obediently because I sense this is what I am supposed to do. But in truth, I understand nothing.

"Give me your arm, please."

I hold out my arm to him and he takes it in his hand. I have not been looking at anything but his face before now, but the touch of his fingers causes me to glance down. I notice immediately that my arm is green and that a fringe of silken hair with tiny leaves grows on the underside from shoulder to wrist.

Before I know what he is doing, he injects me with a syringe, pumping a fluid of some sort into my body. I flinch at the way it stings, but he holds my arm fast until all the liquid is inside me.

We stand facing each other in silence as he withdraws the needle.

Then we wait.

Time passes.

Nothing happens.

"It isn't working," he hisses, clearly displeased.

He disappears, and I am left to wonder what it is he is attempting to do. I examine myself—arms, legs—and find I am green all over. Oddly, I find this both normal and troubling. I want my father to explain what is happening.

Perhaps I should leave now before anything else happens. But I am his dutiful daughter, and I wait for his return.

I SLIDE IN AND OUT OF SLEEP AFTER THAT FOR A SHORT TIME, NEVER fully awake, never fully unconscious. I am aware of all three sisters working on me, hands holding mine, stroking my brow, as their probing gently but steadily explores my thoughts—discarding most but holding on to a few. I relax, soothed by the comfort their ministrations provide, unbothered by their soothing presence in my mind. They do not intrude; they simply observe. I know they are seeing things from my past that I do not; finding memories that are either already mostly present or unnecessary to help reveal my past.

"Here," one whispers to the other two, and something is extracted and examined.

"Oh, dear!" another exclaims.

"Hold it steady now," another orders.

Silence, and some further searching. They are intense in their efforts but not incautious or rough. I know they are seeing everything about me, but it does not feel as if they are judging or flinching. I see some of the memories they explore, but all of these are current and already known to me.

One is different. It is the last one they recover and I view it with them, shocked and frightened.

This memory is a more fully realized rendering of my recurring dream.

I STAND IN A DIFFERENT ROOM BEHIND A PARTIALLY CLOSED DOOR, CONcealed from the two people who converse with lowered voices in an adjoining room—my mother and my father. I cannot see them, but I know their voices. There is a clear urgency to their words that I cannot ignore.

"They know," my father says. "They will come for me soon. You must take Auris and flee."

"I won't," my mother answers, and there is a firm insistence in her voice, a determination. "We can send Auris away, but I will stay with you."

"They will take you, as well, if they find you. Please. It was a valiant effort, but it failed. You need to take Auris and leave. I will follow shortly."

"But what about Auris? What about her condition?"

"She's fine as she is for now, but I can't be sure of the drug's long-term effect. I can't know how she will respond when it wears off. I'm not sure when her memories will return. You have to be patient, but you need to do so in a safe place. You need to take shelter—go into hiding."

"Where? Where can we go?"

"Anywhere but here. Away from the compound and the madness that is taking root all around us. I can't do what they want anymore. I won't. So take Auris and go—now!"

His voice has become desperate, as if this is a life-threatening situation they are facing. But I don't know what the situation is. I want to ask them, but at the same time I don't. I am conflicted for reasons I cannot entirely understand.

Then I hear my mother say, "Dennis, we have to send her back!"

"No!" my father replies immediately. "No, I won't do that."

This triggers a strange understanding in me. I can sense there is something about me that my parents find deeply troubling. Something hidden is threatening to be revealed. Something that poses a threat of monstrous proportions—something that could destroy us all.

I step into view, confronting them.

As I do, the front door of our house explodes inward, and I freeze in place. A clutch of armored soldiers surge forward. My parents are seized and forced to their knees.

I hear myself screaming.

I COME OUT OF MY TRANCE WITH A JOLT OF REALIZATION OF WHAT my recurring dream is about. I take a moment to let my vision adjust and then I focus on the faces around me, one by one. Harrow is last—my rock, my assurance of safety.

He still holds my hands tightly.

"Did you see what I did?" I ask the sisters, who are clustered together before me.

They all nod. "That, and much more, child," Dreena answers. "Such a tangled web, and no clear path forward. No certain answers, and only a strong sense of what to look for. Did you feel it, sisters?" she asks them.

Maven and Benith nod immediately.

"That memory is also a dream I have been having for years," I tell them. "It explains more than I knew from the dream, but still not enough."

"What your dreams also reveal, when taken altogether," Maven says to me, her ancient face crinkling with emotion, "is that at some point in your life, while you were still quite young, you were taken from us. Perhaps by your parents, perhaps by someone else.

Your father did not specifically say you came from Viridian Deep. But woven in his words and his emotions—all of which we could read easily enough—he revealed that you are one of us. You are Fae. No matter how you look now or ever did look for that matter, you are a Sylvan."

"But you are something else," Benith adds, glancing from one sister to the next. "Did you sense it, too, sisters?"

This time they both shake their heads no. "What did we miss?" asks Dreena.

"Sisters," Benith says softly, now looking directly at me. "I think Auris is a Changeling."

TEN

A CHANGELING!

I hear Benith speak the name clearly enough, and I abruptly recall what a Changeling is, which is a creature that up until now I was pretty well convinced lived only in fairy tales. A Changeling is supposed to be a fairy child exchanged by deceitful adults for a Human child. I sit there still half-dazed by the rapidity with which I recovered this lost memory and at the same time try to take in the possibility that what I have just been told could be true. But I know it could be. I know because I am living in a new world—in a world I also didn't believe existed. The world of the Fae was imaginary, too . . . right up until I found myself standing in it. Is it so difficult then to believe that if there are Fae creatures there might also be Changelings?

The problem is that I still find it difficult to believe I am one of them. If I am a Fae child sent to the Human world, then why do I look Human? Is this solely the result of my father's experiments? I don't remember a childhood of experimentation and trauma. But then my memories are suspect, and those snippets the Seers managed to dredge up seem telling. Somehow, in some way, I was experimented on as a child. And how can that be the act of a loving father? From my reactions to him, it was clear that I loved him deeply. But how do you love your abusers? And were those same experiments the ones that had cost me my memories?

I am left with more questions now than when I set out to find the truth about myself. Yet wasn't this what I wanted? To be connected in some way to the Fae and Viridian Deep so I could stay here? So I could stay with Harrow?

"There is no other reasonable explanation for what we have found in your memories, Auris," Benith says a moment later. "In the first memory we recovered, you don't remember much of anything—not even your name. Your father appears and tells you it is Auris and that you are home and he is your father. In your second memory, he injects you with something, but it doesn't seem to work as he wishes. What you most clearly remember is that you have arms like Sylvans—greenish and fringed. But in both dreams I sense you are out of place and even somehow out of your own skin, not who you seem to be. There is a clear displacement that suggests you were Fae but somehow became Human. An injection alone would not achieve that—not to the extent that you demonstrate. On the surface—and in almost every other way that involves your appearance and behavior—you *are* Human."

I am suddenly terror-stricken. Is it possible Humans have developed a formula that suppresses your true nature so your identity can be stolen from you permanently?

Dreena intervenes. "That said, Auris, all three of us sense that you are not Human. You look the part, but your memories say otherwise. Your mother, in your last memory, said to your father: 'We have to send her back.' That supports what our instincts tell us, and our instincts never lie. You are Fae. So how can that be? Easily enough, if you are a Changeling. You see, the Fae use the word in two different ways—either to designate a Fae child switched out for a Human child, or a Fae who can transform their appearance at will. In your case, the first is obvious and the second still unproven.

But some kind of ability to transform seems innate in your physical makeup—and while Sylvan Changelings are rare, there have been a few."

I have never heard this second definition, but I don't question it. Much of what I have learned since discovering the Fae seems equally strange.

"But there is much more we need to examine before we fully understand how you got here." Now tiny Maven is speaking. "There is the discussion between your parents in which your father talks about a drug you took that will at some point wear off. Yet after several years in a Goblin prison, it has not done so—or not in any noticeable way. You still appear Human. You still have no memories of your past. So what exactly was this drug supposed to do? There are still questions to be asked and answered, and it may take some time to do so. But as long as we have you here with us, we can continue to look for those answers. What we need to report to the High Council as soon as possible, however, is that Harrow was right, and you are unmistakably Fae. We can attest to this much, at least."

"But how will we ever discover the rest?" I ask. "If my parents are dead—which it seems they are—then is there anyone who *can* supply the answers we need?"

The sisters look at one another, but no one speaks. I know what they are thinking. They are not sure what it will take to discover who and what I am. They are not sure how it can happen. Maybe it won't. Maybe it *can't*. There are limits to what even Seers can use their talents to reveal.

Harrow is still holding my hands, and he gives them a small squeeze. "Whatever you need, Auris, we will all work together to help you find it."

I squeeze his hands back, wanting him to know how much it means to me to be able to count on him. This man from another world, another culture, and another life has given me so much, when he would have been fully justified in walking away once I was safely free of the wastelands. Yet instead he chose to help me discover the truth about myself. How many people have I met like that in my life? I will never be able to repay or even thank him enough. I hope that even with Ronden in his life, I will always have him for my friend.

As I sink into the warmth of comfort he provides me, I realize suddenly that I have forgotten something. In the last memory Dreena recovered, my parents were planning to go into hiding. They knew they were in danger, and their conversation made it clear I was in danger as well. After they were killed and I was sent to the Goblin prisons, did the Humans responsible forget about me entirely? It is a big assumption to make. But if they didn't and word reaches them of my escape to Viridian Deep, won't they come looking for me so they can take me back? How important am I to them? Have I been in danger the whole time I have been here and just not realized it?

"I think I need to go lie down for a while," I say, a deep-seated weariness sweeping over me. "Can I go back to my cottage?"

All agree this would be a good idea. After thanking the sisters for sharing their time and their gifts with me, I leave with Harrow for what I do not intend to be a lie-down at all, but an out-and-out escape. I am traumatized by what I have learned—all of it so wildly impossible that I know I need to sit down by myself and think it through. I woke up this morning feeling certain I would gain the insights I needed to understand what has happened to me and why I am here. I woke certain that the answers to my questions would surface if the Seer was given a chance to bring them out. Instead I am burdened by more questions now than I had going in, and a sense that I know less about myself than I thought.

I don't talk to Harrow, and he is wise enough to know when to let me be. I need to think about what I have learned—at the very least in order to get used to it—and he knows not to intrude. We retrace our steps, and I lose myself in trying to make sense of the idea that I was born in Viridian Deep but somehow either cannot remember or was made to forget. The conversation between my mother and my father strongly suggests that I was taken away and possibly hidden—and that my presence in my parents' world was a violation of rules or laws that, if discovered, would lead to punishment for us all. And not only *would* but *did*, with my parents killed and me confined to the Goblin prisons. But why would this have happened? My mother said I had to be sent back, yet if being sent back meant being returned to Viridian, why was I taken from there in the first place? Was I kidnapped? Is it possible the mother and father I saw in my memories are not my real mother and father at all, but my kidnappers?

How suspect *are* my memories of a loving childhood in a Human world?

I arrive back at my cottage hardly aware of having made the journey, my thoughts racing and my speculations veering wildly about. I thank Harrow for escorting me, go inside without looking back, and close the door. I cannot think with him present. I have to work this through on my own, and then perhaps later we can talk it over.

I stand just inside the door for several minutes and try to calm myself. Whatever else happens, I should be allowed to stay once the sisters tell the High Council I am a Sylvan—even if there is not one visible shred of evidence that this is so. Even if I do not feel anything like what I am supposed to be. Even if I seem to have no real past and only a small shred of a future.

I sit on my couch and try to reason things through—try to order them properly—to pull loose threads together and weave them into a pattern that helps me make sense of everything I have learned.

I fail. I am too tired to think. I decide to lie down after all. My bed feels incredibly comfortable, and I find it so easy to let go of my good intentions. My mind drifts, and in moments I fall asleep.

THE AFTERNOON HAS FADED INTO TWILIGHT WHEN I WAKE. I FEEL rested, and after splashing some water on my face I feel I am again a reasonable approximation of myself. Walking over to the cold box I extract an apple and some cheese and sit at the small dining room table to eat them. The crisp tartness of the fruit brings me back to myself a little more. When I finish I feel ready to return to the outside world.

I open the door to find Harrow already sitting on the bench, waiting for me. He glances up, smiling. "Better now?"

I nod and sit down beside him. "I haven't done much other than sleep."

He smiles. "Sleep might be what you need most. A session with the Seers takes a lot out of you."

"You say that as if you've had the same experience."

"I have. A few years ago I was having some troubling dreams, and I was pretty sure they were trying to tell me something. I mentioned it to Benith while I was there on another errand—actually, she divined something was wrong and questioned me about it. In any case, she sat me down and did a retrieval. It was . . . well, like you, I was worn down at the end of it."

He shifts so he is facing me directly. "I took the details of our meeting with the sisters to the High Council office and had the scribes write them up to present to my mother and the others. Hard to tell what they will decide to do now, but it won't involve you leaving. For a Sylvan to be dismissed from Viridian, you'd have to commit a major breach of rules or contravention of Fae laws, and you've done neither. You are under my protection, and that is all that is required for now. But there is something else we need to talk about."

"Something that is going to force me to take to my bed again?" I ask, only half joking. I've had enough of surprises for one day.

"That's for you to decide. But you must have considered at some point that you might still be in danger from whoever sent you to the Goblin prisons. I think we need to take some steps to prepare you, in the event you are forced to defend yourself. I can be there most of the time, but not always, so I would like to start training you in the Fae arts of self-defense. It would help if you had the use of magic, but even without that protection you can still learn important skills that will help if you are threatened or attacked. I don't like having to talk about it, but I think it would be a mistake to pretend the danger doesn't exist. Are you willing to let me teach you?"

I nod eagerly. "I would very much appreciate your help. But do you have time for this?"

"I have a week. After that I have to go back out on patrol for two weeks—across Roughlin Wake to the wastelands. I will have someone else watch over you in my absence."

For a moment I consider asking if I could go with him. No matter whose care he leaves me in, I would feel safer if I could stay with him. But I realize it is unfair of me to ask him to assume responsibility for me while he is charged with the responsibility of keeping watch for dangers that might threaten his homeland and his people.

"I will be fine," I assure him. "But I would appreciate the week of training you are offering in the meantime. Can we start tomorrow?"

He nods. "A week is not a great deal of time, but I should be able to teach you a little about how to protect yourself should you be threatened, and a little more about how to keep it from happening."

"Can we accomplish anything meaningful in just a week?"

"You are fit enough, Auris. You showed that by surviving the prisons and crossing the desert when few others could have managed either, let alone both. You are agile and strong; you have good coordination and sharp eyes. I think you will learn a lot in a week."

"You make me sound more capable than I feel," I say, laughing. "Mostly, I feel like I would be lost without you."

He rises. "That will never be true. You are a survivor—and whatever dangers or troubles or difficult choices you face, you will always overcome them. I believe that. And you should, too."

He looks around. "It's getting dark. How about something to eat?"

I find I am surprisingly hungry.

———

THE FOLLOWING MORNING I START MY TRAINING. AND FROM THE first, almost nothing goes as expected.

We begin with Harrow talking about how I must train every day—even when he is gone—following the exercises he will set for me. The goal is to get stronger, quicker, and faster, and become less reliant on experience and more on instinct. The latter is important. The Fae are instinctual creatures, and their ability to react without thinking is legendary. If I can master using instinct when I am faced with an enemy, I will have a better chance of surviving.

I don't much care for the suggestion that my ability to survive might be tested when all along I have believed myself in a safe place. That is, until the Seers had revealed that someone was after me. "Isn't it enough that I am inside Viridian Deep and surrounded by Fae?"

"When you are faced with the possibility that you are being tracked by enemies and likely will be discovered, you cannot rely on anyone—not even me. You will always be your own last, best line of defense."

Mostly I have to learn how to use Fae weapons. For the next week I will work with him on gaining proficiency with knives, short swords, bow and arrows, and perhaps—if we can channel it—my *inish*.

"You think I have *inish?*" I ask. "Just because you think I am Fae?"

"All Fae possess *inish*, but each of us accesses it on a different level. It is very personal to the individual, and that won't be any different for you. To this point, there has been no indication that you have any means of accessing it, but that may be more because you didn't know it was there than because you cannot summon it. We have to find out."

I shake my head. I've never felt anything like what *inish* is supposed to be. I've never sensed I had any special powers. Mostly, I've always thought of myself as ordinary. But I realize that this was while believing I was Human—which I somehow cannot stop thinking I am—rather than a Forest Sylvan. It will be hard to shift my sense of self from what it has always been to what it apparently always was.

"All right," I respond. "I'll do the best I can."

What follows is an object lesson in how to never assume.

Harrow loads up on weapons and we hike into the woods. We walk for what feels to be at least a mile, well away from the settled parts of Viridian Deep and all the way over to a canyon wall where we find a reasonably large open space allowing for safe usage of the weapons with which I am to practice. The day is overcast and threatens rain, but Harrow doesn't want to delay my training. We don't get to choose the weather in which we might have to defend ourselves, so we might as well train in bad as well as good weather. I watch him spread out a piece of heavy canvas and lay all the weapons out in rows. There is enough variety that he might as well be an arms merchant as an instructor.

But an odd thing happens while he is unpacking. I watch him produce each weapon and lay it on the canvas, and as he does so I name each silently, one by one. I have no idea how I can do this. I am reminded about my odd familiarity with spitfires while I was fleeing the Goblins with Tommy and the others. There is information tucked away inside my brain that would indicate I once knew weapons far better than I do now. I wonder if I should say something to Harrow, but I hesitate. Just knowing their names doesn't mean anything by itself, does it?

He takes a target and walks it about fifty yards away from where I am standing. Then he looks back at me questioningly. I immediately shake my head and motion for him to move farther away. Why do I do that? My reaction was automatic, as if I didn't think the challenge hard enough. I am beginning to suspect the truth now, but I can't quite bring myself to admit it. When he reaches a hundred yards I find myself tempted to tell him to keep going, but common sense tells me I am already well out of range and signal him to stop.

He pins the target to a tree and walks back. "You do like a challenge, don't you?" he says.

"I know. It's silly. But I guess I reacted to . . ." I shrug. "Just let me try. Then you can move it closer again."

I have tied back my hair and rolled up my tunic sleeves. He selects a bow he thinks appropriate and hands it to me. I heft it experimentally and hand it back. "Feels kind of light. What else do you have?"

He is staring at me suspiciously by now, but he remains silent as he picks up a different bow—one that demands a stronger pull. "Try this."

I take it and find that it immediately feels comfortable in my hands. I grip it with one hand and test the tension in the bowstring. Good. (Just like I felt when I held the Goblin spitfire!) Then I reach down and pick out an arrow and sight along its length.

In a single fluid movement I notch the arrow in the bowstring, bring up the bow, sight along the shaft, pull back, and release. My arrow finds the exact center of the bull's-eye.

It all takes less than five seconds.

Harrow stares at me with a deadpan look. "You've done this before, haven't you?"

I shake my head. "I don't think so. I don't remember it. But it does *feel* strangely familiar."

"Try again."

He hands me a second arrow and I repeat the process in about the same amount of time—all too quickly for a neophyte. This arrow strikes right next to the other.

"You are too comfortable, too quick, and too sure of yourself for you *not* to have done this before," he declares. "I don't think there is much else I can teach you about using a bow. Let's try something different."

After walking to the target to retrieve the arrows and moving the target to within thirty yards, he returns with a speculative look on his face, picks up a throwing star, and hands it to me. "Do you know what this is?"

I do, of course. I know them all. I recognized them the moment he laid them out. I feel a breeze blow across my face, cooling the flush that has suddenly appeared. What is going on? "I don't know what to say," I confess. "I don't remember ever knowing any of this, but somehow I do."

"Just show me how you would use it."

I hold the star just so, lower my arm to my side, and fling it underhand at the target. Just off center. He hands me a throwing knife. I repeat the motion, this time overhand; same result. Everything I am doing is automatic, and I cannot understand how this could possibly be. It all feels so familiar. It all suggests I have done this many times before. So why don't I remember any of it?

We run the gamut. I take up every weapon from sling to crossbow, and I show remarkable proficiency with each. I do not have to stop and think about it; I just know what it is and how to use it. Harrow tests me in any number of ways, and when we have exhausted them all he gives me a wry grin.

"You are very good with weapons, Auris," he says. "Better than good. Someone has taught you well. But you don't remember anything about this at all?"

I shake my head. Not one single thing. But I have demonstrated that Harrow's assessment is right. I know too much about weapons not to have trained extensively. I just wish I knew when and how.

"Whatever happened to make you forget about your time before the prisons also seems to have stolen away your memory about training. But your muscle memory is still there, and that does not appear at all diminished. Let's see how you do with hand-to-hand fighting."

He takes up a pair of stout wooden staffs and gives me one. "Feel familiar?" he asks me.

It does, but I feel less comfortable this time. I think it might have something to do with fighting a flesh-and-blood opponent. Or at least with fighting Harrow. But he senses my insecurity and shows me how to hold the staff to defend myself, how to plant my feet, and how to move in response to his moves. He walks me through it all, explaining.

"Your best defense is always to keep away from your opponent, especially if they are bigger than you are. So it is best to use your weapons to stop them before they get close. But if that fails, don't ever let them grapple with you. Once you are that close, your quickness and agility won't do you much good. You have to move away and dodge and weave until you can strike."

I am uncertain at first, and I find myself on the ground quickly for the first couple of bouts. But then I begin to adapt to the fighting style, and start to recognize, through his initial movements, what he intends. We go back and forth for a time, but I tire quickly, my energy used up within minutes. It appears I am still recovering from my time in the wastelands.

Finally he signals a halt. "Enough for now. I honestly don't think there is much more I can teach you about traditional weapons. You might be every bit as good as I am, and that is after years in a prison with no practice or exposure. Remarkable. You are full of surprises, Auris."

I blush at the compliment and shake my head in denial. "I don't feel remarkable."

"Maybe not. But that's how it feels to me. I am still surprised by how skillful you are with a bow and arrows."

I feel a measure of relief at the praise. Discovering I have real training with Fae weapons leaves me a little more confident, but at the same time confused. How was I trained and by whom? My father didn't seem to be a man who was familiar enough with weapons to be able to train me. Besides, Humans rely on spitfires rather than Fae weapons, so it isn't likely . . .

Abruptly, I decide to tell him. "Harrow," I say sharply. "While I was fleeing the prison with my friends, I used a spitfire to try to stop the Goblins coming after us. I remember thinking I wouldn't be able to do much with it, but I could. Just like today, I seemed to know exactly what I was doing. I felt comfortable with a weapon I don't ever remember using before."

Harrow thinks about it, then shakes his head. "It is odd. It makes me wonder if perhaps this isn't a hint about the strength of your *inish*. Maybe this is an indication of its potential."

He glances at the sky, checking the position of the sun. "We have time still before we lose the light. No rain yet, either. Would you like to see if we can access your *inish* a little more?"

I would. I *very much* would. I remember what Harrow was able to do to help us escape the Goblins and reach Viridian Deep. His ability to access his *inish* had enfolded their much larger vessel and sent them careening off into an illusory black storm cloud. That I might be able to summon magic to do something even close seems wildly unlikely but, oh, so enticing. If I had a staff to direct my *inish*, that would render all other conventional weapons ineffective by comparison. I know nothing about how to make this happen, but maybe Harrow can help me learn.

He makes it plain that he thinks this is possible.

"First, I think you can learn to channel your *inish*. You have too much talent otherwise not to be able to do so. The difficulty comes in finding out how to make this happen, because every Sylvan who has achieved mastery over their *inish* has done so differently. We just need to find the right path for you."

He pauses. "So we should begin with the most common denominator for those who have already succeeded. It comes easiest when the user is relaxed. It sounds easy, but it isn't. You have to teach yourself to let go of all of your fears and doubts, as well as any tendency toward panic or loss of control. It is one thing to relax when there isn't any stress, but that almost never happens when you are under threat. This means you have to overcome these responses simply by teaching yourself to skip right past them. Let me show you what I mean."

He seats us on the ground across from each other, legs crossed, hands resting loosely in his lap. "Close your eyes and picture something calming and restful—a beautiful place, a memory, anything that quiets you and makes you feel at peace. Once you have that image, just sit quietly until I tell you to open your eyes."

I do this. It is easy enough to find such an image—I go at once to my first night in Viridian Deep: entering this magical city, seeing the lights flickering everywhere like fireflies, watching the carriages flying as they are drawn by wonderfully strange creatures, feeling at peace with myself for the first time in years. But maintaining this image is not so easy. Other images want to intrude. Concerns about my future surface and try to edge their way in. Ronden's beautiful face shoves into view, with Harrow beside her. I remain settled, but not entirely calm. When Harrow tells me to open my eyes and asks me how successful I was, I tell him the truth—while carefully avoiding the specifics.

"You begin to see how difficult it is to maintain a state of disassociation. To do so instantly is even harder, but it becomes easier with practice. I wish we had more time to work together, but we don't. We have seven days. So let's continue to experiment with achieving this state with no more than a thought."

We try for the rest of the afternoon. Harrow provides me with every trick, skill, and strategy he knows. He is patient and determined, and he does not rush or criticize me or in any way disparage my efforts. But I fail at every turn. I try as hard as I can, but it seems—though he does not say it—that I am simply not one of those with the talent to summon their *inish*.

By nightfall we are trudging back through the growing shadows and descending darkness with the problem unsolved. I am pretty flattened by my inability to show even a little progress.

"Do not be so glum, Auris," he tells me. "Look at what you have learned today. You discovered you've had extensive training with all sorts of weapons *and* in hand-to-hand combat. You have showed yourself so capable in both areas that I have no more to teach you, and we can just use our six days to hone and practice your skills. And use of *inish* will come with time. Patience is a large part of acquiring mastery over the power that resides within us. It doesn't just happen because we want it to. It doesn't always happen just because we practice hard. Sometimes it happens for no good reason at all."

"I wish I believed that," I tell him. "But to have worked so hard and not made any progress at all is discouraging. What more do I have to do to discover whether I will ever have this power? Was it this hard for you?"

He gives me a small smile. "Nothing has ever been easy for me, Auris. I am a poor example to look to."

He turns to look into the trees, and we walk the rest of the way back in silence.

ELEVEN

For the next six days, Harrow and I practice my combat skills using weapons and hand-to-hand exercises. Because I have shown familiarity and experience with both, Harrow concentrates on specific areas where he thinks I might improve with further practice. He is a patient instructor, and when I fail to understand or perform successfully he is always quick to provide me with a new way of approaching the problem. He walks me through every step, always explaining the reasoning. His knowledge is vast, and he is excellent at conveying just what he wants me to do.

These six days are long and hard, but wonderful, too. Hard because the work I do leaves me both physically and mentally drained, and wonderful because I get to spend my time with Harrow. He is so much a part of my world by now I cannot think of him ever not being there. My concerns about his relationship with Ronden are pushed to the far corners of my mind, and I live in the present as if nothing will ever cause that to change. Though foolishly, at night, I lie awake thinking of what could be. I am besotted by my dreams and at the same time unmoored by my realization that it could all vanish in a moment. I like to think I am a hard-core realist, to come out of the Goblin prisons alive when so many of my friends did not, but at the same time I persistently indulge in fantasies I have no business contemplating.

There was a time in the beginning when I found the Fae to be strange, alien creatures. Their culture, their connection with nature, their rejection of technology in favor of *inish* are so far removed from Human experience. But I was not then nor am I now put off by this—and certainly not in the way I might have expected when first exposed to it. Especially where Harrow is concerned, it doesn't seem to matter in the slightest. My attraction to him runs deep. The differences in our features—or the color of his skin or the sweep of dark hair that falls to his shoulders, sprouting tiny leaves, or the tendrils of silk that grow along the undersides of his arms and down the backs of his legs or a dozen other distinctions I can identify—are never troubling.

By now I barely notice them, and when I do I find them endearing. I like the slant of his features and the little leaves that sprout in his hair. I want to run my fingers through the fringe that grows along his arms. I want to know how that feels. But what matters to me most is the person he is inside—the one behind the serious face that can melt, in a moment, the chill of the insecurities I still experience; the one whose steadfast belief in me never wavers; the one whose eyes—those eyes, my God, my God!—draw me in and make me a willing prisoner of all my ongoing fantasies.

Understand, I have never been in love before. I have never had a boyfriend or indulged in anything more than furtive kisses. I have never allowed myself to consider a relationship with someone that was anything more than temporary. In the prisons you try not to get too close to anyone. Other kids come and go, and what you have to remind yourself is that what matters first and foremost is finding a way to stay alive. Commitment to that sort of life has the chilling effect of shutting out everything and everyone else save in the most peripheral of ways.

Now I am free of all that, escaped from the prisons and placed in a world where my time and my space are my own and I am not living each day in fear for my life and the lives of my friends. I have opportunities and choices. I have a chance to make friends and experience real relationships. I have hope for an ordinary life.

The irony of this recognizably hollow belief does not escape me. Here I am, training to stay alive—learning combat skills and weapons usage because there is every possibility my life is still at risk. Here I am, too, aware that everything I have come to love could be snatched away from me by a woman who clearly does not like or trust me and has determined that I am an obstacle to the safety of her people and so do not belong.

Still, as long as Harrow believes in me, I can live with all of it.

Until the day I finally lose him to Ronden for good. Just now, that doesn't seem imminent—even though it increasingly appears that he is already lost to me. But I ignore this as best I can.

My days are filled by his presence. He still works with me on drawing out my *inish,* but we make little progress. If I have the capacity for doing so, it is failing to manifest itself. I try every suggestion for accessing it that he makes, and nothing works. I cannot even seem to feel its presence. I am unable to summon even the smallest hint that might persuade me I should have hope. Harrow makes it seem so easy when he demonstrates what it can accomplish, yet for me it remains nothing more than an elusive possibility.

After the fourth day of trying, I am ready to admit I will never be able to do anything with *inish;* I even begin to doubt that it is present inside of me. Harrow insists I am mistaken when I voice my fears; his instincts, he confides, tell him otherwise, and his instincts are never wrong.

On the fifth day we are back on the training course, back to exercising and practicing with weapons when quite abruptly, halfway through the day, he orders a halt. "We are going to try something different today," he announces. "Put aside your weapons."

I do so, laying them out quite carefully on their bed of canvas, each in its place as he has instructed me. Ordering things, he says, both physically and mentally, will save your life more often than you realize.

As I turn to him, my task finished, he hands me an astonishingly beautiful black staff. "This is yours," he tells me. "It was carved from ironwood and then fire-hardened and sealed to protect it from the elements and any breakage. From now on, you will carry it with you everywhere. Once your *inish* surfaces, you will channel it through your staff. Your staff will respond to your thoughts—a direct transferal of inner energy into power."

I take the staff from him, turning it over and over in my hands. The ironwood has been blackened by the hardening and sealing. I do not know types of wood well, but this gleams with such a deep gloss that it seems as if I can see all the way down to its core. Its surface is smooth, but gnarled with bolls and knots and twists so that it is easily gripped. The entire middle section is carved with symbols, which I cannot translate but which radiate meanings and beliefs that are unmistakable in their power.

"I took the liberty of carving those runes," he admits. "I used what I have learned to be true about the world and added the things I have found to be true about you and your beliefs. They are written in the Sylvan language, which I know you cannot yet read but which I think you one day will. Soon you will begin to write your own truths."

I am overcome with gratitude and pleasure. "I love this staff," I reply, smiling and shaking my head in disbelief. "It is the most beautiful gift I have ever been given. I don't know that I deserve it, but I will do everything I can to earn it."

"So I believe," he says, beaming back at me. "Starting right now."

We sit together beneath a shade tree, and he tells me what he is going to try. "You have not had any success summoning your *inish*, so I begin to wonder if it has in some way or other been blocked. I was holding back on giving you the staff until you had found a way to unlock your *inish* without it, but now I think we should see if possession of an *inish* staff will aid in your recovery."

"I don't feel blocked," I tell him. "I just don't feel anything happening."

"Which is even more odd. Every Sylvan possesses some degree of *inish*. It may not be accessed in a meaningful way for many, but it is always there. Were we not convinced by now of your Sylvan heritage, I would wonder if you really were Human. But I think this is something more. So we will test it."

"Using the staff?"

He nods. "I want you to walk to the center of the clearing." He points. "Stand in the sunlight where you are fully lit and close your eyes. Relax. Focus your thoughts inward; try to summon your strength and your concentration. When I tell you to do so, open your eyes and react as you think best to whatever you see."

I rise and walk to the place he has indicated and turn to face him. He motions for me to turn farther and face off to his left, into the trees. I do so. He tells me to close my eyes. I obey. And I wait.

When I hear him call to me, I open my eyes without hesitating and find myself face-to-face with a pair of armored Goblins, crouched low as they advance on me.

I stand perfectly still—as if stillness will save me—thinking through my choices at breakneck speed. I have no weapons; they are all lying neatly arranged on their canvas blanket. I could run, but Goblins (back when I had a chance to see them in action) are very fast over short distances in spite of their bulk and seeming lack of agility. I could call for help from Harrow, but since he obviously put me in this situation it will only serve to demonstrate how truly hopeless I am.

Then abruptly I realize the Goblins aren't real. My instincts tell me this almost immediately. If they were real, they would already be on top of me. This is Harrow's way of testing my response to a surprise attack.

Except it is fake, and I know it. So I decide to pretend it is real and just see what happens.

My hand tightens on the staff and I hold it in front of me like a protective talisman and summon my *inish*. But I don't know what I am doing and nothing happens. The Goblin twins are watching me carefully, still moving closer. I try again. Same non-result. I take a deep breath. I am in no real danger, so none of this matters.

I sigh as I watch the Goblins disappear.

Harrow joins me. "You didn't feel any response from the staff?" I shake my head. "Not even a twinge?"

"Not even that."

I am a failure; there is no other way to put it. I have been given every opportunity, every reason, and every incentive to summon my *inish*, and I have not been able to detect even the smallest trace of it. Harrow must be wrong about me after all. I lack the ability to summon and convert my inner strength in even the smallest of ways.

"I thought the staff would make a difference," he says. "I will need to think about this."

We return to our regular routine. I am hot, sweaty, tired, and disappointed. I have progressed in every area of my training save one—but it is a failure that haunts me. I try very hard not to think about what it means. Not to have the use of *inish* as Harrow does would mean admitting that, even if I am a Sylvan, I will never be viewed as an equal. I will be cheapened by my lack of ability and therefore labeled an oddity. To be stared at by other Sylvans as I was by Zedlin and his Sprite companions would be a constant humiliation. I cannot imagine how I will deal with this. I might as well pack and leave, abandoning any hope of ever finding a home in Viridian Deep.

And in one day more, Harrow will go out on patrol for two weeks. I do not see how I can manage without him. I do not begin to understand what sort of progress I can expect to make without his patient instruction. But maybe this last day will change things. Maybe my *inish* will finally reveal itself. Maybe my need for it will become strong enough that it will have to show itself.

Day six comes and goes, however, and my *inish* remains a stranger, unwilling to visit for even a few brief seconds.

That night, Harrow sits me down. His lean features tighten and his eyes reveal the uncertainty he is feeling. "I wish I didn't have to go, Auris. I wish I could stay to work with you on your training. But that won't be possible, so I am handing you over to Ronden. She will be your instructor until I return."

My heart sinks. *Ronden.* Her name has barely come up of late, but just the mention of it is enough to cause a fresh burst of despair. I am not at all happy to learn that Harrow intends to replace himself with her.

"Couldn't we just postpone my training until you return?" I ask. "I was just getting used to working with you. I will have to start all over with Ronden. What if we don't work well together?"

"Ronden helped train me. She has been my partner for a long time. You won't miss a thing I could teach you by working with her." He pauses. "And discontinuing training, even for a few weeks, would be a mistake. This isn't something you can put off. *Inish* or not, you don't have enough time to learn everything you need to as it is. You have to keep practicing."

I don't hear anything after "partner." In a mindless daze, I nod my acquiescence and resign myself to training with Ronden—all the while wishing it was anyone else but her.

I SLEEP POORLY THAT NIGHT, CONSUMED BY DOUBTS AND WORRIES, very unsure of how to handle myself in this awkward situation. If she wasn't so beautiful, I might feel differently. If she wasn't older and more experienced in the Sylvan world, I might feel a tad more confident. But nothing of what I am compares favorably with what she is, so as dawn arrives and I still lie awake, dithering about the whole mess, I resolve to shove it all aside and do the best I can.

Then, perhaps, I will try to learn to fly.

I meet Ronden for the second time when I step out the door of my cottage the next morning, carrying my *inish* staff, and find her waiting for me. Statuesque, willowy, and incandescently beautiful, she makes me feel instantly inadequate. "Good morning, Auris," she greets me with a broad smile.

"Good morning," I respond. Her words are filled with warmth and sincerity, and I find I cannot help smiling back at her.

"You carry a beautiful staff," she says admiringly. "I see Harrow's workmanship clearly displayed. He must think a great deal of you to put in the time and effort required to craft such a treasure."

She seems genuinely pleased that he has done this for me, and I am infuriated that she demonstrates no jealousy whatsoever. I grit my teeth and nod silently.

We walk together down through the city and out to the training ground. She is dressed in loose clothing and bears a canvas case that I know must contain fighting weapons because it matches the one Harrow carried with him each day he was with me. In fact, I realize suddenly, it is the *same* case. The stains and smudges on the canvas are unmistakable.

Something about recognizing it as Harrow's is demoralizing. I exhale sharply, thinking about how they are so familiar with each other, how being partnered would mean that they share everything. I have been so foolish. I have been deluded in thinking he might one day be interested in me for something beyond my value as another of the Fae and his moral responsibility for having rescued me from the Goblins.

We reach the training field about an hour after sunrise, and Ronden suggests we sit and visit for a bit before we start. She asks me in-depth questions about what Harrow and I have worked on and how much progress I think we have made. She mentions a few of the weapons we have been using and asks me to describe my comfort level with each. I do my best to comply, all the while wishing I were somewhere else. We talk a bit about my loss of memory and why I think I am proficient in the use of weapons yet cannot remember anything about my training.

I shake my head. "I wish I knew. I was so surprised when Harrow gave me that bow and I was able to wield it so comfortably. I still don't understand it. Yet just seeing it—holding it—triggered a memory of exactly how I was supposed use it. The right way to grip it, the proper stance, how and where to place my fingers, how far to pull back on the bowstring—it was suddenly all right there."

She nods. "A miracle of instant knowledge. And Harrow was every bit as surprised as you. He thought he was going to have to teach you to use Fae weapons from scratch, and that teaching you anything more than the basics was going to be impossible in the week he had." She chuckles. "You certainly shocked the pants off him when you promptly picked up one weapon after the other and used them all as if you were born to it."

I find it odd, but already I like her better than I thought I would. She is calm and steady in the same way as Harrow. She is warm and open in our conversation, and I am quickly relaxed enough to speak with her as if we are old friends. I sort of hate it and love it at the same time. It is very unexpected. I was prepared to tolerate her at best, but nothing about her allows that. In some very strange way, it feels as if we could become close.

"Harrow tells me you are struggling with channeling your *inish*," she says suddenly.

All the air goes out of me. I had hoped to keep that confidential. I lower my gaze and shrug. "It isn't as if I want it that way. Just the opposite. I want to be able to do what Harrow thinks I can, but nothing seems to work for me."

"Including the *inish* staff you were given?" She frowns, an expression of determination lining her features. "We have to discover why."

I blush in spite of myself, humiliated just by the thought of her knowing of my failure. I face her bravely. "Does Harrow think it's possible?" Then I quickly add, "Do you?"

She shrugs. "I don't see why not."

I do. But if working with her will help, I won't let how I feel about her stand in the way. "I admit I may not have a clear idea yet of what it takes to summon my *inish*. But if Harrow and you both insist it is there, I intend to keep trying."

"He's very persistent," Ronden says. "When he makes up his mind about something, he does whatever it takes to achieve it. He is also mostly right about things like this. Those instincts of his, you know. Even when he was little, he had this amazing ability to detect what was hidden. He certainly pulled that trick with me often enough."

"You knew him when you were younger?"

She gives me a funny look. "Of course. All our lives."

All our lives? In that instant, I decide to take the plunge. "He hasn't told me much about you, but it was obvious to me right from our first meeting that you were close. How did you meet?"

"How did we meet? I was there when he was born, Auris. I didn't have to *meet* him; he was *thrust* upon me." She giggles. "That's how these things happen. Don't you have any brothers or sisters?"

"I don't know," I admit. "I can't remember if I ever . . ."

And then, abruptly, I realize what she has just said. "Harrow is your *brother?*"

"Of course! Didn't he say so? Who did you think I was?" She stops talking and stares. "Wait, did you think he and I were . . . ?"

"Promised," I manage to whisper, flooded with such a wild mix of feelings I cannot begin to sort them out. "Char said you roomed together, and I thought you were . . . maybe, partners."

Ronden breaks into peals of laughter, and even though I know they are at my expense, I find myself laughing with her. Eventually the laughter tapers off as—rather wonderfully—she leans forward and embraces me. "Oh, Auris! I am so sorry you misunderstood! No, we are not promised to each other or partnered or anything— well, save for being partners in training. Did he mention that I trained him? But otherwise, we are just your ordinary garden-variety sister and brother."

I feel deeply foolish and at the same time terribly relieved. My understanding of Ronden's relationship with Harrow has simply been a misunderstanding, and what I had once thought possible and then been forced to accept as unlikely is suddenly possible again. Harrow might have mentioned it and saved me the embarrassment of making this mistake, but then, too, I could have asked about it more directly and avoided all the agony.

"I feel pretty foolish," I admit.

"You shouldn't." She takes my hands in her own and squeezes them. "How could you know? When you heard we lived together, it must have seemed as if we were . . ."

She trails off and studies me silently for a moment. "Gods of Fae- and Faerie-kind, you're in love with him," she whispers.

I shake my head instantly, but the deep blush that heats my face gives me away. "I didn't want to be . . . didn't plan to be . . ." I stutter.

She makes a motion of dismissal. "No one ever does. It just happens. I should have seen it earlier. He finds you in the wastelands and saves you from the Goblins. He brings you to Viridian, makes sure you have a place to live, says he thinks you're one of us even when you don't look anything but Human, stands up for you with the High Council, and gets permission to take you to see the Seers. Spends virtually all his time with you. Why wouldn't you be at least a little in love with him? Anyone else who went through what you did certainly would."

I find myself fighting not to smile and at the same time wishing I could sink into the earth. This mix of relief from knowing the truth and fearing it will come to nothing anyway is strange and new, but wonderfully enthralling. I want it and don't, both at the same time.

"Maybe we could keep this between us?" I ask hopefully.

She nods at once. "I like you, Auris. My brother could do worse, and I am constantly afraid he will. My mother likes to think she can determine the direction of our lives, especially where Harrow is concerned, but she is wrong. Harrow told me, by the way, what happened at the High Council."

"It was a bit uncomfortable."

"Ancrow is a formidable woman. She is an icon to some and a witch to others—and sometimes both at the same time. But my brother walks his own path."

"Maybe she will change her mind about me."

"Maybe—especially now that the Seers have determined you are definitely Fae. She will still be expecting demonstrable evidence of it, but Harrow would never let that stop him. You just need to be patient. Give things a chance to work themselves out."

She stands and pulls me up with her. "For now, let's see what we can do about helping you learn to defend yourself better."

We go back to work at once, starting with weapons practice and moving on to exercises and finally to a discussion about making tactical choices in dangerous situations. Now that I am unburdened by irritation with having her as my instructor and mistaking her relationship with Harrow, I can accept her efforts more willingly, and I find myself bonding with her quickly. She is less intense and more relaxed in her teaching, which puts decidedly less pressure on me than when Harrow was my instructor.

"Harrow didn't spend much time on this, so I will. He looks at defending himself differently because he's a man. But a woman can't rely on strength in the same way, so I've spent considerably more time on tactics than he has, and I'm better suited to teaching you what you need to know."

We work for four hours on weapons and exercises, most of it now familiar enough that I barely have to think before acting. But tactics is another matter altogether, and Ronden takes time not only to introduce her favorites one by one, but also to explain the reason why they are valuable tools for a woman, and how each one has several variations that relate directly to the nature of the threat.

"If a man comes at you bare-handed, relying on his size and strength to overpower you, you can use that size and strength against him. Various holds and throws, spins and drops, kicks and punches can put him down before he knows what's happened. If a man comes at you with a knife, however, the first thing you have to do is disarm him. For that, you use arm locks, pressure points, and twists. If you are out in the open, you use speed and agility, movement and deception. If you are pinned against a wall, you have to let him get close enough that you can cause him such pain he will lose heart. Eyes, nose, crotch, fingers—all good choices."

"But if he is too much for you even so? If his skills are a match for yours? Then what?"

"You have to kill him on the first strike or hope help arrives."

I do not find this at all reassuring. "You've told me what to expect from a man and how to react to it. Will it be different with a woman?"

Ronden shrugs. "Maybe. Maybe not. A man sees you as a physical inferior. A woman sees you as an equal. Her skills are more likely to be a mirror of your own. Combat is fluid and you must adjust your tactics with each new challenge you face. But if you study tactics now, you won't have to wonder what to do later. Your body will respond on its own once you see what you are up against."

"I don't know if I can do that, if I can be that person. I think I am strong, but I don't think I am a killer."

"You shouldn't think of yourself that way, Auris. You should think of yourself as a *survivor*. It's what you are, after all. That's what got you here. You survived when others did not. It is a harsh reality, but this is how you have to look at it. There are enemies who will try to kill you, often for no better reason than who and what you are. Or simply that you are in the way. You need to be able to protect yourself. But how wisely you choose and how well you have trained will determine most outcomes. Injury or death are always possibilities, and you need to keep a healthy respect for both whenever you fight, but the more you train, the less likely that you will have to kill."

We go back to work, and she walks me through a variety of situations and tactics. I have no trouble understanding the thinking behind it, but I do have a certain resistance to the idea of using the more deadly of the defenses and retaliations I am being taught. In practice, I can make believe they will be there when I need them. But in a real situation, I wonder.

As the sun slips west, we finish up and walk back toward the city. Neither of us talks, lost in our own thoughts, until finally Ronden begins to speak once again about my failure to summon my *inish*.

"I may not have the same strong instincts Harrow does, but I do have some. What I see of your abilities tells me he is right about you possessing a strong *inish*—one that I think will manifest itself sooner or later. What I also think is that something has happened to lock it away. Maybe it was an incident in your early life. Maybe it was a magic created to tamp it all the way down. Maybe it was something else. But you are blocked in some way, Auris. We just have to find a way to unblock you."

"Harrow couldn't do it."

"My brother might be the wrong person. You love him enough that you rely on him, and he is always there to protect you. I can't explain how that matters, but I think maybe it does. Maybe being away from your real home helped keep your *inish* tucked away, and it has been locked down for so long it doesn't know how to surface. Or something of that sort. I keep thinking about ways we might change that. Some sort of trigger is needed, so we need to keep looking for it during these next two weeks."

I think it over when she goes silent again. She may be right, but I can't imagine what might accomplish what she's asking of me. I cannot think of a way to even look for my *inish* so that I might find a release for it. But if I do not do so, or if I fail to find it, what becomes of my hopes for a life in Viridian? It is all well and good for Harrow to reassure me that nothing will change if I fail, but I think maybe it will anyway.

And if it does, the intensity of my feelings for him will not be enough to make up for it.

TWELVE

IT HAS BEEN A LITTLE MORE THAN TWO MONTHS SINCE MY ESCAPE from the Goblin prisons, and enough time has passed that I am irretrievably altered. I no longer dwell on my old life, on my years behind walls and bars, on my brutal treatment at the hands of my jailers or the deprivations I endured during my imprisonment. I haven't dreamed of my parents once since the Seer sisters revealed my enhanced memory of our last minutes together. This does not mean I no longer think about it now and then. It does not mean I no longer cry for all that happened in that dark and brutal existence I have managed to escape. It only means my sleep is once again my own, and I have something good to hold on to to help me put all the bad to rest.

But it also does not mean I am able to live without fears and doubts—that I am now free of all worries in the present. Life does not give you a pass from upheavals even in the best of times. Life gives you living—which is messy and uncertain, constantly shifting your place in the world and your expectations of what waits just around the next corner.

I am in a good place now, but not a perfect one. I am mostly happy and content, but not free from knowing that it could all change so quickly. If there is one thing I have learned, it is this: Life is never settled.

I've spent the days continuing my training with Ronden, who is now my new best friend. Next to Harrow, of course, but her brother is something more to me than a friend, at least in my daydreams and sweet wishes. Instead, she has taken me under her wing as she would a sister, and she has made it clear that she intends to help me not only in the mastery of weapons and combat skills, but with the direction she knows I hope my life will take. We work hard on the training field. She is a skilled practitioner of hand-to-hand combat, and we spar with each other constantly. At first I am so inept she overcomes me every time. But gradually that begins to change until I have learned enough to become a reasonable match. Little by little, I gain ground until I can feel at every practice and with every challenge that I have a reasonable chance of emerging as the victor.

These sessions are not life-and-death events for me, but they take on real importance from knowing that one day they might be. Ronden is demanding and insistent—more so than Harrow was—but it produces results that his more cautious handling might not have. She understands the nature of a woman's toughness, and she spares me nothing in providing me with my education. I do not ask for quarter or shy from doing her bidding. I am tough already, both mentally and physically, from my years in prison. What I lack in skills and experience I make up for with determination and endurance.

But it is not all hard work and sore bodies and tired minds. It is also laughter and joking. It includes intimate truths amid quiet conversations. She becomes my sister in fact—the only sibling I have ever had and the best I could ever ask for. We bond quickly and easily following my discovery of her true relationship to Harrow, and while I do not mistake the nature of the shift in our connection, I also do not underestimate the importance of its impact.

"Come to dinner tonight," she suggests a week into our training as we sit together at midday eating a light lunch. "You've already met Char, and now you can meet my other sister, Ramey. They've asked after you repeatedly, and I think it is time to satisfy their curiosity."

"Oh, then I am to be a curiosity to entertain them?" I joke. "How lucky for me."

She shakes her head. "It may very well turn out that they will be curiosities for you. You've met do-it-all Char, but Ramey is another story. Will you come?"

I have never been invited into their home. I assume this has much to do with the fact that the youngest two still live with their mother, Ancrow, who does not much like me. While the rest have embraced me as a friend, she has remained distant and mostly absent from my life, apparently still thinking of me as an intruder and a member of a people she detests.

I shake my head. "What does your mother think about this? Or does she know?"

"What my mother thinks or knows is irrelevant. She will be gone. This is a sisters' dinner, and you are going to be one of us. Please come."

I smile broadly, gratefully. "Thank you. I will."

We finish eating and go back to training. The remainder of the day flies by. The only negative is my continued failure to access my *inish*, which we experiment with summoning for over two hours, only to achieve nothing.

I return to my cottage to shower, and end up spending an inordinate amount of time afterward just wrapped in a towel in front of my mirror, brushing my hair with long, languorous strokes. The rhythmic brushing is soothing, and I realize how very lucky I am. Look at how much good fortune has come my way! I have found a home I never knew I had. I have found a family that considers me one of them (well, mostly). I have found someone I love and may one day spend the rest of my life with. I wonder at the odds of the latter, but I do not feel they are insurmountable. I was meant to be with Harrow; it was why he was fated to find me and I driven toward him. We are already close friends, even though I cannot yet be certain of any other feelings he might have for me.

Now I am going to dinner with his sisters at their invitation and with the knowledge that they are anxious to spend time with me. Really, I would do anything that would give us a further opportunity to bond. I want them to like me; I want Harrow's family to know that I belong with him. I can do nothing about his mother as yet, but one day I will find the opportunity to do so.

I dress in loose-fitting pants and shirt and prepare to exit my home. Just before leaving, I remember Harrow's admonition to never go anywhere without my black staff. So far, I have done so on every occasion, even those that do not involve training. There is no reason to change things now, so I go back to retrieve it, then head out once more.

From there, it is only a short walk to my destination. As I reach the front door, I am smiling in anticipation of spending an evening with Ronden and her sisters, getting to know them all much better, laughing and joking with a family—even if it is a family that is not really my own.

But when I knock on the door and it opens, my heart sinks. It is not Ronden who stands there to greet me. It is Ancrow—tall, imposing, and stern-faced. Trouble waiting to happen.

"Good evening," I manage, hoping for the best.

"Go home," she says at once. "You are not welcome here."

I shrink from her and then steady myself. "But I was invited by Ronden to . . ."

"Ronden doesn't live here anymore. She may be my daughter, but this isn't her house and she has no business inviting people over without my permission."

I look past her. "Is she here? May I speak to her?"

"You may not. You may turn around and go back to your cottage and stay there. Understand, *little girl*. I do not care what those old women think or what Harrow thinks, either. You are not a Fae. You are not a Sylvan. You are not one of us. *You. Are. A. Human!* And no Human will ever be welcome in this house. So accept that, and do not come here again."

She means to demean me, and she succeeds. "If you would give me a chance . . ."

"Go away!" she snaps and slams the door in my face.

I stand there a moment, unable to move. I would cry if I was not so angry. As it is, I am not sure I can make myself leave. She has thrown the tattered remnants of my hopes in my face, and I want to throw something in hers in reply. But I have nothing to throw and no answer without talking first to Ronden. She was sure her mother would not be there, so something must have gone wrong with Ancrow's plans. I feel bad for Char, who I know has been looking forward to this dinner. I feel bad for all three daughters and myself for the injustice of it all.

Finally, after long minutes, I turn around and walk back to my cottage, go inside, and sit staring into space for long minutes. I want to find Ronden, but don't know where to look. I could wait, but doing nothing feels like defeat. I am suddenly hungry, so I decide to go out and find something to eat. Alone is fine. I know the area by now. I know several places to dine and enough of the language to order a meal.

So with my ironwood staff in hand, I depart my cottage for the second time and walk along the tree lanes to a favorite establishment. It sits another level up in the giant hardwoods, set out on a pair of broad limbs that look out over the city all the way to Promise Falls. Because it is almost dark by now, I can barely see the falls, but there is more than a little of the lighted city to content me. I am greeted in my own tongue and offered a table out on the edge where I have a clear view. I order a glass of hunter's ale (which Harrow introduced me to) and sit staring out at the lights, thinking things over.

I am beginning to wonder about my future with Harrow—not only if there *is* one, but also if one could even be possible. His mother is a formidable obstacle, and she seems determined to see me packed up and gone—or at least denied any chance of ever being accepted into the Sylvan community. And as much as I love Harrow, I don't want to be someone who breaks apart a close-knit family, even if I am in the right and there is something between Harrow and me that would be worth exploring.

On the other hand, I am not the type to give up and walk away without a fight. I just have to find some way to convince Ancrow of at least two things—that I am Fae, and that I am worth having as a part of her family. This seems a tall order, given her firmly settled opinion that I am neither. In her eyes, I clearly look Human. And to her way of thinking, right or wrong, Humans are the enemy.

A server comes to take my order and I give it in passable Sylvan. But I still sound like what I am—a visitor to another country. Or in this case, to another world—a world that two months ago I did not even know existed. I wonder exactly where I am. Where in my known world is Viridian Deep located, and why has no one ever mentioned it before? I realize such talk might be strange among prisoners locked away from the larger world, but wouldn't you think someone would have said something about this place during my years of incarceration, given how close it lies to the prison?

Surreptitiously, I watch the other diners. Mostly, they talk among themselves, paying no attention to me. But now and then one looks at me and quickly away again. I am a curiosity. I am an outlander. I wonder what it will take for that to change. I wonder if it can ever change. I suppose if I am here long enough and become a familiar sight, the curiosity might dissipate. But how long does that take? When you are one of a kind, how can you ever be anything but a curiosity? When you look so entirely different, how can you ever find a way to blend in?

The answer, I suppose, is that you can't. You just have to learn to live with it. You have to find a way to fit in, even in spite of your differences. I am not sure I can do this. I am pretty sure I do not know how.

I eat my food and drink a second glass of ale. I probably shouldn't, given my current emotional state, but the heady liquid seems to take the edge off the evening's disappointment. I had been looking forward to my time with Ronden, Ramey, and Char, and Ancrow snatched it all away. If Harrow were here . . .

But he is not.

An hour passes, and full darkness sets in. Still I sit at my table and ponder my fate and what I might do to change it. There has to be a way. There must be something I can do to turn things around. My *inish* staff leans against a chair across from me, gleaming black wood with deep-carved runes clearly visible even in the dimmed light. What do these runes say exactly? I must find time to learn the Sylvan language so I can read them. I will never have the facility to understand other languages as the Fae do, but I must at least do the best I can with the one they speak.

Another hour passes, and I decide I should go back to my cottage and try to sleep. The tables are emptying out; the crowds both inside the eatery and out on the tree lanes have thinned to a trickle. I have finished my second glass of ale and declined the offer of a third. I am new to alcohol, not sure how well I can handle it in more than small amounts, and this seems like a poor time to experiment.

I rise, pick up my staff, and walk to the entry to thank the manager and express my appreciation for being allowed to linger. I do so passably well and go out into the night. Lost in thought, I wander toward my cottage, following the path I took coming in. When I descend to the next level down, I find the tree lanes practically deserted. The Sylvan people tend to retire early, I have discovered, except if there are special celebrations or holidays. How these days are determined or what they are meant to recognize is a mystery to me. Odd as it might seem, they do not seem particularly concerned about what day of the week or month of the year it might be. Time seems to be of no special importance. There are no timepieces to be found. There are only morning and night, light and dark, and the in-betweens. To me, this is not strange; it is familiar. In prison, you don't pay attention to time, either.

I am wrapped in thought as I walk, saddened anew by the mem-

ory of my dashed expectations for the evening. I can still see Ancrow's face and hear her voice as she stands in the doorway of her
home, confronting me. I can still hear the venom in her voice.

It is less than a hundred yards to my cottage when I look up. A
pair of Goblins has appeared right in front of me. I stop in my
tracks, wondering if they are real. But they are—I sense it immediately. I do not know where they come from; I am caught completely
by surprise. What are Goblins doing in the heart of the Sylvan
home city? Harrow's whole job is to prevent this from ever happening, so how could they even get here without an alarm being
sounded? How could they manage to find me?

But there is no time for speculation.

Reacting instinctively, I assume a defensive stance, my staff
held protectively before me. I am in an open space, and there is
room to maneuver. What I lack are weapons of any kind. All I have
is the staff and my training in hand-to-hand combat, so these will
have to be enough. These attackers, each twice my size, must not
be allowed to get within arm's reach or I am finished.

I shout at them in challenge, trying to demonstrate I am not
frightened and at the same time hoping to summon help. The Goblins show no reaction, but separate from each other slightly, arms
spread wide as they take a step toward me. A surge of fear rushes
through me as I tighten into a crouch and prepare to make a break
for safety—perhaps back to my own cottage, perhaps to somewhere
lower down on the tree lanes. I realize suddenly how alone I am.
There is no one around and no lights on in the surrounding houses
and cottages. The entire area feels empty of life.

I am poised to run when I feel arms come around me from behind, pinning my staff to my body and yanking me off my feet.
There is a third Goblin! Two seconds more and the three have me
immobilized and are hauling me away so quickly I have had no
chance at all to escape them, or even use my staff as a cudgel. I am
enraged and terrified; I will be taken back to the prisons. Why have
I not been more careful?

Then abruptly the front door of Ancrow's house bursts open and little Char rushes out, yelling like a wild thing. "I'm coming, Auris! Don't be afraid!"

Well, if I wasn't afraid before, I am now. She's running heedlessly toward me at reckless speed, and the Goblins stand between us.

And then—suddenly—a miracle occurs. Perhaps willed to life out of desperate need alone, I feel something palpable rise within me—a churning of life, a bubble bursting, a surging of such intensity that it feels as if my blood has ignited and fire is running through my veins. I gasp at the impact of its unexpected awakening, curling up against myself in an automatic response to an unfamiliar sensation. I wonder what is happening to me.

Then abruptly, I know. I do not stop to doubt myself. I do not pause to wonder if I am mistaken. I react instinctively. I summon my *inish* with a single thought and channel it through the length of my rune-carved staff, which is still jammed against the length of my body. Flames erupt! I am on fire! But no, it is not me that burns; it is just the *inish* staff. The grooves that form its runes are filled with tiny flames that lick out hungrily. It takes me another moment to realize my hands are still gripping the staff tightly, yet I do not feel its fire. But the Goblins that hold me drop me in shock and back away, their growls and snarls filled with anger and fear. I tumble onto the tree lane pathway and scramble up. I see the Goblins gathering for a rush at me, but they are too slow. In three short, deadly bursts my *inish* propels them backward with such force that they simply fly off into the darkness and disappear.

Char—still racing to save me, a club of some sort gripped in one hand—skids to a halt. Her mouth opens in disbelief and then breaks into a broad smile. "You did it, Auris! You found your *inish*!"

I manage to slow my breathing and collect myself. I smile back. After days of struggling, after constant disappointments and failures—after standing on the brink of accepting it was never to be—I have found my *inish* and successfully summoned it. I have managed to pass the most important test I set for myself.

"I found it," I confirm.

As soon as she sees my smile, she rushes up and hugs me around the waist, burying her face in my chest. "I knew you would!" She looks up. "Those were Goblins, weren't they? They had you surrounded. I heard you calling, so I came." She exhales sharply. "But I was so scared!" she admits.

I nod and stroke her leafy hair. "Me, too."

A figure appears in the darkness behind her, tall and dark robed as she moves into the light. Ancrow. She has heard the commotion and come for a look. I have no idea how much she's seen.

She moves closer. "Char, please go inside now. Everything is fine. Go on."

Reluctantly, Char releases her grip on me and walks away. Ancrow stays a moment longer. "I think we need to have a talk. Tonight seems a little precipitous. I'll come by tomorrow morning."

I nod, although part of me wants to suggest she stay away from me. She turns to leave, but takes only a few steps before she looks back, her face so tightly shuttered I can read nothing of her emotions.

"I may have misread you, Auris," she says.

Then she continues on, leaving me staring after her in silence.

THIRTEEN

ON THE FOLLOWING MORNING I WAKE EUPHORIC AND GRATE-
ful. Before rising, I replay my memories of the previous
night, considering what really happened and what it means. I was
confronted by Goblins and taken prisoner, then Char came running to save me, and I acted instinctively and almost without
thinking. Perhaps it was stress or anger that unblocked me and perhaps it was simply fear, but I managed to summon my *inish* when
everything I had tried before had failed. I don't know how I managed it, but my *inish* surfaced just in time to allow me to free myself
from the Goblins and cast them so far away I still have no idea
what became of them.

As a result of this, I can now tell myself I am a Sylvan inside
no matter how I look on the outside. But how I got this way, I have
no idea. Nor am I at all sure what will happen next. Besides Char,
who else knows what I have discovered about myself or what I have
done? I can't be sure about Ancrow, even though she said she was
coming to talk to me this morning. I haven't seen Ronden and
don't know where she was during last night's drama. I am supposed

to train with her today as always, but has she talked to Char or her mother yet? What happened to those Goblins I flung away? Does anyone in the city know that somehow Goblins have found a way inside their city, and that they have come there because of me?

Some answers arrive with a knock on the door right after I have showered and dressed but before I have eaten even a bite of my breakfast.

Abandoning food and drink I walk over to answer, expecting Ancrow and finding Ronden standing there instead.

"Well, you had quite a night," she declares, stepping inside and giving me a warm hug.

"You heard?"

"Everything, I imagine. Char was at my door at sunrise, pounding away as if she might break it down, dragging me from my sleep, talking as if she might never stop, going on about Goblins and your amazing discovery. Once I got her calmed down, I was able to understand most of it."

"So you know I found my *inish* and used it successfully." I make it a statement.

"I know you found it, used it, saved your own life and Char's foolishly impetuous life in the process. This is so wonderful, Auris! I am so very happy for you."

"I'm pretty happy for myself," I admit. "Do you know what became of the Goblins?"

She nods. "All three died falling from the tree lanes."

"But how did Goblins get so far inside the city without any warning? They shouldn't have been able to do that, should they?"

"No, they shouldn't. Someone must have helped them. Apparently not everyone likes the idea of an apparent Human in Viridian. It will be difficult to find out who did this, but at least we can be pretty sure how the Goblins found you. Still, there are a few questions that need answering."

It never occurred to me that there would be those who hated the idea of a Human living among them so utterly that they would try to do something about it—even if it meant reaching out to their own ancient enemies. "I don't much care for the idea of someone hating me so."

Ronden smiles. "We'll find out who it is, I promise. Right now, we have to concentrate on getting you out on the training field and seeing what you can do with your newfound *inish*. I admit I am anxious to see. But first tell me what happened with my mother."

I heave a resigned sigh. "I went over as planned, knocked on the door, but your mother answered and told me to go away. I said I was invited to dinner, and she said I was never going to be allowed in her house."

"Oh, I know all about that. I was listening from the other room with Char and Ramey. I meant afterward, when she came out to get Char. Char was banished inside and couldn't hear. What did my mother say? Does she know about your discovery?"

"I don't know. She didn't tell me. She just said she was coming over to talk to me this morning." I pause, thinking back. "At the end though, as she was walking away, she did say something about misreading me. I'm not sure what she meant."

"Guess you'll find out when she gets here." Ronden stands. "Then you can tell me. I'll tell her to come now, so we can start today's training. Isn't it exciting?"

And she is out the door before I can respond.

Somewhat bewildered by the speed of her departure, I try to bolt down my breakfast before Ancrow appears, trying my best to remain calm. Even the thought of being in this formidable woman's presence is daunting, and I don't expect that whatever she plans to tell me will leave me feeling any more certain about my future in Viridian Deep.

As I eat, I study my ironwood staff, which rests against the empty dining room chair across from me. Its polished length gleams with such brilliance, it is hard to believe it has ever seen use. Yet last night it saved my life. It channeled my *inish* and prevented my return to the Goblin prisons. It cemented my place as a member of the Fae people. But I know it wasn't the staff alone that accomplished this. The staff simply gave direction to my *inish*; I was the one who unlocked it. The staff is a symbol of what I now carry inside me. The power is a part of who I am now, and a part of my heritage. It all still feels a bit unreal, but at the same time utterly right.

Today and in the days to come I will be given a chance to explore the limits of that power and to learn to use it wisely and comfortably. I will become the person I know Harrow saw me to be—the person that I want to be. No one can take that away from me now. No one—not even Ancrow—can deny what is rightfully mine. I feel reborn into the world in the same way as I felt when I escaped the Goblins and found Viridian Deep. I no longer see myself as I have for so long—a Human, a prisoner, and a lost soul. I am a Sylvan, a free woman; I have found a way to begin living again.

Breakfast consumed, I rise, walk to my bedroom and spend long minutes studying my face in the mirror. I see myself looking back, and I am physically the same person I was the night before. My dark eyes, dark hair, olive skin, and familiar expression have not changed. I am ordinary when I look at myself, yet today I feel special. My newfound abilities have revealed themselves; my confidence in myself is high and my future is my own. Everything that lies ahead feels fresh and new and exciting, and I want to hold on to this feeling forever.

I determine in that instant that I will do so.

I snatch up my staff and exit my cottage. I will not wait for Ancrow to come to me; I will go to her instead. I will meet her on my terms and not her own.

Crossing toward her home along the platforms and lanes, I mark the spot where I fought and prevailed the previous night. It was here my *inish* surfaced and signaled the start of my new life. I flush with a happiness I have never known. To be able to have these expectations is a gift.

I reach my destination and pause, struck suddenly by a fresh oddity. I know Harrow and his family only by their first names. What is their surname? Do the Fae possess a family name? How can I not know this?

Moving to the front door to announce my presence, I am caught off guard when it opens before I can reach it and Ronden emerges.

"I have settled things with Ancrow so that we can get on with your training. She will see you tonight instead. Come."

She starts away, and I follow wordlessly. No confrontation for now; the matter is postponed. I am both disappointed and relieved. But I know there is no need to rush, because the result will be the same whether it is revealed now or later. Better to focus on what really matters. Better to concentrate on what I can now expect to accomplish. What can I do with my newly found *inish*? What are its limits, and how much will it change the direction of my life?

We walk through the city and continue on through the forests to the training field where Ronden and I begin our familiar routine of weapons and hand-to-hand defense training. When that is done—not quickly enough in my estimation—we begin to experiment with my *inish*.

We begin slowly, and soon I begin to realize that possessing magic—as much as I had desired it—comes with a huge moral responsibility. Like any weapon, how you use it has consequences—and Ronden does not hesitate to point those out. We talk about defensive and offensive uses, of emotional involvement, of need versus desire, of my life versus the lives of—or the cost to—others.

Having the use of *inish* carries with it responsibilities I hadn't thought about and now know I must. Almost, I find myself wishing I had never managed to access it at all.

"Once you use your *inish* as you did last night, you are infused with knowledge of how that usage feels. Do you understand?" she asks.

I nod. "But I want to see if I can do it again."

"You can and you will. But first you must see clearly the danger that this presents. The urge to employ your *inish* power is enormous, and you cannot allow it to rule you. You must always be in command, and you must always exercise great care. If you fail to do so, you risk spinning out of control and causing something terrible to happen, either to you or to someone else. You must keep your *inish* tightly checked always, and only carefully released when needed. Its use must be judicious and practiced and well considered. Response is all too frequently automatic, and to not have thought through the consequences ahead of time would be a grave mistake."

She smiles—that wonderful smile that brightens her face and mine with it. "I have some understanding of this because I have experience from accessing my own *inish*. But, Auris, your power is new and your ability still raw. Both require careful tending. The responsibility you exercise now will go far in determining how skilled you become."

So she has me use my *inish* to create shields, and then she tests their strength against her efforts to break them. She tasks me with moving objects much too heavy for me to lift, using my inner strength to overcome my physical weakness. I surprise myself with the amount of weight I can handle. I am given locks of increasing complexity to open using only my mind. I am shown how application of *inish* to familiar weapons provides speed, range, accuracy, and impact beyond what I could have managed otherwise.

When we are done with these exercises she has me set aside my staff and do one summoning after another using only my hands and my thoughts. At first, the lack of the staff makes these efforts feel awkward and even daunting. But soon enough I am able to call up my *inish* without the staff—even though directing it creates problems.

"You use the staff to channel your power, and for the most part it is the more reliable choice. But sometimes that choice is not an option. So mastery requires that you feel confident enough that you can summon and make use of your *inish* even when you don't hold the staff. Let's stand over here."

For another hour she has me summon my *inish* using my hands only to spark a fire that strikes specific targets—each increasingly smaller, and each increasingly requiring more nuanced control. Then we expand both distance and spread, and then abrogate any visual fire and concentrate on force alone. I am reminded how I did this with the three Goblins the previous night when I flung them away by sheer force of will. But that was done automatically, in response to a threat. Now I learn how to control it.

"This is more difficult than I thought it would be," I offer at one point.

"Difficult but necessary," Ronden corrects me at once.

We work the rest of the day, using trial and error, repeating failed efforts until I get it right. It requires arduous amounts of concentration, and by the time the afternoon is waning, I am exhausted. I have not summoned a single major concentration of *inish* even once during this period, yet I am wrung out and light-headed.

Sitting together in the shade as the sun slides toward the western horizon, I drink copious amounts of water and take deep breaths to steady the beating of my heart. I have learned so much today. I have discovered things I never considered before, and found all of it to be important and necessary. My skills have improved immeasurably, as has my understanding of what I am dealing with. I thought Harrow to be a good teacher, but Ronden is better. In part it is because she is a woman and has a more in-depth appreciation of how a woman's body and mind function, which gives her a better appreciation of mine. Then, too, Harrow was more direct while Ronden is more nuanced.

I am lucky, I know, to have had the benefit of both.

"You are invited to dinner tonight," Ronden says suddenly. "Again. But this time it is Ancrow who extends the invitation, perhaps because she wants to make up for her rudeness yesterday. Or maybe something else; it's difficult to know with my mother. Do you want to come?"

I hesitate. "Char and Ramey will be there, too?"

She nods. "The four of us. Are you brave enough?"

I smile. "I think so."

DINNERTIME ARRIVES QUICKLY.

Ronden and I return to our respective homes to wash up and change clothes before going to Ancrow's, promising to meet first at my cottage so we can walk over together. She makes the offer without my having to ask, which speaks volumes about how uncomfortable she knows I feel about this evening after what happened yesterday.

Although, upon arriving at my door, she surprises me by saying, "I know you wonder about Ancrow's purpose in making this offer, but I saw something in her eyes when she told me. A hesitation, maybe even an uncertainty. I don't see that often. She doesn't quite seem to know how to react to you. This evening should be interesting. But I think you should give her a chance and see how things work out. I will support you, if matters get out of hand."

I thank her for her offer. With Ronden there to buttress whatever unpleasantness might arise, I am reassured. Enough so that I am prepared to put aside my misgivings and simply assume everything will be fine. After all, Ancrow invited me herself this time. And if she wanted to attack me, wouldn't she have done so by confronting me alone?

We make the short walk over and are greeted by an exuberant Char, who ushers us into a living area where we are invited to sit and enjoy a fruity drink of some sort that she has prepared for us. There is also a plate of crackers and cheeses, along with some fruit I don't recognize but like very much. A few minutes later, Ramey appears, and I meet the final member of the family. After having met the others, she is something of a surprise. Older than Char by maybe five years but much younger than Harrow and Ronden, she is a slender, quiet girl with a serious demeanor and a no-nonsense approach to conversations. When you ask a question or offer an opinion, you had better be ready to engage with the topic in a serious way. I worry at first that she might be too stern, but her smile when she lets it out of hiding is a revelation and we are soon fast friends.

At one point I decide to test her sense of humor and ask her the family surname. I tell her I know everyone only by their first names, so maybe we could move on to the second. She is astonished at this lapse, but then quickly replies in her deadpan fashion, "But we don't know yours, either."

We all four stare at one another for a moment before breaking into spontaneous laughter. Which brings Ancrow out just in time for me to say, "My full name is Auris Afton Grieg."

We all stop where we are, and I see a flicker of hesitation on Ancrow's face. Then she walks right up to me, reaches down to take my hands in hers, and says in an impossibly serious voice, "Welcome to our home, Auris Afton Grieg."

I am completely stunned by this turnaround—the invitation notwithstanding. I feel like I am talking to an entirely different woman. I just sit there, staring at her. For some reason this causes Char to break out in fresh peals of laughter, and even Ancrow permits herself a small smile.

She moves at once to sit next to me on the couch I am occupying, which is a strange wood-and-vine woven affair with dozens of cushions. There is plenty of room for two, so I cannot move away on a pretense of providing her with more space. I sit where I am, momentarily frozen.

A moment later, she leans over surreptitiously and whispers, "Don't worry, I won't bite. But that doesn't change things. I still don't know what to make of you."

I don't reply. I don't even look at her. I can't bear to find the serious look of disapproval that I am very afraid I will.

The conversation continues around me, but I don't volunteer anything more and neither does Ancrow. Now and then a question from one of the other girls is directed my way and I answer as briefly as I can, wanting to move away from Ancrow and at the same time wanting to stand—or sit—my ground. If Ronden notices anything, she is not revealing it. The two younger daughters talk mostly between themselves, throwing occasional looks my way.

Dinner can't come soon enough at this point. And when it does, I am on my feet immediately, only to have Ancrow take firm hold of my arm and bring me about. She stands close. "Let's talk a bit later on, just the two of us. I think it will serve a useful purpose."

I nod. On this, we agree. Talking might help. I can't imagine how it could make things any worse.

At dinner, I sit next to Char and across from Ramey, so I am spared any further surreptitious comments from Ancrow, who presides alone at the head of the table. Ronden occupies the other end, closest to me. The meal is delicious. To my surprise it is not Char who cooks it but Ancrow. I think unkindly of being poisoned as retribution for my insistence on remaining in Viridian, but my thoughts are not serious. We talk and laugh and spar as we dine—everyone but Ancrow. It feels the way I think family gatherings should, and I join in rather than shrink away in fear of the matriarch. I am entitled to a little fun and relaxation after what I have gone through these past few days, and I make up my mind quickly not to deprive myself.

The conversation drifts around to my imprisonment, driven there by Char's curiosity in spite of Ronden's caution that perhaps I might not want to talk about it. I don't, but Char is so endearing that I find myself eager to please her. So I give her the answers she seeks in general terms and without any of the graphic details I would like to forget. I tell her that being imprisoned is hard and that Goblins are uncaring jailers who mostly ignore you. I don't tell her about the torture racks and the isolation tanks. I tell her I remember my friends and miss them, but I don't tell her they are all dead. I don't tell her about the nightmares I experience as a result of my imprisonment. I try not to look at Ancrow while I am speaking, but now and then cannot help but glance her way. Every time I do, I find her looking down at her plate in silence.

We finish dinner, enjoy a crumble for dessert, and retire back to the living room for tea. After that, Ancrow sends the younger girls off to bed. When they both rush to hug me good night, she does not interfere.

But once they are gone, she tells Ronden she wants to speak to me alone. Ronden hesitates, glancing my way, but I nod my agreement. Better to get this out of the way. I can take care of myself. I am more confident of this than I was before I discovered my *inish* and my right to call myself a Sylvan.

Ronden gives her mother a hug and whispers just loudly enough for me to hear, "Manners, Mother. Auris is our guest."

Her mother gives her a cold smile and turns her toward the door. In seconds Ronden is gone, and her mother and I are alone.

I am sitting in a chair by now rather than on the couch, and Ancrow sits in the chair closest to me, positioning it so we are facing. Looking at the door Ronden has just closed, she says, "You don't appear to be someone who needs looking after. Am I that frightening?"

I smile as she turns back to face me. "Not this time. At our first meeting in the High Council chambers, you were."

"I believe in speaking my mind."

"I've had a taste of what that means. Am I to be lectured again?"

She makes a face. "So blunt. Having discovered your *inish* and put it to good use, you've gained a stronger backbone." She pauses. "I want to thank you for saving Char from her reckless behavior last night. She is too quick to act and too slow to think. Still a child."

"A wonderful child," I venture.

"A mother would have to be churlish indeed to disagree with that. But her impetuous nature is going to get her into trouble one day. In any case, my thanks are overdue, so I am offering them now. You saved my daughter's life. To have your *inish* appear as it did, so unexpectedly, was a gift. It must have surprised you, surfacing like that."

Her hawk face is intense and her eyes penetrating. I cannot help but feel intimidated all over again, but I refuse to give in to it. "A surprise unlike any other I can remember. Are you still questioning my Fae origins?"

"I'm questioning everything. Wondering how someone like you is possible. That you have *inish* appears to be incontrovertible. It certainly suggests you have a Fae connection of some sort. But what is it exactly? You look in every way possible like a Human. You look nothing like a Sylvan. The contradiction is inexplicable. How can such a thing be?"

"Have you spoken to the Seers about what they found? They insist I am Fae. Have you asked them what was revealed in the memories they recovered?"

"I have spoken neither to them nor to Harrow. I was waiting to talk to you first. Would you be willing to tell me what they discovered? Maybe it would help me understand. Maybe it would even reveal something I could believe."

Something I could believe? I am on my guard now. She still thinks I am a Human. Even with all that's happened, she is still not convinced.

But I need her to be, so I will open up to her. I have to find a way to persuade her to accept me into the family. She has refrained from asking either the Seers or Harrow in order to ask me first, and if I decline it will suggest I have something to hide. But I have nothing to hide, and much I do not understand. And I want desperately to change her mind about me.

So I tell her everything the sisters saw in my recovered memories; I lay all of it bare for her to examine. I hesitate more than once in my telling, anxious not to make a mistake, but I leave nothing out. I hold nothing back. I think she might know if I did. I think she can sense such things.

When I am done, I ask anxiously, "What do you think? Can you help me with any of it?"

She is already shaking her head. "Not without thinking it all over first. You tell a complex, confusing story—and much of it unbelievable. If a Sylvan child went missing, we would know—even if it was taken by Humans. No child is ever lost that we do not account for. Yet your story suggests you were taken from here without anyone knowing, which is impossible. Even so, why do you not look like us? There is simply no reasonable explanation for any of this, Auris. It doesn't make sense!"

"I know that!" I snap in reply, losing patience. "Benith said I was a Changeling. Is it not possible I was able to change how I looked? One vision was of my father giving me injections to tamp something down. There was talk of medications. Is it not possible these were meant to keep me from changing? Maybe under their influence I wasn't able to look like a Fae. But now that the injections and medications are no longer being used on me, maybe one day I will."

"You're talking nonsense now. Changelings are a myth. There are no Sylvan Changelings! If you are one, why don't you change yourself back right now? Go ahead, change!"

Her voice is rising, and I sense something quite clearly in its strident tone. She is afraid. But what is there for her to be afraid of?

"Why do you think you ended up in the Goblin prisons?" she asks suddenly. "Can you remember anything of why you were sent there—anything of what you or your parents might have done to deserve this? You wouldn't have been sent there without a reason."

But many were, of course. In a world where Human children are expendable, you don't need a reason to imprison them. Children seized, parents killed, families destroyed because Humans and Goblins made an alliance of the darkest kind. I shake my head. "I don't remember anything clearly from before I was sent there. Everything from before is shadowy or lost. I have my few recovered memories, and that is all."

A shading of the truth, but on impulse I deem it necessary.

"And you remember no names? Not even those of your father and mother?"

"My mother called my father 'Dennis' in one of the memories."

Although Ancrow tries to hide it, hearing the name startles her. I want to ask her why—if it is somehow familiar to her. Nevertheless, I decide to hold off on asking any more questions.

"I might have to go back there," I say instead. "Back to the prisons or to my old world to find the answers I need. But I don't want to do that until I know I have a place to come back to."

Ancrow looks distraught. "What are you asking? No one can ever know if they will have a place to come back to once they leave. There is never any guarantee. In any case, leaving Viridian for any reason is a bad idea. Stay here with us. You belong here. I admit to some reservations about your origins and your identity, but I also know my family admires and likes you, and that counts for something. Why not give yourself time to find out more?"

What have I said that troubles her so? There it is again, in a sudden shifting of her eyes away from me as I attempt to look directly at her.

"That would be much easier to do if I didn't have to keep looking over my shoulder for a Goblin or two waiting to haul me back to the prisons."

She nods. "Understandable. I will put a watch on your cottage and have you shadowed as you move about the city. You will never see your shadow, but he or she will be there, watching over you. That way you can go about your business without worry."

"Don't do that to me," I say at once. "I had that done to me in prison for five years—Goblin eyes on me all the time. I don't want it done to me here."

"But you won't even know . . ."

"That is not the point, Ancrow! I don't want to feel like I am back in prison! And you're wrong about my not knowing. I will know. I always know. Don't do it."

She smiles a dark, challenging smile. "No one gets to *tell* me what to do, Auris."

"Just do what I *asked* you to do. I will know if you don't."

"You didn't know when those Goblins came to catch you."

"They caught me off guard. But if you send your spies to shadow me, it will be different. Why can't you understand? I don't want eyes constantly watching me now that I am no longer in prison. Is that so difficult to understand?"

"I think you better go home and get some sleep," she says, turning away. "We can discuss this later."

"Discuss?" I call back, tromping off for the door. "You won't listen anyway. Your mind is made up."

"Then give me a reason to change it, Auris," she calls after me. "You're hiding something. I want to know what it is."

I slam the door on my way out. She's wrong about me. I'm not hiding anything. But I think she is.

FOURTEEN

THE BEDROOM WINDOW IN MY COTTAGE FACES THE FOOT OF THE
bed so that when I go to sleep the last thing I see before drifting off are the huge trees that surround me on all sides and, through the screen of their leafy boughs, small glimpses of the stars. Sometimes night birds will fly past in quick flashes of wings and feathers. On occasion, one will alight on a branch that is within my view. Now and again an owl will peer in at me, its lantern eyes bright yellow in the darkness, and provide me with a small hoot or two.

On this night I lie in my bed and look out my window, but I do not drift off. I do not sleep at all. I am too wound up, too angry, and too disappointed. Nothing went the way I thought it would—even the part where Ancrow admitted I must be a member of the Fae nation and the Sylvan people. Although I did not show it, her rejection of my request not to be shadowed hurt me deeply. It was as if she was letting me know that it didn't make any difference what I wanted; she would impose her will on me whenever she wished. She might as well have been saying that I belonged in Viridian Deep only if I did as she wanted.

So I bounce from feeling to feeling, from memory to memory, from one set of hurtful words to the next, replaying the evening and wondering what I can do besides lie here and seethe. I know I will not fall asleep—not for a while at least and maybe not at all if I don't come up with a plan for how to handle my disappointment. I could ask Ronden for help, but that would be putting her on the spot and this isn't her problem. If Harrow were here I could ask him, too, but it would be the same as asking his sister. The problem is not theirs to solve. It is mine. Whatever relationship I am ever going to have with Ancrow has to be worked out between the two of us. No third party is in a position to do more than complain, and complaining isn't going to solve anything.

After I have gone through the whole conundrum three times, I finally manage to rid myself of my harsher feelings. Distancing myself from my initial reaction, I start to reexamine things more calmly and dispassionately. Ancrow accused me of hiding the truth, but what is *she* hiding? The first thing that pops into my mind is how startled she was to hear the name Dennis. She knew that name . . . and likely knew the man (a Human almost certainly) to whom it belonged. She also seemed alarmed by the idea of my going back to my old world to try to find out more about where I came from and how I ended up in the prisons. I can't help wondering why, if she wants me gone, she didn't just tell me to go, hoping I would never come back. Instead she tried to argue me out of going, insisting I should stay, trying to persuade me that she had changed her mind and believed Viridian should be my new home.

A complete reversal of what she had indicated in our previous meetings.

And then she became angry when she discovered I was not going to allow her to put a watch on me. Even though she insisted it was for my own protection, I can see clearly enough it is also a way to monitor everything I do. Why else would she be so determined to have me under constant surveillance? She has to know I can protect myself now that I am learning to channel my *inish*. She has to know I am almost always in the company of either Harrow or

Ronden. But that isn't enough, is it? No, she looks at it as a chance to keep me under her thumb and safely tucked away from any further investigations about my origins and her involvement in them.

I stop myself right there. Because she *is* somehow involved, isn't she? I can sense it. She knows something about my past, and she is very determined to keep it a secret.

I have my way forward, I decide. I will find out what she is hiding. But I will have to learn something about the history of the Sylvan people first and how it is they have so little to do with Humans. There is so much about the Fae I still don't know.

I will start there. I will ask Ronden in the morning to tell me more about the Fae history and how the Fae have managed to remain so isolated for so long.

I fall asleep quickly after that and do not wake until morning.

I AM WASHED AND DRESSED AND HAVE FINISHED BREAKFAST BY THE time Ronden comes knocking on my door. It is early still, but we are scheduled for another day of training and I know she will be anxious to hear about how things went the previous night with Ancrow.

Indeed, it is her first question as she steps inside, and I lead her to the couch where we sit facing each other. "It went badly," I confess, searching for the least harmful words to describe to Ancrow's daughter what has transpired. "It started out well enough, and I believed we were both seeking common ground. She even accepted that I did indeed have use of my *inish*. But matters deteriorated when she insisted on putting a watch on me and I objected and asked her not to."

Ronden huffed irritably. "What is wrong with Mother? She isn't usually so stubborn. What brought on this rejection?"

"What sparked it all was when I suggested I should go back to my old world and try to find out something more about my origins. She tried to dissuade me and then insisted on the shadow—even after I told her I did not want it, that it would be like I was in prison all over again. But honestly, it felt as if she wanted to be able to monitor me so she could know what I was doing at all times."

"But why would she want to monitor you? How does she think that will help?"

"You know her better than I do. But I will tell you this, Ronden— she is afraid of something. Twice I saw her startled when I told her about my memories. She asked me to tell her what I remembered, and so I did. I thought it would help settle things between us, but I was badly mistaken. When I mentioned the name Dennis, which I think might have been my father's name, and again when I mentioned the possibility of going back to my old home, she was visibly upset. I think she knows something about both, and I want to find out what it is."

"I will ask her," Ronden volunteers. "I will demand she tell me the truth."

"Which I don't think for one minute would persuade her," I answer quickly. "Do you?"

Ronden shakes her head. "No, you're right, it wouldn't. Not her."

"Is there someone else we might talk to, someone who would know the Sylvan history and how it matches up with that of Humans? Someone who might know your mother well enough to at least guess at what she is trying to hide?"

"You ask a lot of me. I cannot do anything that would make me feel I had betrayed her."

"I don't seek a betrayal. I only seek enlightenment. I know so little of Sylvans or even of myself. If there were someone who could speak to both—even in general terms—I might discover something that would help explain what is happening. But I would never ask you or anyone else in your family to bring harm to your mother."

A long silence hangs between us. "I think she hides secrets from all of us, Auris. And I'm not sure I want to discover any of them. I'm not sure I have that right."

"Can you tell me more about Sylvan history then, or introduce me to someone who can? Can you at least do that?"

Her fierce expression softens. "I would never deny you a chance to discover the history of our people. You should talk to the Seers."

"But don't I need permission for that?"

"Not if the only purpose for your visit is to just take tea and converse. You can't ask them to use their magic without permission, but you wouldn't be asking for that."

"I wouldn't. But would you accompany me to make sure I don't overstep? That way, you can stop me if it feels like I am betraying our bargain."

"I think you should do this alone," she says quietly. "If you wish, come back and tell me about it after and we can talk further." She sighs. "I expect you want to do this right away?"

"If possible. I don't think I can focus on anything else until I know the truth."

She nods and stands. "I will arrange things." She moves toward the door. "Wait here for me."

When she is gone, I go outside and sit on the bench to enjoy the sunshine. I am worn down from lack of sleep and the trauma of last night's visit with Ancrow. I imagine there will be no more dinners at her house—at least, not until I have found a way to show her how wrong she is about me. It's funny, but I thought the worst was over once Harrow brought me out of the wastelands to Viridian Deep. Now I am beginning to wonder if one nightmare hasn't replaced another.

I am alone for maybe five minutes before both Char and Ramey appear, crossing the tree lanes to reach my cottage. When they arrive, looking very uncomfortable, I motion for them to sit next to me. They do so, one on either side. Ramey is as solemn as usual, but Char is thoroughly distraught.

"Mother yelled at me!" she snaps. She is almost in tears. "I hate her."

"No, you don't," I reply quickly, taking her hands in mine. "No matter how mad we get, we never hate our mothers."

"But it isn't right," Ramey says calmly, shaking her head slowly.

"She got angry when we asked about you. I think she is afraid of you. She thinks I can't see it, but I can."

"She thinks you are too stubborn," Char goes on grimly. Her lips tighten into a thin line. "I told her she should get to know you, and she said she knows you well enough already."

"Char thinks she can stand up to anyone," Ramey points out. "Even someone as strong as Mother."

I sigh wearily. "Char, you have to be patient with your mother. You might be right. She might be afraid of me. But we have to show her she shouldn't be."

Char is adamant. "I'm still coming over here whenever I want!"

"Me, too," Ramey declares.

My heart is filled with a sweet ache in response to the kindness of these two young girls. "I will ask Ronden to speak to her about this. Perhaps she can persuade your mother that I am not a bad person."

They look at me doubtfully, but nod their agreement. I am putting a lot on Ronden these days, but I have no one else to look to with Harrow away. I lean over and give each of the girls a hug. "Go home now. It will be all right."

They linger a bit before going, talking about other things as young girls will, stalling for time. Finally I shoo them along and go back to waiting for Ronden. I cannot believe Ancrow can be this upset about me. Why can't she see that the last thing I want to do is hurt her or her family? Why can't she see me for who and what I am rather than as something I have proved I am not? She keeps insisting I am Human, and while for a time I still thought I was—in spite of what Harrow and the Seers said—I now accept this radical change in my life, a change that requires me to see myself in an entirely new way. After all, how much better is it to know who and what you are than to think yourself something you aren't? I had no past, no memories, no clear understanding of myself beyond what I knew from my time in the Goblin prisons. Now I have a path toward understanding and acceptance that will give me a wonderful new life. So what if I don't look the part? So what if I still appear to be a Human? At the base of it, Fae and Human are only words. It is what's inside that matters.

I am weary of Ancrow and her doubts and fears and displeasure. I am not obligated to prove anything to her. But I will do so because I care for her children and they care for me. This relationship is too important to be cast aside solely because it is challenged by a single person—no matter who that person is.

Ronden returns a little while later. She comes up to me in something of a rush, a little breathless, seeming almost disconcerted. "It is all arranged, Auris. Benith will speak with you now. Come."

I rise. "I want you to hear for yourself whatever she has to tell me. Please, come with me."

"I don't know . . ."

"Please."

She hesitates and nods. "All right."

We set out for our meeting, and I feel a strange lightening of my troubles. I have no reason to. I cannot know if I will discover anything, but it feels at that moment I have a reasonable chance of doing so, and that is enough for now.

WHEN WE REACH THE TIERED HOME OF THE SEERS, BENITH IS WAITING for us, sitting on her doorstep, working on a piece of embroidery. Her kind face lifts and she stands to offer greetings. She looks exactly as I remember her from before—quite elderly, yet sprightly too, her ancient features a pale green and deeply lined, but her eyes young and bright.

"Auris," she says happily. "Back again so soon? I knew you would come, but I thought it might take longer. Ronden has explained much of what is troubling you. Shall we go into the garden?"

She leads us along a path that leads to the rear of the stack-box cottage and a profusely flower-laden garden with arches and benches for sitting and even a small turreted pavilion with clematis growing up its trellised sides. We sit, and I take a moment to admire gardens that are wild rather than arranged, but which seem on reflection to be more appropriate for these elderly ladies.

"I do not tend the gardens," she advises me, using a voice that is almost a whisper. "Maven does that—or likes to think she does. I have retained gardeners to provide help. She is getting on in years, after all."

As are you all, I think, unable to conceal a smile. "They are very beautiful and just right for the three of you."

"Flowers are a necessary part of life," Benith advises, giving Ronden a wink.

"She is chiding me for not having a garden of my own," Ronden says with a tacked-on sigh. "But a Watcher is away too much of the time to tend a garden in the way it needs to be tended."

"As your mother has discovered is also true about raising children."

Benith leaves the sentence hanging and gestures toward the house where the third sister, Dreena, is emerging with a tea tray and some small cakes. Hospitality is not lacking in this home.

"Black currant, if I remember correctly," Benith says to me, and I nod in agreement.

Dreena deposits the tray on a small table, pours three cups, and departs without a word. We sip our tea in silence for a few minutes, looking out over the flower beds and bushes, breathing in the fragrant smells of roses and lilies.

"Ancrow is a bit of an enigma," Benith says finally. She smiles at Ronden. "I am not overstepping myself, am I?"

Ronden snorts. "Hardly. Mother is a constant source of confusion and contradiction. Never more so than now, with her reaction to Auris."

"Yes, that is puzzling behavior." Benith looks back to me. "Ronden has explained how Ancrow has treated you and given me a brief description of your conversation last evening. It is odd—but then Ancrow is odd in other ways, as well. Do you know she has never come to us to retrieve her memories of the past? Even though we have suggested it might be a good idea?"

"Which the sisters almost never offer to do," Ronden adds.

"Is there a reason you think she should?" I ask.

"Oh, yes. Did you know that, like yourself, she was once made a prisoner? Not of Goblins, but of Humans?"

Now this is interesting. I knew, of course, that she was made a prisoner, but I thought it was Goblins acting on the orders of Humans, not by Humans themselves. I am reminded that I know next to nothing about Ancrow's life beyond her reputation as a warrior and a leader. "When was this?"

"Quite awhile ago. Twenty years, perhaps? She was taken in a raid of a Watcher camp. She was a Watcher herself back then. Her male companions were all killed, but she was taken back to the Human world and kept there by them for months until she eventually escaped and found her way back to us. Very much like you, Auris."

I stare at her. "Is this why she hates Humans so?"

Benith stares back. "What do you think?"

I look at Ronden. "Has she ever talked about it with you?"

"Not in depth, ever. She claims her captors tortured her. She claims she killed them all before she left. Other than that, she refuses to say anything. I was very young when this happened, but I remember her being gone and then coming back. I was told she might never return. So I asked her what happened, but she only told me those few details and said it was over and to forget it. She was pregnant with Harrow, however, when she was taken, and he was born a few months after her return. Our father's last gift to her, she said."

"Odd," Benith repeated.

Odd, indeed. I try to think what this means in terms of how she sees me and can conclude that I am only an unpleasant reminder of the time she spent imprisoned and pregnant. But somehow it feels more personal than that.

Benith breaks into my thoughts. "Let me tell you something about the history of your people, Auris—and by that, I mean something about the history of the Fae. I think it would help you to better understand the relationship between Fae and Humans. Would you like more tea?"

I accept another cup with a smile. This is exactly what I needed to know, and I am thankful again that Ronden has brought me here.

As I sip my tea, she begins to talk.

"The Fae are referred to by most—Humans included—as the Old Folk. We came into being before the Humans existed. In the Old World—the non-Human world—we practiced magic and relied on it for everything that we needed to sustain ourselves. Magic was drawn from earth, air, fire, and water—the four major staples of our existence. We created it from within ourselves and from an understanding of nature. We never ventured into seeking advancement through any form of industrial exploration. For the Fae, this was a sacrilege and a betrayal of our promise to protect and preserve nature in all her various forms. Industry destroys nature—through either pillaging her resources or damaging her gifts.

"Humans—once they were born into the world—were of a different mind-set. They were determined to make their lives better not by adapting to nature, but by subjugating her. The entire history of their evolution has been centered on taking from nature what they needed to improve their lives without regard for how it might damage nature herself. And eventually they evolved into a people that have become so industrialized and so dependent on machines that to forgo that mind-set and adapt to ours is beyond them. This lifestyle is furthered by an unshakable belief that Humans are superior to all other beings, giving them the right to exercise domination over the entire world."

Benith allows herself a small smile. "Humans have blinded themselves to the reality of what they are doing. When you closely examine the path they have taken, you come to realize it leads directly to extinction. Sooner or later nature will have no more to give them. She will turn on them and they will perish. Humans do not believe this is possible; they turn a blind eye to what is happening to their world because of the choices they have made. They have no real connection with nature beyond a reliance on what she can provide them; they have no sense of responsibility for her safety and protection. They view her as theirs to exploit and dominate, and they see themselves as invested with the right to use her in any way they deem necessary.

"To most of them, the Fae are not real. We do not exist save in fairy tales and myths. To those who know better, we are inconsequential save as an interesting, but troubling, oddity."

"And their minds cannot be changed?" I ask.

"As yet, no. So we separated ourselves from them by moving away from their part of the world entirely and isolating in our own, which you know as Viridian Deep. Do you understand what I am saying, Auris? Once you crossed Roughlin Wake with Harrow, you left the Human part of the world to come into ours. We no longer share our world with the Humans, but live in a place in which Humans have no presence. Our worlds are linked still, but few can make the crossing from one realm to the other. We coexist in the same time period, but not the same place. We are one step removed. We have consciously distanced ourselves from all the damage they have done to their own part of the world. The territory that belongs to the Fae is what theirs could be, had they not chosen the path they did."

I am stunned. "How can you have managed something like this? How could you even find a place like Viridian Deep in the first place?"

"Oh, Viridian was always here. Even before the Humans."

"But to keep it separate? To hide it from them?"

"Magic, Auris. Magic."

I look at Ronden. "Did you know of this? Is this history familiar to you? To others of the Fae?"

She nods. "We know who and what we are, and what danger lies in venturing outside the boundaries we have established."

"But what about the Goblins . . ." I trail off, trying to think it through. "They already cross that boundary all the time, don't they?"

"Goblins are a type of Fae, but they have no magic of their

own," Benith replies. "They think allying with Humans will help give them access to our magic. Right now, their way of life borders on that of early Human existence. They are users of fire and furnaces, of machines and weapons made of metal. Theirs were rudimentary tools at first, but once they made contact with the Humans and entered into an agreement to work with them, they were gifted with the more terrible weapons that have become such a staple of Human existence. Now they are more Human than Fae, and for them there is no turning back."

I am horrified. "But won't they show Humans the way into Viridian Deep?"

"They do not possess the power to do that," Ronden interjects. "No one who isn't a true Fae can come into Viridian Deep unless one of us shows them the way. We are protected well enough."

"The way into Viridian Deep is secret," Benith adds. "And to those who don't know it, entry is denied by a formidable set of obstacles. Any attempt at passage requires crossing through the wastelands and then over the waters of Roughlin Wake. The Roughlin is unpredictable, filled with riptides and whirlpools. It hides creatures that can bring down the biggest ships and will do so if they sense an intrusion from anyone who is not Fae. The winds that blow across the waters are dangerous as well, so attempts at flying over Viridian pose a considerable risk, too. Understand, Auris, long ago we conjured these barriers to protect our land and our people. Goblins can come into Viridian because they are themselves Fae, but Humans cannot. So the Goblins can invade us and have done so repeatedly, though we have always been able to fight them off. Now they simply keep to the wastelands and the far northern stretches of Viridian Deep."

"Mostly," I correct her gently. "The Goblins who came for me the other night came right into the city."

"That was an anomaly—and how they found you remains a mystery. But they went to a lot of trouble to try to recapture you."

I am worried anew. "And no one knows what happened? How they found me?"

She shakes her head. "Questions surround you, Auris. I think you will eventually be able to answer most of them, but it may take time. You have discovered how to channel your *inish* and have established yourself as one of the Fae. Ancrow may question your place here and your right to call yourself a Sylvan, but she does so without a reason."

"Or at least a reason we can determine at present," Ronden adds. "Which is galling."

"Ancrow has had a difficult life," Benith says. "She has always been a warrior, a defender of her people. Even if we don't know the details, we can imagine she suffered badly at the hands of the Humans to whom the Goblins delivered her. She has seen many of her friends and fellow Sylvans die in the Goblin wars. She lost her life partner in a particularly savage reprisal. She has been celebrated for her efforts and her deeds, yet at the same time she has paid a terrible price."

She pauses and looks away for long moments, and I think she will say nothing more. But then she whispers, "I think you will have to tread softly, Auris, if you want to discover what she hides."

We talk some more, but the talk drifts to other subjects—my training in particular—and we leave behind the reason for my coming. I choose to let it go; I think I have learned enough for one visit. I sense that coming back to speak again with Benith will not be difficult. I have a lot to think about in any case, and I need to do so in private. But what I have learned has persuaded me that it is more necessary than ever to discover the truth about my past. There is a big revelation waiting—an explanation for everything that has happened to me in the past and has brought me home again. That I have come to Viridian Deep was fated. That I have found my way to where I belong is clear.

Now I need to discover why I belong here and why I was kept away for so long.

WE ARE STILL VISITING AND DRINKING TEA WHEN RONDEN STANDS, signaling it is time to depart, and as she does Dreena and Maven come out of a rear door of their home and walk quickly toward us. Their joint appearance is unexpected, and the look they share suggests something is wrong.

"The *Inish* Reveal tells us there has been an incident on the far shores of the Roughlin," Dreena advises, lips pressed tight and brow furrowed. "Goblins have taken Harrow."

I feel my world drop away.

FIFTEEN

RONDEN IS THE FIRST TO REACT. "DO YOU KNOW THIS FOR CERtain? No mistake?"

Dreena nods solemnly, her aged features tightening. "There is no mistake. The Reveal never lies."

"Do we know when this happened? Where he was when they took him?"

"A little over four hours ago, somewhere along the shores of the Roughlin. He was apparently on patrol. They must have laid a trap for him. He was taken swiftly and brought down without much effort."

Ronden's face is a tight mask of fear. "Is he alive? Was he hurt?"

"He is alive," tiny Maven says. "There is no darkness on him."

"Do we know where he is?" I ask impulsively.

"He was transported to a Goblin prison. He only just arrived."

It must be the one where I was locked away. Where I was held for so long. The prison that is closest to the shores of the Roughlin. I shiver at the memories these thoughts induce and fight back against my fear.

Ronden seems to consider what she's been told. "Does anyone else know of this? My mother?"

"No one knows yet but us," Dreena says.

"You know what Ancrow will do once she finds out," Maven adds.

Ronden nods. She knows. As do I. Ancrow will go after her son and bring him back or die in the attempt. I look at Ronden, and she looks back. We are thinking the same thing. Ancrow is not who she was. She remains a warrior at heart, but she is too old now. She is too close to her son to be able to keep her thoughts clear while carrying out a rescue.

"We have to go," I say to Ronden. "We have to bring him home."

Ronden shakes her head. "I have to go. Not you."

I am stung, but I stay calm. "No, both of us. Me, especially. Harrow saved my life, Ronden. What does it say about me if I do not now save his? I have to go. If I want to live with myself, I have to go. I have to try, no matter what it takes."

"You have no experience." She is firm, determined to leave me behind. "You are too new to your powers."

"But I have experience you do not. I know the prison. I was there for five years, and I know everything about it. You know next to nothing. If you try to find him on your own, you risk being caught as well. You must take me with you."

"Auris . . ."

But I am beyond hearing anything that would deny me this right. "I have been trained by you and Harrow. I am fit and have command of my *inish*. I am strong and capable, Ronden. I will not slow you down. You have to take me!"

The Seers are standing by silently, watching to see what will happen. I wish one of them would say something to support me, but I understand why they don't. This isn't their business. This isn't their family. They know better than to interfere unless they are asked to.

So I turn to them. "How strong do you judge my use of *inish*? Am I capable of undertaking this rescue with Ronden?"

Dreena frowns and shakes her head. "You are very young still, Auris."

"You are more than capable," Benith announces suddenly. "Your *inish* is very strong. That you were able to defeat those Goblins who tried to kidnap you speaks to your power. Ronden should take you with her."

I had all but forgotten Benith, but she has come to my aid. I want to give her a hug in response, but I simply stand there with my eyes fixed on Ronden. She has to understand. I cannot bear to lose Harrow. I have lost so much, and now there is a good chance I will lose him, too. I would rather die first. I will give my life, if that is what it takes to save his. But I can do nothing if I am left behind. Ronden must let me come with her. She must.

She says nothing for a long time, then she gives me a quick nod. Relief floods through me, and I smile in response. The bond is forged; our fates are joined. We will find Harrow together and bring him back. I do not consider the possible alternatives. I refuse to.

"Can you forbear from speaking of this until we are well away?" Ronden asks the sisters. "Can we keep this between us for now?"

"You ask a lot," Dreena declares, frowning in disapproval.

"Because it is necessary."

"For how long am I to keep quiet?"

"Give us a day. If we cannot get him out on our own, then you must reveal everything. But give us time to try this first."

"If we are asked about him, we will have to answer truthfully," Benith says after a long silence. "But we understand why you ask for this delay. We understand, as well, that risking more lives to save Harrow's is likely pointless once he is inside the prison. But Ancrow will insist on going anyway. She will end up throwing her life away."

Ronden nods. "I want my mother safe. If there is any way to make this happen . . ."

Benith comes forward and takes her hands. "There is always a way. Go. Do what you must. Come back safe."

We hastily leave the gardens and emerge onto the pathway

leading back into the city. We do not talk. We are lost in our separate thoughts, plagued by our personal doubts and fears, but we leave them unspoken and remain silent. I am fortified by my determination to see this through and see Harrow brought home. He must be saved. For the first time, I allow myself to admit what I suspect was true from the moment we met: I cannot imagine a life without him. I love him without reservation. I have no need to provide myself with reasons for this, and for whatever time is given me in this life, I will come to love him more.

I cannot tolerate the prospect of losing him. I cannot.

"How will we get there?" I ask finally. "Isn't it at least a three-day journey on foot?"

Ronden nods, tight-lipped. "But we are Fae. We can be there before nightfall if we use a wormhole."

I have no idea what that means for the Fae, but the term is familiar to me. "Isn't *wormhole* a scientific term? Isn't it a Human word—a reference to a time-warp phenomenon?"

How do I know this? I speak before I think to question myself, remembering without knowing why.

She makes a rude noise. "The Fae invented the term and applied it to a form of travel we learned to conjure long before Humans even walked the earth. They stole it from us—or at least claimed it as their own—to apply to a different form of technology entirely. They're quite good at laying claim to things that were never theirs to begin with."

I want to say she sounds like her mother, but instead ask, "So how long will it take us to reach the prison?"

"Three hours, if you can provide me with a description of what our destination looks like and where you think it might be. But first we need to outfit ourselves. We need weapons, healing supplies, and food. We don't want to rush into this blindly."

I guess not, but I hadn't thought of it. "Will we take anyone else with us?"

She glances over. "What do you think?"

I don't have to think. I know. The fewer, the better. It will be hard enough to manage to gain entry for just two and then make a subsequent departure with Harrow in tow. I am already trying to figure how we can accomplish this. I had five years to think about escaping the Goblin prison. The obstacles and barriers of trying to break myself out are not so different from those Ronden and I will face trying to break in.

I have some ideas, but none of them have ever been tested.

"I'm still not convinced that taking you with me is a good idea," Ronden says suddenly, striding a bit faster as if to make sure I can keep up.

I reach out impulsively, grab hold of her arm, and pull her around so we are facing each other. "I know how to get inside the prison. I know where Harrow is probably being held. I know how to get there and get us out. You need me."

Then I stride ahead of her without any clear idea of where we are going and force *her* to keep up with *me*. There will be no leaving me behind, not for any reason.

The city is busy, and there are Fae everywhere, going about their business. But they do not bother with us; most don't even spare us a glance. If they knew what we were about to do, it might be different. It is odd how we lead such separate lives so much of the time, keeping our thoughts to ourselves. We are connected by relationships and place and time; we are connected by shared experience. But in the end we are each our own person and ultimately alone.

We navigate the tree lanes and skywalks, the ladders and stairs, and avoid coming close to either my cottage or Ancrow's. We do not wish to be seen and possibly detained. We go to Ronden's home, retrieve the supplies, weapons, and a few additional pieces of protective gear we might need, including all-weather cloaks, and go out again. The afternoon is still early, but Ronden says that by the time we reach the location of the wormhole and pass through it will be sunset. It doesn't matter to me what time it will be; it only matters that we reach Harrow as quickly as possible. Coming to rescue him too late would be every bit as bad as not coming at all.

With our gear organized and packed and our *inish* staffs in hand, we set out. Ronden is clearly stricken by the thought of what has happened to her brother, her fears no less than mine, and she wears a mask of determination that I recognize. It is a mirror of my own. We do not say much; there is no good reason for talk. Our destination, Ronden tells me, lies to the south not the east, although it is east that the Roughlin, the wastelands, and the prison that is our ultimate destination, lie.

"Wormholes are tricky forms of magic," Ronden explains. "They cannot be created just anywhere. The mix of elements must be just right—air, fire, earth, and water. It takes a long time to create a wormhole that will not disappear as soon as it is created. We have three in Viridian Deep. From any one of them, you can get to wherever you choose quickly. But the magic that creates them is fluid, so we have to make sure they are strong enough to hold together with repeated use. If they are, then you can extend or retract them. And you can control where they will take you."

"It must take a great deal of Fae magic to do all that!"

"It does, so you can see why there are only three. To make one is a massive undertaking, and there is always the chance of the entire project collapsing. It has happened more than once. Magic is mostly ephemeral, and creating a wormhole is no exception."

She leads me out of the city along pathways and trails I have never taken, and for an hour we walk through the ancient trees of the forest, listening to the birds that live there. The birds talk, she tells me. They know things we do not and see things we cannot. They can keep us safe if we pay attention. Sometimes, they can save our lives.

I find myself thinking about the Fae way of life and how much I still do not know about it. I am as innocent as a newborn child in the ways of this world, and I wonder how long it will take me to grow up. Even with my *inish* unlocked and my identity confirmed, I do not begin to possess the knowledge I will need in order to survive.

At the end of an hour, we reach a wetlands. It is broad and

winds through uneven terrain where water glimmers all about us, but the trees hold fast to the earth anyway—tall sentinels amid the glistening of the shallows that stretch away into the distance. I think I am about to get my feet wet, but Ronden knows a path that is invisible to me but clear to her. We proceed for a time as if walking on water, but the soil we tread is no more than a few inches below. Different species of birds reside here—some of them waterborn, some long-legged and long-necked predators of the things that live within the waters. There are snakes and reptiles, too. There are tree mammals scurrying across branches and down trunks as if haste means everything. I want to look everywhere at once, but instead am careful to place my feet where Ronden does so I will not topple headfirst off the hidden pathway and into the waters.

When we reach our destination, I recognize it for what it is immediately. Sunlight breaks through the canopy overhead to form a strange halo effect atop the surface of a wide space that plants and animals alike seem to avoid. Within that space lies a bare mound, sun-brightened and shimmering, earth and water both reflecting back at me. There are hints of fire here and there—flickers that are not actual flames but suggest their presence.

"We go there," Ronden says, pointing to the bare space. "But before we do, tell me where it is we are going. Describe the prison as best you can. Describe what you remember about its location and surroundings. Tell me where it is we should be standing when we get there—what we will see and why you think it a safe place for us to reappear. Bring us as close as possible to where we need to be to gain entry. And try to place us in a spot where we will not be seen by guards."

I do all that she asks to the best of my ability. I choose to bring us out at a service entrance to the east side—the back side—of the outer walls. It will be darker there at sunset, and the chances of encountering any Goblins outside at that hour are minimal. Their attention will be occupied with bringing prisoners from their cells to the dining hall, serving them meals, and then locking them away again.

Ronden has her eyes closed as I talk, I assume to better envision what she is looking for. When I finish, she opens them again. "I have found it. Give me a moment to summon the wormhole we need. Then we can go. But stay close to me. Once we are standing on that bare mound, do nothing to interfere with what I do or what happens as a result. Place one hand on my shoulder and keep it there. Ready?"

I nod. We step away from our invisible path into the waters surrounding the bare space, but again they do not seem to be more than a few inches deep. Staying close to each other, we make our way to the center of the bare space and stop. I place my hand on Ronden's shoulder as instructed and wait. Nothing happens at first, and then I feel a stirring of wind and smell sulfur. The sunlight deepens and the world about us disappears. I am aware suddenly that Ronden is singing, her voice audible but her words too soft to make out. Her arms lift as if to embrace something I cannot see, and the waters around us stir. Bubbles rise and break as they surface, and colors fill the air. There is a strong sense of everything about us changing and a strange look in the air before us as it breaks apart to allow glimpses of a long empty passageway leading into a vast nothingness.

Ronden begins to walk, and I follow in her footsteps, my hand still on her shoulder. It is a bit awkward, but manageable. I concentrate on keeping contact with her while ignoring the way the air about us shimmers and changes colors constantly—a mix of blues and purples, blacks and grays. I hear sounds, but I cannot identify their source. I feel heat and cold in spurts that suggest we might be passing from one climate to another, yet it feels as if we are barely moving.

Our journey is over much faster than I would have expected. It feels as if we have been walking for perhaps only thirty minutes, but apparently time is fluid in a wormhole. As the world reappears around us—taking on definition once more—the light fades to darkness. Night surrounds us where we stand next to the walls of the Goblin prison. Stone blocks fused together by weight and ce-

ment rise up, tall and massive barriers against intrusions by anything made of mere flesh and blood.

We stand in deep shadow, right up against the prison walls. I
have chosen this point deliberately because it is just beyond the
reach of the cameras that survey the outer surroundings. Wherever
you are inside or outside the fortress—with very few exceptions—
you can be seen. The cameras will be our most formidable obstacles
to overcome if we are to reach Harrow and free him.

I draw Ronden close. Even our voices can give us away to the
sound detectors that the perimeter security includes. "There are
visual, voice, sound, and movement detectors everywhere," I whisper in her ear. "If we move from the space we are in, our movements will be detected and we will be seen. If we enter any of the
doors in the outer wall, we risk setting off an alarm. If we climb
higher than eight feet on these walls, we set off an alarm. If we attempt to tunnel under, same result."

She looks at me in horror. "Are you sure?"

"I spent years trying to figure a way to get out of here. I made it
a point to learn everything—either personally or through my
friends. Now I know how to defeat all of it. I can bypass or disable
the alarms and detectors using my *inish*. Let me do what is needed
as we go. Stay right behind me; there are places where I will need
your help."

She nods her understanding. "Just tell me what to do."

"One other thing first." I step close to her and place my hands
on her arms as if to hold her fast, but really only to emphasize how
serious I am. "If we are captured, the outcome is almost certain.
The Goblins will dismember us piece by piece in front of the other
prisoners. They do this to anyone caught trying to escape, and I
doubt it will be different for someone trying to break in. I have
watched this happen many times, and it is horrendous. I am not
about to let it happen to me. So I want your promise that if I am
unable to escape and will be captured, you will kill me. I do not
mean to be unkind, or to display any sort of false bravado, but I
cannot go through this again. Will you promise me?"

"If you will promise to do the same for me," she says in response.
My smile is faint and hard-edged. "I will."

"Understand this," she says. "I do not intend to fail. I do not
intend to die. I do not intend to let you die, either."

"Nor do I intend for any of it to happen." My whisper is so faint,
I am not sure my words are audible. "But I know it could."

She shakes her head. "Anything can happen in any given situation. But we don't have to believe it will."

"No," I agree, "we don't. Are you ready, sister?"

"I am glad to have you for my friend, Auris," she whispers. "I
like hearing you call me sister."

I cannot help myself. Tears fill my eyes. I reach out and hug her
against me, overcome with gratitude. The solid feel and bright
warmth of her body are immensely reassuring. But the cold of a
memory intrudes. I remember my other friends who exchanged this
same promise—friends who are now all dead. The risk of entering
this place of cruelty and suffering is daunting, and there are so very
many ways you can die here. I have a momentary sensation of
hopelessness—of understanding that no matter what weapons I
have at my disposal, or what courage I am able to summon, it may
not be enough.

But I break the chains those fears would place upon me and
straighten, looking Ronden in the eye. "Let's go find Harrow and
bring him home."

SIXTEEN

I TURN TO THE SURVEILLANCE CAMERAS MOUNTED TWENTY FEET up on the walls and reach out to them with my *inish*. Exploring their workings, I discover they require codes to disable them, but I have a better way. Relying on my training with Harrow and Ronden, I use my *inish* to fuse the relays, conjuring a blackout. No alarm sounds; no warning is given. Eventually, someone will notice, but I can only hope they will think it a minor malfunction or mechanical failure of some sort, because on checking the motion detectors they will find no sign of activity. This is because I have disabled them, too.

They will not try to fix the cameras at night but will wait until morning when they can see better. They will wait because there is no apparent need for haste. At least, this is what I hope.

I step from the shadows with Ronden at my shoulder and walk to the door through which we will enter. It has a camera to identify those who seek admittance, but I have already disabled it along with the others. The locks on the door are formidable, but they can be released by entering a specific code on a keypad next to the door.

I bypass all this through use of my *inish* to release the lock, and we are inside.

We stand in an entry portal that is sealed off from the rest of the prison. The Goblin sentry on the other side of a wall of protective glass frantically works buttons as he glances from one countertop screen to the next in an effort to find out why the exterior door has opened for no apparent reason. He does not look up right away, but when he does, I bring him down at once with a quick strike of disabling magic that passes right through the protective glass and renders him unconscious. I have learned a few things in my training, and determined possibilities for using a few more. This is one. I am much more capable than even a week ago, and I am immensely grateful for it.

I turn my attention to the locks on the doors leading out of the entry portal and into the control chamber and, using *inish*, once more release them. We pass from the entry portal into the control room and then are inside the prison. There we find a small storage room for replacement equipment. Ronden drags the sentry inside, closes the door as she exits, and I fuse the lock so it will not release.

Telling Ronden to stay where she is, I walk to the hallway and spy the cameras. They have to be disabled, but this second round will almost certainly draw unwanted attention. We will have to act fast from here on in. We are not all that far from where I believe Harrow is being held, so we should be able to reach him quickly. But even once we do, we will still not be clear of the prison walls— and we'll be facing danger every second we remain inside.

Still, there is no help for it. I explain this to Ronden, who simply nods. We will do what we must.

I start to disable the next set of cameras and then stop as another idea occurs to me. Why not leave the cameras on but scramble the lights? What if I make them blink rapidly and blindly so that they will hide rather than reveal us? There is no security alarm attached, and we can find our way using a were-light. If we go quickly enough and keep the were-light pitched just ahead of us to illuminate our way, we will not be clearly visible. If the alarms don't trigger, maybe the guards on watch won't feel worried enough about a few lights blinking to bother doing anything about it.

Maybe. But I feel an urgent need to leave now. This will be the second malfunction in the same area, and they are going to begin to speculate about what might be happening.

Again, I tell Ronden what I think we should do, and again she agrees. I scramble the passageway lights so they begin to flicker in quick, haphazard ways to throw off any guards keeping watch in the control room. Then we each summon a were-light to guide us and are off, moving swiftly down the passageways I lead us through. We hold our *inish* staffs at the ready in case we encounter anyone, our eyes on the darkness just beyond where the passage lights begin to go off and on all up and down the length of the black nothing. Because it is night and almost everyone is asleep, I do not expect us to encounter anyone.

The familiar, unwelcome smells of the prison wash over me. I had thought I had left them behind forever, but now here they are filling my nostrils, brushing up against my skin. The air is rank with them, and they trigger memories I had hoped I would never have to endure again. But I cannot let this impact me. I have to keep moving.

We advance as if in a dream, the overhead lights continuing to flicker erratically as we make for the heavy-security section of the prison. This is where they keep the most dangerous prisoners, and Harrow will certainly be considered such. We are closing in on our destination, and so far no one has appeared to stop us. I cannot believe our good luck. I am feeling better about our chances. We have broken into a Goblin prison, disabled its protective devices, outwitted its guards, and suffered no interruption of our efforts.

We are invincible.

Or so I think . . . until I discover otherwise.

We reach the high-security area and begin our search. After disabling the surveillance cameras once again, we break every lock on every door and release every prisoner we find. Most do not even glance up, they are so broken. None attempt to leave their cells.

The sight of these defeated souls breaks my heart. I want to help them, but there is nothing further I can do if I am to save Harrow. I have to leave them. I have to leave them all.

But Harrow is nowhere to be found.

By now, alarms are going off. We have been detected in one way or another, and they will be coming for us. What are we to do? I try to think it through. If Harrow isn't here, where would they have put him?

I begin to panic. *Think! Where would they have put him?*

Then I know. Just like that, I know. They have him in one of the punishment boxes. Those they want to break, those they want to make an example of, are locked away there. Those they feel will better respond after a few weeks of minimal food and water with no bed or sink or toilet or room to move about—no sunlight and no contact with another living soul—those they put in the boxes. The boxes are solid iron with no openings other than tiny slits that will allow just enough air to breathe, each one a solitary unit built into the stone of the walls deep underground in the cellars. I was never there, but Malik was. They kept him locked away once for a week before they brought him back out. He was shaking for days afterward—big, strong Malik, who was afraid of nothing else, was very afraid of the boxes.

Now Harrow is there.

I go cold all over. I don't know what to do.

The boxes aren't in one location. They are scattered all through the cellars of the prison, no two together. There is no way we can find out which one holds Harrow in the time we have. I start to panic and wheel back to face Ronden, explaining the problem in a halting voice. Alarms continue to sound all around us, and I imagine I hear Goblin boots pounding on the prison floors as our would-be captors draw closer.

"I know where he is, but not how to reach him. Is there a way I can find him?" I am almost in tears by the time I finish my explanation. "Do you know how we . . . ?"

"I can find him," she interjects quickly. "Just give me a moment."

She closes her eyes, both hands wrapped tightly around her *inish* staff. The runes that mark it begin to glow, and blue light runs up and down its carved length in ripples. She is searching for her brother. I think of the power of their sibling connection, and I know she is using that to seek him out.

Then her staff goes dark and her eyes snap open. "There is a recognizable Fae life force right below us. It must be Harrow. Is there a quick way down?"

Again we set out. I disable everything in sight as we go, thinking that confusion will serve us best at this point. The Goblins are not fools. They will have guessed that we have come for Harrow; that this is the only reason there would be a break-in of this nature. Goblins will be waiting for us in the cellars by the time we get down there. More will follow in order to trap us. We are hunted animals in an enemy warren from which there would seem to be no escape.

But I am calm again, determined anew, become once more as hard as steel. I take Ronden down a loading ramp that allows for deliveries to the cellars, avoiding the stairs. The Goblins might have guessed why we are here, but I am betting they have not guessed that a former prisoner is one of those they seek, and do not expect me to know the prison layout almost as well as they do. They will block the obvious ways in and out, but not the ones I choose to follow.

At the bottom of the loading ramp, I lift the chute door and peer out. No Goblins in sight. The box in which I am all but certain Harrow is imprisoned is down the corridor to our left. But there are bound to be Goblins there by this time, so we need to catch them by surprise. First, though, we have to get much closer. The air vents that spiral all through the cellar levels give us a way to do that.

There is a vent entry in the corridor ceiling not a dozen steps away. We hurry over, and the vent cover lifts off easily once I have melted the securing bolts. Ronden boosts me up, hands me her staff, and leaps for the opening, her hands grasping the edges so she can lever herself inside. We take time to close the cover once more and begin to crawl. It is a swift journey through an empty chute, and we are there in less than two minutes, looking down through another vent opening. Peering through the slats, I can make out a clutch of Goblins just ahead of us, milling about one of the punishment boxes.

Harrow. It has to be where they hold him.

Then I realize something else. There are too many guards standing about just to watch one caged prisoner. This is a trap. But there is no help for it.

Ready? I mouth.

Ready, she replies.

We don't stop to think further. I release the locking bolts and slide the cover aside soundlessly. After a moment's hesitation as she positions herself, Ronden drops through the opening. A few Goblin heads turn, but she is striking out with her *inish* staff the moment she lands, leveling the four who stand closest so quickly they have no time to bring their automatic weapons to bear. I follow on her heels and take down the remaining three. Not a single weapon has been fired. I strip the guns from the Goblins and toss them aside. We leave the guards sprawled unconscious and set about opening the sealed box they were guarding.

Kneeling before the slits and bending close, I whisper, "Harrow, move back from the opening. Ronden and I are going to get you out."

I hear a shuffling inside, and Ronden quickly releases both locks and hinges with quick bursts of fiery magic. The door falls away— heavy enough that if it struck the floor, the resulting sound would send a booming echo down the hallways. But Ronden catches it in a web of magic and lowers it slowly and silently.

Harrow's lean face appears in the opening, scratched and bruised from his ordeal. His familiar smile, though fleeting, is there. He says nothing but begins to crawl free. Even with our help, he moves gingerly and slowly; he has probably been both beaten and drugged. As a result, he doesn't make it all the way out before more Goblin guards appear, coming toward us from either direction along the passageway.

The jaws of the trap are closing.

Ronden and I move quickly as we see their weapons lift and point. Standing back-to-back we conjure our *inish* and blow the Goblins twenty feet back down the hallway, leaving them limp and unmoving. From the direction we came, I can hear others approaching. There is no time or opportunity to go back that way. Another choice is necessary.

I make it quickly. I am the one who has to; I am the one who knows the way. We shoulder Harrow between us and get him on his feet, then shuffle away from the sounds of reinforcements. I know where we are, but not what awaits us up ahead. When we find a second loading ramp not far from where we started out, I trigger it to open so we can scramble up the ramp and back to the main floor. There are shouts and guttural snarls joining the sounds of the alarms by now, and it is clear that the entire prison watch is awake and searching. All we have in our favor at this point is that they cannot be sure exactly where we are, because all the devices that might have tracked us are disabled.

Still, it is easy enough to know which section of the prison we are in, and the trick now is to convince them they can catch us there.

We move quickly away from the Goblin approach, but Harrow is flagging. Disoriented from being crammed into the punishment box, even for those few hours it held him—and, from the look of his eyes, definitely drugged—he is struggling. I feel a fresh surge of anger, but there is no time for it now. Escape is all that matters. We need to get back outside the wall, to where the wormhole awaits.

Deception, I think. Deception is our best alternative.

The sounds of pursuit rise up, harsh and insistent. Another loading ramp door comes into view and I burn the locks away. We go through, then scramble, claw, and push our way up its rough surface and into a different passageway. Once through and standing momentarily beneath yet more cameras, which I am quick to disable, I try to orient myself. I do so quickly because I have scrubbed the floors of this section countless times over my five years as an inmate, and I know it like the back of my hand. Trying to ignore the chaos threatening to close in about us, we make our way down the darkened passageways as I continue to disable lights, cameras, and motion and sound detectors, leaving us with nothing more than a small were-light that Ronden pitches a dozen steps ahead. I do so as a precaution in case we are found anew, which proves prescient. We have gone no more than several dozen yards when automatic weapons fire lances toward us from out of the darkness ahead. Ronden grunts, struck at least once, but she doesn't falter. I use my staff to bring down our attackers, lashing out blindly into the darkness. I hear howls and groans and then silence. Clear enough now, I think. I hope.

It feels as if we struggle on forever, even though I know it is only minutes. I grow weary but never once consider stopping. If we stop to rest, we are lost. We keep going, encounter no one else, and finally reach the door that leads into the garages. We go through and are immediately attacked again. This time the Goblins are waiting for us. This time, they choose to come at us using brute strength alone. Ronden's magic brings most of them down, but the others close in. We collapse in a heap, our bodies entangled with theirs; a blow to the head fells Harrow. Ronden and I thrash in a cluster of arms and legs, and I can already tell I am in serious trouble. Goblins are much stronger and heavier than I am. My staff is gone, ripped from my grasp, and powerful hands already have a firm grip on my legs and body.

Panic threatens to overwhelm me. The lights in this room still work, and I can see the cruel faces of those who hold me fast. I am terrified, but I am determined, too. Going momentarily limp, letting my attackers believe I am subdued, I summon my *inish* using only my fingers—employing a technique Ronden taught me—and will my magic to life. Its power explodes out of me from everywhere at once: a fiery, blinding brightness that frees me instantly. My captors tumble away like straw-filled scarecrows, tattered and stunned.

Momentarily depleted, I yank a knife from beneath my belt and scramble to help Ronden. I do not remember ever actually using a knife, yet I reach for it instinctively. This is Ronden I seek to help, and those who attack her would kill her with no hesitation. They are creatures that think nothing of hurting those who cannot defend themselves. I have watched them do so on more than one occasion. I have watched friends die at their hands. They are animals. They are predators.

Three of them fight to hold Ronden down, hands about her neck, choking the life out of her. I react instinctively. I use the knife first on the attacker closest to me, then on another. One quick strike to the neck severs a spinal cord, and another cuts a throat. Goblins are armored with scales and the toughened hide of reptile predators, so each strike must be true. Mine are. My targets grunt and go limp. I feel the dampness of blood on my hands and clothing, and I have to fight to keep from gagging.

Ronden fights off the final attacker and uses her *inish* to toss it away. As one, we struggle to our feet, breathing hard and staring at each other with something that conveys a shared gratitude. Picking up her staff, Ronden moves to close the door through which we entered the garage and seals it in place. I grab my staff in turn, and we get Harrow back on his feet. His head lolls; he is barely conscious, his green flesh turned dark and swollen on his forehead, where he took a heavy blow. Ronden is bleeding now from several bullet wounds. She sees me staring, and the look she gives me says she is not about to let this slow her down. Under my direction we stumble toward the exit, ignoring the vehicles we pass. I do not know what Tommy did under the hood to start them, nor do I know how to drive one. The main thing here is misdirection, to make them think we are escaping by vehicle, as I did before.

I use my *inish* to blow open the main door while Ronden conjures the illusion of a vehicle speeding away, then we go out fast on foot, turning back away from the garage entrance, hugging tightly to the walls and dragging Harrow between us.

"Where is the wormhole?" I demand frantically.

Ronden takes the lead, pointing. The wormhole is not visible, and I take it on faith that it is where she is indicating. Prison spotlights are blazing overhead from atop the walls and we hear vehicles roar to life—the guards tracking Ronden's illusion—but where we travel pressed up against the prison walls is still mostly in shadow. Sliding to a stop, we prop Harrow more securely between us and make a slow advance to where Ronden indicates the wormhole lies. Overhead, we are spotted, and shouts and cries rise up. Weapons fire begins. Pulling Harrow down to shield him, I use my staff to rake the gunports and weapons overhangs with my *inish* and cause each one to disappear in a fiery explosion. Abandoning her illusion, Ronden provides a shield as I do this, and for perhaps thirty seconds we hold our positions.

When the weapons fire from the prison finally goes still, we surge back to our feet with Harrow between us and stumble on. After a few more seconds, Ronden shouts for me to halt and summons the wormhole. When it appears, we move toward it in a rush; renewed weapons fire from the Goblins chasing us all the way.

We don't make it to the entrance. We are still a dozen yards away when I am struck a blow that knocks me off my feet. My staff goes flying. I hear Ronden scream as she sags under Harrow's weight.

I feel nothing at first as I lie prone on the ground, then a furious rush of pain sears my entire right side. I struggle to rise and cannot manage it. Bullets kick up the earth all around me, and I throw up an *inish* shield in desperation. I roll over on my stomach and try to crawl, but my entire right side is so numb I cannot move my arm.

"Leave!" I scream at Ronden.

She has formed a shield over Harrow and herself and looks as if she intends to come for me. But she is a dozen yards away from where I lie, and I can hear vehicles approaching. "You have to go!" I scream. "Save Harrow!"

She shakes her head, and I scream at her again. "Get out of here! You can't help me!"

I know what I am doing. I know what this means. The one thing I did not want to happen is happening and there is no help for it. Ronden cannot save me. I cannot save myself. My fate is decided.

I scream the words I never thought I would. "Kill me! You have to!"

But I can tell from the look on her face she won't. She shakes her head, and shouts, "I will come back for you!"

I don't want her to. I don't want her to risk it. I don't want her to die for me. I scream in rage and frustration, but she is already guiding Harrow into the wormhole.

A final look back at me tells me everything I need to know about how determined she is. *I will come back for you.*

Then she turns away, and the wormhole disappears.

I fight one final time to climb back to my feet and fall into darkness.

SEVENTEEN

WHEN I WAKE AGAIN, I AM LOCKED IN A HIGH-SECURITY CELL. I remember enough from my previous imprisonment to recognize what it is right away. A small, dark cubicle with a triple-ribbed slant window for air, a heavy iron door locked tight against all possibility of any rescue, and furniture consisting of an iron cot, a mattress and blanket, and a bucket for personal relief. And that's it.

My first thought is one of amazement: I am still alive. My second is one of sad recognition: Escaped prisoners caught and returned are always dismembered.

I am aching and stiff when I manage to sit up and discover that I have been stripped of my clothing, and my damaged right arm, shoulder, and ribs are wrapped in a very professionally applied bandage. I am surprised the Goblins bothered, but quickly decide it will be more entertaining for them if I am dismembered after I have been given a chance to heal.

Still, I've never known this to happen—this effort to help an inmate recover from an injury.

I think back to the events of the previous . . . well, whenever I was last conscious. I can't be sure since I don't know what day it is or how long I slept. I can tell from the light that seeps through the slant window that it is daytime, but nothing else. I close my eyes and feel the impact of the weapons fire that sent me spinning away and left me too damaged to escape. I see Ronden's look of anguish as she realizes she cannot help me. I see her lever a barely conscious Harrow to his feet and stumble into the wormhole with her brother clinging to her. I see her final look back at me, remember our shared knowledge of what it meant to leave me behind.

I hear again her final words: *I will come back for you.*

Then she was gone, and now here I am, back where I swore I would never return—back in this hellhole I escaped once already and must now try to find a way to escape from again. As if. Escape this time is a dream. I won't live long enough to come up with a plan, let alone to try to execute it. I am sitting up well enough, but I can already tell I barely have the strength to manage that.

But again, the Goblins didn't just kill me outright, so that's a plus. It suggests someone wants me alive. Maybe the same someone who bandaged my shoulder. Maybe I am not to be dismembered after all. But what fate is planned for me, if not that?

I sit pondering this question for a long time, then finally a gnarled hand pushes a tray with food and drink through a slot that swings open by the floor. The metal tray scrapes along the stone until it is inside and the slot swings shut, locks falling into place. Footsteps fade into the distance.

I am suspicious of anything I am fed, but I am also hungry and thirsty, so I take a chance and consume it all. If they wanted me dead, they wouldn't waste their time on poisons. But they do have something else in mind for me. Once I am done with my meal, a great weariness steals over me. I barely make it into a prone position on my narrow cot before I am sound asleep.

Time passes. When I wake again it is dark out. My sleep was deep and untroubled, and I am sure there was something in my food or drink to facilitate this. It could be it was intended to help me heal. It could also be that they don't want me to cause any more trouble. But what do they think I am capable of doing while locked away like this? Do they have any idea what I am now capable of? I don't think so. Otherwise I would be in chains, pinned to the floor. They have taken my *inish* staff, so they must suspect that it harbors power. When they see me, they see a Human, not a Fae. They cannot know what I am inside—what I have only recently discovered for myself. They see me only as an escaped prisoner who never once displayed any indication of Fae power during my previous five years of incarceration.

Yet they keep me alive for some mysterious reason.

Sure, I think. *Sure, they do. They keep you alive so they can take you apart piece by piece and laugh while they do it! Why are you kidding yourself?*

I go back to thinking about Ronden and Harrow. Already exhausted, they face a difficult walk through the wormhole to get home again. How can they manage it when both are injured? It is a daunting task for Ronden especially, no matter how determined she is to see her brother safe. There is a limit to what even she can manage. Hauling her brother, who is mostly helpless, while she is wounded? She will falter before they are safely arrived. What happens, I wonder suddenly, if you are inside a wormhole for too long? I don't think I want to know. I just want them to find a way out as soon as possible.

By now, of course, they must have done so. Or died trying—but I refuse to contemplate this. Besides, failure is difficult to imagine for those two. They will have found a way to return safely to Viridian Deep. They will be telling the rest of the family of my fate and trying to decide if they can somehow save me. I hope they do not try. I can stand the idea of *my* dying to save *them,* but I cannot bear the thought that *they* might die trying to save *me.* Some possibilities are too awful to contemplate.

I sit up, thinking things over, surprised to find I am already feeling much better—stronger and more able. Many of my aches have disappeared, my weariness has lessened, and even my wounds seem to have begun to heal. Over the next little while, I eat and sleep and think about my life without knowing for sure how much time passes until finally a man in a white smock walks into my cell unannounced. He is slight, diffident, and unimposing. His brown hair is starting to thin, and his bearded face shows signs of aging. The door remains open as he stands looking down; two Goblins bearing automatic weapons are stationed just outside, on watch. Feeling instantly threatened, I get to my feet and stand facing my captors.

"How are you feeling, Auris?" the man asks, his tone gentle and concerned.

But I am suspicious of everyone and everything in this place, so I scowl at him. "How do you know my name?"

He smiles. His smile is warm. "It wasn't so difficult to check the records. You are a former prisoner, after all. Now tell me. Are you better?"

"I feel better," I admit.

"With your permission, now that you are awake and able to give it, I would like to change your bandage and examine your wound."

I give him a hard look. "Are you a doctor?"

"I am. I treated your wound after your jailers carried you in here. Now the dressing needs changing. I don't think there are any unpleasant surprises waiting, but we ought to make sure. Please sit back down while I take a look."

I do as he asks and allow him to kneel in front of me and gently remove the heavy wrapping from around my upper arm, shoulder, and torso. I am near enough to being totally naked to feel uncomfortable, but being naked in front of jailers is nothing new. I sit quietly, staring straight ahead, looking right past his shoulder and off into space. I feel what he does rather than watch. He touches my arm and shoulder several times and presses against my ribs at various points. Each time he does this he asks if it hurts. It does, so I nod. He speaks over his shoulder to the Goblin guards, and one of them goes off briefly and then returns with a bucket of water and bandages. The doctor takes them and shoos him away as you might a troublesome pet. When we are alone he washes the injured areas of my body carefully, applies a salve, and wraps me back up again.

Then he calls to the guard a second time, and again the Goblin disappears. When he returns, he bears a shawl and clothing. The doctor takes the clothing and sets it aside, then wraps me in the shawl so I am covered up.

"For when you are alone again, a fresh change of clothes," he says, patting the items he has laid on my cot next to me. "You are lucky you were not more badly injured. The bullets missed your bones and passed right through muscle. Enough damage to shock you, but nothing that won't heal with time. But you will need to continue to rest, so I can't allow you any freedom right away."

"You say this as if it matters," I snap.

He is taken aback. "Well, if you wish to live, it matters quite a lot."

I shake my head reprovingly. "Don't you know what happens to prisoners like me? Prisoners who have escaped but are recaptured? The Goblins dismember them."

"A vicious practice," he allows. "But that's not going to happen to you."

"How do you know? Are you the warden here?"

The doctor smiles and stands again. "No. But if I say you won't be harmed, you can believe it. Rest now. I will be back tomorrow and we can talk some more. I think we have a lot to say to each other."

He turns and walks away. I watch him go, confused by his self-assurance. "Don't count on it!" I shout after him,

The door to my cell closes and the locks click into place. I am alone again and left to wonder if what he promises is actually going to happen.

I EAT AND DRINK THE FOOD THAT NIGHT WITHOUT RESERVATION, thinking that perhaps I *am* going to find a way out of this. I don't for one minute believe this doctor has my best interests at heart—unless I assume my best interests are the same as his and whomever he works for—but I am willing to play along to discover his true intentions. Because he does have something very specific in mind, given the way he is treating me, and I need to find out what it is.

Sleeping through the night is no problem because I am tired and still recovering from my injuries. I don't dream, which is a blessing, because I don't need the attendant stress. When I wake, there is breakfast waiting, and within an hour after that—after I am dressed in the new clothes my benefactor has provided me—he enters for our talk.

I have been thinking about how I should handle this. I want him to open up to me, but he will not be keen to do so. Yet I know a thing or two about deceptions, and I will engage in a few here. I rise to greet him, framing myself with my hands to show off my new clothes.

"It was kind of you to give me these," I say.

He nods without comment and sits on the cot, gesturing for me to sit beside him. "Let me ask you a few questions. I wasn't here when you were brought into the prison five years ago so I don't know much about you. Your records say you were brought here for treason. Your parents were executed; you were imprisoned. What can you tell me about that?"

I have always assumed my parents were dead—even while hoping against hope that I was wrong—but to hear their fate announced in such a flat, unemotional way is devastating.

I bottle up my urge to cry and just shrug. "I don't remember them."

He shakes his head. "Come on now. You must remember something."

"Sorry. I don't remember anything from before my time here. I have no memory of my early childhood at all. I don't even remember what my parents looked like."

This causes him to frown. "Do you think your memory was deliberately wiped or that the shock of losing your parents might have caused you to forget?"

I give him a look. "Are we playing games already? I don't want to talk about my parents."

He shrugs as if this doesn't matter. "I'm a doctor. I have to ask these questions if I am to know how to best treat my patients."

I grimace at his response. He's the worst liar I have ever encountered.

"Think carefully," he continues. "Can you remember where you lived or maybe recall someone you knew from that time? Can you remember the names of friends or relatives? Any people or places or experiences from your childhood? There must be something."

"There isn't. You can ask until the cows come home, but my answer won't change. I don't remember anything." I can lie, too.

"Then let's talk about when you escaped. You and your friends managed to tunnel out, steal a vehicle, and flee into the wastelands, heading for Roughlin Wake. But the Goblins caught up with you, disabled your vehicle, and killed all your friends. Why weren't you killed, too?"

"I was thrown from the vehicle before it crashed. I rolled into the brush and lost consciousness. When I woke, the Goblins were gone. I found my friends dead and the vehicle disabled, so I started walking. Eventually I got to this lake—what did you call it? Roughlin?"

He ignores my feigned ignorance. "Where one of the Sylph Watchers found you. Do you remember his name? Or the name of the place he took you?"

I've had enough. "Yes," I answer.

He waits for more, then when I say nothing he asks again. "Can you tell me, please?"

"No."

He considers this for a moment, then says, "I can use drugs that will make you tell me."

His patience is apparently quite limited. "Go ahead."

In truth, I am not as brave as I sound. I know he can do what he says. But perhaps my *inish* is powerful enough to protect me from such techniques even when I am drugged. Though this is blind faith at best, and this alone would not be reason enough to defy him. What I really want to do is test the extent of his commitment to protect me from dismemberment.

"Will you tell me anything at all about where you have been and what you have been doing?"

When I am silent, he just smiles.

"It is, perhaps, not too hard to guess. You returned here with one Fae companion to rescue another. You have been to Viridian Deep, have you not?"

"And what is that to you?" I snap back, but my heart is pounding as I see the walls of his trap take shape. Benith said the Humans were interested in Fae magic. And his next words confirm it.

"What interests me—as a medical man—is that while your green friends don't have the use of Human weapons, they are very capable in other ways. Our soldiers have done battle with them on a few occasions, and they are a formidable enemy. I wish they weren't. I wish we could be friends, but they don't seem interested."

"I don't think they trust you," I offer.

"Oh, you can speak their language?"

I don't answer. I just stare at him.

"You don't seem to want to help me," he says, looking a bit sad about it. "Why is that?"

"Do you work for the Ministry?" I ask.

He nods. "As a doctor and adviser."

"Then why should I help you? The Ministry are allied with the Goblins, and the Goblins want to see the Fae destroyed down to the last man, woman, and child. The Ministry also keeps the children of its citizens locked away in these prisons. Why would anyone do that? I would consider helping you if I thought for one minute you deserved it. But that's not what I think."

He purses his lips thoughtfully. "You are well informed—if not accurately so. I told you I was your friend, and I am. I've promised to keep you from being dismembered. Doesn't that count for something?"

"Then give me back my staff and let me go. That would count for something. Otherwise, all I have is a promise you can renege on the moment I cease to be of use. Do you have a name?"

He nods. "Dr. Allensby."

"First name?"

He just smiles. Two can play this game.

"Dr. Allensby." I speak his name slowly and precisely. "I don't trust you."

"You should."

"Because you say so? Please."

"Because I am the only friend you have here."

"So you claim. But from my standpoint, I have no friends here."

"Then maybe this is a chance for you to make one. You have to start somewhere, right? Why not take a chance on me?"

I go silent, and then say, "Are we finished? This conversation doesn't seem to be going anywhere."

His smile this time is just a shade harder. "Give it time, Auris."

We spend the next two hours fencing with words, covering much of the same ground we already have. We also establish that he actually is a doctor and not someone pretending to be, but he is something more as well. He holds some position in the government of the Humans that built this prison and have allied themselves with the Goblins.

"The Goblins are a primitive people," Allensby allows, "but that makes them more reasonable. If we give them what they want, they don't question what we ask of them. In the opinion of the Goblins, those green people—Sylvans, as they call themselves—are the real enemy. If we find a way to make an agreement with their enemy, perhaps we can help the Goblins make one, too. It all works out to everyone's benefit."

This is such a load of total crap I don't bother responding to it. The good doctor's attempts at bringing me into the fold would work better if he were more straightforward about what his superiors are trying to do. I am willing to believe they are not representative of the entire Human race, but I cannot know this for sure. So I keep quiet about what I have learned from the Seers and my newfound Sylvan family. It becomes clear that Allensby intends to wear me down gradually, to wait for me to open the door just a crack so he can stick his foot in. He's doomed to disappointment. He will get nothing from me.

For several days of "conversation" he tests me over and over, and I do not bend one inch. Nor will I ever.

So I promise myself. So I believe.

Until he shows me why I am wrong.

We are perhaps a week into our daily conversations—which by now have shifted a bit closer to interrogations, although threats or warnings are still absent—when Dr. Allensby comes in and immediately lays out how he intends for our newest session to go.

"We are covering the same ground too often," he begins. "While I enjoy our little talks and our verbal games, I need to make a bit more progress. What I have told you about myself is the truth"—no, it isn't—"and what I have promised about keeping you safe will not change because of anything that happens today." He is lying again. "But we have to move ahead.

"So let's review. What I have refrained from talking about is what I know for a fact to be true. In the course of events following your escape, you gained considerable knowledge of your green rescuers and their homeland. You have lived there for weeks; you must have learned something significant. You have also carefully avoided saying one word about your return with a second Sylvan to rescue the Sylvan we had locked away. You didn't just *happen* to come back here to rescue him; there is a reason you came. Whoever this man is, he means something to you. You would never have taken the risk you did otherwise. No one would have. So tell me about him."

I hesitate, and I am on the verge of denying him even a single scrap of information when I see how pointless that would be. What he suggests is beyond obvious. "He was the one who found me in the wastelands and took me to his homeland," I admit. "I owed it to him to come back."

"And the woman with you?"

"His sister."

"Now, see? That didn't hurt a bit, did it?" He seems genuinely pleased. "A little more cooperation between us, and things will go so much more smoothly. I really am your friend."

"If there is to be cooperation, when does your side of the bargain begin?" I ask.

"A fair question. Here is something I found out yesterday after I left you. Actually, I have been seeking this information for almost the entire time we have conversed. Your father apparently worked for my government as a scientist. In that capacity, he performed an illegal experiment of some sort. He did this without revealing his work to his employer—which you can understand was a serious violation. On top of that, he transgressed in some other ways. I don't know the details, but whatever he did, it branded both your mother and him as traitors and cost them their lives. And it deprived you of your freedom and apparently your memory; you were taken from them and locked away here."

I stare at him suspiciously. There is more, I am certain. More that he knows; more that he is holding back. This is how he works. Reveal just a little; hide the rest. But I sense what he tells me is probably true. The memories recovered by the Seers support this scenario. It squares with what little knowledge I possess of the fate of my family.

"Let's continue," he says, the smile back in place again. He is practically drooling with anticipation. "I will share a secret with you—one that will help you better understand your position as my patient. I know about your staff. I know it holds within it considerable power. You were seen wielding that power during your attempt to escape. Somehow you have learned how to master and make use of Sylvan magic, and I want to know how you did that. Please do not insult me by denying what I have just told you. It took me awhile to piece together the truth—interviews with a raft of Goblins, sorting out facts from wild imaginings—but now I know. So I want to hear the whole truth. What is the source of the staff's power? How did you learn to make use of it and who taught you?"

I decide quickly this is where I must make my stand. "Before I tell you anything, I want you to tell me what you have done with it. I want to know it is safe."

"A beautifully crafted piece of art, that wicked length of wood. But a dangerous weapon, too. You killed and injured a lot of Goblins. Without my intervention, they would have gladly torn you to pieces when they recaptured you. But they know better than to do so now." His smile is a bit too ready. "As to your question, I have your staff safely tucked away in my office. It is in perfect condition in spite of the rough use to which you put it."

So, it is in his office. I wonder where that is. I wonder how I can find out.

"I won't deny what you suspect," I say. "I will admit what you have probably already guessed. I was taught how to use it by my rescuers."

He beams so brightly I want to puke. "As I suspected, indeed," he agrees. "But it languishes there when it needs to be employed. Can you teach me how to use it?"

Now we arrive at the heart of his interrogation. This is what he really wants. Just like that, I see a way out of this mess. But I must tread carefully. "Perhaps. Perhaps not. What will you give me, if I do?"

"Your life?"

"Being kept in this prison is no life. I want you to set me free."

He hesitates. "Very well. Once you have kept your end of the bargain, I see no reason not to let you go."

"With my staff in hand," I add.

"Oh, come now, Auris. It is the staff's power I need to examine and come to understand. If I give the staff back, I can hardly do that, can I? No, the staff stays with me. You can get another."

I want to argue the point, but hold off. "Then I will have to show you. I can't just tell you. There is more to it than a simple explanation."

"You can certainly tell me something . . ."

"I can, but it won't mean anything without a demonstration."

"Would this demonstration involve me being incinerated while you attempt yet another escape?"

"I doubt you would allow that."

He pauses, studying me. "Indeed, I wouldn't." He rises. "Let me give it some thought. I will come back tomorrow with your staff and a chance for you to show me how to use it. But remember, Auris. If you try to trick me or attack me in any way, I will consider our friendship breached and my promise to you void. At that point, I will have no further use for you, and will give you to the Goblins to do with as they will. Are we clear on this?"

I nod wordlessly and he turns to leave. "One thing more. I said I was a doctor and adviser to the Ministry. This is true. But I am also something more. I *am* warden of this prison." He pauses. "Your life is in my hands."

I watch him leave my cell without looking away, but already I am thinking ahead to what I am now certain I must do.

On the morrow, I will escape or die trying.

EIGHTEEN

I HAVE A PLAN, BUT IT RELIES HEAVILY ON MY SYLVAN FRIENDS.
It relies on Sylvan magic. It relies especially on Ronden's
promise to come back for me. Most of all, it relies on faith.

If I am correct about what I think will happen on the morrow, I
will be out in the open surrounded by Goblins with automatic
weapons. Dr. Allensby will be there, but he will want to keep his
distance. The risk would be too great if he were to place himself
within arm's reach of me. I may be small, but he knows I escaped
once already when all my friends were killed, and I almost escaped
again this last time. He knows I can be dangerous. He may not yet
understand where my use of magic comes from—that it doesn't
come from the staff itself, but from within me—but he will be
watching me closely. If he believes he is in even the smallest danger, he will have me killed. So he must be made to believe I am
doing everything he asks of me right up until it is too late.

Next, I have to hope that what I believe is happening back in
Viridian Deep is not just a product of my imagination. What I believe is that Ronden will be looking for a way to rescue me—even

in the face of the danger they know they will face. I am counting on her gaining help from the Seers to keep track of me—to know where I am at any given moment through use of an *Inish* Reveal.

The Reveal is a three-foot-wide basin of magically infused colored sands. When the sands are at rest, they show a representation of the known Fae world that can be expanded to show the lands surrounding it. The sands can then shift and re-form to show the approximate whereabouts of any member of the Fae people. They can reveal what is happening to that person, as they did with Harrow when he was taken. But the Seers alone can interpret the display, as they were the ones who built the basin, collected the sands, and infused them with magic.

Yet more useful still is the way the Reveal can sense any substantial use of *inish* and identify the source. All that is needed is for one of the sisters to be monitoring the basin, as Dreena was doing when Harrow was taken. It can tell them what has become of me. Any substantial use of my *inish* can let them know I am still alive. I am counting on this to happen—counting on it when I have no right to do so, but must if I am to have any chance at all. I am depending on either Harrow or Ronden to understand what I am doing and to come for me.

I believe it is a reasonable expectation in spite of what it demands of my friends. They know me well enough to believe I am alerting them. They will know that even if I have been stripped of my staff, I can summon my *inish* without it. If they are watching, they can come for me instantly using the same wormhole Ronden and I used to rescue Harrow. If they reach me in time, they can snatch me away.

Neither Harrow nor Ronden would ever abandon me. But I am asking a lot of both here; I am asking them to deduce what it is I am asking. I am trusting in them in a way no sane person should, but I have no other choice. I must risk everything if I expect to get out of the Goblin prison alive.

This is a big gamble. It is a *huge* gamble.

There is one thing more that my decision requires. Ronden

could not bring herself to kill me when she knew I would be taken—even though I had made her promise she would. Now I must make this promise for myself. If my gambit fails, I must be ready and willing to give up my own life. My promise must be more than words; it must be a sacred vow that I will not violate. *I cannot be taken alive.* Not again. Allensby will give me to the Goblins, and the horror of what awaits me if I fail to keep my promise to myself is too awful to contemplate.

I sleep restlessly that night, waking often to repeat the steps of my plan one more time, to reassure myself, to prepare anew for the coming of morning. Sometime around dawn, I realize if I wait longer, I risk missing an opportunity that will not come again. I have the power to summon my *inish,* staff or no, and I must do so now. I do not intend to leave without my staff, and at some point I will have it in hand again. But providing Harrow and Ronden with a signal of what I intend does not require it.

So sitting back in a far corner, I close my eyes and bring my *inish* to bear in a rough projection of my face that the sisters cannot fail to recognize, along with a slow beckoning of my arm. It should tell them I am still alive and need help. It should suggest to Harrow and Ronden that they should come to me. It will not tell them anything more specific but, if I am lucky, my friends will deduce what is needed.

I hope. I can't be sure my efforts will achieve anything, or even that my friends will realize what is needed. But it is the best I can do, and I have to trust their instincts, experience, and expectations of me.

I have to hope, too, that the sudden brightening of my dark cell has failed to alert the Goblins. I have to hope none of them were looking in my direction. After a long, expectant wait, I believe I am safe and fall asleep again.

Morning arrives, and I prepare myself for the new day. It doesn't take much to do so—washing up in the basin and dressing in the clothes Dr. Allensby has provided—but I am grateful even for these small comforts. I sit on my cot and go over my plan one more time.

Almost everything will have to happen on the spur of the moment. Almost everything could go wrong. I must remember not to become too attached to any one part of my plan, but to hold myself ready for whatever is needed and to be willing to adjust to whatever occurs.

When the locks on my cell door release, I think I am ready for what will come next. I am wrong.

Dr. Allensby steps inside and faces me, hands wrapped about my staff possessively. A huge Goblin guard stands just behind and to one side of him, an automatic weapon cradled loosely in his big hands.

"We are going out into the exercise yard to allow you to instruct me on how to use your staff, Auris," Allensby advises. "We will be surrounded by Goblin guards—some in the yard, and some on the walls. All of them will have their weapons trained on you. If you try to use the staff against me, you will be shot. Same thing if you turn it on them. You will tell me what you intend to do and how you will do it before you attempt any actions. You will obey every command I give you. I am wearing armor beneath my clothing and will don a protective helmet once we are outside. Am I clear?"

I nod. None of it matters to me. "Perfectly. You don't trust me."

"Of course I don't. I am convinced you intend to escape, so I am giving you as many reasons as possible why you must not do so. There is no escape from dozens of armed guards and impenetrable prison walls. Is there?"

"Apparently not," I concede.

"Then there is only one thing more you need to know. I am only interested in how the staff works and how I can access its power— nothing more. If you give me that, you can go free. Without your staff, of course, but with your life and an opportunity to return to your green friends in one piece."

He pauses. "That said, don't think I am underestimating you or believe for one minute you aren't planning something. I know better. If given the chance, you would take advantage of me. But that is not going to happen. And here's why."

He steps back and to one side and calls out to the guards standing just outside the cell. A hooded figure is shoved forward, stumbling into the room blindly. Dr. Allensby catches hold of whoever it is to prevent them from falling. He gives me an enigmatic look and snatches off the hood.

Khoury.

All the air goes out of me. *Khoury. Alive!*

How can this be? I was so certain both she and Malik had been brought back and dismembered. But here she stands—short-cropped black hair, lean features, and dark-blue eyes. Small even when she was well, she now seems to have shrunk to almost nothing. Her body is thin and her shoulders slumped; she looks beaten down. She looks ruined.

"You want to keep her safe?" Allensby asks. "Then behave yourself."

"She doesn't look very safe to me," I manage. I glare at him. "What have you done to her?"

He shrugs. "Drugs to make her compliant. More drugs to make her talk—what I would do to you if you weren't willing to cooperate with me. Have I made myself perfectly clear?"

I ignore his ridiculous rhetorical question. "She comes with me when I leave."

Allensby nods slowly. "Fine. She can leave with you. She's of no further use to me or anyone else at this point, so you can have her. Just don't disappoint me by doing something stupid. Let's go out into the exercise yard and see if you can keep your end of the bargain."

Still keeping a tight grip on my *inish* staff, he spins Khoury about and marches her out the cell door, not even bothering to see if I am following. The big Goblin guard stays close until I start to move and then falls into step behind me. We walk through the cellblock to the stairs leading up to ground level, and I begin to panic. It is easy enough to picture what I will do if it is just me I have to worry about. But what am I to do now that I know Khoury is alive? What happens to her when I make my break? What if I can't save her, too?

I wonder for a moment if saving her is even possible. I saw her face—blank, expressionless, empty. Is there anything left of her inside that lifeless shell? Has anything of who she was survived all the drugs and whatever else she has endured since her recapture? I cannot be sure. I know only that I cannot abandon her if there is even the faintest hope.

I am aware of the familiar sounds of the prison rising up around me as we reach the main floor. Voices echo down the hallways—prisoners like myself being sent off to work or left locked in their cells for the day. The shuffling of booted feet and raspy growls of Goblin voices. The smells, fetid and raw—of sewage and slop and unwashed bodies and the sense of confinement when locked behind stone block walls—are harsh reminders of what I had thought I had escaped. Memories return in a flood, none of them good. I cannot go back to this. I cannot.

We pass through a heavily armored set of double doors where Goblins stand watch and go out into the exercise yard. It is a broad piece of ground open to the sky but fully surrounded by walls atop which guards stand everywhere. There are no prisoners in the yard now. Only Allensby, Khoury, the Goblins who escort us, and another dozen who surround us with weapons pointed. I am about to be asked to give over the power of my *inish* staff to the doctor when I know it is not possible. But I must let him think it is.

We move to the center of the courtyard where Allensby and I stand facing each other, six feet apart. Khoury stands in the grip of the huge Goblin guard off to the side, too far away for me to reach. I take a deep breath. Time is up. No turning back now, no faltering, no giving in to doubts or fears.

"What do I need to do to make this staff of yours work?" the doctor asks.

Shove it down your throat, I think.

"You need to place your hands on it just so," I tell him.

"Tell me how."

"I can't tell you. I have to show you. Your hands and fingers have to be precisely placed. The separation and angles have to be perfect. You are going to have to let me move your hands into place for you."

He shakes his head. "You are playing games with me, Auris."

"I am trying to stay alive!" I snap back. "I know what happens to me if you can't do this, so you have to let me show you. Just telling you won't be enough!"

He gives me a doubtful look. "If you try anything . . ."

"I know," I interrupt. "Just walk over to me and let me do what you want me to. Nothing will happen that you don't want to."

He nods and walks up to me. I tell him I am going to help him place his hands on the staff in the correct positions and not to make any sudden moves that will get me shot. Then I adjust his hands on the staff, widening his fingers and eventually getting his hands to where I want them—both in awkward positions where a simple twist of my hands would free the staff.

All the while I look him in the eyes, giving nothing away of what I am thinking, keeping all his attention on me.

"Now I am going to place my hands over yours so you won't drop the staff when the magic surfaces. The feeling can be jarring when you are not used to it. Stand still while I do this. Repeat what I say. This takes practice. We are going to move the staff to a vertical position so the magic goes straight up and not sideways into some unfortunate Goblin. All right?"

"Careful, Auris," he whispers. "Be very careful."

I'll be careful, all right. "Sure."

Even though I don't allow myself to look, I am acutely aware of the automatic weapons trained on me, of the Goblins who stand all around, and of the expectation I have managed to hold on to that I will be rescued. I am one small young woman in the grip of powerful creatures and a ruthless doctor who holds the last of my prison friends as his hostage to force me to comply. It is an impossible situation, and I have got to somehow turn it to my advantage.

If not, I have to embrace my own death and join Tommy, JoJo, Wince, Barris and Breck, Malik, and almost certainly Khoury in whatever awaits after life is over.

I close my hands over his so that we are both firmly connected to my staff. Then I mouth a bunch of nonsense and make him repeat each phrase until he has it all memorized. None of it means anything, but Allensby doesn't know this. When he says he is ready, I tell him to say it all at once, keeping his eyes on the staff while he does.

Hesitating as he gives me a final look of warning, he does what I tell him. But it is I who summon the magic, my hands still locked on his.

The staff explodes in a towering lance of blue fire that rises thousands of feet into the sky—an ignition of flammable particles I have gathered from the air. The force of its release knocks Allensby back on his heels, dragging me along with him. Allensby thinks he has done this and his face breaks into a wide grin—not realizing it had nothing to do with him and everything to do with me.

"Holy Mother of . . ." he screams in delight, his voice cracking before he can finish. I order him to hold steady and tell his Goblin guards to lower their weapons, all of which are now trained on me. He does so with frantic shouts, unwilling to release his grip on the staff and leave me holding it alone. He need not worry. With so many spitfires pointing my way, I am not about to set him free in any case.

I terminate my demonstration, shut down my *inish,* and shout at him to stand where he is. He does so obediently, his eyes fastened on my staff, his greed for a further taste of its power transparent. "I want to do it again!" he roars, hands clasping my staff with a death grip. He is practically jumping up and down. Any semblance of the calm, controlled doctor of earlier has vanished.

"Listen to me!" I hiss at him. "You're not ready yet. There are other things you have to learn if you want to do this without killing yourself. We need to practice. Can you do so now? Or do you want to rest first?"

"Can all of your green-skinned friends do this?" he asks, ignoring me. "Can they all make staffs like this one?"

"Not all," I say. "But many. Do you want me to show you more?"

"Yes! Yes, of course! Everything you know about using this staff. Right now! Teach me!"

I have him where I want him. He will do just about anything I want him to. He has unwittingly put himself in my hands. If Ronden and Harrow are watching, I will have the chance I need to escape this place and return to Viridian Deep. I glance over to where Khoury stands, her face empty of emotion, her eyes blank. I have to get her closer to me, but I don't know how to do this. Anything I say to suggest she be moved next to us will warn him.

There is only one thing for it. "I have to stand right behind you," I tell Allensby. I remove my hands from his and lower them. My staff is now out of reach. "Turn around."

He might not have done so if he was thinking clearly, but he is obsessed with the power of the staff and so immediately does what I ask. I move behind him and again place my hands over his, holding him fast to the staff. "Stay calm," I whisper.

Positioning the staff so that it remains pointed up, I have him recite the words, then release the power of my *inish* once more. But this time there is no fire. This time the magic serves a different purpose. It binds Dr. Allensby to me as surely as iron bonds, and we are made one. Any control he had before is gone; all control belongs to me. Only his voice and eyes remain his own.

Then I release the fire once more.

It takes a moment for Allensby to realize what has happened—that he is my prisoner. He screams in fury—but the roar of the fire and the howling of the Goblin guards as they watch the fire blossom into blazing shards that rain down everywhere drowns him out. I am giving them a show, a demonstration of magic, and they watch with rapt attention—all interest in their doctor momentarily forgotten. They have no idea that I have made Allensby my puppet.

Now I need help.

I need Harrow and Ronden.

But they do not appear. So I will have to fight my way clear of these walls using Allensby as a shield. Will the guards care about preserving his life in their attempts to stop me? If I blast down a wall and drag Allensby out with me, will they still shoot us, or will that buy me a pass?

There is no way to know, but I have to try. Already one or two guards are starting to look my way, attracted by Allensby's screams, wondering if something is wrong.

I have to go now.

The heat of the fire has stirred up the dusty floor of the exercise yard to such an extent that there is dust and debris flying everywhere. That screen allows me to edge closer to Khoury and her minder. But Allensby's presence, prisoner or not, is making my efforts too difficult. I realize I will have to set him free if I am to reach her. Even if I can reach Khoury, though, what will I do then? No matter how much damage I cause the Goblins, we will still both be cut to pieces before we can gain safety outside the prison walls.

And I need Allensby as my shield if this is to work at all.

Then the miracle I have been counting on comes to pass.

The air to one side of me blossoms into ripples as if it has been turned to water and the familiar shape of a wormhole emerges from out of the ground a dozen yards off to one side. Both Harrow and Ronden emerge, the latter's *inish* staff forming a shelter around me just as I think my strength will fail. Wrenching my staff from Allensby's hands, I throw him to the ground and turn to find Khoury.

The huge Goblin has her on her knees in front of him, his eyes wild with uncertainty, his spitfire pointed at her head. I don't hesitate; I use the staff to knock him twenty feet away from her, screaming at Khoury that I am coming. Our eyes lock as I reach out to her, and for just a minute it seems as if she recognizes me, her face regaining a look of awareness, her eyes coming back to life.

Then I hear Allensby scream. Spitfires held by Goblins atop the wall erupt in staccato bursts, and before I can do anything to prevent it, Khoury is shot to pieces.

I am not sure exactly what happens after that. I remember my howl of dismay and my wild efforts to go to her. I remember Harrow's strong arms about my waist as he lifts me up and carries me away. I remember our rush to reach the wormhole where Ronden stands waiting to receive us, doing her best to shield us with her magic. I remember the dust and the heat and the weapons fire raining down and somehow not touching us as we stumble into the wormhole. I remember it closing and Ronden leading the way back toward Viridian as Harrow continues to carry me.

I remember breaking down in tears.

I remember my grief for Khoury—grief I already expended when I wrongly believed her dead, and grief now that I know she really is. I remember being inconsolable even as I hear Harrow whisper in my ear, trying to calm me, to soothe me, to give me what support he can manage. To help me weather the storm that is tearing me apart.

But the harsh truth cannot be eased. Khoury is gone, and I am safe.

I cannot make it feel right.

I cannot dismiss my sense of failure.

Then abruptly we stop while still inside the wormhole, and both Harrow and Ronden kneel to hold me tight and let me wail until exhaustion claims me.

NINETEEN

I HAVE ONLY VAGUE MEMORIES OF RETURNING TO VIRIDIAN DEEP, most of them centered on how I am hauled into the city by Harrow and Ronden—barely conscious, sobbing, and exhausted. I am put to bed at once in my cottage—my outer clothing stripped off, my boots removed, and my blankets pulled up to cover me—and then my rescuers slip out the door on cat's paws. I sleep after that, deeply for the most part, waking twice to find it is still dark and immediately closing my eyes once more.

I try not to think about where I was or what happened to me. I banish thoughts of the Goblins and Allensby. I cannot bear to dwell on Khoury. I won't let myself think about any of it. I cradle my *inish* staff close to me beneath the covers and take comfort in its firm, reassuring presence.

When I wake for the third time, it is midday. I can see the sun shining out of a clear blue sky through my bedroom window and hear the familiar voices of Sylvans as they pass my home. I could almost make myself believe it was all a dream, but I decide not to. I allow myself to recall everything now—give myself permission to think through what has happened in its entirety. I cry more than once while doing so, but each time it becomes a little easier to stop. I tell myself I did the best I could for Khoury. I try not to consider what else I might have done or how I might have done it better; it is a pointless exercise to dwell on events I cannot now change. It will have to be enough that I tried. I remind myself more than once that, by all rights, I should be dead, too. I take comfort in the gratitude I feel at still being alive.

Finally, I rise and shower and do what I can to cover the bruises and cuts that mar my face and arms. I check myself over for deeper injuries and am happy not to find any. I eat a bit of fruit and bread, drink a little hard ale, and walk to the door to find Harrow and Ronden. I have taken two steps outside when I become aware of someone sitting on my bench, and I stop and turn.

"I have been waiting for you since dawn," Harrow says as he gets to his feet. He takes my hands in his. "I was so worried about you last night, but you seem better this morning. All that sleep must have helped."

For some reason his words make me blush. "It did."

"I can never find enough words to thank you enough for rescuing me," he continues, his smile widening in recognition of my discomfort.

"You did as much for me, didn't you?"

"You took a terrible chance, expecting us to figure out how to reach you."

"Not so great. I know you and Ronden pretty well. I just used common sense."

"And great courage." He squeezes my hands gently. "Let's promise each other not to let it happen again. Let's make a pact."

I look into his eyes, and once again I am lost. "A pact? Shouldn't Ronden be part of it?"

"Not this one. She didn't have to be rescued like we were. Both times, she helped rescue us. We need a different pact for her—one that promises we will never put her in a position where she will have to rescue us again."

I am smiling widely now. Such nonsense. But he always knows how to make me feel better. "That seems fair. But do we have to take a blood oath to bind our pact? Should we cut our fingers and mingle our blood?"

He shakes his head. "I was thinking of something a little less painful . . . but with a certain amount of touching."

He leans toward me slowly, his face lowering, and his lips press up against mine. As he kisses me, I marvel over the fact that Sylvans kiss the same way Humans do. I close my eyes and kiss him back. I let my tongue run over his pointed teeth, enjoying the strange feeling. I let my hands lift to cradle his head and hold him close, and my fingers find the silky smoothness of his long hair, brushing over the tiny leaves. Like little bits of silk, I think with pleasure. I never want the feelings that rush through me to end.

He pulls away finally. "I do not think I could stand it if I lost you," he whispers.

I mumble something incomprehensible, so filled with wonder and happiness that I cannot make myself say more. I have dreamed of this—dreamed without allowing myself to think it would ever happen. Yet I accept the gift and do not question why it has happened now. I treat it as I would a precious, fragile treasure.

"Come walk with me," he says.

We pass down through Viridian and find a small park not far away where we sit in seclusion amid a stand of conifers and flowering vines that wrap the narrow trunks of aspen. It is another in a seemingly endless succession of beautiful little glades that can be found everywhere in this city. He continues to hold my hands in his, and I continue to let him. I have never been in love, but I know how being with Harrow makes me feel, and I want badly to make up for lost time.

"Tell me everything," he asks. "If you can bear to."

I can bear anything just now, and so I do as he wishes and recount my days in captivity with the devious Dr. Allensby. I tell him of the man's efforts to persuade me to reveal what I know about Viridian Deep, the Sylvan people, my staff's power, and me. I recount what he told me about the fate of my parents, and about what happened in the prison. Halfway through my effort and before getting to Khoury, I break to ask a question that has been bothering me for weeks.

"I cannot forget what Benith said to me that first time we went to see the sisters to find out if my memories could be recovered. Right at the end, she said that I might be a Changeling—a Fae who can change how they look. I keep wondering how this can be. I know I am a Fae—a Sylvan—even if I don't look like one. I've accepted that. But is it possible I could ever have changed the way I look? Could I have learned how to do this? Or could someone have done it to me?"

He shakes his head. "I don't know. I don't have the answers. I don't know what a true Fae Changeling could do. There hasn't been one in my lifetime, and I believe none for generations."

"How could this have happened in any case?" I press on. "If I was taken from Viridian as a baby, wouldn't someone have missed me? And if I were altered so drastically physically—enough so that I would look Human—wouldn't I have some memory of it happening? I just don't understand, and I want to."

Harrow nods his understanding of my frustration. "One thing you need to remember. Benith didn't say you *were* a Changeling; she said you *might* be. That is a sizable difference. I think we need to know more than we do now before we try to figure out how this could be possible."

"But how can I learn more? What more can I do short of going back to where I came from before I was sent to the Goblin prisons?"

Harrow actually laughs. "You are the only person I know who would survive a stretch of imprisonment in a place you had only recently escaped from, and immediately consider going back!"

I nod sheepishly. "I guess that's why you find me so interesting."

"Interesting, yes. But also a bit crazy."

I shrug carelessly. "Maybe. But in a good way?"

"Please do this much. Take another week to rest up and heal, think things through further. You are accepted by the Sylvan now as one of us. You have uncovered and released your *inish* in a way any other Sylvan would envy. You have close friends in Ronden and myself. You have a good life waiting for you. How important is it that you know your past? What will you gain if you are successful? Is it really that important to you?"

I smile and nod in agreement with what he says, but Harrow can't understand how I feel; no one could who hasn't gone through what I have. What I am searching for is an explanation for my life. If I am ever to be at peace with who I have discovered I was meant to be, I have to find that explanation.

We remain in the glade that Harrow has chosen for another hour, our talk shifting to more mundane matters. I ask after Ronden and learn she has taken Char and Ramey on a picnic to Promise Falls, giving them a day off from their housework and studies so Harrow can be alone with me. But then, Ronden already knows how I feel about Harrow—and perhaps more than he knows, as well, about his feelings for me. I have wanted him to kiss me for a long time, but it always seemed out of reach. Today's kiss tells me that sometimes things work themselves out if you just give them a chance to do so.

I AM GOOD ABOUT FOLLOWING HARROW'S ADVICE IN THE DAYS that follow. I sleep late and go to bed early. I do not shy away from napping when I am tired. I walk with Harrow along the tree lanes and avenues of Viridian Deep every day, following his footsteps to new and wonderful places I have never seen before. Gardens profuse with flowers; parks verdant and tree-shadowed; waterfalls that ripple and sing with strange messages; lakes broad enough that I can only barely see their far shores; streams filled with colorful fish; old growth groves so ancient, their giant limbs seem to brush against the sky. Once we climb to the top of a bluff from where we can see the whole of the city revealed below us.

The days are slow and warm, and I drift through them gaining strength and confidence anew, pretending at first that this is my new life and I will always live here, but eventually allowing myself to believe that pretense. Harrow reassures me of my place in Viridian through his words and gestures. We do not kiss again, although I would welcome it if we did. But he seems not to want to rush me, to let me adjust to the life he thinks I will find on my own. I remember how Ronden said that her brother was committed to his life as a Watcher and would never want to give it up. But still, I wonder if maybe she is wrong. Would he do so for me, if it meant making a life with me? Is it possible I can find a way to make him want to do so?

Do I even have the right to try?

For now, I am content to do nothing more than be with him while I can. What I love about him as much as anything is the way he lets me be who I am. He does nothing to try to shape me. When he sees a need, he tries to help me find a way to fill it. He sees I am still troubled about my origins, so he lets me work my own way toward a better understanding. When I need him, I know he will be there for me. When I need him, he will come.

So to some extent I continue to allow life to take me where it wants and to reveal what it chooses, continuing to believe that letting things work themselves out is, for now, the best way.

Still, as I wait for him to come to me on the evening of the seventh day after our return from the Goblin prison, everything changes.

I am in my cottage expecting his visit, our plans for dinner already settled. I am excited at the prospect of his arrival and of the time we will spend alone dining in yet another wonderful place that he already knows well and that I will soon be allowed to discover with him. It doesn't take much to feel happy these days. My time is his and his mine—at least until he is required to go back out on Watcher duty. I try not to think about that. He is being allowed time to recover from his imprisonment, but he will not be turning away from his life's work simply because of one unfortunate incident. Harrow thinks of it as a fluke—a onetime accident that will not happen again. Not to someone as skilled and adept as he is.

But I know differently. Accidents, mistakes, and twists of fate can happen to anyone. If they have happened once, they can happen again.

When his knock on my door sounds, I bound up and swing it wide, anxious to embrace him, and find Ancrow standing there instead. Tall, severe, regal in her carriage, black hair shimmering in the fading daylight with the silkiness of a crow's wings, she gives me a moment to adjust to the idea that she is standing there instead of her son.

"Harrow agreed to let me take his place as your dinner companion this evening, Auris. I am sorry to disappoint you, but it is necessary. I need to talk to you at some length. I need to explain a few things that I have been keeping from you. Would it be all right if we did this over dinner?"

What can I say? "Of course. And I apologize for looking shocked. I don't mean to be rude."

"You're being yourself," she says. "Are you ready?"

We walk through the tree lanes to an eatery that sits deep within the gathered old growth that shades everything beneath its boughs so thoroughly, it requires lights everywhere there are tables. But the owners keep the lights down low and there are numerous private tables set aside within alcoves, so that there is a certain intimacy. Ancrow, of course, is immediately recognized and taken to a table deep within a niche that allows us to feel entirely alone.

The Sylvan who serves us takes a moment to ask what we would like to drink and disappears. Ancrow and I stare at each other somewhat hesitantly. We did not part on the best of terms the last time we were together. We share a history of mutual mistrust and suspicion, and it seems impossible that we can make it through this meal without one of us walking out.

"How are you feeling?" she asks me.

"Well enough. I've been sleeping and resting."

"And spending time with my son. I imagine that goes a long way toward making you feel better as well?"

I do not respond to this. It feels like a subtle accusation I don't care to address.

"I want to thank you for what you did for Harrow." Her gaze is steady and her words carefully chosen. "I cannot tell you how much it means to me. You took a huge gamble to free him and very nearly ended up imprisoning yourself in the bargain. You saved his life at the risk of your own. That took great courage."

"I care about your son," I say. And then, almost without thinking, I add, "I care about all of you."

She allows me a small smile. "I think you do. I think you have a good heart. A brave young woman's heart. I had one, too, once upon a time. I was very different than I am now. Life does that to you. It gives much, but it takes much away in the bargain."

I am suddenly very sorry for her. I don't know exactly why, but it has something to do with the way her tone of voice has changed. How there is a ripple to it that suggests what she is telling me is immensely painful. I can detect the sadness in it.

She sighs. "I have mistreated you badly, Auris," she says. "I have been unfriendly and judgmental. I have spurned you when it was clear to me, from the first, that everyone else in my family likes you very much. But I was struggling with something, and my struggle caused me to misjudge my behavior. I should have been welcoming and instead I chose to be defensive. I apologize for that. I know I was wrong. I've found it hard to admit—even to myself—but I think it is necessary now."

Our server returns with our beverages, and Ancrow orders for both of us. I do not object. I sense that she feels the need to do something for me. She feels she has wronged me in some way— which, indeed, she has—but she is talking about a different wrong than the ones I know. She is working up to something, and I think it best to let her do so in whatever way she finds comfortable.

Our server leaves. Ancrow's dark eyes find mine once more.

"What I am going to tell you is a secret I have kept for almost twenty years. No one alive knows about it but me—not even my children. It has haunted me—a dark memory I cannot find a way to erase. I never thought it would be necessary to confront it again, but life is full of surprises."

She pauses. "I was a young woman not much older than you when I fell in love with a man not much older than me. We were both in the Sylvan Home Guard and rose through its ranks together. We partnered for life, and I gave birth to Ronden. I became commander of the Home Guard, and Carrowen became my second. We fought together, shared victory together, suffered together, and endured together—but mostly we loved each other deeply. We were young and strong and thought our happiness would last forever. We thought *we* would last forever.

"We were wrong. We had twelve years together before it all came to an end. We were on patrol—unusual for a commander and her second, but it was an important mission. We were caught off guard by a much larger Goblin force. We fought hard, but in the end we were taken prisoner. Those of us who survived. The insignia on my jacket betrayed my rank, and I was bound and made to watch as those of my unit who survived—Carrowen among them—were dismembered in front of me. It took hours. Seven altogether, taken apart one by one—and my love last. I could not look away from him. I endured his suffering with him. I tried to give him strength as his life was slowly stripped away. It was the worst thing I have ever seen, and even today it remains so."

Tears are leaking from her eyes, and she takes a moment to wipe them away. "On that day, I ceased to have any respect for or empathy toward or willingness to forgive any Human anywhere. But these were Goblins who killed him, you would point out, not Humans. Which is true. But it was Humans who commanded them, and Humans who encouraged dismemberment as a solution to who and what they thought the Fae to be—abominations!"

I nod in understanding. I would say something supportive, but I am not able to find the words I think she needs to hear. I am horrified and sad for her, but nothing I can think to say seems adequate.

"I wanted to die with him—with Carrowen—but I was taken to the Goblin prisons and from there to somewhere else entirely—to a place where only Humans live. I was locked away and kept there for weeks. I was shackled and examined by my captors as if I were an animal. I think that was how they saw me—as an exotic, intriguing animal. I was stripped naked, probed, injected, humiliated. I understood what they were trying to do. They wanted to know what I was exactly. Why did I look as I did? Why was my skin green? Where did I get my use of magic? From my staff, certainly, but how did I conjure it? What parts of me were the same as theirs and what parts different?

"They performed experiments. They violated me. They used me in the worst ways possible, and then they discussed what it was like for each of them. Supposedly in the interests of science, but for other reasons, too. I could tell easily enough. I wanted to die, but I could not find a way to do so. I hated these men—these Human animals. I hated them for how they saw me. I hated them for what they were doing to me. I hated myself for not being able to put a stop to it."

And as Ronden had told me, she had been pregnant with Harrow at the time. I shivered at the thought of how easily she—and I—could have lost him, given what she had to endure.

Dinner arrives, and she goes silent. When the server is gone again, she continues. "Finally, I escaped. One of my examiners came to me when I was alone to tell me he was sorry about how I was being treated. I begged him to help me. I pleaded with him to set me free. I told him I just wanted to go home. At first, although he listened, he simply went away. But each time he returned, I tried again. This continued for many nights until finally he released my bonds and said he would help me."

Our eyes are locked on each other. Dinner is forgotten. Neither of us has touched it. My appetite is gone; my understanding of what Ancrow has gone through has changed my opinion of her entirely. What must that have been like? How could she have endured it? I was imprisoned, too, but I was not treated as she was. I was worked and mistreated and punished now and again, but I was never alone and violated in quite the same way. Would I be strong enough to survive what she did? I don't think so. But then, none of us knows how much we can endure until we are put to the test. Harrow's mother had been tested beyond anything I could imagine.

"I was given back my freedom and I ran," she says quietly. "I did not know where I was going, but I could speak the language. It took me weeks more, but eventually I found my way back to the waste-lands and the Roughlin and from there home. I returned a ghost, a shadow of myself, ruined inside in ways that could not be seen and were overshadowed by how I appeared on the outside. I was in bed for weeks, cared for by healers and especially by Ronden. She wanted to know more about my captivity, but I could not talk about it. I refused to talk about it. I thought eventually I would, but then something else happened. I had thought the nightmare was fin-ished, but it was not."

She pauses again, this time almost visibly revealing that she is struggling to say—that the rest of what she intends to tell me is even more terrible than what she has said already. Our server comes by to ask if we need something more and, on spying our uneaten meals, starts to approach, but I wave him away. *No interruptions. Not now.*

"I discovered I was pregnant," Ancrow whispers, almost as if wishing she could avoid speaking the words at all. "I should have realized it sooner. But the struggle I was going through to survive my captivity and then to return to Viridian disguised what was hap-pening. By the time I knew, it was too late to do anything about it. I was pregnant. I was already starting to show. But this child was not Carrowen's. This was the child of one of those who had used me, had forced me, had violated me. Because I could not face the truth, I told Ronden that Carrowen was the father. If I aborted my pregnancy, she would know the truth—and quite probably others would find out, too.

"I hated it, of course. How could I not? It was unwanted. It was at least half Human, which in my eyes made it all the way Human and anathema. Perhaps it would look Sylvan in some respects, but that was not enough to make me forget how I had gotten it and from whom. No, I decided. The child had to go. I had to find a way to be rid of it!"

She is suddenly furious, enraged anew by the injustice of it all, but by something more, too. My mind reels as I process her words. That pregnancy must have been the one that bore Harrow. But nothing about Harrow suggests he is in any way Human.

"I carried the child for a short time longer, and then I left. I told Ronden I was going to have the baby on my own terms, that I had to do it that way. I told her it was Carrowen's last gift to me. I reassured her I would return once the child was born. But the birthing of it was something I would do in private, away from everyone. I had made arrangements that I felt would be suitable."

She sighs wearily. "I kept the rest a secret from her. I had found a midwife out in the countryside who would take me in and help me through my delivery. But once this child was born, I planned to give it away—tell Ronden it died or replace it with another. The midwife swore she would say nothing of what I intended to do to anyone—ever. She promised she would see my child delivered and then do with it whatever I asked. I think she knew me; I think she knew my story. She might have guessed the rest, but we never talked about it.

"I stayed with her until I had given birth and the child was brought to me to see for the first time. I knew then what it would look like; I could see it in her eyes as she approached. But I did not understand the extent of the horror I would feel on actually viewing it. My child was entirely Human, with no trace of Sylvan to be found. I knew I had to give it away."

She pauses, and I stare at her. But Harrow is still here and has not . . .

"The child, Auris," she continues, "was you."

TWENTY

In the wake of her words, I am left speechless. Unable to provide a response of any sort, I simply stare at her. She stares back for a moment, and then she signals our server. "Remove these plates and bring us a salad. We are not as hungry as we thought. Also, bring two glasses of Elysian Gold."

The server goes away. "You see why I brought you here," she whispers. "I wanted people around when I told you. I wanted to make certain I would not break down before everything came out. It's harder to cry in public."

I marvel at Ancrow's iron command of her emotions. She is showing almost nothing of what she feels, and she manages to place an order with a server when I know what she must be going through. Clearly, she is leaving it up to me to do any breaking down that's required. Maybe she doesn't know me as well as she thinks.

But if I was the child born right after Carrowen's death, then what of Harrow? Who is Harrow?

"You cannot be certain of this," I manage to say, still controlled enough that I do not scream, although tears begin to run down my cheeks. I do not make my words sound like an accusation, although this is exactly what they are.

"It is not common for a Fae to be born looking exactly like a Human. As far as I know, it has not happened in the lifetime of anyone living. Yet you are the right age and you have certain features similar to mine. You probably never gave the possibility any real consideration."

She is right. I have never considered it once. Why would I?

"A mother knows her child as she knows herself, and there is a lot of myself in you. I saw it from the first time we met. I suspected it after Harrow told me about how you found your way here. I hoped I was wrong when you could not muster your *inish*. If you had no command over your *inish*, then he was mistaken about your Fae connection, and I could find a way to dismiss you. I could tell myself that even if I gave you life, I had no reason to give you anything more."

She shakes her head slowly. "I was wrong at every turn, about every decision, and about everything I did and didn't do. I knew it when your *inish* surfaced during your struggle with the Goblins. I knew it when you went back for Harrow in spite of what it might mean for you. I knew it when you fought your way clear to reach Harrow and Ronden and bring them to you. I knew it when you returned safely. But I was blinded by my hatred of all Humans, by what they did to Carrowen and me. By how they diminished me to the point of leaving me wishing I were dead. By how they dismissed me out of hand as something less than what I knew I was.

"Understand, Auris," she adds quickly. "I do not tell you any of this to gain forgiveness for what I did. I gave you away. I denied your existence and pretended you never had one. I tell you because I owe it to you. I cannot let you continue to struggle with your identity. I cannot justify leaving you wondering about your origins. I can do this much to make up for what was stolen from you."

"But what about Harrow?" I am still reeling. "Ronden told me that Harrow was Carrowen's child, his last gift to you. But if I am that child, then Harrow . . ."

She holds up one hand in a warding gesture. "Let me finish. I had departed home pregnant and a child had been born to me. I had sworn to Ronden that all would be well. If I returned and claimed the child had died, she would never forgive me—or even herself for letting me go alone. So I asked the midwife to find me another child—one that needed a home, one who was virtually the same age as you. She did. The child's mother had died giving birth while in the midwife's care and the father had disappeared on Watcher patrol only months earlier. There were no other relatives to question what I did. I took that child in place of you and claimed they were the same. That child was Harrow."

Harrow, who always believed himself to be Carrowen's last child. A fresh realization pours over me. Harrow doesn't know about any of this. Like me, he is not who he believed. He is not Carrowen's son. All his life he has seen himself as the child of a hero of the Goblin wars. The entire Sylvan community has thought of him that way. Now everything will change. His story will be revealed as a lie. How will he feel about my part in that? Will he be devastated to learn he is not who he believed he was?

"Only the old midwife knew the truth of what had happened," Ancrow continued. "She did not live more than a few years beyond that time. I have kept what I did secret all these years since. I accepted my life with Ronden and Harrow and told myself it was better that way—that it was the right thing to do."

"Yet you had more children afterward. You had Char and Ramey. You must have changed your mind. Did you find another partner?"

"I did not wish another partner. I do not wish it now. Carrowen was the only partner I ever wanted. I made a different choice. Many children are left orphaned in Viridian Deep—by Sylvan deaths incurred in battles with the Goblins, by sickness, by abandonment. This last misfortune bothered me the most. I had essentially abandoned you, after all. I found I could neither forget nor forgive what I had done; I tried to make up for it by taking in other children who needed homes. Ramey and Char were the two I kept. The others ended up in different homes. Only Ronden and you are my blood children, but all my children are equal in my eyes. I have made certain they know this; I have been careful to treat them all the same. The only one I have failed is you."

I think back to our first encounter in the chambers of the Sylvan High Council and how dismissive of me Ancrow had seemed. And again each time after, treating me as unwanted—both as a resident in Viridian and as a presence in the lives of her children and herself. I can understand it better now. She was trying to protect herself, seeking a return to the way things were before I appeared, wanting me to have never come back into her life. The guilt she felt must have been enormous—increasing every time I showed her kindness or gained further affection from her children. After Harrow and I saved each other—with Ronden there to detail every moment of it later—she must have collapsed under the weight of the pretense and realized that living this lie was no longer tenable.

I think, too, she must have been frightened by what my abrupt and unexpected appearance meant.

"You've said very little," she observes, looking away. "Do you wish me to leave?"

I shake my head. "No, I wish you to stay. I just need to think about everything you've told me. I still have questions."

Our salads come, and we eat them in silence. The Elysian Golds are beautifully crafted sunrise-colored drinks that radiate like lamps as we sip them. Apparently, they are an especially fine ale concoction of which Sylvans are very fond. I can understand why. They are delicious, and I consume mine quickly. I had never drunk anything alcoholic until coming to Viridian Deep, and little since my arrival. I do not think I should make it a habit, but tonight the numbing, slightly off-balance way this one makes me feel is welcome. When Ancrow offers to join me in another, I agree. This is a night of sharing secrets, and I do not want it to end until I am sure I have uncovered them all.

"Harrow doesn't know any of this, does he?" I ask quietly. "None of them do."

"No, he doesn't know. I never found the courage to tell him. I never found a good reason. I wanted him to be the child I gave birth to after returning from my captivity. I wanted him to be Carrowen's child. I wanted to think of him as special—to deflect the guilt I felt about forsaking you. At that point, I was afraid of what would happen to both of us if the truth came out. I was afraid to tell him or anyone else."

She pauses. "But if you choose to tell him, you have my blessing. I am done with lies."

"I think you should be the one to tell him. It's been your secret; it will be better if you are the one who reveals it. I am grateful you've told me, and I think he will be grateful if you tell him, too."

She nods. "And I will be doing something to help you, won't I? I see the way he looks at you. It is important to tell him the truth about himself once he learns you are my child, too. It will remove an obstacle you both will wish did not exist. And doing this for you is a small way to begin making amends."

I am surprised all over again. Not that she notices Harrow's interest in me or mine in him, but that she does not intend to stand in the way of it. I cannot know for certain what will come of the affection we feel for each other, but I know that revealing the truth about the absence of a blood relationship will leave us free to choose. But I am grateful that Harrow's mother has considered it and thought it necessary to reassure me that she will bless whatever friendship, union, or partnering Harrow and I might decide to embrace.

Having momentarily exhausted our discussion about my past, we sit in silence for a time and eat our salads. And drink our Elysian Golds, although I have slowed down considerably on my intake. I don't think that a steady diet of these potent drinks is likely to be part of my future. I am still a bit light-headed, and my struggle to come to terms with who I am and where I come from finish off the job.

But when the salads and the distraction of consuming them are removed, we go back to our discussion about what now binds us closer.

"Will you speak to all of the children about who I am?" I ask. "I cannot imagine trying to explain it myself. I think that, just as with Harrow, the others will like it better if they hear it from you."

She hesitates, looking stricken. "Will it help if I am there with you?" I ask.

She shakes her head at once. "I think I will have a difficult time doing it myself. I don't know if I could do it if you were present, too. Tonight has been hard enough. I am so sorry, Auris. I've made such a mess of things, and all for selfish reasons."

"No, because you were hurting," I correct her. "It was done because you were living a nightmare and could not, in the moment, think of any other way to handle it. I can understand. I lived the nightmare of imprisonment by Goblins for five years. I wasn't as badly treated as you, but I was not treated well, either. Everything that happened to me is a memory I cannot shed. That will never change. But you know what that means: You learn to live with it. You find a way to box it up and stick it in a dark corner. Give me your hands."

She does, and I take them in my own and hold them tightly. Her hands are calloused, worn rough and hard from battles she has fought and survived, from weapons wielded against enemies that would have killed her, from her life's demands. We are the sum of our life's experiences, and our bodies reveal much of what that experience has been.

"Listen to me. As I listened to you, please do so now for me. I am shocked and dismayed by what you tell me. I am stricken by the thought that you made the choice to give me up—that my mother would do such a thing. I tell myself I would never do it, but I cannot know if that is true. I cannot know without going through what you did, and I pray to everything good and kind that fate never puts me on that path."

My grip on her hands tightens, and hers on mine tightens back in response. "I have suffered in the prisons, and I know what the grief and pain can do to you—how desperate they can make you feel," I whisper. "So I forgive you. I forgive you everything, all of it, the whole of what you did. I lost you and I thought I would never have you back. I thought my parents were dead and gone—but Humans were not my parents at all. I have found the home I thought I would never have. I have been given a miracle, and it is a miracle I want to celebrate. I am grateful you have the courage to tell me everything. I forgive you, Ancrow. Tell this to Harrow, Ronden, Ramey, and Char. If I can forgive you, surely they can, too. Tell them I want them to. Tell them I need this as much as you do."

Tears are streaming down her cheeks. In that moment, there is nothing left of the hardened warrior leader who has fought and won so many battles on behalf of her people. Nothing of the woman who lost her great love and was defiled in the process. Nothing of the embittered, frightened mother who has judged me so harshly and done so much to try to ruin any chance I might have for becoming a Sylvan and finding a home in Viridian Deep. What is left is a supplicant who has sought and found rebirth through repentance and forgiveness.

She walks around the table, draws me gently to my feet, and embraces me fully, sobbing into my shoulder, holding me as if she might never release me again. "You have suffered so much because of what I did when I gave you away. Every bad thing that happened to you afterward is my fault. I cannot pretend otherwise. I cannot begin to find a way to forgive myself, but if you can forgive me it would help. Do you really forgive me? Please, say you do."

My mother, begging for what is already hers.

"Yes, I forgive you."

She presses her lips to my ear. "I love you, Auris. I wish I had been better at showing it before. I will try hard to do so now."

I am willing to believe this. I would like to think that, even in spite of the wrong she has done me, I will one day be able to love her back.

I RETURN FROM MY STRANGE AND WONDERFUL DINNER WITH ANcrow, my thoughts a whirlwind of surprises and shocks. I am a bit tipsy from the Elysian mind-muddlers, but I go to bed happy and sleep in late the following morning. My slumber is deep and untroubled. I am not sure I would have risen at all if a loud pounding on my door hadn't brought me awake and a familiar voice begun shouting, "Auris! Get up! Open the door! It's your sisters!"

I open my eyes to bright streamers of sunrise slanting through curtains and a bit of a headache throbbing behind my eyes. I climb from my bed and throw on a robe over my nightdress before trudging to the front door of the cottage, already smiling. Some things cannot be kept waiting. Small bundles of endless energy need to find a release.

When I open the door, one of those bundles flies into my arms, shrieking with laughter. "Auris, we're sisters! Isn't it wonderful?"

Well, yes it is. Char is in my arms, practically climbing up my body to hug and kiss me, her exuberance a clear testament to the fact that she has already been informed by her mother of who I am and has found it way beyond acceptable. She is laughing and crying at the same time, her emotions pouring out of her like a cluster of brilliant shooting stars. Ramey stands behind her, watching this display with furrowed brow, studied reticence her fallback to every situation. Still holding on to Char, I step forward to reach out and draw her into my arms as well.

"I am so happy," I whisper as I draw them inside and nudge the door shut. "How could anything be better than this?"

We hug and kiss for a bit. We cry tears of joy and disbelief. Then I sit them down and ask them to be honest with me and tell me seriously what they thought when their mother told them. With Char, there is no hesitation. She has thought of me as family from the first day we met. Having it made official is a dream come true.

"I always knew we were sisters!" she exclaims. She gives Ramey a meaningful look, so she will know she is included in this proclamation. "All of us family—Ronden and Harrow, too. We belong together!"

Ramey is less enthusiastic in her response, and I have to press her a bit to get her to open up. She is by nature more reserved, and her emotions are not always discernible. It becomes clear she is happy to have me as a sister, but she is disappointed in her mother.

"She should have told us," she says solemnly. "She shouldn't have kept it from us."

"No, she shouldn't," I agree. "Telling you would have been better. You are both very grown-up and smart. You would have understood. But I think she was afraid to admit what she had done—that maybe you wouldn't love her anymore. Even last night, she had trouble telling me. She was so upset, she cried."

Both girls stare at me. "Ancrow cried?" Ramey manages to ask, clearly shocked.

"Copiously," I affirm, and then we all break down in laughter.

"Besides, Ramey," I add with a smile, "isn't finding out we are sisters more fun this way? Isn't the surprise more wonderful?"

We talk some more, sharing our feelings about this new discovery, opening up about how it makes us feel to learn the truth. Ancrow has told them the whole story—clearly deciding that holding back at this point would be a mistake. She has glossed over or skipped some of the details—everything surrounding her violation and treatment by the Human scientists and her Goblin captors and the death of her life partner. She has instead emphasized how happy she is to have found me again and to have made a fresh start with her life. Both girls comment on how happy she seems, and Ramey notes her mother seems relieved to have opened up about it at last.

"She is very different this morning, now that she's told us. I could tell. Ronden will be over shortly; she's anxious to see you, too. But Char asked her to wait. She wanted the two of us to come see you first."

"She told all of you together, then?" I ask. "Harrow was there, too? Was he pleased?"

Char shook her head. "He just stared at her. He didn't say anything."

"Then she took him aside and talked to him some more," Ramey added. "We couldn't hear what they were saying. But when they were done talking, he walked out the door."

"I think maybe he was angry," Char said.

"He looked more shocked than angry," Ramey corrected. "I think he just wanted to think about it."

I am worried now. I had hoped this discovery would make him happy, but I might have been mistaken. His whole identity has been shaken now, and I cannot decide what I should do. But the problem is solved when Ronden appears, insisting she has waited long enough, and repeats pretty much everything Char and Ramey have already said with equal enthusiasm.

Hugs and kisses are exchanged first, and then she says, "Well, you wanted to know, didn't you? But having found out, I hope you are happy. I know the three of us are. Having you for our sister is a blessing of the best sort, Auris. It seems the most wonderful thing that could possibly happen."

I am crying again, and I ask them to wait while I wash and dress so we can talk some more. While I am dressing, Ronden slips into my bedroom with an apologetic smile, apparently wanting to talk to me alone. I know at once why she feels the need.

"You didn't ask about Harrow," she says at once. "At least not while I was there."

I nod. "Char told me he went off alone. Is he unhappy about this? She thought he might be."

Her smile dims as Ronden comes over to hug me again. "It's hard to tell. He pretty much just walked out when she finished. Didn't say a word. With Harrow, you never know. He keeps things bottled up, and never wants to say much about how he feels. I can imagine he is shaken. It can't be easy to discover you aren't who you thought you were. He was so proud of being Carrowen's son. It was why he became a Watcher. It has defined his whole life. But I know how he feels about you, and he has to be happy you are not blood-related. I think he'll be all right. I expect he'll be back around to talk with you before the day is over."

Her smile returns. "Do you want to take the girls over to Promise Falls for a picnic today? We can celebrate having a new sister."

Picnic? Harrow must have taught her that word.

I smile back. How can I refuse an offer like that?

ALL DAY I WAIT FOR HARROW TO COME TO ME, IF ONLY JUST TO LET me know he is all right. I wait for him after returning from Promise Falls with Ronden and the girls, and through a dinner I choose to eat alone; then, beginning to worry now, I go out to find him. But while I look everywhere I can imagine he might be—even going all the way to the training field—I find no sign of him. I spend the remainder of the evening sitting on my bench in front of my cottage watching the rest of the world—or the Sylvan part of it at least—pass by. The sun slides into the horizon, the light in the sky changes from the gold of the sun to the silver of the moon and stars, and the city about me brightens with lamplight. I listen to the voices of the Sylvan people and pick up what I can of what is being said. I grow a little better every day at understanding a language I have had to learn from scratch, proud of myself for having been able to do so.

When full dark descends and the lights in the surrounding homes begin to wink out and still Harrow has not appeared, I decide to stop waiting. I go inside, undress, and change into my nightclothes. I sit at my kitchen table to drink a cup of tea and ponder what his absence means. I am worried that he has disappeared so utterly. Is it because of what I have brought about by coming to Viridian? An inquiry with the girls earlier this evening revealed that he has not reappeared all day. I don't like to speculate about what that means, but I am troubled by not knowing.

Why hasn't he come to see me?

I am in the process of washing out my teacup and resigning myself to a night when I know I will not sleep when there is a knock at the door. I know before I open it what I will find. Or at least I hope I do.

I am not disappointed.

Harrow walks through silently and turns to face me. "I'm sorry. I should have come sooner. But I couldn't. I had to think about things first. I had to come to terms with what Ancrow told me—not just the part about you, but also the truth about myself. We've both lived with false beliefs about ourselves for almost our entire lives. Does it matter? Should it? Does it matter that we've been lied to?"

His amber eyes are so sad that I go to him and wrap my arms around him, holding him tightly. "It doesn't change anything that matters. It doesn't change how I feel about you. It doesn't change how the girls love you and think of you. It doesn't change the love your mother feels for you. She wanted you to be her son, and she took you in and made you so. That is the kind of love all of us want from a mother."

"But she didn't give it to you!" he retorts. "Forget about me for a moment. It is you who have been cheated out of so much. She cast you out as if you were nothing but trash. She gave you away without even knowing to whom you'd be given. You were sent or sold or exchanged for me—the Changeling girl that Benith suggested you might be. How do you feel about that? What does that make you feel about Ancrow?"

His hand is stroking my hair and I let him continue for a moment, comforted by the feeling it provides. Then I release him and step back so we are looking at each other.

"I am hurt and saddened by what she did. I probably will continue to be hurt for a while yet. But she was frightened and anguished by the death of the man she loved most, and all that made it impossible for her to accept me. I was a reminder of what she had suffered and lost—and would continue to be a reminder every day of her life if she kept me. She did the only thing she could in giving me up. I have forgiven her. I cannot bring myself to hate her; I won't give that response space in my life. It is enough that she has come to me and admitted what she did. That cost her. It was very hard for her."

"I don't know," he says, looking doubtful. "It's easy enough to confess guilt without feeling any. Remorse is easy to pretend."

"Harrow." I speak his name firmly and with emphasis. "She is your mother. Did you really sense pretense in what she told you earlier? Did you not see the pain in her eyes and hear it in her voice? Because I did when we sat together last night and she told me. She could barely make it through her confession. What she said and how she said it was real. The hurt was real; the truth was real. We—you and I and the girls—we have to forgive her or everything is lost."

I reach up and put my hands on his face. "You have been treated as badly as I, and it can't be any easier for you than it is for me. I know it is hard to discover that you aren't who you thought you were. Who would know this better? But those things you learned do not change the fundamental truth of who you are. You are still the same person, in spite of everything. Nothing about what I know of you has changed. At least, this is how I choose to see you."

He smiles. "This is how I see you, too."

"So are you in any way sorry that you found me and brought me back here? Because none of this would have come to light if I had stayed away. It is my return that has brought it all about."

He shakes his head slowly. "I would never wish that. I am glad you are here."

"It's important to me," I tell him. "My life is here, in Viridian Deep, with you and your family and the Fae. I don't care how I look to others. I don't care that what I thought was true about my life isn't. I don't care about the past. I won't let knowing it change my future. But I don't want it to change things for you, either, unless that change is for the better."

He pulls me close once more, and I nestle into him. I love him so much. I can admit it freely now. I was unsure at first on coming here, reticent to consider the possibility, wondering if I even belonged. But all that is behind me, and I will not waste what I have been given.

"Will you stay with me tonight?" I whisper.

There is no hesitation, no hint of uncertainty. Just a smile. "I will."

TWENTY-ONE

WHEN I WAKE THE FOLLOWING MORNING, HARROW IS GONE. I find this out when I rise from my bed, put on my robe, and walk to the living room to discover he is no longer sleeping on the couch. Last night didn't exactly turn out the way I imagined. He stayed the night, all right—he just didn't sleep with me. His explanation was something about honor and tradition and Sylvan expectations regarding unmarried men and women. I might have understood at the time—or perhaps I was just too tired even to try—but on waking I am not exactly sure what happened.

Although I am very sure about what didn't.

I wash and dress and take my time doing it, thinking back on what I remember of our conversation and Ancrow's revelations and the shock and hurt and anger it caused me, and my closeness to Harrow when he was pressed against me and the way I knew nothing could ever be so wonderful. The last of these memories are only a girl's ruminations about a boy, but I am not a girl nor is he a boy—and such thoughts, while pleasant distractions, only point out the depth and breadth of the fantasy I have fallen into.

Sure, I love him. I love him to pieces. I've known this right from the beginning. But I'm drowning in disappointment, and the wounds caused by the sharp edges of my shattered expectations are painful.

Then, abruptly, I am irritated with myself. Even now, I am sure he loves me. But what matters is whether or not he loves me enough to want to partner with me and commit to sharing our lives together even if it means giving up his duties as a Sylvan Watcher. Yet what right do I have to expect this from him? If I were in his shoes, would I give up my life's work for him, assuming I had a life's work to give up? I shove the question aside, not wanting to explore the answer too closely. This is where I need to take a big step back, pull myself together, and charge back into the fray.

Washed and dressed, I eat some fruit, a bowl of grain cereal with milk (of some sort), drink some cold water (a lot, in light of the aftereffects of those Elysian concoctions), and taking up my *inish* staff go out to find the man that I believe—with all my heart—is the one I am meant to spend my life with. Walking out the door, I half expect to find him on my bench, waiting for me. But he is not there, and so I make my way along the tree lanes toward the cottage he shares with Ronden. No one home. I retrace my steps to Ancrow's. No one there, either.

Great. Just great.

I stand there looking down at my feet for a moment, trying to decide what to do next. I come up with nothing. So I go back to my cottage and sit on the bench and wait for something to happen. Usually this works, but not today. Dozens of Sylvans pass by, but none of them are the ones I am seeking and none show any particular interest in me. Before, they might be inclined to stare a bit, but by now I have become a familiar enough sight that few Sylvans are excited to find a Human (looking) person in their midst. Now I am as common as the trees that surround me.

My mind wanders—as unoccupied minds tend to do—to thoughts of all that has happened in the past few weeks. What have I actually learned about my past in the interim? I am a Fae who looks Human and was given up at birth by my Fae mother, whose elderly midwife took me somewhere that ended up with me being left in the care of a Human family. But how? Then my father and mother fell afoul of their Human government and were likely put to death while I was sent to the Goblin prisons.

That last part bothers me. Did anyone know I was Fae? Was the secret so deeply kept that no one even suspected I was different? I suppose since I looked Human, grew up Human, and thought I was Human, I must have behaved as one. But how was I then given a Fae name? And how did I get put into the Goblin prisons? I can't remember any part of my life after seeing my parents taken by Ministry soldiers, so what happened to me then? And why hadn't my parents made any plans for my care after knowing they were in danger? Did they not have any relatives or friends who might have been persuaded to take care of me? Why wasn't I sent to an orphanage? Why to a Goblin prison?

An awful lot of what I have learned does not make much sense. Dr. Allensby seemed to know a good deal about me when he came to the prison to try to persuade me to teach him how to use my *inish* staff. He said at one point that he was a recent arrival and did not know my past, but he also said later he was the warden. Shouldn't there have been records to tell him about my past? I wonder how much he lied to me about what he knew. I realize he might not know, even now, that I was born a Fae. He might be assuming I was simply a Human that had been taught to use the power of the staff by—as he put it—my green friends. But he never asked me about it, did he? He seemed to care so little about finding out.

I am in the grip of this muddle when Ronden finally appears, walking out of the bright sunlight to take a seat at my side. "How goes it, Auris?" she asks brightly. "You seem very deep in thought."

I shrug. "I am. I have a lot to think about. For all that I've learned, there still seems to be a lot I don't know. Do you know where Harrow is, by the way?"

"I do. He came by early this morning and told me to let you know he was sorry about last night." She pauses long enough to cock a questioning eyebrow. "He also said he would be gone for a few days and not to worry about him. What happened last night?"

"Nothing." *Regrettably.* "Do you know where he's gone or what he's doing?"

"I don't. And apparently you don't, either. What really happened last night? I know it was something, Auris."

"Actually, it wasn't—which is the problem. Do you want to train with me today?"

She nods. "When?"

"Right now." I stand. "Let me get my gear and we can stop for yours and be at the field in an hour. Gives us half the day."

So off we go, an impulsive decision for me and maybe for her, too, but neither of us says so and neither of us brings up Harrow and last night again. My mind slips back to my earlier thoughts about how little I really know of my parents or what happened to me that I ended up in the Goblin prisons. I run through everything I know on our way to the practice field, but huge gaps in the story are hard to avoid. Even given what Ancrow told me about how I came to be a Fae in a Human world, I am mostly in the dark about how I got there in the first place, and know virtually nothing at all about what happened once I did, save for my time in the prisons. It might be that she doesn't know, either—or didn't care to know, for that matter—so she couldn't tell me even if she wanted to.

But something crucial in all this is missing, and I have a nagging feeling that it is important.

When we reach the training field, I shove all this to the back of my overworked brain and turn my attention to training. We loosen up first—stretches and sprints—and finally engage in our one-on-one combat exercises. Ronden is taller than I am and very fast, so I lose every race we run. But I do better at wrestling and throws because I am quicker and more agile, and I can get inside her guard faster than she can get inside mine. Although I know that if she really wanted to overpower me, she could probably do it.

Marksmanship is another area where I excel. I have always been good with bow and arrow, spears and knives, slings and nets, and I can more than hold my own with her there. We are evenly matched for the most part, even when we employ our *inish* either to shape or strengthen our attacks, or to provide us with fresh energy when weariness starts to set in. We do not ever skirmish with blades or heavy implements. We have promised that we will never do anything that might cause serious damage to each other. This is training, not actual combat.

We practice for about four hours before we both decide that is enough and sit down to chat before starting back.

"Tell the truth," she demands. "Did you sleep with my brother?"

I break out laughing. The way she says it strikes me as both odd and funny. She waits on my answer with a rather severe look of disapproval.

"No." I shake my head for emphasis.

"You probably could have, if you really wanted to."

"Hah! I seriously doubt that. We didn't even come close. I'm not even sure he thinks it's a good idea. He likes me well enough, but he keeps me at arm's length most of the time. Maybe it's for the best, given what we've found out about each other."

Ronden makes a face. "I would think you would both be relieved about that. You're family, but you're not related—something that would have been a problem. But Harrow is odd—that's true enough. Mostly, he just wants to be out on patrol, working as a Watcher. Still, the way he looks at you . . ."

"Yes. He looks at me, and I want to melt. He's always had that effect on me. But I don't see him acting on it. And why doesn't he ever tell me how he feels? He never says anything."

Ronden shakes back her hair and ties it with a band. "He said some pretty wonderful things about you after we rescued him from the prisons. You just weren't around to hear them. He was devastated about leaving you there. I think he was scared to death he might lose you."

"In probably the same way he would feel about losing a pet. I can see him now, wandering the night: *Here, Auris. Come on, girl. Come on home.*"

My companion laughs. "I like the image. Maybe I'll tell him you said that. He might turn even greener than he is."

"Do Sylvans blush in green?" I ask, suddenly curious. "Do they blush at all?"

She stares at me. "What does *blush* mean?"

WHEN WE ARRIVE BACK IN THE CITY, TWILIGHT HAS SETTLED IN and the lights have come on along the tree lanes and in the dining spots and residences. The foot traffic is heavy as people stream home for the night, and I find it all comforting and reassuring. I have never had this life, not even before I was taken to the Goblin prisons. Or if I did, I have forgotten it along with almost everything else from before. It is all strange and new to me, but there is a predictability and a purpose to it that seems as if it is the way life should be for people—whether they be Fae or Human. I wonder if I will ever lead this life. It is hard to say at the moment; everything feels uncertain and ephemeral. While I believe I can safely call myself one of the Fae, I still have no discernible purpose waiting for me in the days ahead.

In fact, I wonder suddenly, just what exactly am I to do now that I have been rescued from the prisons? I have the use of my *inish* and the skills Harrow and Ronden have taught me. I have a family that cares about me, all of them willing to help in any way they can . . . I think—although I am still uncertain about Ancrow. The feeling I had earlier that I still wasn't understanding something critical about my past now resurfaces, and this time it points directly at my newfound mother. I do not think she lied again, but I am wondering if she is still keeping something back. It feels that way. Some part of what I learned about myself remains incomplete.

Ronden takes me to yet another new dining place, this one on the forest floor close to Promise Falls, where it is tucked away in a grove of flowering cherry trees and surrounded loosely by stately elms. It serves its fare indoors and out, so Ronden and I find a table at the edge of a hedge-enclosed patio from which you can smell the flowers. We sit among other diners, the restaurant filled to near capacity, not caring who looks at us and judges our relationship or hears us laugh and joke, which we do more than a little this night. The food is all vegetarian, the drink another odd concoction—this one distilled from the juices of something called an asnin vine— which Ronden tries and fails to explain to me adequately. Something about maple and spirits distilled from barley.

Dinner passes in a leisurely fashion, and I am relaxed and happy. But it is somewhere in the middle of eating that I realize what it is that has been troubling me. It is all I can do not to tell Ronden and ask for her thoughts, but I decide not to. Harrow is the one I need to speak with; he was there when the Seers retrieved my hidden memories. He will be able to answer me best.

So instead, wanting to talk about something else, I ask Ronden a different question. "How is it that Humans don't know the Fae are here?"

She gives me a flat look. "Oh, they know. Or at least some do— though most think we are a fable for children. But no one knows *exactly* where we are."

"Benith said the Roughlin and the air above it are magically enhanced to help keep Humans away—with sea creatures in the water and protective winds in the sky. But doesn't their technology reveal you to them? Aren't you afraid it will tell them how to find you?"

Ronden glances around. "No. As Benith told you, what really protects us is our magic. From the first, magic was summoned from the elements and infused into the air and water all around us. Think of how our *inish* protects us. Much of the magic that we summon is what screens us from Humans."

"But not Goblins? What if they told the Humans where we were? Or showed them how to get in—maybe even guided them?"

Ronden smiles. "They can't do that. They lack the magic that would allow it. And even if they could, look at what they would be giving up by doing so. Their value as Human allies lies in their ability to come and go freely in Viridian. After all, they are Fae, too. So why would they consider surrendering their one advantage by sharing it with a dangerous ally? What both want is access to our magic, but neither knows how to obtain it. And even if either did, they would want to keep it for themselves. The one advantage Goblins have is that they can come and go freely while Humans can't. Humans would be happy to dispatch the Goblins as quickly as the rest of the Fae, otherwise."

Her smile widens. "Let me give you an example of what that means. The magic that protects Viridian Deep and the Fae was created by Sylvans specifically to prevent anyone other than Fae—either by invasion or by use of technology—from entering. Humans have tried to bypass this prohibition before—repeatedly. The last time was only a few years ago. The Goblins provided Humans with a hand-drawn map for the purpose of directing a guided missile into our city. It was to be a demonstration of how much more powerful they were. Can you guess what happened?"

"It all went wrong?"

"Spectacularly. The magic corrupted the guidance technology and the missile was sent back to where it came from. The Humans lost most of their technology specialists that day, along with a control center and everyone working in it. A few unfortunate Goblin mapmakers were subsequently put to death as punishment for their failure to provide accurate information, and there haven't been any further attempts since. Not of that magnitude, anyway."

"Yet someone who was one of the Fae, and who had use of magic, could show them the way?"

"It is possible. But very unlikely."

"Harrow brought me into Viridian. He took a big chance when he did that."

"I don't think he saw it that way. I know he wanted to help you, but there were other ways he could have done so. I think he suspected your origins from the first and acted on that. If he had been wrong, you would have been allowed to heal and then sent back to Human lands."

I am impressed by this. I knew Harrow wanted to find a way to protect me, but I had no idea that it might prove difficult if I were not one of the Fae. He took a rather large risk in bringing me to Viridian Deep, not knowing how the prohibitive magic might engage if I were Human. Then I wonder why, if he could sense that, he can't sense how I feel about him? Or is it just that he doesn't feel the same way about me?

I return to what I realized earlier about my past and what I need to ask Harrow, and I think that maybe that question will answer itself when I speak with him.

The next several days pass slowly as I wait for his return. I take Ramey and Char to Promise Falls for a day in the park. I exercise with Ronden on the two days following, slowly regaining my strength and setting my mind on a path that will require me to do something I did not think I would ever do again.

I must leave Viridian Deep.

FIVE DAYS PASS BEFORE HARROW RETURNS. I WAKE THAT MORNING, wash and dress, eat my breakfast, and go out the door to find him sitting on my bench once more, looking for all the world as if his unexpected appearance is the most natural thing in the world. I am speechless—outrage and relief warring each other for control of my voice. But what I do is sit down beside him, lean forward, and kiss him on the lips. "I missed you."

"I expect you are angry with me," he says, "but there was something I had to do, and I wanted to complete it before I saw you again."

He looks embarrassed; I know him well enough by now to recognize all his looks. "Which was?"

"When I was taken by the Goblins, they took my staff. When you and Ronden came for me, there was no time to get it back. It is there still."

I had been so intent on getting Harrow out, I now realize, that I had forgotten all about his staff—and he hadn't exactly been in a position to mention it. "Do you want to go back for it?"

If so, I will go with you, I am thinking. *For you, I will do anything.*

But he shakes his head, reaches behind the bench, and pulls out the most beautiful length of carved wood I have ever seen. This staff lacks the runes mine possesses, but has in their place scenes of events he deems important. One by one, he points them all out. Most I don't know about because they happened before my time with him, but the last two I recognize immediately. One depicts our initial meeting in the wastelands, his hand outstretched to mine and mine to his; I look considerably better in the rendering than I did at the time. The second scene shows me bringing him out of the prisons toward the wormhole, guiding him to safety. Ronden stands in the background, her staff held ready. I understand. He saved me; I saved him. Those two moments bookend our time together.

"How long did it take you to carve this?"

"Five days. Once you begin the shaping and then infusing it with the magic that allows you to create an *inish* staff, you don't want to quit until it is completed. My old staff served me well, but it is foolish to contemplate returning to the prisons to retrieve it. So I made this one—which better reflects who I am now, anyway."

I run my hands over its length, feeling the deep grooves and tracing runnels, brushing over the smoothness of the lovingly polished sections surrounding the carvings, and finding it to be a thing of exquisite workmanship and beauty. The wood is a deep chocolate color streaked with vibrant violet that in places becomes almost black. Harrow has completed a wondrous joining of art and function, and this staff is every bit as wonderful as the one he made for me.

"I forgive you everything," I whisper in stunned admiration. "You were right to complete your work. I am in no way angry with you. I love your new staff."

He smiles, and I fall into his eyes. "It no longer felt right," he says, "having a staff in which you had no part."

I look again at the last two scenes that he has carved into it, linking us, and brush my fingers over the wood. Warmth flows through me. "Every time you use it," I breathe, "it will remind you of me. I cannot think of a greater gift."

He gives me a funny look. "You don't believe I am sufficiently reminded of you already? You don't realize you are in my thoughts when I am awake and in my dreams when I sleep? I think of you constantly!"

The words are out of his mouth before he can think better of them, and for what seems to be an endless amount of time we stare at each other.

Then I reach toward him and offer my mouth. He leans down and kisses me. He takes his time. It isn't enough.

I am pretty sure it will never be enough.

When we break apart again, I give him back his staff. He takes it, looks down at it for a moment, and then looks back at me. "I probably said too much," he confesses as he draws back again.

I smile, hearing the reluctance in his voice. "I think I can handle it."

We walk together after that. We make our way through the city until we reach one of our favorite parks and find a bench on which to sit. I smell the greenery and the flowers that surround us, and I look at his new staff and marvel at how our lives are linked. There are so many things I want to say to him, but I hesitate. I know that door is open, but is it open far enough? And shouldn't he be the one saying them to me?

A long silence falls between us, so I eventually start talking about something else instead. I've been saving it for his return, and I don't think it's a good idea to put it off any longer.

"While you were gone, I remembered something about my recovered memories," I begin. "In one of them, my Human mother called my father by his name: Dennis."

Harrow nods. "I remember."

"Later, when Ancrow and I spoke of my past, I told her about that memory. When I mentioned the name Dennis, she was startled. She knew it. She tried to hide it, but I noticed. She recognized his name. Then, when she confessed to what she had been hiding about our relationship, she said she had just given me newborn to someone who would find me a home. She never said anything about knowing my adoptive father, so she was lying."

He gives me a long look. "Are you sure about this? Is it possible she just forgot?"

I shake my head. "I don't think so. I think she is still hiding something."

He sighs. "Ah, my mother. I love her still, but she has always been difficult and secretive, and it's no surprise to hear that none of that has changed. What are you going to do?"

"Go to her. Speak with her. Ask her to tell me what she knows about my parents. Find out the truth."

His amber eyes fix on me, and I cannot look away. "I will go with you," he says.

TWENTY-TWO

OUR DECISION MADE, WE LEAVE THE GLADE AND WALK BACK to Ancrow's home. We say little. We know what this confrontation will require, and it feels daunting, but the need to know the truth propels us. This dissembling and relying on half-truths has to end. Ancrow has revealed much, and I do not undervalue what it must have cost her to do so. But she still holds something back, and that is not right.

We ascend to the second level of the city and follow the tree lanes to her front door. There we pause, exchange a quick glance, and knock.

It is Char who opens the door. "Auris! Harrow! Are we going to Promise Falls?"

Her enthusiasm nearly undoes us both, but it is Harrow who steps in. "Not today, little one. We are here to speak to Mother."

"Pooh," she says and steps aside to let us in. A frown follows, then, "Maybe we can go tomorrow?"

"We'll see," I allow.

"That means no," Char declares and stomps away.

We enter the living room and find Ancrow emerging from the kitchen. Her smile is warm and genuine for an instant; and then she sees something in our eyes and it disappears entirely. "Is something wrong?"

I know it is my place to speak of what is bothering me. "It is," I say, taking a step forward. "I need to ask you something. About my birth—and about what you said. Or rather, what you didn't say. When I told you that all I knew about my parents from the recovered memories was my father's name, I saw something in your eyes. Recognition. A bit of knowledge. I forgot about that in the rush of your subsequent revelations. I am not here to criticize you. I am grateful for everything you told me. But I want to know what you *haven't* told me. What do you know about Dennis, who claimed he was my father?"

Her face turns stony. "Nothing. Nothing I haven't already said."

"Mother, I know you too well to believe that," Harrow interjects. "Tell the truth. If you don't want me here while you do, I can leave."

"Please," I say quietly. "I don't want any other secrets between us. I want to know about my father. If you can tell me something—anything—it would mean the world. I have spent my entire life not knowing anything about my parents. Now I know about you. What can it hurt for you to tell me about Dennis? Who is Dennis to me?"

"Tell her, Mother," Harrow adds quickly. "Either we are your children or we aren't. If we are, we deserve to know. Look what Auris has been through to get to Viridian. Look at what she has done for us. She saved Char's life. She saved my life! She's earned the right to know. You cannot pick and choose what you wish to tell her. You have to tell it all. You can't deny her this."

"Maybe I think I *have* the right. Maybe I am protecting you both."

"Then let me be the judge of that!" I practically shout. "At least respect me enough to let *me* decide if I want to risk it. I won't love you any less, no matter what it is. Please, Ancrow."

She is expressionless as she looks at me, but her eyes betray the anguish she is feeling. She stares at me with a mix of admiration and horror, then shifts her gaze to Harrow before turning back at me. She nods. "I owe you this, don't I? Complete honesty about your life and mine? Very well. I will do what you ask. I will tell you what I have been holding back. Char! Ramey!"

The girls come running, worried looks on their faces. "Don't worry. Everything is all right. But Harrow, Auris, and I have to talk alone. Will you please go outside and play for a bit? And try not to peek in the windows or listen at the door. This is not about you."

The girls exchange a look and leave without a word. I am pretty sure they will try to find out what is going on later, but I think they will stay clear of the house for now. Ancrow is a force of nature when crossed.

"Let's sit down," she says, leading the way to a pair of couches.

We sit on one, Harrow and I together, and Ancrow sits across from us. She takes a deep breath. "I did not tell you the truth about escaping from the Humans who held me prisoner. The Humans were scientists, as I said before. As such, they saw me as a valuable specimen and were not about to release me. That is also true. But it was not one of my jailers who freed me. It was a scientist working in another division—one specializing in genetic alterations. He was invited to observe several times while I was being experimented on. He never stayed long, but I was always aware that watching made him deeply uncomfortable. Eventually, when it became apparent I would never be released but held imprisoned and used as an experiment for as long as I had life left in me, he decided to free me."

She shrugs. "To pretend I fully understand his reasons or his nature would be lying. He took me away one night all cloaked and covered so there was no way to tell I was Fae. He hid me in his home and said I would have to stay there until I regained my strength and arrangements were made to take me home. I didn't argue or object; why would I? He was going to set me free.

"I think he must have loved me—at least a little. His deference, his solicitude, and his obvious affection were made quite clear in the course of spiriting me from my prison and during the few days that followed. I was weakened from my ordeal and still very afraid. And I must admit that I found some comfort in his arms when he tried to reassure me that everything would be all right, that he could get me to safety. I just needed to be patient, he said. I believed him. During the time I stayed I think I came to love him back, at least a little."

She pauses, gathering herself. "On the third night of my stay, I sought . . . more from him."

Stunned silence. This is Ancrow, warrior on dozens of battlefields, a woman who has forged her own path in life and who professes undying hatred of Humans as I do not imagine any other Sylvan ever has. Yet she is saying she made advances to one? I cannot look at Harrow. I cannot bear to see what is on his face.

Ancrow has lowered her eyes to where her clasped hands rest in her lap. "I'm still not entirely sure what made me do this. Perhaps it was just loneliness or desperation, or perhaps it was my way of giving thanks. He wasn't like the others, I told myself. He was kind and considerate. He was saving me. But I will not lie to you; I also took some comfort from it, some sense of security. I did not love this man as I had Carrowen, but he was an island of hope for me."

Neither Harrow nor I say anything. I start to, but I feel his hand grip mine and tighten in warning, silencing me.

Ancrow begins to cry. "I did not tell you this before because I am deeply ashamed. I tell you now because you need to know that your father was a good man. He saved my life when he had no reason to do so other than he knew what was being done to me was wrong. He was a Human, but he is also your father and you should keep him in your heart."

I cannot stand seeing what this terrible admission is doing to her, how she reviles herself for this one choice she made. But I have lived in prison. I know how it breaks you down. Why would I question her actions? Why would I think I have the right?

"Mother," Harrow says, but she cuts him off.

"Let me finish, Harrow, while I still can. My rescuer kept his word; he found a way to get me safely away from my captors and to the shores of the Roughlin. He left me there, and I never saw him again. But when I found out I was pregnant not long after my return, I knew he was the father."

She looks at me, her eyes revealing new anguish. "His name was Dennis."

SO NOW WE KNOW. MY MOTHER BREAKS DOWN COMPLETELY, AND Harrow and I rise as one and go to comfort her. She resists, but only briefly, and we hold her as she cries, her sobs heartbreaking. Char and Ramey reappear, and I go quickly to meet them at the door and ask them to wait. Mother is all right, I tell them. She just needs to be alone with us a bit longer. I will come get them when it is time. They look at me doubtfully, but go back outside.

I am seeing Ancrow with fresh eyes, revealed now as a more vulnerable and real person. Before she was all stone and sharp angles, all harsh words and stern looks. When she admitted she was my mother, there were cracks in her façade that gave me a look at the walls she had built to protect herself, but even then she could not speak of this further humiliation. I suppose that forcing herself to reveal what she has been hiding for almost twenty years enables her to speak about the rest now. I know she is sincere when she says she wants no more secrets, but this one is massive. If it were to be revealed to the larger part of the Sylvan community, it would change everyone's perception and leave her reputation in tatters. She would no longer be the Ancrow of legend, railing against the Human taint. She would be diminished in the eyes of her community thanks to her perceived hypocrisy, and we cannot allow that to happen.

"No one will ever hear of this again," I promise. I glance at Harrow, who nods his agreement. "Not from us. We will keep this among the three of us. But I have to ask you one more thing, so please bear with me, Mother. And please be honest with me. Will you do that?"

She cannot speak yet, but she nods her agreement.

"How is it that, after I was born, I ended up back with my real father? How did you know where to find him?"

"I didn't. Someone else found him for me."

"Someone in Viridian Deep?" Harrow presses.

"It was a Water Sprite who helped me. I needed this to remain a secret from those who knew me, so I asked someone who wouldn't tell anyone in Viridian. His name was Trinch. He was a . . . a facilitator. When you needed someone to do something questionable, you called on him. I had known him from another time in my life."

"But how did he know how to find my father? How did he manage it?"

She gives her son a stricken look. "I didn't ask. I just wanted it to be over and done with. I told him to look for a scientist named Dennis. I told him where to find him. I don't know how he did it, but it seems he managed. He never explained, and I never asked. He just took Auris and that was the end of it."

She heaves a long sigh. "Until your arrival. Until it has become clear that everything I did wrong then requires righting now."

"Is this man, this Trinch, is he still alive?" I ask impulsively.

Ancrow is immediately on guard. "Why? You're not thinking of trying to find him, are you? Wait, are you thinking of trying to *find* your adoptive parents? Don't do that. They're probably already dead. Why else would you have been in a Goblin prison?"

Dr. Allensby had said as much to me, but I wasn't sure I believed him. "And what if they are not? Maybe Trinch could find the truth for me."

"I heard that Trinch died several years ago," Ancrow says hastily. "Please let this alone, Auris. The past should be left buried. It is all I can do just to live with the knowledge of it." She looks miserable. "Don't let it burden you as well. I wish I had been thinking more clearly when I gave you up. I wish none of this had happened. I should never have done what I did."

I wish the same. I wish Ancrow hadn't done a lot of things. But in this case I am not willing to think her entirely wrong for her choices. Yes, she gave me up when I was newborn, but she also went to the trouble of finding my father, whom she knew to be a good man, in order to be sure I was given to him. That demonstrates a level of caring that was not apparent before. Initially, her actions felt random and bereft of any concern. Now I see her differently once again.

"No one can undo the past," I say, taking her hands in mine. "We can only try to understand and accept it. I have done so; I have forgiven you so I can begin to heal. Now I want you to do this for yourself."

Harrow and I stay with our mother awhile longer, and the matter of my departure is not mentioned again. I think it is because Ancrow does not see a path forward for me, now that Trinch is dead. But I am not so easily dissuaded. I cannot pinpoint the reason for my insistence on wanting to know more about my father, and perhaps it will all come to nothing, but some part of me will never be satisfied until I am assured of the truth. When you have lived a lifetime of lies about your family and yourself, you need to set things right in your own mind, if nowhere else. I have my birth mother back; now I wonder if in some small way I can get one or both of the parents who raised me back as well.

Harrow senses this, and we are not far from Ancrow's home, following the tree lanes to a small dining space where we can enjoy something to eat, when he says, "I know you well enough, Auris, to anticipate what you intend. You're going back, aren't you?"

"I would if I knew how to get there. I need to discover the truth about what happened to my father and mother, but that doesn't seem possible right now."

"So what are you going to do?"

I shrug. "Try to forget about it? Try to learn to live with it? Keep looking for another way to find out about my father?" I stop and look at him. "I know I am probably being foolish, but when you have a need to know something as strongly as I do, it is hard to give it up. There are still so many unanswered questions—and some are very troubling. Supposedly, my father took me when my mother didn't want me, and he and his wife raised me. But raised me how? What was he doing with me that I have this memory of him examining me and giving me medications? Was my father experimenting on me? And if so, why was he doing this if he was the decent man that Ancrow claims? Also, how did I end up in the Goblin prisons with no memories of my childhood? Was he responsible? Or was he trying to protect me and paid the ultimate price for doing so? Do you understand?"

Harrow nods. "I do."

His arm comes around my shoulders, and we walk on in silence. We reach our destination and are seated. I am sitting across from him, studying his lean face, my thoughts in turmoil, my emotions a wild mix of relief and sadness, when he says, "Mother was lying."

I am not sure I hear him right. "What did you say?"

"She was lying about your father—and maybe the rest of what she was telling us, too. I know her too well to be deceived. Maybe her lies were outright, and maybe they were lies of omission. But she was lying."

"She didn't sound like it," I say, my mood already darkening. She's lied so many times already, and each time I have believed she was finally telling me everything. "Are you sure?"

Harrow looks weary, but he gives me a smile. "Mothers always lie to their children. Ramey told me that a few years back. They do it not out of malicious intent but out of love. They do it because they think it is necessary. They believe they are sparing us from the truth."

"But she was so convincing!"

A shrug. "She always is. But for Ancrow, lying is a way of life. It is how she gets by." He reaches for my hand across the table. "I might know a way to find your adoptive parents, but I am not sure I should tell you what it is. If I tell you, you will want to go back into Human country—back to where you came from, back to the very people who locked you away in the first place. You would be risking your life all over again, and I don't want that."

He is speaking very softly, his fingers tightening possessively around mine. I take a moment to steady myself.

"I would be careful," I tell him. "I look Human, after all—and I am one to all appearances. I would fit in easily. Remember, I have spent my entire life thinking I was a Human right up until you found me in the wastelands. I know it is dangerous, but I don't think I can pass up a chance of finding the truth. If I can't get it from Ancrow, I have to get it elsewhere." I pause. "Harrow, this is important. You have to tell me how I can do this."

It is not entirely out of the question that he will refuse. He has saved my life twice already, and I do not think he would look kindly on having to do it a third time—especially if he feels I am being reckless. I know he cares about me; he will not want to put me in danger. Yet he is the one who has opened the door.

Once again, he surprises me. "Trinch might not be dead."

I stare at him in shock. "But Ancrow said . . ."

"I love my mother, but she is not to be trusted. She may have said he was dead simply to dissuade you from doing something she clearly doesn't want you to do."

I know this is so. My mother has lied to me over and over. I reach impulsively for his hands. "Can you find out if he is alive? Could you make it possible for me to speak with him?"

"I can try." He pauses. "But I have two conditions. I know you, after all. You are talented but impulsive. You are determined, but not always wise. Reckless behavior will not serve you well in this instance, so we must make a bargain. You must promise that you will not attempt to find your parents without a very definite idea of where they can be found, and if you then choose to go looking for them, you will take me with you."

I sigh in dismay. "Now who is putting themselves at risk? You do not look Human in even the slightest way. You would never fit in. You'd be exposing yourself to far more danger than I would."

"Let me worry about that. I can protect myself better than you think. My conditions are firm. Do you agree to them?"

I think it through, but I already know what I will say. "I agree."

"Your word is your bond, Auris. You must keep it."

I nod. "How soon can we find out if Trinch is still alive? Can you locate him?"

"I cannot. These are Water Sprites we are talking about, and I am not intimately acquainted with them." He pauses. "Whether Trinch is alive and where he might be found are not things I can find out on my own."

I smile my understanding. "But you know someone who can?"

He smiles back. "As a matter of fact, we both do."

Right away, I know who he is talking about.

TWENTY-THREE

THE GOBLINS COME FOR ME AGAIN THAT NIGHT, THIS TIME waiting until I am asleep. I have returned with Harrow, our plans for the following day determined, the hour of our departure set for just before sunrise. Harrow kisses me and holds me close and tells me he will be with me until this matter is settled, no matter what, and I tell him I will not pursue my search for my father if it becomes too dangerous. But while I believe he has been truthful, I have not. At least not entirely. I do not believe there is a level of danger that will dissuade me at this point. I go to bed regretting my shading of the truth, but at the same time justifying it to myself. I am stubborn that way, but I know I will never rest until the fate of my father has been determined. I cannot do more this night, however, and so my eyes close and I am quickly asleep.

And then the Goblins appear.

As they expect to find me sleeping, they believe I pose no real threat to them. But my instincts have been much more acute since my discovery of my *inish*, and I am awake the moment they enter the cottage. I know right away—without knowing who or what intrudes—that I am in danger, and I fling back the covers and stand to meet it.

I am barely upright before the Goblins burst through my bedroom doorway, intent on dragging me from my bed. There are five of them—big, armored head-to-foot, and much stronger than I am. They fill the small bedroom with their combined bulk. They think themselves sufficiently prepared for whatever they might encounter. But when they find me standing before them with my *inish* staff in my hands, its tip alight with blue fire, they hesitate for half a second. Then the closest two launch themselves at me. Two more crouch down protectively, and the last hangs back, waiting for his chance. But none of them reach me. My magic snatches up the two who come directly at me and sends them spinning out the bedroom door. The two who have gone into a crouch wait for an opening, but the Goblin hanging back produces a heavy net and flings it over me. The weight drags me down, and I lose control of the staff, which skitters away. By now all five Goblins are on top of me— those I flung in the other room abruptly returning—and all five of them rush toward me as I struggle beneath the net.

Even without my staff, I reach for my *inish,* but then I falter, suddenly weakened, my strength failing.

A moment later, the Goblins snatch me up and bundle me out my bedroom door, hastening to make their escape. I claw and scratch and kick and scream, but they are big creatures, impervious to anything I might do, and simply ignore me.

But when they reach my cottage door to make their escape, they find someone waiting—someone they cannot dispatch so easily.

Harrow!

He uses his staff to separate me from the Goblins while spinning them about and slamming them into nearby tree trunks with such force that all are rendered unconscious. I drop onto the upper-level platform with the wind knocked out of me—still tangled in the mesh net. He comes over to me and his strong hands reach down to free me. Harrow. Come to save me one more time. My struggle must have woken him and brought him to me. Or have we bonded in some other way? I like thinking that we have. I like thinking we are bonded in a special way that makes it possible for him to always be there when I need him.

I feel my mind clear, and my strength flood back as the net lifts away. "Are you hurt?" he asks.

"Only my pride. I had things under control and then all of a sudden I didn't." I sit up, shaking my head. "I don't know what happened, but I seemed to lose strength all at once. I was using my *inish* to protect myself, and suddenly my magic just faded away."

He kneels in front of me. "That would be because the netting the Goblins used is woven with a special metal they favor—one that weakens the Fae when it touches them. The Goblins would have been affected, too, but they wear heavy leather gloves." He sits back on his heels, smiling. "So all's well?"

"Well enough." I notice for the first time that he has rushed to my rescue so fast he apparently didn't have time to put on anything more than a pair of pants. The tiny leaves woven through his black hair where it falls across his shoulders and runs along the undersides of his arms shimmer, and the greenish skin of his sculpted body gleams in the moonlight. I try not to stare. "How did you know I was in trouble?"

He shrugs. "How could I not with all that screaming?"

I punch his shoulder lightly in rebuke. "You were there before I screamed. You were waiting. Seriously, how did you know?"

He looks pensive. "Good question. Instinct, I suppose. But I just knew. Let me ask you something. Why do you think the Goblins are working so hard to recapture you? Is there some reason for this—something you haven't told me or maybe forgot?"

I shake my head slowly. Is there? I can't think of anything, but that doesn't mean there isn't something else about myself I don't know. Why have they come back for me a second time? Why are they bothering?

"Maybe they miss me," I joke.

Harrow doesn't smile.

WE LEAVE THE NEXT DAY. WE TELL NO ONE WHERE WE ARE GOING. We don't even tell anyone we are leaving, except for Ronden. We tell her because—having told her about Ancrow's latest revelation—it is a good bet that she will figure it out anyway. If she does, we do not want her coming after us; we want her to remain behind in case we get into trouble and need help getting out.

"If something goes wrong and we need rescuing—which you know can happen easily enough with either of us—it will be up to you," I say lightly. "Pact or no pact."

She gives me a look. "I hope you know what you are doing, but even if you don't, you are too stubborn for me to try to tell you what to do. Just remember to reach out if anything goes wrong."

We have a code for emergencies by now, one created in the wake of our last mission: Two quick bursts of *inish* followed by one long one. The Seers will read it in the *Inish* Reveal; Ronden will have them looking for it. It is an imperfect plan for mounting any sort of rescue, since we are going to be outside any part of the country that can be reached by wormholes. Wormholes, Harrow explains, can be used in the wastelands because this is border country between the Fae and Human worlds and therefore accessible to both. In any case, we can't rely on them to provide an escape if we get caught.

One reason I feel more confident than I did at first is that Harrow tells me he has gone into Human lands before as part of his duties as a Fae Watcher. For the most part, he stays along the borderlands on the far side of Roughlin Wake. But now and again he finds it necessary to venture farther, and he has been in the cities and towns that lie closest to the Roughlin and the far sides of the wastelands. He knows enough about the Human world in general to think we can find our way, unless my parents lived too far away to be safely reached. But we will have to find that out from Trinch, if he is indeed still alive.

Yet while I desperately want to know the truth about my adoptive parents, I am not anxious to go back to a people and a country that has imprisoned me twice, very nearly killed me both times, and will likely try to kill me again if they get their hands on me. I know what the risks are, and they are considerable. It would be one thing if my search were happening in Fae country, but another altogether to return to an unfriendly country already actively engaged in trying to bring me back. While I once believed I was Human, I now know I am not. I might look it, but both physically and emotionally I am Fae. I am still who I always was, but not who I thought. I am resigned to a life in which I appear one thing on the outside and am another within. But there is one crucial difference between the Fae and Human lands. In the one I am at least somewhat protected; in the other I will be in constant danger.

So why deliberately put myself and Harrow in such danger? I think it is because I realize that to ever rest easy about my new life I have to know about the hidden paths that have brought me here. There is so much I do not know. Apparently, my father was deceiving the authorities of his own country to take me in and make it seem as if I was his daughter. He was a medical man, and he was giving me medications for something for reasons I don't yet understand. What was he doing with me? His wife wanted to send me away—for their safety or mine? Yet he persisted in keeping me with them. Then he was found to be harboring me and apparently killed. But what happened to my adoptive mother, whose efforts to protect me failed? And why was I sent to the prisons?

Too many questions for me to step away from and claim they don't matter. They do. They are secrets I need to uncover, and there is only one way to do this.

We set out at dawn, slipping from the city into the surrounding countryside to begin our journey into the lands of the Water Sprites. Sylvans share a good relationship with Water Sprites, but they lead very different lives and do not interact on a regular basis. Sprites are water creatures and need to live in places where water is readily available. Water is essential to their survival. They must submerse themselves regularly in order to maintain their health, and many of them live entirely in water all the time. Hence, the first leg of our journey will take us to where the largest portion of the Sprite population makes its home.

We don't walk far before my thoughts shift back to Harrow's words about finding an old friend once we reach our destination.

Old friend, indeed!

"I cannot believe I have to put up with Zedlin again," I grumble once our departure is under way. "I thought I'd seen the last of him."

Harrow smiles in an indulgent way. "Whatever happened between you, set it aside. Zedlin is a valuable source of information— and one we need. He knows every single one of the Water Sprite people, where they live, and how to find them. How he manages this, I have no idea. But if anyone knows whether Trinch is alive and can tell us how to reach him, it is Zedlin. He's young, but he can be trusted. That boy is our best chance of finding your father."

"Maybe so. But he's also a boy who has already crossed a line."

The smile drops away. "What do you mean, *crossed a line?*"

I could kick myself. I have forgotten that I lied to Harrow about my encounter with Zedlin and his crew. Harrow didn't need to hear about it then and he doesn't need to hear about it now.

I force a smile. "He just got a little pushy with me, but it means nothing. I've forgiven him. Actually, it might be nice to see him again."

It is a weak explanation, and I am not at all sure Harrow is buying what I am trying to sell. He gives me a long look, and for a minute I am certain he is going to pursue the matter. But then he lets it drop and I breathe a sigh of relief.

We walk for two days to reach the Sprite village where Zedlin lives, and by the time we arrive on the second day it is almost sunset. The village is small and well kept, and I can smell the lake even without being able to see it. Sprite homes are built at the ground level, not elevated into the branches of trees like Sylvan homes, even though there are forests everywhere and the trees are frequently of the same species. There are no tree lanes or overlooks;

the homes are mostly connected huts framed of wood and sealed with thick swamp grasses. I cannot imagine what those who live in the water do for shelter. I glance around at everything, and as I do I cannot help but notice that the Sprites we pass are taking a close look at me. But no one approaches. Without being able to say why, I sense that they know Harrow well enough to leave me alone while I am in his company.

But perhaps, too, it is because I carry the very distinct and recognizable *inish* staff that marks my ability to use magic.

The first thing I notice is the water. It saturates the village in ponds both large and small, in culverts and streams, in springs, and in one case a small reservoir.

As we progress I become increasingly aware that everything is laid out in what seems to be haphazard fashion, with no clear indication of what anything is. Some buildings are clearly homes; the lights in the windows and the movements within signal the presence of families. Some are dark and empty, so I assume at first that they are businesses, but they look exactly the same as the lighted ones. Size seems irrelevant to usage, since all are single-story. Almost all consist of multiple connected buildings—some as large as six or eight buildings. Save for a stray toy or rope swing, there is almost nothing to indicate who resides where.

"How do you know which homes are residences and which are not?" I ask Harrow. "Everything looks the same."

"That's the idea," he replies with a smile. "The Goblins prey on the Water Sprite people in the same way they do on Sylvans. If attacked and overrun, they simply disappear into these buildings and go underground into tunnels that interconnect them and run all the way to the shores of the Roughlin. Once there, they flee into the water where the Goblins cannot reach them. Their larger cities are underwater—in vast, sealed domes where they can keep safe. The greater number of Sprites live there, and in smaller bodies of water scattered throughout Viridian Deep. If this village were to be attacked, the people would simply disappear underground and go to the domes. If their huts are destroyed, it doesn't matter. It's easy enough to make new ones."

"That seems an odd way to live."

He chuckles. "Humans live in structures built of stone and iron. They live behind walls. Sprites would find that equally odd."

We walk until we are at the far eastern end of the village, where a series of five connected buildings—all pretty much the same size—appear. Windows and doors are open, and voices are audible from within.

"Wait here," Harrow tells me. "This is an orphan residence. I will try to find out where Zedlin is. It might be better if you stayed back."

He disappears for long minutes, and I am left waiting in the dark. But I don't mind the dark or the waiting. I am used to them. I've experienced plenty of both inside the Goblin prisons, and re-visiting them here is much more pleasant. Besides, it gives me time to think. I try to imagine what life must be like for these people. It is so foreign to me that I think I would have to live here awhile in order to find out. How do they grow food in this swampy ground? How do they live aboveground if they are water people? What do they eat? What do they do to school their young? Why don't they have streets or signs or gardens like the Sylvans? I don't have the answers, but I am new to this world and still know very little about the Sylvans, let alone the Sprites. I have a lot to learn.

Harrow returns. "Zedlin is off somewhere with his friends."

"Probably getting into trouble." I can't help myself.

Harrow gives me another of those looks. "Why do you say that?"

I shrug. "No reason. Do we wait or go find him?"

He shakes his head. "We don't have to find him. I know where he is."

He starts off without waiting, and I fall into step beside him. His impatience is obvious, but I cannot tell if it is directed toward Zed-lin or me. We walk for a time into the deeper forest until we reach a glade where a large pond is filled with splashing Sprites and a fire is lit to ward off the chill of the night air. Dozens of young people are shouting and playing. Some are close to my age; most are much younger. No one watches over them, but I notice some of the older kids standing apart at regular intervals, apparently there to act as sentries and peacekeepers. One of them spies us and walks over. He is heavily muscled, short and stocky, and looks capable enough to restore order if things get out of hand.

"Watcher," he greets Harrow and gives me a long look. "Can I help you?"

"Zedlin?" Harrow asks.

"Oh, that one. Wait here. I'll bring him."

He disappears into the crowd. "This area is for young people only," Harrow tells me, eyes on the crowd. Always on watch, I think. "They are charged with monitoring one another. They manage well enough, for the most part. If you step too far out of line, you are banned—and no one wants that. These gatherings are called *alle confres* in the Sprite language, or youth conclaves in the Human tongue. Free zones for kids."

I look about. Everyone does look pretty free. There are no adults anywhere, but no signs of acting out, either.

A few minutes pass and Zedlin appears. He is dripping wet, stripped down to pants only, his young face shining with the damp. His chest is heaving, and his neck gills are opening and closing rapidly. He sees Harrow first. "Well met, Watcher!" he greets him. Same self-assurance, same cocky attitude. Then he sees me and his expression turns wary. But his recovery is quick. "A big Watcher and a little Watcher. What do you need from me?"

"Do you know a Sprite called Trinch?" Harrow asks.

"Old Trinch? The 'barter man' we call him. I know him."

So he's still alive. Ancrow *was* lying.

"We need to speak with him."

"Tomorrow ought to be . . ."

"Tonight. We must see him tonight, and he must answer our questions."

Zedlin starts to object and then shrugs. "Well, it is late, but you've done a lot for me in the past. Trinch is a surly old dog at best, but maybe I can soften him up a bit. Will that help?"

Harrow nods. "Lead the way."

As Zedlin goes for the rest of his clothes and his boots, Harrow stands silently beside me for several long minutes before he says, "I rather like that boy."

Truth be told, he is beginning to grow on me, too.

We walk all the way to where Trinch has his cabin on the very northernmost edge of the village. His cabin sits all alone in a stand of conifers with no other homes in sight. I can tell that this site must remain heavily shaded even in daylight, with a canopy of overhanging boughs interlocking. They almost droop to the rooftop, and tree trunks crowd about from all sides. There is a light in the window facing us, and another emanating from a lamp hanging just off the porch front. The cabin is secluded, and there is a lonely feeling about it that is unmistakable. Harrow and I glance at each other as we draw closer, but Zedlin seems unperturbed. He is clearly familiar with its location; he never once hesitated while guiding us here. I wonder how he came to know a man like Trinch well enough to feel comfortable bringing strangers to his doorstep without checking to see if it was all right first.

As if reading my mind, the boy asks us to wait while he goes ahead to announce our presence and request a meeting. Harrow and I stand side by side and watch him climb the porch steps and knock on the door. The sound of his knock is hollow and empty, and it makes me think that the cabin is unoccupied in spite of the light. But then the door opens, and Zedlin stands talking to whoever is within for a few minutes, their voices pitched low, their conversation impossible to hear.

A few minutes later he beckons us over, and we enter the cabin. "This is the man you came to see," he announces as we stand just inside the doorway. "Trinch, this is Harrow and Auris. They have important questions to ask you." He pauses as a very old and gnarly

Sprite glares at us doubtfully. "I'll leave you to your business and wait outside until you are finished."

As he leaves, he gives us a wink. He'll wait outside, but with an ear to the door, I suspect. The cabin door closes and Harrow and I are left facing the old man.

"Sit," he orders, rather than invites. The no-nonsense, little-patience-for-strangers tone of his voice is easy enough to read. As he lowers himself back into his tattered easy chair, Harrow and I sit on the facing couch. I take in the cabin's interior with a single glance. Old, faded, and cluttered, and it's been a long time since anyone bothered cleaning. The furniture is minimal and all of it in the same poor condition as the easy chair. Books and papers are scattered everywhere—a mess that only the occupant could possibly tolerate. The man himself is a match for his habitat: so old I cannot guess his real age, his body crumpled in on itself, his skin deeply lined and age-spotted, his hair not much more than two white tufts—one on his chin and the other on the top of his head.

"What is it you want?" he demands, his gaze wandering.

"We need to find someone," Harrow says.

"I'm not in the business of finding people."

"This is someone you know."

Trinch harrumphs his disinterest. "I know a lot of people. Some don't want to be found."

"Do you know Ancrow of the Sylvan people?"

The old man goes still. "Not a good idea to go looking for her. You're Sylvan. You should know."

I force myself to stay quiet and let Harrow take the lead. He will have better luck with this old man than I will. Since we entered his cabin, he has barely spared me a glance.

"About twenty years ago, Ancrow brought you a baby. A Human. A girl. You were asked to find her father and present him with his child. She told you his name was Dennis."

Trinch stares at us. "She told me it was to be our secret—that I was never to tell anyone about it. She told me she wanted it to remain that way always—the secret ours and ours alone. But she told you?"

"She told me," I say suddenly. "I am that child. I am looking for my father."

"Are you, now?" he whispers.

There is a long silence, and then Trinch laughs. His laugh is dark and unpleasant, and he points at me as if I were a curiosity. "She never told you the rest of what she asked, I warrant. Never mentioned what I was to do when I found your father and showed you to him, did she? Never mentioned what she told me to say to him?"

I shake my head. I already don't want to hear what is coming. I can sense it in his wickedly gleeful tone of voice. This man, this Sprite that Zedlin calls the barter man, trades things—some of them apparently babies.

"I run a business," the old man continues. "I buy and sell. I barter and trade. I don't give or do anything for free. Ancrow knew this. She paid, as I knew she would; I could see the desperation in her eyes when she asked her favor. She paid, and she paid well. She said to do whatever I needed to do to be rid of you. She said to tell the man I gave you to—your father—that he could do whatever he wanted once he had you, but he was not to bring you back. When I told him this, he insisted on examining you. He seemed very interested in how you looked. He studied you very carefully. He was a doctor, he told me. I think he saw you as an interesting specimen."

His grin is a rictus of glee. "When he said he'd take you, I told him I wanted money. Needed to be paid for my trouble in bringing you all that way. He agreed. I sold you to your father, little girl. You were goods, and I sold you as such."

He pauses, his voice low and cruel. "And when I told your mother, she thanked me."

TWENTY-FOUR

"HOW DOES *THAT* NEWS TASTE?" TRINCH CONTINUES, A NASTY grin on his wrinkled face. "Poor, unwanted baby girl."

I am almost out of my chair and at his throat when Harrow places his hand on my arm and, by that simple act, conveys the need for restraint. But I hate that old Water Sprite at this moment—hate him so badly I could easily kill him.

"Is your memory as sharp as your tongue?" Harrow asks calmly, but there is an edge to his voice, too. "Do you remember the father's name?"

The hard eyes shift to find my companion. A slow nod follows, and a new kind of smile emerges. He senses opportunity. "I might. Good chance I could, if there were reason enough."

"And if there were reason enough, would your memory stretch far enough to recall where he could be found?"

A shrug. "Depends on the value I attach to the reason, I'd say. But I think maybe I could do even more. Might be able to draw you a map to help guide you, you being a Sylvan trying to find your way around in the Human world. You really brave enough for that?"

Harrow ignores the taunt. "There was a wife, too. At some point, this man was married. Was she there on your visit to return the baby no one wanted?"

"Might have been."

If he is experiencing the same frustration I am, Harrow is doing a good job of hiding it. His voice and his manner remain calm and unruffled, his eyes still fixed on the obstreperous old man. Trinch is silent, giving himself time to consider what Harrow might choose to do, intimidated perhaps by the Watcher as he is not by me.

Harrow reaches into his pocket and produces a gold coin—one used in the Human world—and holds it up, just out of reach. "Reason enough?" he asks softly.

Trinch considers for a moment. "A good start. A down payment."

A flick of his fingers, and Harrow is holding up a second gold coin that matches the first. "Before you say anything more, this is four times the value of what I am asking you to provide, and as yet I have no idea if you have anything useful to offer."

"The man's name was Dennis. His wife was Margrete."

Trinch holds out his hand, palm up. Harrow drops one of the coins into it. The hand stays where it is, open and waiting.

"I will keep this second coin until I have a chance to discover if you are telling me the truth. Draw me that map you promised."

Trinch shakes his head. "Not until you give me the coin."

"What if I squeeze your head hard enough to force the information out of you instead?"

"Might work. But I have a weak heart. Don't think I would last long enough to tell you much. You might get nothing. I wouldn't chance it, if I were you. Remember—I am the only one who knows where I took your friend when she was newborn, the only one who knows where Dennis and Margrete might be found."

Harrow drops the second coin. "I'll keep my options open until I have a look at this map."

Trinch locates pen and paper and works up a rough map with a few directions written on it. "Harbor's End. That's your destination."

"We'll find both parents there?"

The old man cackles. "That's where they were back then. Don't know where they are now. That's your problem." He tucks the coins in his pants pocket. Then he glares at Harrow. "Don't think for one minute you frighten me. Threatening to come back and do bad things to me if you decide I'm lying? Poor old barter man, you think? Crack him like an eggshell? Well, maybe. But hear this. You don't frighten me, because I know something you don't. Once you've set foot in the Human world, you've made a choice. And you won't be coming back after making it. A green-skinned Sylvan wandering around with Humans? Think they won't spy you out, won't know you for what you are? You're a fool! There won't be enough of you left to spread on toast!"

He pauses, his gaze shifting momentarily to me. "Why're you doing this for her anyway? For this nothing girl, this throwaway? Good for only one thing, and she's probably already given you that. Why risk your life? For a chance to find a man who's probably dead and a woman who wishes she was?"

I grit my teeth. This old man talks about me as if I'm not even there. He thinks himself free to say hurtful things and pretend it doesn't matter. It is almost more than I can stand, but I force myself to sit quietly, inwardly seething.

Harrow gets to his feet. "Our business is concluded, old man. But hear me. That 'girl,' as you call her, could kill you in a minute if she wished it. I'm surprised you're still breathing as it is. Don't get too used to the idea. If you've lied or deliberately misled me, I will be back. Come, Auris."

Then we are out of the door, Harrow slamming it so hard it rattles on its hinges, both of us anxious to put this evil old man and his foul mouth as far behind us as we can manage.

Zedlin falls into step beside us. "You can trust him, you know. His livelihood depends on his word being good. If he lied—even once—that would be the end of his business and possibly his life. Word gets around, and grudges run deep against those who lie."

He looks at me and runs a finger across his throat. Then he

laughs and skips ahead. I follow him with a dark look, but Harrow bends down to kiss my cheek. "Let him go. He's just having fun with you."

Fun? If he wants to have fun, I wish he'd do it with someone else. But I do what Harrow suggests and let the moment pass. I might still be angry with Trinch, but there is no need to take it out on Zedlin, who is just being himself and does not mean me any real harm.

We walk back into the village, continuing on to Zedlin's home. Once we get there, Zedlin slows and waits for us to catch up. "So, Watcher, what are you and this 'throwaway' girl going to do next?" he asks, grinning at me.

Harrow waits to catch his eye. "The first thing *you* are going to do is never say that about Auris again! She is not the girl you encountered when she first came into Viridian, and you do not want to find this out the hard way. You will treat her with respect."

Zedlin clearly thought he was being funny, and is shocked by Harrow's response. He turns to me at once. "I was wrong to speak of you as I did. I apologize."

This surprises me, but I accept his apology and tell him we will be friends from here forward. He looks relieved—especially when he looks over and sees Harrow nodding in agreement.

"I need your help, Zedlin," the Watcher continues. "First, a place to sleep tonight for Auris and myself, and second a way to cross the Roughlin to the mainland undetected. Do you know of Harbor's End?"

The boy nods. "Been over for a look once or twice. Always stayed in the water, though the map should help you there. But I know how to make the crossing without being seen. Several ways, in fact, though only one of them is reliable. Only one where we can't be seen by the Goblins."

"A submersible?" Harrow says abruptly. "You want us to travel underwater?"

"Wait!" I exclaim, already unhappy with the idea. "Can't we travel through a wormhole? As Ronden and I did to come rescue you from the prisons?"

He shakes his head. "Wormholes can't be formed in the Human world."

I want to ask more about this, but Zedlin is already moving on, intent on showing us our shelter for the night. He takes us to a small cottage behind the orphan complex where he is housed and tells us we can spend the night there. A living room, a bedroom alcove, and shelves and a cold box fully stocked, he advises. Help yourselves. Also, an outdoor privy a short walk from the cottage. He points the way. He will arrange the submersible and have it ready by midday. Members of his gang will crew, so no one else from the village has to know we're here. They've all trained together, so there won't be any problems getting us across.

He says this with confidence. So why do I doubt him?

He wanders off to the main complex as we stand watching. "These submersibles he's talking about, can we trust them?"

"We can. Their ships are fast and maneuverable, constructed of sections of plastek and sealed with glue made of a mix of seaweed and oils boiled down and treated with high heat."

"Plastek?"

"A clear, tough substance that the Water Sprites conjure using their own form of *inish*. They discovered it hundreds of years ago when they were seeking a way to travel underwater. Even then, the Goblins were a threat. Believe me, these craft are very safe. You don't have to worry."

I wish everyone would stop saying this. *Don't worry. No problem.* I do worry, and I do think there could be problems. I am a realist. I did not survive the Goblin prisons by being a dreamer.

But I say nothing once again. I have to trust to those who know better—especially Harrow, who has gotten me this far since my escape and who is making the effort to get me a little further still, even though he is risking his own life to do so. If it was only Zedlin, I think I would suggest we take a surface boat—one that floats, not sinks. If my trust in Harrow was not paramount to all the doubts and fears I feel pushing against me, I might question what I am doing. As it is, I trust him with my life. I've learned I can do that.

We go into the cottage and look around. It is pretty much as Zedlin has described it. Even better, it is immaculate. Whoever cleans it has done a thorough job, and I am amazed at how everything gleams as if it were new. I walk through slowly, pretending to give it a careful once-over, peeking into the sleeping alcove as I go. Two beds. Just as well. Things might be a little uncomfortable otherwise, and Harrow would end up in one of two rockers or on the floor for the night.

Or I would. He's given up a lot for me. It's probably my turn to give up something for him.

We don't say much after that. We forage about for something to eat and find fruit and bread and cheese that suffice. We find a jug of ice ale and share that, as well. We don't say much to each other, carefully avoiding any mention of what lies ahead. Time enough for that later, when we are starting out. For tonight, a little quiet time and small talk seem enough.

We sit out on the porch together for a short time, look at the sky, and talk about missing Ronden and the little ones—wondering how they are, speculating about what they might be doing. But something is beginning to nag at me that won't let go. I cannot put it into words or give it a face, but it troubles me sufficiently that, after a short time on the porch, I announce that I am going to bed.

When I go in, Harrow stays where he is, giving me privacy. I don't require much; I don't have any bedclothes to change into. I strip off my cloak and outer garments, wash my face, and climb into the bed I have chosen, pulling up the covers against the night chill. I lie there for a long time, still searching for a hint of what is bothering me. Eventually Harrow comes in, but I am still awake. He strips down as I turn away and, after extinguishing the only light in the room, climbs into the other bed. Almost right away I can hear his breathing deepen into a slow, steady rhythm, and I know he is asleep.

I lie there without moving, not wanting to wake him by accident. Here is one small thing I can do for him.

And right away I know what it is that nags at me.

It's my selfishness.

Here I am, living a free life in a beautiful land with a man who loves me and whom I love—even if the extent of this affection is not quite settled—but still I am not satisfied. I have to insist on more. I have to know all about my Human family, too—about the family that adopted and raised me. I have discovered the truth about my birth mother but now I am insisting on knowing the truth about my birth father and my adoptive mother. My birth mother, at least, is someone I know. But the Humans are a complete mystery—people I might have known once, but about whom I now have only vague memories.

Finding out would be all well and good if it didn't require such risk. But it does. It requires tremendous risk, and that risk is being faced not only by me but also by Harrow and now these young Sprites. What is wrong with me that I am so ready to drag them into it? I should never have begun this odyssey. I should have put a stop to it right at the beginning. I should have known Harrow would never let me go alone. What if something happens to him? I love him beyond anything words can express, and yet I have led him down this dangerous road as if it were the most natural thing in the world.

I make a pact with myself. If there comes a time when it is necessary, I will give my life for him before I see him die. The guilt otherwise would be unbearable, and I have enough guilt to bear already with my friends all dead and only myself left. I can still see Khoury as she is riddled with bullets and falls in a heap. If I were forced to endure that with Harrow, I would not want to live a moment longer. I am being brutal and perhaps unrealistic with my assessments, but I am also preparing myself.

Whatever happens in the days ahead, I will protect Harrow at any cost.

WE RISE SHORTLY AFTER SUNRISE, WASH AND DRESS AND EAT BREAK-fast, our thoughts fixed on what lies ahead. As if he has been reading my mind, Harrow says over our meal, "You are not to place yourself in any further danger, Auris. You must let me take the lead and assume the risks. You must promise me this."

"I can't do that," I tell him.

"You have to. I could never return if I lost you." He hesitates. "Don't you know how much I love you?"

What did he just say? Oh, those words are magic! And how long have I waited to hear them? I take a deep, steadying breath. "I love you, too."

We stare at each other for long moments. I am happy. I am stricken. To have this truth laid bare, given voice and presence at this moment, is maddening. I knew it all along, sensed it to be so, and yet neither of us has spoken these words for the entire time we have been together. To do so now only deepens the misgivings I have about making this journey.

"It's because I love you that I cannot make this promise." I shake my head, thinking again about how selfish I am suddenly feeling. "I think perhaps we need to stop this endeavor. I think we need to turn back."

He shakes his head immediately. "We're not turning back. Why are you even suggesting it? You were the one who wanted to do this."

"I was, but I made a mistake. It's too dangerous."

"It's exactly as dangerous today as it was yesterday and the day before." His anger is apparent. "So what is this really about?"

I can't meet his steady gaze. "I don't want to be the reason that something happens to you. I don't want to put you at risk because of my insistence on uncovering my past. It's not that important."

He sits back, studying me. "What do your instincts tell you? What does your *inish* say?"

"I'm not sure."

"Yes, you are. You rely on your instincts as much as I do. Wasn't it your *inish* that told you to embark on this search in the first place—to find your father and learn the truth?"

I nod. "But I might have been mistaken."

"What does your *inish* tell you now? Be honest with yourself. What is it saying? Step back from the risks and look at it closely. Does it say to turn back?"

"I can't stand knowing that something might happen to you! I won't be able to live with myself if things go wrong. If you're hurt . . ."

"What. Does. Your. *Inish*. Say!"

He is practically shouting. I quit talking and look inward at what I am feeling, at what is speaking to me. No contemplating Harrow or Auris. No being in love and being loved back. But something else. *Is* there something else?

I see it then, peeking from the dark corner into which I have shoved it. I close my eyes against its presence. I cannot speak the words I know I must.

Harrow waits. I stay silent, head lowered with my eyes still closed.

Because the *inish* tells me I need to go. It tells me I must risk what threatens and discover the truth if I am ever to be at peace.

THE SUBMERSIBLE IS NOT VERY LARGE—ONLY ENOUGH SPACE FOR six—and with Harrow and me as passengers and Zedlin, Adderon, Crans, and Porlis as crew, we are at capacity. Our transport is odd, to say the least. It is almost entirely transparent, a series of three bubbles attached horizontally: one where the pilot and copilot sit at the steering and power controls, a second where passengers sit, and a third where the remainder of the crew monitors and operates the propulsion unit. The three are connected so that any of us can pass back and forth from one pod to another, although Harrow and I are instructed to stay in our seats at all times with our safety restraints firmly in place. We do as we are told, placing our *inish* staffs on the floor between us. We are cautioned that the currents can be strong, the lake waters rough, and our safety could be compromised if we try to loosen the restraints and move about.

I have the curious feeling of being in a very large fishbowl.

We set out from one of the Water Sprite tri-pads: launching sites that are anchored just offshore and used to house and repair the submersibles. Until you are right on top of them, they appear to be islands overgrown with vegetation. But once atop one, you become quickly aware that you are standing on something much harder and firmer than ground. There are hatchways leading down into the waters, to compartments and storage pods. In some tri-pads, I am told, whole villages reside.

"Don't the Goblins know about these?" I ask at one point. "Can't they build them, too? Aren't the Sprites afraid the Goblins will attack them underwater?"

He shakes his head. "The Goblins lack the skill and the *inish* to do much of anything that doesn't rely on fire and iron. They are primitive compared with other Fae—which is another reason why they hate us so. Their *inish* is poorly developed, and their understanding of it is limited. This is why gaining possession of Human technology is so important to them."

"Danger from Goblins is part of life," Zedlin opines, as if offering wisdom. But his flippant attitude disappears when he sees the look on my face. "We reduce the chances of encountering them as best we can. Our submersibles travel underwater and cannot be easily detected. Goblins rely on their surface craft and cannot find us when we go deep. The tri-pads are movable, and we reposition them on a regular basis. Unless the Goblins get right up on top of one, a tri-pad appears to be just another ordinary island."

Of which there are many along the lakeshore in this part of Viridian, Harrow goes on to explain. Hundreds of all sizes and shapes, the fake impossible to distinguish from the real. These islands have proven to be nature's gift to the Water Sprites, who can live among them almost invisibly. Now and then one of the islands breaks its anchors and has to be resecured, and very infrequently the artificial buoyancy fails and the pad sinks, but escape is simple enough. These are water people, after all, and their ability to live as long as they choose underwater, breathing through their gills, negates any danger of drowning.

"We are in greater danger on land," the boy continues. "We can't be out of the water for more than six days at a time without reimmersion—and staying dry even that long is pushing things."

I experience another surprise once we get under way and our submersible begins to move into deeper waters. While Harrow and I sit warm and dry in the center compartment, the front and rear compartments slowly begin to flood. At first I think they are leaking, and I look around quickly, searching for a crack. But Harrow quickly points out that this is how Water Sprites prefer to travel when underwater. It is more uncomfortable for them to be confined in an air-filled compartment than in one filled with water—their natural element.

It feels odd to be this exposed, but it also allows for clear views of everything surrounding us. While Roughlin Wake is only a lake and not an ocean, there are vistas on all sides in its surprisingly clear waters. There are no reefs but there are grasses and plants and thousands of fish and other forms of life. I can see much farther out into the distance than I would have thought possible from the surface. There is a clear sense of being in another world entirely. The uniformity of colors particularly catches my attention. Down here, the world is predominantly blue and gray, with spots of bright color from fish and sea plants. Above, the world is much more varied, from the yellow sands of the wastelands to the lush greens of Viridian.

I sit beside Harrow and we look out through the clear skin of the plastek, our conversation mostly confined to Harrow identifying what we are seeing of life underwater. I notice that the propulsion unit on our craft makes surprisingly little noise. It offers up a dim humming sound but otherwise is silent. I ask how it works, and he says that the unit swallows water at the front of its intake pipes and spits it out at the rear of the vessel, propelling us ahead. Valves can be opened or closed to maneuver, and fins and a rudder facilitate control over the steering.

Mostly, he adds, movement and control rely on the skill of the pilot. Zedlin has been training in submersibles since he was ten.

His instincts and his quick decision-making have earned him a widespread reputation as one of the best.

We travel through the day. I have no way of knowing how fast we are going. At times it seems we are going faster than your standard watercraft. I also have no way of knowing how far we have gone, because everything looks pretty much the same. When I ask Harrow about this, he tells me we change speeds as the currents direct and our trip to Harbor's End will take us somewhere around six to seven hours. As for the sameness of our surroundings as we travel, he says not to worry. Water Sprites have learned to see identifying landmarks that land dwellers would not even notice.

The hours pass slowly. We are provided with food and water by Porlis, who comes forward to feed us from her place in the rear bubble. She is small and slight, and her features are striking. She wears her black hair long and loose, and her fingers are so delicate that they appear entirely flexible. The other three members of the crew are older boys, thicker in build and well muscled. They mostly stay in their assigned pod, which causes me to wonder how Porlis got out of hers. When I watch her emerge a second time to take away our trays, I see her merge with the plastek wall and just appear to melt through its surface.

"Their magic and their physical makeup allow them to do that," Harrow explains, noticing my surprise. "While of a different sort than ours, it has power of its own."

Finally, we draw near our destination and Zedlin slows our approach. I cannot see any real difference in our surroundings, but Harrow assures me we are close. Then we stop altogether, and through the skin of the bubbles I can make out a huge, shadowy apparition just ahead, an indistinct form suspended deep in the lake waters.

Zedlin melts through the wall of the pilot housing and comes back to us. "Harbor's End is just ahead. But something new has been added since I was here last—something that sits right across the harbor mouth. You can just make it out. Whatever it is, I don't think we want to draw its attention. I'd guess it's one of their mechanical creatures—and this one has a predator's look. It was probably placed there to guard the harbor entrance. Regular traffic would carry identity signals, but intruders will be destroyed. Still, we have to get past it, whatever it is. We can't fight it; it would crush us if those jaws got a grip. Our safest choice is to drop down near the bottom and slide under it. We might escape notice if we go that deep. We can lower our speed, try to hide our presence."

Harrow shakes his head. "I don't much care for being down so deep. What if it does track us? Then what do we do?"

"Pick up speed again quickly and get clear before it can stop us." Zedlin frowns. "The only other option is to surface and let you swim past it. But I wouldn't risk it."

Not to mention that I cannot swim. I say nothing; I wait on Harrow. He will know what we should do. But whatever that turns out to be, he also knows I am not turning back.

"Take us deep," he tells Zedlin.

Zedlin bleeds back through the plastek wall and takes his seat at the controls. We drop to the lake floor. I can't tell how far down that is, but I can still make out the jaws of the huge thing floating not that far above us. As we inch forward, I keep my eyes on it, watching for unusual movement, almost hypnotized by the willowy, lethargic way it hangs there, rolling slightly in the current.

Then suddenly I notice we have stopped moving. Harrow leans forward abruptly. "Zedlin!" he hisses. The boy is working the controls frantically, but nothing seems to be helping. "Something has hold of us!" Harrow snaps, recognizing the danger. "We're caught fast!"

Now I panic. I glance quickly upward to where the jaws continue their rhythmic dance. But then abruptly the guardian begins lowering. We have been detected, and it's coming for us. I watch it descend in the same leisurely fashion—slow, unhurried, reacting to programming, prepared to carry out the work it was built to do. It knows we are trapped; it knows we are intruders. Its intentions seem pretty clear. Those jaws will close on our craft and crush it— with us inside.

Then suddenly the skin of our submersible begins to ooze out-ward a thick clear liquid that releases from hundreds of tiny pores and quickly coats the entirety of the three pods. The lake waters do not wash it away; it clings with sticky determination.

Harrow turns to me. "Zedlin's released a fluid that will make the submersible so slick it will be almost impossible to grip. He thinks that might help escape whatever has hold of us." He looks doubtful. "But I don't know that it's enough to save us."

Just as he says this, however, the submersible breaks free of whatever impedes it and begins to move forward again. The dark shadow of our predator hovers over us, descending more swiftly in response, huge and implacable. We are no longer held immobile, but the jaws of our pursuer are opening. We will be seized and torn apart. I feel scared, but angry, too. I will not sit by idly while it hap-pens. I will not die trapped like this.

I seize my *inish* staff from where it rests against my seat and grip it tightly. A hiss of fury, a deep pull from within where my magic stirs to life, and the staff glows dark blue. Harrow is shouting some-thing at me, but I refuse to be distracted. I fix my attention on the descending jaws and send my magic off in two sheets of black light that wrap those jaws about, binding them in place. The predator thrashes and twists frantically, but it cannot free itself. Sparks shower from its joints like fiery water bugs, and the monster goes still. Slowly, it begins to sink. We are moving ahead now, the hum of the propulsion unit increasing, though I don't think we are mov-ing quickly enough. Our attacker falls to the lake bottom and lies still, but we are still badly exposed.

"Auris!" Harrow calls, and I see the tip of his staff glowing. I lock into his *inish* with mine.

In response to our magic, the submersible shoots forward with a huge lurch that nearly throws me from my seat. We shoot ahead into darkness—the breath knocked out of us, the momentary prox-imity of a barely avoided death sending a palpable chill down my spine. But the jaws are behind us.

The whole effort takes maybe a minute—a surreal escape from

what seemed inescapable. I release my *inish* and collapse in my seat, drenched in sweat and riddled with fear. Our end was certain, yet we have escaped once again. Harrow looks over at me, his own magic leashed, and nods his shared understanding of what I am feeling.

We are saved from the mechanical predator, but somewhere monitors will be registering the malfunction of their watchdog at the harbor entrance. Soldiers will be dispatched. By the time they arrive, however, the magic will have dissipated and the submersible will be long gone.

For the moment we are safe.

Once back on land again, my search for the truth can resume.

TWENTY-FIVE

Now that we have reached the shores of the Human world, my sense of urgency increases. I have returned to the land and the people I once thought were mine—to everything I have been forced to recognize as false—leaving behind any real safety. I feel myself to be something of a chameleon—able to be something more or less than what I appear. On the surface I look Human, but beneath my skin I am Fae. I am not part of this world any longer.

Zedlin steers the submersible through the harbor waters at a speed that allows us to become a virtually silent presence. We have escaped the mechanical jaws and their promise of a crushing death, but there are other ways to die if we are discovered, and other dangers that wait. The harbor is a busy place, with ships and men at work. But Zedlin says there is a landing point he has used before where some small expectation of safety is possible. We need only find it and take shelter beneath heavy boughs and shadows that overlap the waters of the Roughlin where they brush up against the shore. There he and his crew and the submersible will be concealed until our return.

Harrow and I must go on foot from there into the city of Harbor's End to find the place Trinch has marked on the map—the home where my father last lived. How far we can trust this map—or Trinch, for that matter—is up for debate. But we trust both because we must; they are all we have to rely on.

I glance at Harrow, but his strong features are calm and reveal no hint of worry. His steady presence is reassuring, and I borrow a modicum of his confidence for myself. We will find our way. Together we will succeed.

We leave the submersible through a topside hatch that I don't even know is there until Zedlin somehow triggers its release. Harrow goes first, springing up to grab the sides of the opening and pull himself through. He reaches down for me and hauls me up after him. We crouch down amid the shadows and the overhanging branches of a cedar, and then with Harrow leading we step off the submersible where it rests against the lake bank and onto dry land.

We are now on our own.

We look at each other in a measuring way. We are both dressed in Human clothes brought with us from the Fae storerooms where such things are stockpiled. Fae ventures into Human territory are uncommon but not unknown, so the Fae have learned to come prepared. We both wear coats with hoods; it is cooler here than I expected—much cooler than in Viridian. We wear gloves and boots both for warmth and to hide Harrow's hands. He pulls up his hood to shadow his face. Someone would have to stand directly in front of him to discover the truth about his identity, but still we have to take steps to see that this doesn't happen, because if he is found out, we are finished.

"We have one thing working in our favor," Harrow tells me. "I didn't say anything before, but I know this city. I have been here a number of times in my duties as a Sylvan Watcher, and I have spent enough time inside the city proper to know my way around. We have the map from Trinch, but we don't need to rely on it completely. Harbor's End is laid out geometrically. All the buildings—homes and offices—are numbered sequentially. I think we can find the home where your mother and father lived before they were taken by the Ministry."

We set out as the sun is sinking into the horizon, walking along the outskirts of Harbor's End. It would be quicker to pass directly through the city, but that way there is also a greater chance of discovery. So we stay on the byways—as Trinch's map and Harrow's familiarity with the city allow us to do—encountering only a limited number of passersby as we proceed. Almost no one even looks at us. Everyone is on their way to somewhere else, be it home or work. Our progress is unhindered but cautious. The layout of the city is distinctly Human. Streets and alleyways crisscross the residential areas we pass through in precise geometrical formations—all parallel lines and neat circles. There are houses everywhere, all with the same look, all with fronting lawns and fences and gates and driveways with cars parked in them, some with pets and children's toys in their yards.

I remember none of it, but feel an odd kinship anyway. I lived here once—in neighborhoods like these, with people like these. My memory provides no clear visuals, but I know this nevertheless. It is an odd feeling. Everything is different here than it is in Viridian Deep. There are no lush forests and green glades, no waterfalls and ponds, no meandering paths or tree lanes. Nothing that is even remotely Fae is visible.

Yet I cannot deny that being here almost makes me think I remember such scenes from another time, when I was still little and had not yet become aware that something was wrong in my father's life or that one day I would be sent to the Goblin prisons. But none of it triggers any feelings of nostalgia or helps me recall my past. My life began with my imprisonment, and everything from before then could just as easily belong to someone else.

The twilight deepens and the presence of other people noticeably diminishes. We move more quickly now to reach our destination, no longer quite so worried about being noticed. We have brought our *inish* staffs because we know they are our best protection if we are threatened, though we have been using them like walking sticks in order to deflect unneeded interest. Our plan is tested when a very young boy runs over and asks if he could have a closer look at one. Harrow draws back, but I hand mine over; we can't afford a scene at this point. The boy turns the staff over and over in his hands and then gives it back, grinning madly, looking very much as if he has taken a dare and lived to tell about it, shaking his head as he runs off.

Other than this one incident, we are left alone.

When we finally reach the house we have been sent to find, we find it boarded up and closed away. Clearly, no one lives there. The house is in a state of disrepair, and the yard is overgrown with weeds. We glance at each other in dismay. It is too much to hope that someone would still be living here, I suppose, but we had to start somewhere.

Then I see an old man raking leaves in the yard next door. Why not take a chance and ask him what he can tell me? I walk over and draw his attention. "Do you know what became of the people who were living there?" I point to my old house as he turns.

He frowns, shakes his head, and says, "Don't remember hardly anything about those folks. Didn't ever get to know them well."

But the way he answers suggests that the question makes him uncomfortable, and my instincts tell me he does indeed know something but is uncertain about sharing. I decide to take another chance. "Please, the man and woman who lived there were my parents. I would be grateful for anything you can tell me."

A slight stretching of the truth, but close enough to not count as a lie.

He studies me a moment, then nods slowly. "Okay, then. I have to be careful, you know. It's dangerous to talk about such things, but you don't look like anyone from the Ministry. So I'll tell you what I know if you can prove who you are. You say you're their daughter? Well, you look to be about the right age. Can you tell me your name?"

"Auris," I reply.

"Right you are. I remember you when you were just a squirt. Never heard that name again. Even your mother didn't speak it. She told me you disappeared and she never saw you again. Always wondered about that."

His face is seamed and spotted, and his body bent and withered. I sense he will not be long for this world by the way he holds himself and the feeling I get from standing close. "Do you know what happened to her?" I ask. "And to my father?"

Harrow walks up beside me and stops a safe distance away, his face completely in shadow. The old man gives him a glance. "Friend?" he asks me.

"Husband," I say—maybe because that feels safer, maybe just because I want to hear how it sounds. "Can you tell me your name?"

"I'm Edward. Mostly, people call me Eddie."

I extend my hand and he takes it. We grip hands for a moment, then he releases me and looks down at his shoes. "I have some bad news, I'm afraid. Your father is dead. He was charged with treason for doing some experimental work that was prohibited. Never talked about it with me, but I heard. The Ministry took him away and never brought him back. And we all know what that means."

He trails off.

"And my mother?" I ask.

"Your mother's still about."

"Alive?" This is unexpected.

He nods. "But she keeps quiet about her identity. Calls herself Davinia now. You can find her easy enough. Just walk east to the next neighborhood, go to Thirteenth Street, and look for Number Eight Eleven." He points out the direction he wants us to go. "She lives there—or at least she used to. Haven't seen her for some time."

I thank him for his help and wish him well. He has no idea about my real purpose in coming, but he has given me what I needed. With Harrow in tow, I set out with renewed determination.

What is odd is how hopeful I feel. I know that is probably wishful thinking, but I cannot help but believe that some of it is instinct, telling me an important truth lies ahead if I just keep pushing toward it. My instincts have always been good, and are probably even better now. Finding my *inish* has helped. Harrow and I are kindred in that, both possessed of an undeniable ability to recognize hidden truths and lies, concealed secrets and pretenses.

The neighborhoods of Harbor's End spread out from the center of the city in three directions, fanning away from the harbor. Edward's neighborhood sits on the northern edge, so it seems likely Davinia's does the same. We depart through a neatly tended green space and arrive at the next neighborhood over. We walk into a steadily deepening darkness, reading house numbers by streetlights, proceeding quietly through the gloom. We encounter no one. My *mother*, I keep repeating to myself. My other mother—the one who raised me in childhood. Once Margrete, now Davinia. What has her life been like?

When we find the house, there are lights on within, and movement as someone passes back and forth behind drawn curtains. I ask Harrow to let me go in alone. I sense Davinia will respond better to me if I approach her by myself. Then I hand him my staff. Better if he keeps it for me, I tell him. I don't want it to distract or frighten her. I want this to be about nothing but the two of us. He agrees to both requests, then looks about and says he will watch for me from where he will not be seen. Where that might be amid crowded houses and open yards I cannot imagine, but I am not about to question him. His skills at hiding in plain sight are formidable.

I go up to the door and knock. There is a short pause, and then the door opens. The woman who stands before me is a stranger, but she is old enough to be my mother, so I ask, "Are you Davinia?"

She nods, a strange look crossing her face as she stares at me. I think now that she might be the woman in the final memory the Seers recovered from my past. It is all I can do to continue.

"Were you once Margrete?" I add softly.

She emits a small gasp and retreats a step. "Auris? Is it really you?"

I smile and nod. "It's me."

She holds out her arms and we fall into an intense embrace. I can feel her shaking, hear her sobbing. "I never thought I would see you again! I thought I had lost you forever." She breaks down completely and for long moments cannot speak. Then, "I'm sorry. I'm so sorry. I couldn't stop them. Those soldiers—they wouldn't listen."

She clutches me tighter, tears streaming down her cheeks. "Thank God, thank God, you're safe!"

She brings me into the house, and we sit next to each other on the sofa. She is gray-haired and heavy about the middle, but she seems healthy enough. Her face is surprisingly young, and her eyes bright through the lingering wash of her tears. She puts her hand on my face, as if seeking reassurance that I am not a mirage. She holds me at arm's length to study me, shaking her head and smiling.

"Where have you been all these years?" she asks at last.

"In a prison," I answer.

She shakes her head. "After they took Dennis away, I was afraid they might send *him* there. But I think the director of the project he was working on just had him killed. I've always hated that man, and I never understood how Dennis could work for someone like that. Evil to his core—you could see it in his eyes. He was the devil himself."

"Can you tell me something about my father?" I ask. "What was he doing that got him taken away and killed? What was he doing with his experiments? I have almost no memories left of my childhood, but I do remember you telling Father that maybe you should send me back to somewhere. And I remember that he was giving me medicines. Why was he doing that? Can you tell me anything?"

She considers her answer for a long time, seemingly trying to decide what she should say. I imagine the shock of my appearance has set her back more than a little, and she takes her time, looking not at me but at the floor.

"This isn't easy," she says finally. "These are memories it took me a long time to forget. Or at least a long time to put aside, so that they did not haunt me perpetually. You were my precious child—not mine by birth, but by chance and good fortune. I could not have children. Dennis knew this, so when you were brought to him by this Fae man and offered for sale, he knew I had to have you. I saw you, and I knew. You were meant to be my daughter. Dennis and I agreed to pay the Fae man his money, and we took you into our lives. We loved you dearly, and there was never a moment of regret. Even when Dennis discovered the circumstances of your birth, I still loved you. You did not look or in any way act as if you were a Fae child, so I just pretended you were ours all along."

I reach out for her hands and grip them tightly. "I was yours," I reassure her. "I was always yours. But you knew about my birth mother?"

She smiles sadly. "Dennis told me. He told me you were her child, born after he had helped the Fae woman to escape and now brought back to us. I was shocked, but grateful to have you. There were no obstacles to our taking you in as our own. We gave you a Fae name but raised you as the Human you appeared—until you reached your teen years and began to exhibit small signs of your birth mother's blood. I was so scared. I was afraid you might change as you grew, show signs of your Fae nature, and then they would take you away from me and experiment on you as they did your mother. You were my child, and I knew I would do anything to protect you."

A shiver goes through me. "But I didn't change. So what happened to prevent it?"

"Dennis worked as a geneticist for a division of the Ministry that specialized in uncovering and neutralizing threats from alien creatures—their words, not ours. Part of what he did was to attempt to uncover the specifics of the genetic makeup of such creatures. He was considered a shining light in those days—a man whose future in the field was endlessly promising. He had access to drugs and chemicals that could alter looks and even behavior. He had been working on their development from the beginning.

"When you finally started manifesting signs of the physical change we had always feared, he started giving you medicines that he said would put a stop to it. They must have worked, because you always stayed the same afterward—and so stayed safe. But they did have an effect on your memory. We had hoped it was temporary, but . . ."

She looks suddenly heartbroken, so I hasten to change the subject. "Why was Father arrested?" I ask instead. "What did he do?"

Her face turns hard. "I never knew for sure. They never told me. Some nonsense about treason—some trumped-up charge that served as an excuse to discredit him. But I knew the truth. It was his superior, the director of his agency, who arranged it. He was furious at Dennis for keeping you from him—for keeping you hidden—so he determined to get rid of Dennis. And that's just what he did."

"What about you? I remember seeing you both taken . . ."

"We were, but they didn't seem to know what to do with me. After a period of questioning, they let me go. I tried to find Dennis, but no one would tell me anything until finally a man I knew who worked for the government came to me in secret and told me he was dead. Executed by the director himself."

"And what happened to me? Where was I?"

"I intended to take you away—to hide you with a woman I knew who would see that you were looked after—but the director's goons found us first and you disappeared. I tried to find you just as I tried to find Dennis after I was released, but it was pointless. No one would speak of you. I got the feeling after a while that no one actually knew what had become of you—that maybe it wasn't the government that took you after all. That you might have escaped them and fled. Don't you remember anything? You were old enough at the time. You must remember *something*."

"I'm sorry, but I don't. I only have a few memories. One of them is of the front door of our home being broken down and a squad of soldiers barging in. You and Father try to stop them, and I . . ." I shake my head. "I don't know. I don't know what happened after, but somehow I ended up in the prisons. I remained there until only a few months ago."

"Where have you been living?" my mother asks me curiously. "Why didn't you come looking for me?"

"I didn't know where I was from. I didn't know if you were even still alive," I answer. Which is the truth.

"It must have been hard, Auris. Losing your parents, being locked up in some prison, knowing so little about your past." Her features are ragged, but then they brighten. "Yet here you are now. Here *we* are. You're staying, aren't you?"

I can't, of course. I don't belong here. In truth, I don't want to be here a moment longer than I have to. My connection with my mother is tenuous at best. She is a figment of memory, a bit of my almost completely forgotten past—a past I think it would be best to leave behind. I belong in Viridian Deep. I belong with my new family—with Harrow.

"I have to leave, Mother," I tell her softly, hands on her shoulders to steady her. "I have another family now and a husband who waits for me. I have to go home to them."

I am lying again. But only, I tell myself, to persuade her I am well looked after so she will be reassured.

She stares at me for long moments, and then she nods. "Of course. Of course you have found a place for yourself. But will you come to see me again?"

This much I can promise, and so I do. Then I say, "I have to ask you something before I go. It sounds like you forgave Father for his part in bringing me into this world, but was it terrible to learn the truth? Was he able to make you understand why he did it?"

She stares at me. "What are you talking about?"

I blink in confusion. "That Father slept with my biological mother. That he is my birth father. Was that hard for you to accept?"

Now she is not just surprised; she is furious. "Who told you that? Dennis loved me, and I loved him. We rescued your mother; that is all. Besides, she was already pregnant when she arrived!"

I hear the words, but do not yet process them entirely. "Then Dennis isn't my birth father? But I was told . . ."

I cut off the rest of what I am about to say. Because of course I was told by Ancrow, who has repeatedly lied to me. Ancrow, who apparently has lied about this, as well.

"I'm sorry," I say. "I must have misunderstood. But if Dennis was not my biological father, do you know who is? Who got my mother pregnant?"

"Who do you think?"

I am beginning to see the truth. "The agency director," I guess. "Am I right?"

"Yes, Auris. The Devil incarnate. He impregnated her—supposedly in the interests of science so he could have a half-Fae child to experiment upon. It was for that child—for you, as much as for her—that Dennis rescued her. He did what was right to help you and your birth mother, and he paid the price for it. We all did."

I feel a chill run through me as something else becomes apparent—something so horrible I can barely stand to think about it.

But my mother is still talking. "He did something else for your mother, too. The director had implanted a tracking chip under her skin that would allow him to follow her. Dennis believed they intended to allow her to give birth to you and then send her back to wherever she had come from while keeping you. And Dennis knew what would happen then."

I blanch in recognition.

"Why keep one Fae for experimentation when you could have an entire nation to choose from?" my mother continues.

Of course. The Ministry would follow my mother into Viridian Deep, using the implant as a beacon that would show them the way. Ancrow would inadvertently become the invitation they needed to enter, and once there they would be able to destroy

Viridian Deep and the Fae people down to the last man, woman, and child unless they gave up the secret of their magic.

I can barely tolerate the shock I feel. But there is one final question that demands an answer.

"What was the Ministry director's name?"

"Allensby," she says, and my darkest fear is confirmed.

TWENTY-SIX

ALLENSBY.
My father.

I am torn between wanting to scream in horror and cry in despair. Of all the possible outcomes of my quest for the truth, this is the worst. It doesn't matter if it was rape or artificial insemination or something else—my mother was violated, and by Allensby. The very man who claimed to know so little about me when we last met. Ancrow and I have had our differences. She has lied to me more than once and apparently is lying still. But no one should be treated as she was. Just the thought of it is horrifying, and the fact that it was *this* man who has been revealed as my father is all but unbearable. I don't know what to do about it. I don't know how I am supposed to live with it.

I am still staring at Margrete, my face horror-stricken, my mind whirling with the realization of what this means. I cannot bring myself to speak about it with my mother. Maybe I cannot speak about it at all, but I know I will have to try when I rejoin Harrow.

Dr. Allensby is my father.

My father is a man I despise—a man I think I could kill for what he has done: impregnating Ancrow, causing Khoury's death. Trying to use me. I can still see his lying face as he speaks to me when I am held captive—twisting everything, shading the truth, using deception to turn me to his purpose. He claimed to know next to nothing about me. He insisted he wanted to help me. But he never cared about me in the least. He is an evil man. Yet he is also my father.

It is a nightmare I cannot yet make myself believe.

It fills me with shame and a strange self-loathing. If my father is a monster, then I am a monster's child. And what does that mean for me down the road? Can I ever be truly free of such a creature? Can I ever be sure that his dark blood has not infused me to one day surface and claim me?

I wish I had something to smash. My father's face would do for a start. Dennis and Margrete did their best to save my mother and then to help me, but all the time my real father was intent on destroying us all.

Abruptly, the front door bursts open and Ministry soldiers pour into the room. I am still in the middle of digesting the fact that Allensby is my father, so I act too slowly. By the time I am on my feet, heavy hands have seized me. And it is too late to summon my *inish* in my defense, because a few feet away, other hands have hauled my mother off the couch. A knife is pressed up against her throat. The rest of the soldiers ring us tightly, their short-barreled spitfires held ready.

A familiar figure follows them in. "Welcome home, Auris," my father greets me. "Stand very still, please. The knife at your mother's throat might slip if you act irresponsibly. Just take a deep breath and stay calm."

I have no choice. Even if I were to free myself and summon my *inish*, it wouldn't be in time to save my mother. I cannot risk her life. Not even to save my own.

"How did you find me?" I ask.

"When you were in the prison, recovering from your injuries—

for which I treated you, just as I said—I took the opportunity to insert a small tracking device into your body."

"Like you did to my mother."

"The Fae woman? That was twenty years ago. Our technology has improved immeasurably since then. Her chip was inserted beneath the skin, so removing it presented no difficulty. This time I inserted a much smaller tracker into your bloodstream, so that it moves about with your blood. Very difficult to find, let alone remove. That assured me you could be found if you returned to our world, which I strongly believed you would. Whatever protects you in the Fae world would not do so here."

"But you couldn't wait for me to return on my own. So you sent Goblins to bring me back, didn't you? That's how they found me."

He nods. "But now I don't have to rely on Goblins or tracking devices anymore. Now I have you personally."

Something about the Goblins finding me twice is wrong. In spite of the danger I am in, I need to know. "But there were two sets of Goblins who came to find me, and the first three came *before* you captured me. I wasn't chipped at that point, so how did you find me then?"

"I don't know what you're talking about. I only ever sent one set to find you."

"But when I first escaped . . ."

"When you first escaped, I had no idea you were even in that prison. It was only when you were recaptured that I discovered the truth." His voice is tight with dismissal. The very fact that he had been ignorant of my original imprisonment seemed to annoy him. "Up until then, I thought you were dead. But once I knew where you had been, it was easy enough to get you back by capturing your boyfriend. And introducing an added bit of insurance, in case you escaped once more—as you seem so adept at doing. But you can rest assured you will not find a way to escape again!"

My thoughts are a whirl as I try to think of a way out of this. Harrow is still out there, somewhere close. But what can he do with so many soldiers surrounding my mother and me?

Margrete is sobbing in despair, her eyes squeezed tightly shut to avoid confronting what is happening to us. "Please," she begs.

Allensby spares her a glance. "No need to cry," he tells her. "We only came for your daughter. You will be released once we have secured what we need from her."

"Don't hurt her!" she gasps.

Allensby looks at me. "No one will be harmed if she takes me back to where she came from. Otherwise, I will hurt you both. Quite a lot, in fact—starting with you, Margrete. Are you paying attention, Auris?"

I want to kill him. I think of how quickly I could do this, summoning magic that would choke the life out of him in seconds. But I know in my heart that, however fast I might be, it would not be fast enough with a knife at my mother's throat and spitfires all around us.

A shadow appears in the doorway, and all heads turn. An old man is standing there, staring inside. Eddie, I realize; Margrete's former neighbor. What is he doing here? He looks around with a scowl as Allensby turns and asks, "Who are you?"

"I might ask you the same question."

"None of your business. Wherever you came from, go back!"

"First, tell me what you think you are doing with these two women?"

"Ministry business!" Allensby snaps. "And if you choose to press the matter, you will find out more than you wish. Get moving."

I want to tell Eddie he should go, that he can't help; that no one can. And then I see something in Eddie's eyes . . .

Harrow!

The old man takes a few further steps inside, shaking his head. "I don't think you understand. That lady your soldier threatens with a knife is my friend. You need to let her go."

Allensby looks at him in disbelief. "I could have you killed for interfering!"

No reply. Eddie looks confused now. My father walks right up to him and puts a hand on his shoulder. "Time to go. I won't ask . . ."

Eddie seizes Allensby and whips him about so he is facing the room with a knife held against *his* neck. Then Eddie disappears as if he was never there (which he wasn't, of course) and a green-skinned, leafy-haired Harrow has replaced him, holding my father fast.

The entire room backs away. A monster. An alien. A Fae. Something terrible and godless.

Even my mother shrinks away.

But who wouldn't? With amber eyes glowing and pointed teeth bared, he looks like an avenging angel. Fury radiates off him, and I find myself working hard not to smile.

Allensby tries to say something, but Harrow clamps his free hand over his prisoner's mouth, yanks his head back, and looks around the room. "If you want to keep this man alive, stay right where you are and don't move," he commands. "If you disobey me, I will bite his head off! Auris, bring your mother and walk over to me."

I cannot believe he is going to get away with this, but as I step over to my mother, the soldier moves the knife away from her neck. I hustle my mother away from him, watching everywhere at once, and walk us both to stand close to Harrow.

He doesn't look at me. "Go out the door and turn right. Then run to the end of the block and wait."

I don't argue. This is not the time for objections. I lead my mother out the doorway, and together we rush as fast as Margrete can manage to the end of the block.

When we turn to look back, everything is quiet. "Do you have friends nearby that you can trust?" I ask her.

She nods, still distraught, but glances back down the block. "Was that your husband?"

I nod, and I see tears fill her eyes.

"Oh, Auris. He loves you, I can tell. Just look what he risked to save you. But . . ."

"He doesn't look Human?" I bite back. "He looks scary? Alien?"

She looks startled. "No! I mean, it surprised me at first, but . . .

It's not that he's Fae. It just . . . It feels like I've lost you all over again, to a world I can never enter. And right when I have just found you!"

She starts to cry once more, and I bend over to kiss her cheek. "I'm sorry, Mother, but you need to hide. As you said, we can't take you with us. Hide with your friends and, when you can, move out of the city." I embrace her quickly. "Perhaps one day we'll find each other again."

"I hope so. I love you, Auris." Then she looks at me, still hesitating. "How will you . . . ?"

Abruptly, her house fills with blinding light. All the downstairs windows blow out and smoke pours through the glassless openings. Harrow bursts into view, leaping through the doorway and racing up the street toward us.

"Go!" I tell my mother. "Run!"

She does so, as fast as her age and legs will carry her. She calls back to me once more, but I cannot make out what she is saying. Then she disappears into the darkness. I know I will never see her again. I wait for Harrow to reach me, knowing already that any escape might be impossible. When he reaches me, he hands me my *inish* staff. "Thought I should leave them outside if I wanted to fool those soldiers into believing I was Eddie. You could tell it was me, though, couldn't you?"

"It was your eyes," I tell him. "Once I took a good look."

He laughs. "Only you would know."

Then we both start running, heading back the way we came, putting as much distance as we can—as fast as we are able—between ourselves and Allensby.

"How did you do it?" I ask. "How did you make yourself look like Eddie?"

"I didn't. It was an *inish* glamour."

"*Inish* can do that?"

"*Mine* can," he corrects me. "You still have some lessons to learn."

Fair enough. I grin like a mad thing. "Still, attempting that deception, walking right in there? That was so brave."

"I had to do something, and it was all I could think of."

I go quiet then for a few minutes as we pass once more through my adoptive parents' old neighborhood. "What happened back there?" I ask at last. "What was that explosion?"

"I triggered a flashbang I had hidden on me and tossed it into the middle of the room. Then I went out the door—helped a bit by the force of the explosion. It was supposed to be a distraction, but the room seemed to amplify the explosion. I don't know what happened to those still inside. There wasn't time to look."

"No, I don't imagine there was." I laugh at the sheer ridiculousness of what he did, the utter bravado. I am amazed that we are still alive and free. "The man you grabbed," I tell him, unable to hold it back any longer. "That was my father!"

We talk back and forth as we run, retracing our steps toward the docks and the safety of the submersible. I use the time to relate what Margrete had told me, up until I disappeared after the Ministry break-in. I explain how Dennis and Margrete worked to raise and protect me right up until then. I don't quite succeed in staying calm when I get to the part about who my real father is, losing myself in rage that quickly devolves into tears.

We stop running, and Harrow holds me as I sob. He whispers what I need to hear—that I am not my father and never will be; that his choices were his own and do not define me in any way; that his time in my life is over and we will never speak of him again—save perhaps to Ancrow. I have revealed to him—because I know I must—that she has lied to me once more. Dennis might have sheltered her and raised me, but he never slept with her, and he is not my father.

"We will confront Mother with the truth when we get back to Viridian Deep," he promises darkly. "And we will demand to know what *else* she is hiding."

But I don't want this. We can confront her, I tell him, but that has to be it. I do not seek any further recriminations. Ancrow must have suffered far more than we can imagine at Allensby's hands—and been forced to live with that shame for all these years. She lied to us because the truth was too painful to speak. To have undergone what she did, to have endured what she suffered at the hands of this loathsome man, must have all but destroyed her. It is likely she lied to me about my father because she couldn't bear admitting the truth. She must have considered that a lie like this would hurt no one, and that having me believe Dennis was my father would help make what she did in giving me up feel better.

Harrow agrees. Then he releases me from his embrace and starts running again, guiding us toward the harbor and the submersible. He sees our quest as over and wants us safely returned to Viridian Deep. I want this, too, but something is troubling me. I have rushed through these past several hours so quickly that I am still not thinking clearly. But I know that something is wrong, and I have to straighten out my thoughts sufficiently so that I can determine what it is.

It doesn't take much. Abruptly, I remember and pull up short, my thoughts coming together in a bitter rush of recognition—which quickly coalesces into a horrible realization.

Harrow turns at once and comes back to me. "What is it?" he asks. "Something else?"

"Something else," I repeat woodenly. "Back at the house, before you saved me, Allensby revealed that he had inserted a chip in Ancrow so she could be tracked later. Then he hinted that he had done the same thing to me when I was wounded and recaptured. What if it is his intention to use me as he intended to use Ancrow, to find a way into Viridian Deep? That I came to him as I did must have looked like a shortcut. The chip must have been how he found me at Margrete's. Now he will use it to find me in Viridian Deep."

Harrow shakes his head. "How do you know he is telling the truth about the tracker? How do you know he didn't find you some other way?"

"Because I know!" I snap angrily. "This monster is my father. It is how he thinks and acts—even toward his own child."

He slows to a walk as we near the docks. "Wait, just wait." He exhales sharply. "You're speculating, Auris. Just because he told you . . ."

"For the first day or so after my capture, I was unconscious. He looked after me, bandaging my wounds. He purposely reminded me of this. He could easily have inserted a tracker then."

"But wouldn't your instincts have warned you . . ."

"Harrow, listen to me!"

He stops talking when he sees the look on my face. I need him to hear what I am saying. I need him to see clearly what I have realized.

"Think a moment. This is a man who violated my mother for no other reason than to create a child he could study as a lab rat! This is a man who let his colleagues use my mother as they wanted under the pretense of scientific investigation. This is a man who lied to me about everything, and pretended to be my friend when he had me under his control. Is there anything this man will not do to use me or any other Fae who fall into his hands if it furthers his research?"

Harrow hesitates a beat. "But if you are right, then you have been carrying this chip around inside you for days now. Why hasn't he come for us earlier?"

"He did. He sent the Goblins after me, right before we left. He needs me, because he wants me to guide him into Viridian Deep. Benith and Ronden both told me that Humans cannot penetrate Viridian Deep even if they have a map. But now we know that Allensby has something better—me! And even if he never gets his hands on me to guide him there—which I would never do!—how long will it be before he finds a way around the magic? The wards might be able to turn back one missile, but what about a hundred? What about an entire invading army? If I go back, try and hide behind the wards, he will find a way around them eventually, and then I will be putting all of Viridian in danger!"

I take a deep, steadying breath. "The Fae are my people, Harrow. I can't betray them. Which is what I will be doing if I return to Viridian carrying a tracker."

"But you also can't stay here if they can find you whenever they want," he points out. "If there is a tracking device inside you, you're not safe anywhere. But at least in Viridian you will be behind the wards, and have friends who will try to protect you. Maybe one of the Fae will know a way to remove the device. We should at least ask. We have healers who might know a way."

Maybe. Maybe not. As Ronden has already assured me, any Human attempts to penetrate Viridian Deep from outside our boundaries cannot succeed, thanks to the obfuscating nature of the magic that protects it. But the fact remains that a tracking device operating from *inside* those barriers will act as a clear beacon—which is precisely what I will become if I return. I will be providing the Humans with an open invitation to follow that beacon to its source. Every day I remain inside those boundaries is a day I place everyone living in my Homeland in danger.

I cannot live with that.

But Harrow is right. If I stay behind, out in the Human world—unprotected by either friends or magic—Allensby will have a sure way of finding me no matter when I go. Or if the flashbang eliminated him, there will be another like him.

I am doomed either way, whatever I do.

Stalemate.

TWENTY-SEVEN

WE STARE AT EACH OTHER IN SILENCE AS I PONDER WHAT TO
do. There is no easy choice, given what my father has told
me. I can't be sure he is lying. I can't be sure what is true.

Finally, I take hold of Harrow's hand and squeeze it reassuringly.
We are standing in the halo of the warehouse lights, and I guide
him into the deep shadows, where he waits for me to speak.

"I can't go back with you," I tell him. "I can't risk having the
Humans track me there—if they haven't done so yet. After tonight,
if he survived the explosion, Allensby will come for all of us."

"He will try," Harrow agrees. "But as both Ronden and Benith
told you, he will not find us easy to overcome. Even if Humans were
to find their way to Viridian because you carry a tracking device
somewhere inside your body—which, given the magic that protects us, seems unlikely—they will find us ready and waiting. They
may have weapons forged in their furnaces, but we are our *own*
weapons, and our *inish* has always been superior to whatever technology they can muster."

I shake my head in disagreement. "Unless what they muster is an army! If they invade Viridian Deep, they will bring war machines and mechanized constructs that will protect Human soldiers from being attacked by *inish* alone. I know this because I have seen a little of it while imprisoned. Armored vehicles were used to track and hunt and kill us when we tried to flee. Mechanical sensors smelled us out of hiding. What they have in their armories in the cities is bound to be much worse. Humans have been at war with one another since the dawn of time. Nothing has changed save one thing—they keep finding better, more efficient ways to kill one another. Even if our people survive, they will never be the same, and Viridian will be ruined."

I pause. I don't want this for the Fae. And I don't want it to happen because of me. Better that I take my chances here. Even if that means death or endless experiments in one of Allensby's labs.

He studies me carefully, those depthless eyes drawing me in, *seducing* me, overpowering my reason. He knows as well as I do what the cost of my staying will be. But I must stay determined, and when I feel that failing, I turn and walk away.

"Why must you persist in doing everything on your own?" Harrow calls after me, bringing me around. "With us, you have a chance. Without us . . ." He does not need to complete the thought, instead adding, "Auris, you disdain the help of those who love you just because you worry something bad might happen. You keep everyone at a distance because you still see yourself as different. But difference by itself is not a reason to alienate those who care. Give us a chance. Accept that the threats you could encounter might be threats we are willing to face with you."

"Threats I have caused," I point out once more.

"Threats that were there long before you were born," he fires back. "Threats that have *always* been there. This would not be the first time Humans have found a way into Viridian Deep. No sanctuary is impenetrable. They have discovered ways to enter Viridian before, but each time we have cast them out again and closed off the entry. Give us a chance to do so now. Come back with me and face what must be done."

I feel myself waver. I do not want to stay here on my own. My chances if I do are slim. If I am not found tomorrow, it will happen the next day or the next or the next. But I will be found, and that will be the end of me—or at least make me wish it were. Yet returning to Viridian Deep holds no promise of safety, either, and leaves me with the unpleasant recognition of the guilt I will have to carry if I lead the Humans to that sanctuary.

Harrow and I stare at each other from a distance of not more than fifteen feet. Neither of us speaks. I do not know what else to say, and I am guessing neither does he.

Then Harrow walks over to me and takes me in his arms and presses me against him. "Auris, I do not want to lose you," he whispers.

"I don't want to lose you, either," I whisper back. "Not since the day and the hour and the moment I first saw you in the wastelands."

We hold each other for long moments, and then I relent. "All right. I will come home with you. But if I decide later that I have no choice but to leave, I want you to honor that."

I feel him nodding his agreement without having to hear the words.

AFTER WE SNEAK BACK DOWN TO THE DOCKS—FINDING NO EVIdence of a search or a trap—we locate and reboard the submersible. We receive warm greetings and expressions of relief that we are safe, then begin the journey back. Harrow and I sit in our seats once more, buckled in place, assured by Zedlin that our craft is fully operational and all damage has been repaired. We slip out of the harbor without trouble, for the mechanical predator still lies dormant at the entrance with no evidence of any repairs having begun.

I hope it remains this way, because I can't help thinking of the terrible damage it might do to others who try to enter or exit once it is operational again. But I know this wish is in vain. The makers of such machines are never content to let them languish. If they cannot fix this one, they will make another more powerful, more deadly. It is in their nature.

I am in a black mood, and I don't want Harrow to see it. My problems are with myself and not with him. I have to find a way to come to terms with what I might be doing. I know the possible consequences, and it doesn't matter what Harrow tells me about family and trust and previous invasions. Nothing really matters but how I end up handling this dilemma. By going back, I am salvaging nothing but my own sense of security. How do I find a way to stop this invasion from happening?

And then I have yet another horrible thought: What if the invasion has already begun? What if Allensby has already sent a Human army with all its mechanized weapons into Viridian to destroy it? What if he knows how to get into my homeland without me to guide him because the tracker has already allowed him to chart the path without me?

For long moments, I am petrified. But slowly I begin thinking it through. There has never been any danger of finding Viridian without someone or something providing its location. If my presence in Viridian Deep for the days after my second escape has already given them a way in, then Viridian Deep is doomed. But if they started tracking me only once I reentered the Human realm, or if they need more time to prepare for their invasion before the tracker will be of any use, then there is hope. I mean, why would Allensby send the Goblins after me if he could come himself?

Besides, didn't Allensby claim to still need my cooperation in order to penetrate the barriers that ward Viridian? Didn't he say he would hurt Margrete if I refused to help him? That suggests he can't do this without me providing a signal or inviting him in—whether it is given willingly or not.

"I want to see Ancrow as soon as we arrive," I announce abruptly. "Alone."

Harrow, who is dozing, opens his eyes and gives me a searching look, but then nods his reluctant agreement.

I sleep for most of the rest of the trip back to the shores of Viridian Deep. Once there, we say goodbye to Zedlin and his crew, thanking them for helping us. They mutter a few incomprehensible replies, and Zedlin actually offers to help us again should we ever need him.

Harrow and I then walk back to our home city, which takes two days. The days are sunny and bright, but my mood remains dark and uncertain. I continue to struggle with the certainty that Allensby will track me here and bring with him a heavily weaponized army. He will kill everyone but me. He will destroy Viridian Deep and the Fae, and I will become his newest lab rat.

I need to speak with Ancrow. All the lies she has told conceal a truth she still hides. I don't know what it is, but I know it is there. She will have an answer that will solve the problem of the tracker. I instinctively know this, and I trust my instincts. But If I am wrong, I need to find out as quickly as possible and then leave this country and my home and my people forever.

We arrive home at sunset of the second day. Viridian Deep is still standing, with no evidence that any sort of invasion has already descended on the city or the surrounding countryside, and I breathe a deep sigh of relief; my worst fears have not come to pass. Not that an invasion cannot happen still, but at least it hasn't happened yet. So there is still time.

I say good night to Harrow and go straight to Ancrow's house. Lights are on when I knock, and an elated, energetic Char greets me with hugs, then bounces about like a loose ball with excitement. Ramey comes out to hug me as well, more subdued, but with her smile every bit as wide. I ask them for Ancrow, and they dart off to find her. I sit on the bench outside waiting, wondering how I am going to say what I need to. There is no easy way to tell someone that you know they have lied to you yet again—and how dangerous those lies might prove to be to everyone they care about.

When Ancrow appears at the door, she is already on her guard.

We are not close, and we are not friends—not in the way a mother and daughter ought to be. She abandoned me as a baby and gave me up to strangers in a strange land. She has purged me from her life for nearly twenty years. Then, when I resurface, she lies to me not once, not twice, but three times when she cannot bear to reveal the truth. She has done her best to make up for it each time, but each new lie has diminished her more and weakened the strength of whatever good feelings I might have harbored.

Her sharp features are stern and her expression tight with mistrust. "You've been away," she says accusingly.

I nod. "Where you suggested I should not go—back to the Human world and my home city. Back to the mother who raised me."

Her face goes pale. She turns back to close the front door and sits down beside me on the bench. "Are you satisfied now? Did you get what you wanted by going back there?"

"You lied to me," I say quietly. "Again. You lied about my father, and while I understand the reason, the lie was unconscionable. Hard as it is to know I was fathered by Allensby, it is harder still to have to hear it from a woman I no longer even remember."

She blinks once, then shakes her head. "You seem to have survived it." Her words are so cold I am stunned. "Why did you have to pursue this? Wasn't it better when you thought your father a good man instead of an evil one?"

"It was not your choice to make, Mother. It was mine. I have lived with lies my whole life, and I expected the truth from you. But you made it almost impossible for me to learn even the smallest part of the truth. You tried instead to drive me away from the home that should have been mine all along. That is hard to forgive—and impossible to forget."

"Well, you have what you wanted now." Her weary voice is bitter. "There are no more lies to reveal, no more truths to tell. I have revealed or you have discovered for yourself everything there is to know."

I shake my head slowly. "That's just another lie. There is at least one thing more you have not revealed, and it threatens everyone in Viridian Deep. When you were impregnated, Allensby placed a tracking device somewhere in your body so that you would lead the Humans here. Dennis found this out, and when he took you away from my father, he removed that chip. But now I discover the same thing has been done to me."

To my surprise, there is real shock on her face—the kind of shock that tells me she is hearing all of this for the first time. I seize her shoulders in an effort to steady myself. "You didn't know? Weren't you told you were chipped?"

She shakes her head slowly. "I didn't know anything about this. Dennis didn't tell me. He must have thought it better not to burden me further. But you have had one of these devices implanted in you, as well?"

"Apparently."

"Yet you came back here? So the Humans are given a means of finding us?"

I am instantly enraged. "I would not have done so but for your son, who insisted I not try to solve this problem on my own! Family and friends and Fae magic will help me, he insisted. And then, if that fails, I can leave. Your son loves me, Ancrow, and I love him. I came back because I thought perhaps you might know a way to remove this tracker. So do not dare accuse me of ignoring the danger to the Fae people—who are my people, too—to satisfy my own selfish interests. That territory belongs to you!"

She flinches, but her hard expression does not soften. "I accept that. And I apologize. I know you are a brave and considerate young woman. It was a momentary lapse of judgment on my part to suggest anything else. But I know nothing whatsoever of these tracking chips. Perhaps Allensby's plan to use them won't even work?"

"That's a big gamble, Mother—especially since he seemed pretty sure it would work. He seemed very confident when he told me what he'd done. This is a threat he intends to follow through on. Of that much, I am certain."

I pause, waiting on her. She stares back. "Can you help me?" I ask finally, my anger and disgust draining away and leaving only sadness. "Is there anything you can do that will allow me to stay in my home? Anything that will prevent me from having to leave and risk becoming Allensby's lab rat as you were? Please, Mother."

She stares at me silently for a long time, then looks down at her hands where they lie clasped together in her lap. "You are right, Auris. I let this happen. I lied and deceived and hid the truth from everyone. I thought I had earned the right to do so after what I had suffered. And I did not give you the protection and love you deserved. I tried to make up for that in other ways, but it was not enough. It was never enough."

She goes silent again, but only for a moment. "Go back to the Seers tomorrow and ask them to consult the *Inish* Reveal to see if they can determine whether or not Humans are preparing to invade Viridian Deep. We need to know what sort of time, if any, remains to us. While you do that, I will consider what might be done to blunt Allensby's efforts—either by negating the effectiveness of the tracker or by somehow removing it."

"Thank you," I reply. I suppress a sudden urge to pull her to me and kiss her cheek and tell her I love her, but I cannot do this. The gap she has opened between us is still too large.

Instead, I choose to address one final grievance. "There is one last thing we need to discuss." I watch her face harden anew. She is already preparing her defenses. "Those Goblins who came for me that first time after I came into Viridian. Allensby didn't send them. At that time, he hadn't yet implanted me with the tracker. He didn't even know I was alive. So how did they find me?"

Her gaze is steady as it meets mine. "Someone must have told them."

"Why would someone do that? Who would want me dead?"

She shrugs, the gesture casual. "Humans are not well liked here. You know this. There were some who wanted you gone from our homeland, who saw you only as an enemy of the Fae. Any one of them might have decided to do something about it."

"Something as drastic as having me killed?"

"Perhaps you misread their purpose in giving you up. Their motives might have been simply to remove you from Viridian. To be taken elsewhere—anywhere else—as long as it was not here."

She pauses, shrugs. "It's what I would have done."

I nod slowly. Would have done, or did? I don't care to know anything more. I think perhaps I know as much as I wish to. The knowing doesn't help. Like everything else she has revealed, it just hurts.

I rise wordlessly and go off to find Harrow.

THE SEARCH IS A SHORT ONE. HE IS WAITING FOR ME ON THE BENCH in front of my cottage. I go over and sit down beside him. "Did you speak to her?" he asks.

"I did. She was not happy, and she could offer no assurances of help, but she promised to try. I will go to the Seers tomorrow to ask them to look into the *Inish* Reveal and see how far along preparations for an invasion have progressed. I think we can be pretty sure they have been under way for some time now."

I pause. "Ancrow says she knows nothing of having been chipped herself and did not realize the danger to me. She said Dennis never told her."

He nods. "Perhaps he didn't. She was injured and emotionally devastated. She was fragile. It's hard to think of her that way, but it must have been so. He might have thought it better not to tell her."

We are silent then for a few moments. I wonder if I should tell him what I suspect about the first Goblin attack and then decide not to. What purpose would it serve?

"Will you go with me tomorrow?" I say at last.

"You know I will."

"I do know. But I just wanted to hear you say it. I love you."

He smiles. "I know. But I like to hear you say it, too."

I hesitate, then whisper, "Will you stay with me tonight? In my bed this time—not in the living room? Just to keep me company, if that's enough for you? Just so I can have you close?"

"How close?"

"As close as you want."

"Sounds dangerous, Auris," he says, straight-faced.

"Maybe. But I know you are very brave. Are you willing to risk it?"

He smiles. "I suppose I am."

I smile back, knowing I am once again allowing myself to imagine a future I have no reason to think will happen. Except when I look into his strange, wonderful eyes, I think maybe somehow it can.

TWENTY-EIGHT

I SLEEP IN THE ARMS OF SOMEONE I DESPERATELY LOVE AND AM now sure is in love with me as well. We do not engage in love-making or in talk of love, or do anything more than simply share space and time while holding each other close, because we know that nothing else is needed. We are both too exhausted by what we have been through to enjoy anything more. And worse, I may have to leave Viridian Deep and everything dear to me. If no answer can be found for the dilemma of the tracker traveling through my bloodstream, I will have no choice. I will never betray the Fae. I will never put my own interests before theirs. I've had a good taste of how that feels, and I do not intend to visit it on others.

But before I drift off, cradled in Harrow's arms, snuggling close against his body, the silkiness of his hair brushing softly against me, smelling the forest in the tiny leaves that adorn his head, I wonder how I can ever leave him. Is he right to question if there even is a tracker? Is my father playing games?

But if the Seers can use their *inish* on my mind to reveal lost memories, surely they can find a way to look within my body to see if any foreign objects have been placed there. I resolve to ask them when I see them tomorrow.

Harrow lies next to me when I wake the following morning, still sleeping—but in my bed this time. I smile, thinking of how things ended up before. I kiss his nose, run my fingers through his long hair, and immediately discover I want to do so much more with him. But I extract myself without acting on my impulse and rise to shower and dress.

When I am ready I find Harrow sitting on the side of the bed, his green body all lean and muscled and incredibly sexy, and I stop briefly to muse about how easy it is for me to find him so. I never met one of the Fae before Harrow; I did not know they even existed. I had always thought of myself as Human and had never envisioned falling in love with someone who was anything else. Yet the falling was easy in spite of our physical differences, and now I find it odd to think I could ever hesitate to love this man.

I brush all this aside and walk over to sit beside him. "I intend to ask the Seers if there is some way they can determine if I am chipped or not. Perhaps their *inish* can discover the truth."

He leans close, places a reassuring hand on my leg. "I don't know what else they might be able to do, but we both know how good they are at recovering memories. Maybe you have one about this tracking device, too."

I hadn't thought of this, but it might be so. I am immediately heartened by this possibility, and I lean forward to kiss him in gratitude. We hold the kiss for longer than is necessary for a thank-you, and when we break it we spend a moment looking at each other with an intensity that is almost scary. When I fall into his eyes this time, I feel more in control. I can extricate myself. I can give myself to him and still feel able to manage what is happening.

"What is it?" he asks finally, a hint of confusion appearing on his face.

But I just smile and shrug. "I'm just happy. It feels good."

We eat breakfast and leave for the Seers' cottage at the edge of the city. The day is clouded and the wind brisk. There is the smell of rain in the air, and I think we will see some before the day is over. But not on this morning. We arrive at our destination dry. As we go up the lane toward the front door, Dreena appears to meet us.

"Harrow, the beautiful heartbreaker," she greets him, then turns to me and says, "And Auris, breaker of heartbreaker hearts." She snorts at her twisting words. "Did any of that make sense?"

Harrow embraces her with a smile. "You always make more sense than any of us," he answers. "Can we speak with you?"

"Me, or my sisters, too?" Her sharp eyes move from him to me and back again. "Is this visit for something more than pleasantries?"

"Much more. But first, I am in need of help with a memory," I answer before Harrow can speak. "A recent one—one perhaps lost in a period of unconsciousness."

Dreena gives me a look. "Auris, you of all people should know that, while we can recover lost memories that we know you once had, we do not perform miracles. Still, you are a kind and considerate young lady, so I think we owe you that kindness and consideration in return. Come inside. I will summon the others."

We enter their charming cottage and go into the living room to sit, finding Benith already seated, knitting and humming. She stops both when she sees us and stands.

"Maven!" Dreena calls up the stairs. "Come down for a moment, please."

Ancient Maven appears so fast I think she must have seen our approach from her upstairs room. Her age-riven face turns suddenly young on seeing Harrow, and I begin to suspect he has this effect on many. She comes over to embrace him and accepts a kiss on her cheek. "What need have you of three old women this morning, love of my life? And you bring sweet Auris with you, too? My, we are blessed today!"

We sit—all of us, save Benith who goes off to make tea. And until she returns and we have remarked on the exceptional flavor of this new brand—something called winter's warmth—we talk of seasons and the warm weather. But once she returns, I begin to speak of what brought Harrow and me to their home. It takes me awhile to cover the necessary ground and to explain about the danger I pose and what it is I need them to do. I am circumspect in my explanation, but not enough so that these sharp old women don't recognize quickly enough how troubled I am.

"This tracking device—if it exists—was placed in you by Humans," Maven says after a moment's silence. "It was placed there so that you could be used to provide them with entry into Viridian. If whoever did this intended to achieve this result, why haven't they done so already?"

"Sister," Benith says gently, "consider the time involved. Auris was chipped while a prisoner of the Goblins, then rescued and brought back into Viridian. But she was only here for a few days before she left again for Harbor's End. If the purpose of chipping her was to find a way into Viridian, then an invasion is clearly intended. But insufficient time has passed to mount such an invasion."

Maven makes a face. "All of which ignores the possibility that the intended invasion has already been mounted and now stands waiting. It may even be possible that Human technology has already pinpointed her location and formed a set of coordinates that would allow for tracking her here even as we speak."

"Not likely," Dreena interrupts the exchange. "You forget our own work on enhancing and improving the defenses originally created to ward Viridian Deep. The magic—which infuses both the air and the water surrounding our homeland—is a powerful barrier, full of misdirection. So those who think to rely on predetermined coordinates are in for an unpleasant surprise. Any attempt to follow such coordinates will find themselves in places no sane person would think of going. Humans have tried this more than once before, both with soldiers and with missiles, only to pay a very high price for the lessons they were taught."

I am surprised at their familiarity with Human technology. They speak of it as if they are as well versed in it as they are in their own *inish*. But then to enhance the ancient magic of protections in-stalled by their ancestors, they would need to be.

"Well, then," says Benith. "First, let's see if we can determine if there *is* a tracker involved. Auris, come sit beside me, please."

I get up and go over to her. Maven rises from her usual chair and comes to join us, so that one sister is on either side of me. Then Dreena kneels at my feet, placing my hands in hers as she looks into my eyes.

"All quiet now, Auris," she whispers. "Close your eyes and think of this device floating through your body. Do not try to find it; just make it a generalized search. Be calm and relaxed. Do not think about what we are doing. Concentrate on the device."

I feel their hands begin to move over my body, so softly their fingers are barely touching me, traveling slowly and methodically about. I feel their combined *inish* surface, penetrating my skin like the warmth of the sun, and I grow drowsy in spite of myself. I direct my thoughts to this unknown device I bear, trying to feel its presence—just as the sisters have asked.

Time slows and then fades from my consciousness. Even the feel of the hands moving on my body disappears, and I slide into a state of near-sleep. I can feel the rush of my blood through my veins and the beating of my heart in my chest. I can sense my own breathing as I inhale and exhale in a steady rhythm. Nothing around me in-trudes on my sense of peace, on my passing into myself as if I were nothing more than the air around me, all weightless and become a part of my slow-moving thoughts.

I am lost to myself when I finally wake, held upright by four pairs of hands, a limp and helpless creature. All three Seers and Harrow gently lower me onto the couch and let me continue wak-ing at my own pace. I see their faces and feel their hands immedi-ately, but have nothing else to tell me what is happening. I come back to myself slowly, and have little sense of how long I have been gone or what exactly has happened.

When I try to speak my throat is tight and my voice so hoarse

332 • TERRY BROOKS

that Benith silences me with a hand over my lips and instructs
Dreena to bring me a cup of tea. They help me to sit up again then,
and I drink the life-enhancing liquid in steady, careful sips, the
warmth of it rushing into me and helping to restore my strength.

Fortified once more, I say to them, "Could you locate a tracking
device?"

Maven nods, looking troubled. "We think so. There *is* something foreign inside your body. Whatever it is, it seems to be
everywhere—which would suggest it does in fact travel in your
bloodstream. It is not life threatening and it is decomposing—
although at what rate, we cannot be sure."

"I think we can say for certain that something has been put inside you," Benith continues. "If Allensby says it is a tracking device, I would suggest that he may be telling the truth."

I nod, managing to keep my composure. So no idle threats, after
all. The tracking device is inside me, and it will be used to track me
here if Fae magic cannot redirect it.

"And there is no way to dislodge it or cause it to dissolve more
quickly?" I ask, already knowing the answer.

"No," Benith confirms.

"But if I go elsewhere, then Allensby could not track me here,
even if the device has provided him a way before?"

"Correct," Benith says once more.

I nod my understanding. "Then I have one more request of
you—and it is the most important. In fact, it's the main reason I
came here today."

"We are old and of limited endurance," says Maven, her ancient
face stern, "but we are not yet dead, and we are not yet in a place
where it is asking too much to help a friend. Tell us what you want."

"This one is not for me, but for all of the Fae. Can you look into
the Reveal to discover if a Human invasion is in progress?"

"We can look," Maven confirms. "But how much we can tell
about this invasion will depend on what stage it is in. Please wait
here until I return. Benith, another cup of tea for our guests?"

So Harrow and I continue to sit in the living room with Dreena and Benith, drinking tea and talking about everything but what I am thinking. The information that comes from the Reveal is my last hope. If there is no invasion pending or if it is in its early stages, I do not have to leave. At least, not immediately. Which means the process dissolving the tracking device may progress quickly enough in a week or two that I can stop worrying. Without it, there is no way the Humans *can* track me to Viridian, if what Dreena said is true. They may launch an invasion anyway, but there are enough traps and pitfalls waiting that a blind attempt will be almost certain to fail. It is when they can find a trail such as Harrow and I used that the risk increases dramatically.

So I sit and smile and visit and pray for deliverance. I need a miracle. I have been given a few before now, and I hope it is not too much to ask for yet one more.

By the time Maven returns, I am awash in tea and small talk and practically jumping out of my seat. I want a resolution. I want to know I will be free of my fears. Maven takes a seat and scans the room, meeting each of our eyes in turn. I know from her first glance that my hopes are about to be dashed.

"An invasion is being prepared inland from the coast, on the wastelands. Lines of defense have hidden all preparations from our Watchers, but at a guess, it was probably initialized a day or so after you arrived back from the prison after being rescued, and now it looks ready to be launched. I would say it is coming within the week. The council must be informed. The Fae army and its allies within Viridian must be assembled and made ready to repel what's coming. I am sorry, Auris."

I am on the brink of tears as I thank them for their efforts and their friendship and get to my feet. I have to get out of there before I break down. "Harrow," I say, reaching for his hand. "Will you walk me home?"

WITH HARROW SUPPORTING ME, WE DEPART THE COTTAGE AND THE sisters. We get as far as the end of the lane before I hear footsteps behind us. Benith comes running to catch up, so we stop to wait for her. There is an intensity of purpose about her that is arresting. But I do not think I can stand to hear anything more about my impossible situation.

"I forgot to mention something important, Auris," she says even before she reaches us. She stumbles to a halt, breathing hard. "Once I told you I thought you might be a Changeling. In the Fae culture, a Changeling is one who can assume a different look or identity at will. And even though you have not shown these powers as yet, I still think it is possible. If so, it might mean your body will behave in ways that are different from what any of us suppose. It is not unreasonable to think it might even be able to inhibit the workings of this device implanted inside you. The device might not function as the Humans think because of who and what you are."

I stare at her, thinking through the ramifications of what she is saying. "But I cannot tell this, can I? I cannot know what my Changeling blood will do. None of us can. I may still be a beacon that leads an army into Viridian."

She nods. "I'm sorry. But I had to tell you once more that my instincts suggest there might still be hope. You are not yet bound to any one fate."

I know she means well. I know she wants me to understand that there is still hope for me. But I see only one path forward, one way to be sure that I will not cause a disaster. Even so, I take her in my arms and hold her close, whispering in her ear. "Thank you. Thank you and your sisters for trying to help. I wish I knew more about myself than I do, but your words are important."

We break our embrace, and I watch her walk slowly back to the cottage. I know she came after me to give me hope, but I feel no hope at all. I begin to sob.

Harrow turns me into him and I melt into his arms. I am devastated all over again. My Changeling self has not manifested if it is indeed present, and there is no help for me. All I can do is depart quickly before all of Viridian is lost. It is the conclusion I most feared, and it has come to pass. There is no compromising; there is no second best choice. My fate was decided when my father inserted the tracking device and made it impossible to remove it from my body.

Like my mother, I feel violated. Not sexually, but very personally nevertheless. That he could have done such a thing has made it clear I can never consider him my father—not even if his blood and mine are the same. I cannot bear to think of us as being anything alike. His choice to use me so callously is unforgivable. He will never be my father; I will never accord him that right. Not even if he was, for some reason, to come to think of me as his daughter and not just a means to an end. He will always be Dr. Allensby, and I will always hate him.

"We are not done yet," Harrow says quietly.

I pull back in shock. "What are you talking about? I told you I would leave if the sisters could not find a way to remove or disable the tracker and if I would lead the invasion here. And you promised you wouldn't try to stop me."

"There is still Ancrow. She might have found a way to help. We need to go to her before we give up. She has solved other problems arising from Human attempts to conquer Viridian Deep. She might be able to solve this one."

I find this to be wishful thinking, but I respect and love him enough that I do not spurn his advice. When I needed help most—back when I had escaped the Goblin prisons and was facing a slow wastelands death from lack of water or recapture by pursuing Goblins—he was there to save me. Plus, there was that instinctive sense I had on the submersible, that Ancrow somehow held the answer.

"Let's go to her right now then," I tell him. "There is nothing to be gained by putting this off."

We start to walk to Ancrow's home, but as we near the city proper, I pull him aside and hold him firmly at arm's length, not daring to risk drawing him closer. "Listen to me," I say. "If Ancrow has no answer, I must leave, and I want you to promise to let me go. Don't beg me to change my mind or offer to come with me. I will have to go back into the Human world, and that is no place for you. Please promise you will honor this request, no matter how we feel about each other. I am not strong enough to follow through if you insist on stopping me. So promise me you will let me go."

He studies me carefully, his lean features intense, his body held still in my grip. "I promise, Auris."

I release him and we walk on. We do not speak further, lost in thought, already contemplating what we will find when we come face-to-face with Ancrow once more. I am dreading what I know I will hear. I am already preparing myself so that I will not break down. I do not want her to see me cry. I do not want to appear weak in front of her.

As we walk, I look around at everything we pass, taking in as much as I can of this city, this forested world, and the people—my people—who live here. So many wonderful moments have I enjoyed here; so many are still waiting to be experienced. Once I had nothing—no family, no home, no past, and no future. All this I have found in Viridian. All that matters in this life is here. I can take a little comfort from this in the time I have left. I can celebrate what I have been given, even if I am not going to be able to hold on to anything more than memories.

Harrow is going to be hardest of all to leave. I love him, and I always thought we would build a life together. We worked so hard to make that happen—even when our efforts were directed not to that end but to other goals entirely. Making me well after he saved me. Teaching me skills that would keep me alive and safe. Coming to each other's rescue. Making it possible for me to have a new family. We have shared so much in these past months, and it is all coming to an end.

We reach the city center and climb toward the upper levels, to our destination. I harden myself against false expectations and remind myself that nothing is forever and nothing is given without cost. Whatever is asked—or demanded—of me, I will give willingly if the results will help Viridian Deep and the Fae.

My thoughts drift. I think again of Benith's comments on the possibility of my Changeling identity somehow making a difference in how my body responds to the tracking device. I have never completely accepted myself as a Changeling—at least not according to the Fae definition. The designation is real to me only by the Human definition—that I was a Fae child who was given away to a Human mother—but even then it was not a true exchange of children, and whatever wickedness there was relates solely to my mother's decision not to keep me. What feels more likely, when I consider the contradiction between what I look like on the outside and how I feel on the inside, is that I am who I am: a half Fae who just happens to look all Human. In spite of what some of my recovered memories once said.

Yes, I have the use of *inish*, as do all Fae. But I remain Human in all other ways, and nothing has happened to change that from the time I discovered the truth about myself. So what Benith sees and how she interprets it remains a mystery. All I know is that I have discovered no way by which I might free myself of the tracking device.

We climb to the tree lanes that will take us to Ancrow's home and proceed on a quick and silent journey. Once there, I walk up to the door and knock without hesitating. Better to get this over with. Better to hear the bad news and move ahead with my plan to leave Viridian. Some small preparations will be needed, then I will say goodbye to Ronden, Char, and Ramey.

And Harrow. Always Harrow.

Ancrow answers promptly. "I've been waiting for you. Come inside."

Waiting? I exchange a confused glance with Harrow as we follow our mother into the living room and sit on the couch across from her. She has that determined look that could mean several things—one of which is the offer of yet another unwanted apology for failing me. I hope she does not intend this, because I have had all the meaningless apologies I need from her. But I stay calm, my expression blank. There is nothing to be gained by starting a fight before I hear what she has to say.

"Were the sisters able to help?" she asks.

"Auris carries a tracking device within her. The sisters do not know how to remove it. And preparations for the Human invasion are already well under way." Harrow's voice is clipped, irritated. "What help do you have to offer, Mother?"

"More than they have," she replies. "Although perhaps not exactly what you have been searching for."

We wait, giving her time and space to explain in her own words. I doubt we will like what we hear, but you never know. Odd solutions have come from odd places and people before.

"I have not thought of a way to remove the tracking device, either," she begins. "I am sorry, Auris. I tried to think of something, but nothing suggested itself. So I think it would be better for us to assume it's going to remain inside you and use that to our advantage. How long do we have before the invasion launches?"

"Perhaps a week," I say.

"Then we will try to work with that. Listen carefully. We will not send you away because we need you here, as bait for our trap. We will choose where in Viridian we want Allensby to find you. Let him bring his soldiers, mechanized armor, weapons, and all the rest of what he would use to destroy us. Let him come right to our doorstep."

"Mother, this is hardly what we were hoping for," Harrow breaks in. "What is the reason for letting them find Auris and Viridian Deep?"

Now she smiles. "Because once we have them within our reach we will crush them."

TWENTY-NINE

THAT NIGHT I DREAM ONCE MORE.

I stand in the near-darkness of the tunnel entrance waiting for Ancrow. This is not where I am supposed to be, but it is where I am anyway. I can hear the sounds of the approaching Human army—the shouts and cries, the grinding of wheels and treads, the clank of armor and the sharp reports of weapons fire echoing down the passageway. I know what I am supposed to do, and I am doing it. But my *inish* is sluggish and weak. I have created the illusion as instructed, but it wavers and fades, as if it might fragment entirely at any moment. Nothing I can do helps. Everything feels like it is beginning to fall apart around me.

This is the plan we agreed upon, but so much seems to have gone wrong already.

I see Ancrow now, running toward me, dark hair flying behind her as the wind catches it, her lithe body and long legs stretched out to reach safety. For her age she is incredibly fit; as a result she is also very fast. She is pursued, yet looks untouchable. Weapons discharge in an effort to bring her down, but her *inish* shields her. I already have my protective shield in place, guarding against errant missiles and bullets, warding off the dangers the Humans throw at us. They will try to kill us; they are so trusting in their armor and their weapons that they think they can. But we will kill them first.

Ancrow reaches me and wheels back to face her pursuers. At our backs stands the whole of the Sylvan army, armed and ready. Compared with the number of Human soldiers who rush toward us, they seem too few. And they aren't real anyway, so no help there. I have created the illusion of an army, but it will offer us no protection. It is only a ploy to fool our attackers—a momentary deterrent to those who are now closing in. I look at Ancrow, suddenly desperate for reassurance, but she gives no indication of seeing me. She simply stands where she is and faces her enemies, hard and steady and unyielding.

Not enough.

We're going to fail.

I scream.

She laughs wildly and suddenly rushes the hordes approaching as if she will take all of them down single-handedly. The rush to reach her does not falter. If anything, it increases in speed—an inexorable force bearing down on two lone women. Seconds later Ancrow is run down and disappears beneath booted feet. I hear her screams, and then nothing more.

I am alone.

I call for Harrow. *Save me!*

But he does not hear my plea. He does not come to my aid, does not witness what happens as my shield fails and bullets rip into me, penetrating my body, tearing into my flesh, emptying me of life. I am aware of falling to the ground. I am aware that I am dying. All of my efforts—all *our* efforts—have failed.

Viridian Deep and the Sylvans are lost. And I am lost with them.

———

THE DREAM GOES ON, BUT I LOSE THE THREAD AND LET THE VISIONS slip away. I wake shaking and sweating, my sheets rumpled and damp, my mind whirling. I have just died, but only in a dream. I have just failed to save my people and my homeland, but not for real. I am adrift and powerless in these first few moments after waking, and I can hardly bear the feeling that sweeps over me. I survived the dream, but I know as well that the dream is warning me that I will not survive what's coming. Tomorrow approaches, and our plan to save Viridian Deep will be tested and found wanting. It might be viable in theory, but—just as my dream presaged—it is going to prove unworkable. When that happens, the three of us— and all the Fae people—are going to pay the price.

But Ancrow says not. Ancrow is confident—more confident than I have ever seen her. She is determined to the point of irrationality. I like her show of strength and conviction, but I fear that her insistence is misplaced.

This is how she explained it to Harrow and me yesterday:

"We have the perfect opportunity to destroy Allensby and his army and stop any threat of invasion by Humans for years to come—if not forever. The invaders want to come into Viridian? Then we let them. They will expect to find our army waiting to repel them and will muster everything they have at their disposal against us, so we will let them think they can. All we need do is set a trap they will not recognize."

"A trap?" I spoke the words doubtfully. "What sort of trap?"

"The kind that relies on Fae magic. The kind that Humans won't expect or recognize. We will put them off their guard; we will make them think they have outsmarted us. For that, we need to employ a lure—in this case, a Fae army standing in their way, bravely determined to stop them and clearly inadequate to the task. But that army won't have to stop them. Auris and I will do that alone."

Except this really didn't explain word one about what her plan was. I didn't understand what she thought the two of us could do alone, and I told her so. She offered me one of her cold smiles in response and explained more fully what would happen. I wished I hadn't asked.

"We will set our trap just off the shores of the Roughlin, at a point that lies midway between Spawn Ridge and the Strewlin. There is an open shoreline between the two that offers a perfect landing site for their transports. We will be waiting there—the three of us and the Fae army. The forest begins less than a mile inland, and the path to reach it at that location is broad, flat, and open. Our army will be waiting at the forest edge, clearly visible. The Humans will take notice of its small size and be unable to resist attacking."

"But how do we . . ." I interrupted.

She held up her hand to silence me. "I haven't finished. The Humans will attack, thinking to crush us easily. But when they are close enough, our efforts at resistance will seem to fall apart. The Fae defenders will retreat into the trees, apparently routed and running for their lives. At least, this is how it will appear to Allensby and the Humans. But they will have been deceived, for our army will be doing something else entirely. Unsuspecting, the Humans will continue their pursuit, and for a time it will appear they are gaining on us. But once they come after us into the forest—which you and I will have used our *inish* to manipulate, making it appear to be something other than it is—they will discover the truth. Bang! The trap will snap shut."

I stared. "What trap?"

"A wormhole."

Now both Harrow and I stared at her. "A wormhole?" Harrow finally asked. "What good does a wormhole do us?"

"It does a lot of good if, once they go in, they can't get out again. I will make it collapse and crush them."

"Can you do that?" I asked in surprise.

"No, she can't," Harrow said at once. "*Inish* can summon a wormhole, but it can't trap anyone inside. And it won't collapse, even supposing the entire Human army is inside and both ends close tight. Mother, don't do this! Don't risk our lives thinking you can do something you can't."

She shook her head slowly. "Oh, but I can, Harrow. I've already done it."

"When? When would you ever do such a thing? And why would you even try?"

Her face turned ugly as her lips twisted, giving her a cruel look. "If you were forced to watch the man you loved dismembered in front of your eyes and were hauled off to Human prisons to be debased and violated, impregnated with a Human's child, then found a way to escape but still had to make your way through Human country, how would you get home? If you were Fae—and you were I—you would find a wormhole. I did so by traveling out of the Human lands and into the wastelands. Once I was there, once I had summoned that wormhole and was finally in the clear and safely away, all I could think about was closing it back up so tightly a gnat couldn't get through it again. That's when I found out what my *inish* could do with wormholes."

A long silence followed, the three of us looking at one another, the air charged with the vitriol and dark intensity of Ancrow's words. She had settled on this solution, and she was clearly committed to it. To me it felt like a new form of suicide—a plan where so many things could go wrong, it was hard to count them. But all seem destined to result in the same unfortunate ending for both Ancrow and me.

It was Harrow who pointed out the most obvious flaw. "If you will be closing the wormhole, you will need Auris to create the illusions that will draw the Human army into it. But she has never used her *inish* to create an illusion before, and this will be a massive endeavor. How do we know she is even capable of it?"

Ancrow was dismissive. "I know well enough what she is capable of. And she has time enough to practice before we set out. Besides, I will only need her to hold shreds of the illusion together; we can have *inish* masters maintaining it up until the army flees. But in the end it must be only we three who risk our lives. My *inish* says it must be so."

She went on to explain that we would escape at the far end of the wormhole once the enemy had followed us far enough inside, and the Fae army—which would appear to follow us in but actually wouldn't—would have faded into the surrounding trees on either side of the entry and circled back around to block any escape from the entrance. No one would be allowed to leave the wormhole— and when it collapsed, the entire Human army would simply disappear along with it.

I was immediately tempted to tell her to forget this mad plan; it was way too unpredictable. It would be better if I just left and drew them off as I originally intended. But it wouldn't be better; not really. "Better" would mean putting an end to this threat to my country and my people forever. As long as Ancrow's plan stood a chance of working . . .

Harrow surprised me by asking Ancrow if she knew of an existing wormhole that would serve our purposes. She said she did. He then asked if it was stable enough that it wouldn't collapse until she made it do so. She said it was. An existing wormhole already waited not far back from where the forest opened onto the flats—one that must have been used regularly in the early days of the Fae. Some of it had eroded away over the centuries, but what remained was huge and perfectly suited to what we needed. It was why she had chosen to lure the Human army to this particular point. She was confident she could do what she said and trap the Human army inside this wormhole. Was he convinced? A slight nod of his head and the look on his face told me he was. He believed her. He was usually so careful, and this seemed so risky, but he had made up his mind. And given his unfailing instincts, I had to consider that his willingness to allow both his mother and me to take this risk counted for something.

We explored all the details of Ancrow's plan for several hours afterward, and all the while I was looking for an excuse to back out.

I thought I'd find one, but I was wrong. By the time we talked it through for the third time and I exhausted both questions and concerns, I was persuaded. The plan did have a chance of succeeding. And if it did work, the Human army would be no more, and the Fae would be safe in spite of the tracking device in my bloodstream. There would be no invading army, and no way for those who remained behind in the Human world to know what had happened unless there were survivors—which Ancrow was determined there would not be. Allensby and his army would be annihilated so thoroughly they would seem to have disappeared from the face of the earth. And then I could have the world and the life and the home I wanted so badly instead of spending my future as Allensby's lab rat or a dismembered corpse.

If I had to gamble, I couldn't think of a better gamble than this one. Ancrow had her failings, but believing in this bold plan didn't feel like one of them.

Even so, I felt an unmistakable reticence that I could not quite understand. Even though the plan seemed straightforward, there was still something about it that was deeply troubling. My *inish* warned me that something was wrong. But try as I might, I could not pinpoint what caused this feeling. All I could manage to deduce was that my *inish* was troubled not so much by the plan as by . . . something else. I was missing something important, but I couldn't figure out what. So without dismissing my uneasiness entirely, I did what I thought was right and agreed to what Harrow had already approved. I told myself this did not mean I couldn't change my mind if I discovered a sound reason to do so. It did not mean I couldn't back away if I was once again deceived by my frequently duplicitous mother. It only meant that I was prepared to go ahead with it when the time arrived.

And that time, it seemed, was fast approaching.

I WASH AND DRESS AFTER WAKING, AND FIND HARROW SITTING ON my doorstep when I emerge. He went home last night after our talk with Ancrow to tell Ronden what was happening and to give me some time alone. I would have welcomed him had he chosen to stay, but sometimes Harrow knows what I need better than I do. Now he is back, and I invite him in for breakfast with a kiss on the lips and a tug on his arm. We talk once again about the plan—and even though the details of how Ancrow will achieve her part remain vague, we both feel it has a chance.

I am still not sure about the nature of the conjuring Ancrow's plan requires or the way in which we intend to trap an entire armored, mechanized army consisting of everything from small weapons and robotic giants to rolling fortresses that carry cannons and rocket launchers. But Harrow insists such weapons will not prove so successful in the part of the country where we intend to lure them.

"Allensby will rely on the tracking device to lead the invasion force to us. And we will make sure to temporarily weaken that part of the magic so his readings will be accurate. But he will never get close to you; I will see to it that he doesn't."

I hope he's right about this. Allensby is not someone I ever want near me again.

Then Harrow has an additional thought on our preparation.

"We need to go back to the Seers and tell them to keep a close watch on the invasion. We need to know when the Humans begin transporting their army and by what means they do so. I assume they will attempt to cross the Roughlin using watercraft, but we can't be sure. If we are to prepare ourselves, we need time to make ready. Not beating them to the battlefield will sink the whole endeavor. We need to be in place so they can track us to where we want them to find us."

Breakfast finished, we go off to visit the Seers at their cottage.

Dreena is out on the balcony watering the flower boxes and looks up as we approach. There is reflected on her face that by-now familiar look of mixed irritation and resignation. Always prepared for us, yet never quite satisfied that we should be there in the first place. The sisters are so different from one another, I think. Perhaps it is because of their differences that they are able to work their *inish* together so effectively. Perhaps their individual talents complement one another. I don't begin to understand all the specifics of how *inish* works. Almost everything I know is about how *mine* works, and it is hard enough to get a firm grip on that.

As we come up to the doorway, Benith is there to greet us and invite us in. Maven offers tea and cookies. Dreena stays out on the balcony—although I have the feeling that she is somehow listening in.

We ask about monitoring the invasion, and Benith assures us this is possible. Maven goes off to take an immediate reading, eager to help us deal with the threat to Viridian. She returns with a shrug and a shake of her head. "It looks much as it did yesterday. Preparations continue, but everything is taking place inland, away from the coastline and hidden from our Watchers' eyes. I suspect the army waits on its leader."

Allensby, I think at once. They need him to read the tracking device. They need him to tell them where they should go before they launch their invasion.

Harrow and I depart with thanks and go back into the city. I tell him that I need to talk to Ancrow further—alone. I can't explain what it is I intend, because I am not sure myself. But I think I am seeking some form of reassurance. Harrow nods and tells me to come look for him at my cottage when I am done. He gives me a kiss, and we part upon approaching our mother's home.

Just the thought of speaking with Ancrow alone leaves me feeling uneasy. Nothing new there. I try unsuccessfully to gather my thoughts, but end up settling for determination. Some things you do because you lose something of yourself if you don't.

As I go up to the door, it flies open to disgorge an impassioned Char who rushes out impetuously to intercept me. Hugs and kisses from the little girl, and then a warning that Ancrow is in a bad mood today. No other explanation is offered—though I am not at all sure Char would be able to provide one. Even to her children, Ancrow is a mystery. I ask Char to leave me alone with her mother and go outside until we are finished talking. She pouts, but nods her agreement. I ask if Ramey is about, but she is visiting her grandmother. *Grandmother,* I think. I didn't even know she had one. Is this my grandmother, too?

Stepping into the house, I call out for Ancrow to announce my presence.

When she appears, she does indeed wear a dark visage and walks toward me with purpose. But as she comes up to me the darkness disappears, to be replaced by her smile.

"You've heard?"

I shake my head. "Heard what? I've been with Harrow and the Seers all morning."

"I've been given command of the Fae army. The defense of the city and her people is in my hands."

"As it should be, Mother." I speak the words, but wonder if this is true. It has been a long time since she was a soldier, and she has suffered greatly since. Does she still have the strength and determination a leader needs? Is she still capable of leading?

She hugs me to her. "I'm happy you've come, Auris. I need to talk to you."

She leads me into the living area and sits us side by side on the couch. "I need to talk to you, too," I tell her. "This plan to trap the Human army seems such an impossibility. I worry for both of us."

She nods. "I worry, too. But my plan is our best option, and I think it will work if we are strong-willed enough. I have to admit I don't think I can employ the *inish* alone; I need your strength as well to make it work. I have been a poor mother to you, Auris—poor in every sense of the word. I regret so much of what I have done, and I know that you still wonder if I'm holding something back. But I'm not. Not anymore. I want a new beginning for us—for whatever time we have left together. I want you to know I admire and respect the young woman you have shown yourself to be. I want you to know, too, that I am pleased that Harrow loves you as much as he does—and that you love him. I want you to be happy together, and I will do whatever is needed to help this happen."

Where is this coming from? Weeks of being an intruder, a pretender, a hated Human, and a presence she found anathema have left me doubtful about anything she says. Duplicitous in her behavior, constantly lying about my father and my life and our relationship, she has sought to deceive me at every turn. I want what she says to be the truth, but a part of me cannot accept what I am hearing. Rather than feeling reassured, I am immediately on my guard.

"I would like that," I reply, which is true enough. "But I still wonder how two women can undo an entire invasion. I know how accomplished you are, but I am still just learning to use my *inish*. There are so many ways I could fail that I feel I am a poor choice for this role."

"You won't fail. *We* won't fail. Mother and daughter—two very different but very committed women who have found each other in spite of everything. I have watched you, measured you, and found you supremely capable. You might not yet be as skilled or experienced as I am, but you are still the one I want by my side when this happens. One day soon, you will be better at using *inish* than I am. One day, you will astound yourself with what you can accomplish."

She takes my hands. "I have been thinking about what the Seers told you: that you are a Changeling. I think they were right; I think that power is somewhere inside you. But like your *inish*, it just needs something to bring it out. I also think you came to Viridian Deep because you were meant to. I dismissed you at the beginning, but now I see how wrong that was. You found your way here because—as much as you might have needed us—we needed you more. You are the key to our survival, Auris. I know how this sounds. I know it seems a gross exaggeration. But this is what I believe."

I am now speechless. I found my way here because I was trying to survive, and Harrow found me and rescued me. I never even knew Viridian existed before that. I had no idea I was born here and was a Sylvan and not the Human I appear. The thought that I was guided here to fulfill some important role in my Fae homeland just seems far-fetched and unreal. I am a nineteen-year-old girl whose past remains a mystery, whose present feels ephemeral, and whose future I measure in days. Ancrow invests me with an importance I neither believe in nor deserve.

Still. She is my mother.

"If you believe in our chances and if you want me with you, then you have my support. I will trust you, Mother. Again. Once more. I will put aside our unfortunate past and my lingering doubts, and I will trust you. But do not lie to me again. Do not betray me again. And do not disappoint me again."

She takes my hands in hers and squeezes them reassuringly. "I won't. Not ever again. I promise."

I wonder if this is a promise she can keep. I wonder if she is even capable of keeping it. She has failed thus far, and the consequences have been extremely painful. All I can do now is hope.

I have forgotten what it was I came here to say—if in fact I ever knew what it was. Perhaps I have already said it. Perhaps it doesn't matter. What she's said, what she has made me believe might be possible, is sufficient. Without knowing anything more than I did before, I feel reassured. In a day, maybe three, we will stand together for the first time against a common enemy—an enemy that has plagued us for years—trying to wipe its presence from our lives. Do I speak of Allensby? Yes. Do I include the Humans who hunt and kill us? Yes, again.

But maybe I also mean to try to redress the wrongs we have both suffered and lived with for far too long.

Perhaps, I think, this is how we might finally heal.

THIRTY

THREE DAYS LATER—THREE INTENSELY TRYING DAYS ATTEMPT-
ing to master a form of *inish* I have never used before, and
whose application leaves me exhausted and wrung out every
evening—we receive word from the Seers that new activity has appeared on the wastelands; preparations are actively under way for
the Human invasion. But the invasion is to be launched not by
sailing across the waters of the Roughlin but by flying over them.
Giant transports have landed at the assembly site, and supplies and
vehicles are being loaded.

Ancrow acts quickly. She asks the Seer sisters to further weaken
the wards that might affect the ability of the transports to reach our
designated point for their landing by opening a channel that will
guide them to us. Flight in any other direction will throw their in-
struments into chaos, so they will have little choice in the matter.
Perhaps they will sense this is a trap, but there is no help for it if we
want our plan to succeed.

She already commands the Sylvan army that will defend Viridian Deep, and after leaving the sisters she immediately calls her

soldiers together. Fully assembled by midday—Harrow, Ronden, and I included—our army marches east for ten miles, to where a wormhole opens to allow passage directly to the coast. We exit within the trees a mile back from the shoreline, between the imposing bulk of Spawn Ridge to the north and the deep swamp of the Strewlin to the south. It is the most suitable delivery point for an army of this size for miles in either direction, by water or by air. The remainder of the coast consists of hills and rugged forests that will prevent hovercraft from finding another sufficiently large piece of flat ground on which to land. Here, there is sufficient space to maneuver. Here is where they will determine—by Allensby's reading of the tracking device, now uncovered by the magic—that I and the Fae will be found.

Once in place, we assemble with our backs to the trees and the wormhole hidden behind us. As Ancrow has promised, at the start of this endeavor, the illusion is maintained not just by me, but by a handful of *inish* masters—those Sylvans whose command of magic is exceptional enough to separate them from their fellows. I have trained hard over the past few days, and learned fast, but the scope of this illusion is too much for a single *inish* user—especially one who has trained for only three days. Once the trap is sprung, I will have to maintain the illusion alone and from inside the wormhole, as only Ancrow, Harrow, and I will be going down its throat.

I can only hope I am equal to the challenge, though Ancrow has assured me that, in the chaos of battle, a perfect illusion is not needed. I hope she is right.

Then, with the illusion established, we wait.

Allensby is not a fool. He will suspect that we are trying to trick him by using the tracking device as a lure, and he will be prepared. But Ancrow feels certain all his preparations and foresight will still not be enough to save him. He will find the Fae army waiting and automatically assume they have come to fight. He will judge them to be of insufficient size and number to withstand the strength of the force he commands. He will rely on battle machines and mechanized warriors and advanced weaponry to overcome any magic we might wield. He will survey and test the ground that makes up the battlefield to be sure there are no traps waiting. He will scan the forests and find nothing—for the wormhole is hidden away. He will decide these savages—as he once referred to the Fae in my presence—are overestimating their ability to withstand what is coming, and he will attack.

If all goes as Ancrow believes and all the pieces of the deception fall into place, his army will be destroyed.

What are the odds?

I don't dare think about it too closely. In a direct confrontation with the Human army, ours would be cut to pieces. Their weapons and armor are far superior. But if they are not given a chance to use their vaunted killing tools and machines, it might be a much different story.

We establish our defensive formations—archers on the wings, spearmen and slingers front and center, and swordsmen held in reserve until they are needed to lead the forces when the retreat begins. Scattered everywhere among them are the majority of the *inish* masters—those not working with me to maintain the illusion. Initially these men and women are given one duty and one duty only—to form the shields that will serve to protect the Fae forces.

Ancrow, Harrow, and I stand at the center of the formation. Ronden has left us to take command of the Watchers—a position Harrow would assume had he not been asked by Ancrow to remain with me. We appear for all intents and purposes a formidable fighting force—one that would intimidate any enemy that dared to challenge it.

But then the transports appear in the eastern sky, becoming visible against the horizon as the afternoon wanes, and I can feel my confidence begin to slip. These airships are hovercraft—massive metal disks that seem to float as they begin their descent to the shoreline and the battlefield beyond. I have never seen anything this big, and wonder how such monsters can even manage to leave the ground, let alone hang there in the sky as if weightless? How many soldiers and how much equipment and armor must be aboard each one? There are three of them, and each appears to be the size of a small city. I watch them as they lower and settle, parked in a row along the mile of shoreline, all facing us. I watch as hatchways open and ramps lower. I watch as the disembarkation begins.

I feel a growing sense of hopelessness as their numbers grow. This enemy is too huge, too monstrous, too inexorable, and too inevitable for us to resist. I watch thousands of soldiers march off the vessels in tight formation, all of them armored and bearing weapons. I cringe as the jagged-edged battle machines roll down the ramps with a grinding squeal of wheels and treads, their prows like blades. There, to the left, the mechanized warrior machines tromp into view, twelve feet tall and fully automated. Any one of them possesses the strength of ten of our lightly armed Fae. Human soldiers join them. Company after company of soldiers form up their lines, filling the plain with their massive presence. I am left stunned as the transports empty and their passengers transform into a chilling display of Human achievement that promises certain annihilation for us all.

"Scary," I mutter to Ancrow as we stand together watching.

"Doomed," she replies, and I look over to see fury and determination in her expression.

The Fae army does not move. All of us stand there as if nothing the Humans have displayed provokes even the slightest concern. Here and there I sense the presence of *inish* as protective shields fill the air, invisible and undetectable. Looking far to the left down our lines, I see Ronden standing front and center of her Watcher command. She looks back at me and nods.

Artillery is brought forward, carriages rumbling. The cannons are set into place as shells are inserted into firing chambers. The clank and screech of steel on steel fills the air as the loading progresses, then finally gives way to silence. Overhead, I detect the shields linking up.

When the artillery ignites and the shells streak toward us, I hold my breath. My first instinct is to flee the field and find shelter. But like everyone else, I stand firm. I will not give way to my fears. This is only the first attempt to intimidate us. It will get worse when this fails.

And it does fail. Spectacularly. The shells explode on contact with the *inish* shields—although it appears to the Humans that they explode in midair. The smoke rises, the debris from the exploded shells drifts away, and nothing has changed.

Fire is next, extruded through hoses and tanks of flammable fuel. Gouts of it jet from elevated nozzles, arcing through the late-afternoon sky to fall in sheets over our waiting army. But once again the shields protect us and the fire burns itself out in midair. The attack tapers off, and once more nothing has changed.

I feel a small ray of hope work its way through the layers of fear that threaten to undo me. Maybe we *can* withstand this invasion after all. Maybe the Humans will become so discouraged that they will give up and go home. Wishful thinking, I know. But I cannot help myself. I cling to this small lifeline to see if it might draw me clear from the dangerous waters to the safety of the shore.

But Allensby is only just beginning. He has us in his sights now, and he is not about to let us go.

As if reacting to my thoughts of a safe ending, the entire Human invasion force begins to move toward us. Mechanized war machines form a front line behind which follow hundreds of units of regular soldiers, all advancing in lockstep, all bearing automatic weapons. I can see exactly what this is intended to accomplish. Now that the shields Allensby and his generals were anticipating have been revealed, he will know a successful attack requires testing them not just from overhead but also from the front and sides. He will pound on them until they break. Then the superior size and strength of the Human army will punch through, and the Fae will be overwhelmed.

As I watch this juggernaut roll toward us, I experience a feeling of unreality. What am I doing here, a nineteen-year-old girl with no previous exposure to war and its horrors, standing against power the like of which I have never even imagined possible? I should be anywhere else. I should be gone from Viridian as I had intended to be, and none of this should be happening. It is too late to consider this now, but the thoughts are there.

The sounds of the advance grow louder as the enemy draws closer—the thud of booted feet, the grind and clank of armor, the squeal of treads and wheels, and the sudden howl of sirens all clearly intended to shatter our nerves. The sounds fill my ears and crowd into my head until I want to scream back at them in fury. I wish I had armor and a weapon. I wish I had machines warding me. Instead, I have only my *inish*, and Ancrow and Harrow standing rocksteady next to me, and I know these will have to be enough.

My mother leans down. "You know what we have to do," she whispers.

"I do," I respond. She asks not for the answer itself but for reassurance of my readiness. "Now?" I ask.

"Now," she answers.

As she speaks, she taps the shoulder of the aide standing next to her, and a red flag lifts to where all can see it. Slowly, but steadily, the Fae begin to fall back. Our shields shift their positions, now protecting the Fae on all sides.

The *inish* masters hold the magic they have summoned steady to mask the presence of the concealed wormhole, the forest at our backs forming an unbroken line that fools the eye. Soon now, Ancrow will signal for her soldiers to break and run, the *inish* masters outside the wormhole using their magic to make it seem as if they are all racing toward the same area of the forest—which in reality is the wormhole. Allensby and the Humans will have no idea of the trap they are being drawn into.

Then it will be up to just the three of us—Ancrow, Harrow, and me—to lead them into its throat, drawing them so deep inside our trap they will not be able to escape it.

All of the various parts of our plan must be perfectly executed if it is to work. The Fae soldiers who are already fading into the trees must vanish entirely as my mother, Harrow, and I retreat into the wormhole. Once inside, Ancrow and I must use our magic to make it seem as if we are following our imaginary army. The forest extensions the *inish* masters have created must continue to conceal the wormhole long enough for the enemy to pass into it without realizing what they are doing, and my *inish* must maintain that illusion from the inside. Harrow must shield the three of us from weapons fire while Ancrow and I focus our *inish* on maintaining the deceptions we are perpetrating. If any one of us falters, any chance of this plan succeeding becomes decidedly smaller.

At the edge of the forest, the last remnants of the real Fae army vanish into the trees. In the same moment, the *inish* masters' fake army appears to break formation and flee to where Ancrow stands at the still-concealed mouth of the wormhole. The *inish* masters continue to hide its presence, to give it the look of just another part of the forest—a clearing, an opening leading back through the trees. Artillery has begun firing again, but the remainder of our *inish* masters have remained just long enough to use their magic to block it. Some of the trees are struck and catch fire. Some go down entirely. Smoke and debris starts to drift over the battlefield—which, as Ancrow claimed, will make my illusions easier to maintain.

"Go!" Ancrow yells at Harrow and myself as the *inish* masters direct the last of the fake army into the wormhole and we follow it in, taking over the illusion from the inside as the *inish* masters move away to safety.

Pausing a few steps into the wormhole, I layer my deception in place, hoping it will not fall apart before the whole of the invading army is inside. Time enough if they attack now, I think. I turn to run deeper inside when the whole world explodes and sends me flying. An enemy shell got through our protections, I realize at once. I fall hard and tumble forward. I am dazed, but I drag myself to my feet. Smoke and ash swirl all around me amid thick choking clouds of debris. I start moving in the direction I think I am supposed to be going, summoning my *inish* to protect me, extending the smoky illusion, searching for my family. Ahead I hear coughing, and I spy a reddish flickering. I stumble over to Harrow, who lies motionless and on fire. I fall across him, frantically trying to beat out the flames. His heavy leather gear saves him from severe burning, but he is weakened from the smoke, and I have to help him to his feet. Behind us, roars of anger and the thudding of boots are closing in.

The enemy is almost upon us.

Odd that it was their shell that did this to us, I think dazedly. Why would that be? If it fell on us, it must have impacted them. It's a callous, risky measure for a commander to take, disregarding the safety of his own men like that. Allensby must be growing desperate. I take a moment to picture him, his face a mask of rage and fear. I hope he feels both now. I hope he chokes on them.

Clouds of smoke and debris fill the air. My illusion is easier to maintain, all the smoke and ash helping me add to the confusion. I do not see Ancrow and I can't be sure what's become of her. In desperation, I use my *inish* to throw up a fresh image—this one of a Fae army milling about in the fake trees, hundreds of frightened Sylvan soldiers stumbling about, the clouds of both illusory and real smoke masking any flaws in my rendering. I try to give life to men and women terrified by their situation and seeking to escape. The Humans and their mechanized warriors must see this and be drawn to it. We need them all to enter the wormhole after us. We need them to be fooled a little longer. The images and the swirl of smoke and debris will help mask the truth.

I shoulder Harrow to his feet, taking his weight as I struggle ahead. I am moving too slowly, and the sound of pursuit is right behind me. Without slowing or turning to look, I send a howling wind tearing into those closest, sweeping them off their feet. Cries of distress confirm that I have slowed them a little.

Harrow is coming around. "Auris?"

"You have to help!" I shout at him. "You're too heavy for me!"

He straightens and uses me to support him a moment longer as his strength and sense of balance return. Now we are clear of the smoke, and Ancrow comes limping toward us out of the wormhole's hazy gloom like a wraith. All black, her face as dark as her hair and her clothing, she gathers us in, hissing her relief as if all the air might be going out of her.

"You frightened me!" she gasps. "I thought you were dead!"

The sounds of pursuit are back. I can hear the swish of sword blades and shouts of surprise as those chasing us close in on our soldier phantoms. Ancrow hustles us away, half carrying the still-woozy Harrow by herself. I throw up more images, toss off more magic-formed explosives, trying to maintain the fiction that the entire Fae army is in retreat through the smoky forest. We are all three of us operating in a near-dark miasma of roiling smoke as we push deeper into the wormhole.

Surprisingly, the invaders keep coming, even after realizing the Fae they are encountering are not real. If anything, it seems to enrage them. They know—because they saw it come this way—that the Fae army is somewhere just ahead, and they are determined to catch it.

We stumble, hobble, and drag ourselves onward for long minutes, always battling the fear of being caught. I begin to tire. I don't know how I lasted this long, but my strength is fading trying to mask the inside of the wormhole with only Ancrow to help, and with it the last of my hope. We cannot keep this up for much longer.

Then the floor of the wormhole unexpectedly rises before us in a gentle slope. We climb slowly, unable to move any faster, and the higher we get, the clearer the air is. It becomes easier to see what is happening behind us when we reach the top of the rise and turn back. Mechanized giants appear—five of them—striding toward us, unhindered by smoke or debris or the effects of any explosions. All three of us use our *inish* to form shields, but the giants push through, unhindered. Harrow steps forward. He means to engage them one-on-one—or, in this case, five-on-one.

I grab for him. Just miss.

Ancrow is quicker. She seizes his arm and yanks him back. "Auris!" she shouts. "Clog their gears!"

She takes up the illusion as I instantly summon a substance that will do this and send it seeping into their joints. One by one their machinery seizes up so they cannot move, and they grind to a halt. But behind them come a mass of armored soldiers. This time it is Ancrow who acts while I take back the illusion, knocking our attackers backward with swift blows to their body armor. The magic tumbles them off their feet, leaving them thrashing about in an effort to rise. But even with these small successes, the situation is deteriorating quickly. The wormhole is clogged with Human pursuers and a fresh batch of mechanized warriors, all still coming for us. Ancrow drags me away before any of them can reach us.

"How much farther?" I gasp, the burn in my legs growing stronger.

Harrow looks dazed. "Too far."

Ancrow stops us where we are, hands against our chests. She is gasping for air. "Harrow, I want you to take Auris and go on ahead. Wait for me at the far entrance. I will provide a rear guard."

"No!" I say at once, not even pausing to think. "We stay together."

"Together," Harrow affirms.

Ancrow shakes her head. "Both of you are injured, and I can do this better alone. I can move faster than you can when it is time to catch up."

"No," I repeat. "I won't leave you."

"Nor I," Harrow agrees. He starts stumbling away. "Come on. We go on together."

Ancrow shrugs, suggesting she doesn't care to argue, but I see the look in her eyes and it says something else entirely. She wants us to go ahead. She wants us to leave her.

The chase continues, and the sounds of pursuit grow steadily closer. Our efforts to outdistance the Humans are failing. We are losing this race. I think for a moment about how this will end. If we are caught and brought back to Allensby, he will torment us forever for what we have done. I must avoid being taken alive, no matter the cost. We all must.

Ancrow seems to read my mind. She stops us again. "Wait

here," she orders then walks back a dozen steps. I start after her, but Harrow grabs my arm and pulls me back. "No. Let her be."

Ancrow stands in the center of the wormhole's passageway as I maintain the illusion around her. Armored soldiers and mechanized constructs lumber toward her. I cannot decide what she intends, but I sense her *inish* surfacing as heavy shielding begins to encase her. She is going to attempt to stop the entire army, though I cannot imagine how. Then, suddenly, I can—and I gasp in dismay. I have to do something.

Too late. The leaders of our pursuit emerge from the gloom. One figure shoves forward: an armored soldier wearing a commander's insignia. His visor lifts, revealing a familiar face.

Allensby.

"Give it up!" he shouts at my mother, his smile hard and satisfied. "You and your daughter and all the others will die if you don't. I don't know what chance you think you have. How can you possibly believe you will escape? You can't! There is no escape! It all ends here!"

Ancrow's arms spread wide and lift slowly, almost as if she is signaling her surrender. But I know better. I can feel the magic emanating from her body—huge and gathering strength. "Harrow!" I hiss in dismay.

But Harrow continues to hold me firmly in place and does not respond.

"You've used my child and me for the last time, monster," my mother replies. "It all ends here indeed—but not the way you think."

"Kill her," my father shouts.

Dozens of weapons fire on my mother. I scream in anguish, waiting for her to be ripped apart, but her *inish* shields hold. When the firing ceases and while Allensby is still staring at Ancrow in disbelief, her magic extends to the walls and ceiling of the wormhole and attaches, and suddenly the whole tunnel begins to buckle.

I drop the illusion; there is no point to maintaining it anymore.

Heads look up and to either side as cracks appear and the walls begin to close. Fear surfaces on Allensby's face. My mother is doing now what I thought she would wait to do until we were all clear. She is taking a risk I never believed she would.

She is collapsing the wormhole with us inside it.

Harrow snatches me off my feet, tucks me under one arm, and—in spite of his injuries—begins to run. As we flee, everything turns chaotic. The whole of the Human army is backing away from the impending collapse, unable to accept the obvious, trying to deny what cannot be denied—that they are too deep into the tunnel and too tightly jammed together to get out in time. Cracks are spreading all up and down the entire length of the wormhole— toward the entry we came in through, and the exit we are still trying to reach—the whole of the tunnel tightening down, the walls and ceiling rapidly shrinking. Mother stands before them like a wall, her concentration complete, her arms extended, directing her magic so that it will collapse everything. I call back frantically, screaming at her to run, begging her to save herself. But the frantic cries of the trapped Humans are overwhelming, and nothing else can be heard.

I struggle to break Harrow's grip, but I cannot get free. I try to use my *inish* to free myself, but fail, too exhausted by the loss of what I have already expended. "Harrow, no!" I beg. "Let me go! Please, please, Harrow! Let me go back and save her!"

But there is no saving my mother. She stands where she is as the wormhole collapses around her. She knows she cannot save herself if her efforts are to succeed. Perhaps she always knew. For the Human army to be destroyed, she must sacrifice herself. Perhaps she thought at some point she might not have to. Perhaps. But I don't think so. I think this was always her intention.

Allensby is charging toward her, believing perhaps that if he can reach her in time, he can stop the collapse. Directly above Harrow and me, the wormhole is splitting apart, the forest appearing through the sudden break on either side. Seeing a way to reach safety, Harrow releases me and we leap through the opening together. Tumbling into the foliage, we crouch close together as the edges of the tunnel begin to fold inward, sealing off the Humans and Ancrow. Mother has given us our lives in exchange for hers. Her choice to personally deal with Allensby and his determination to see the Fae destroyed is clear. It began for her more than twenty years ago. Now she will bring about its end. We are to live on, Harrow and I. It is our mother's final gift to us.

My last view of my mother shows Allensby still trying to reach her as the jagged flaps of the wormhole, which has trapped both my parents and the invading army inside, shrink down to almost nothing. Swallowing screams and howls of terror like a snake swallowing its prey, the tunnel winds backward through the trees and disappears.

I squeeze my eyes shut and try not to see anything more.

THIRTY-ONE

I WALK WITH HARROW ON WHAT MUST SURELY BE ONE OF THE
most beautiful days of the year, winding our way along the
wide avenues of our Sylvan home in the Fae land of Viridian Deep.
We pass from the bustle of the traffic that clogs the city's center to
where businesses and shops give way to residences and green spaces.
The sun shines down on me from out of a cloudless blue sky, warming my face and my heart, reminding me how good it feels to be
alive and safe and in love.

The object of my affection looks over and smiles. Almost a
month has passed and his face is almost healed by now, the burns
faded, the cuts and bruises gone. We are both mostly healed—at
least, on the outside.

"I have a surprise for you," Harrow told me earlier when he appeared on my doorstep. "A good one, I think. But you have to put
on especially nice clothes before I can reveal it."

I did so. I wear pants spangled with silver stars that reflect the
sunlight and a silk blouse that drifts about my upper body like a
shimmering cloud. Slippers adorn my feet and bangles hang loosely

on my wrists. I feel pretty for a change, no longer the damaged girl I was when trying to learn to use *inish* or protect my home and family. That part of my life is done. Now I have all the freedom and hope I could possibly ask for. I spend my days playing with Char and Ramey in the parks and walking with Ronden. But mostly I spend them in the company of Harrow.

So much has happened, and time is needed to soften the hard edges of my memories. I will heal, but it will take time.

"You're very quiet," I say to Harrow as we stroll out of the city toward the parks and gardens of Promise Falls.

"I'm thinking," he informs me.

"About what?"

"About you."

"Good thoughts, I hope?"

He glances over again and shakes his head. "You should know by now I never have bad thoughts about you."

After the wormhole closed, swallowing the bulk of the Human invasion force and Ancrow with it, Harrow and I started to walk back toward the Fae army, guarding what was once the entrance to the wormhole. Ronden found us shortly after. She asked about her mother and we told her. She seemed less shaken by the news than I would have expected. I imagine she believed this was what Ancrow intended all along—her way of making up for her failures. She had been unhappy for a long time; she had been living in a shell where she could not be reached by anyone until I appeared. That she chose to sacrifice herself for her people and her family is how facing up to her past and being given a choice of what to do to set things right affected her. Maybe by doing so, she at last found peace and redemption for her tortured mind.

The remnants of the invading army were quickly found and dispatched. The mechanized warriors, the armored vehicles, and the artillery were all rolled, hauled, or dragged to a section of the shoreline where the Roughlin is known to be deep and swift before being dumped into the roiling dark waters to sink from sight. The transports were seized and held; the Fae will take a closer look at how they are built and operated. The few soldiers who remained alive were placed in a small watercraft and warned never to return. Each one was marked, and the marks will be with them forever. If they are found again on Fae shores or if they reveal anything about what happened here, the Fae will know and come looking for them. This last was stretching the truth, but the admonition would have the desired effect.

We returned to the city together, the three of us. The remainder of the army found their own way home at their own pace, and word got around about what had happened and how the Human army had been destroyed. We gave all the credit to Ancrow, and a celebration of her life was held. We also told Ramey and Char what had transpired. I had already resolved that I would be the one who told them; it would be asking too much of Ronden and Harrow. Perhaps they would end up blaming me or disliking me because of what they heard, but I didn't think so. Not for one minute. Our bond would not allow for it.

All this was over and done with more than three weeks ago, but the memories linger and I know this will continue.

I am still not sure how all that has happened and all that I have learned makes me feel. I am struggling with much of it. That my mother might have achieved some form of closure with her past pleases me. That I have lost her forever haunts me. I believed, all along, that what she intended to accomplish did not mean she would have to die. I had been so certain that—even if she failed—we would all somehow come out of this madness intact. But now I have lost all four of my parents—three of them to death and the last to a world I am no longer part of. My family now consists of my sisters and my friends. And Harrow, of course—but he is something much more to me than the others. He is the child with whom my mother replaced me, my rescuer when I was lost in the wastelands and hunted by Goblins, my teacher and trainer in my early days in Viridian, and the one who believed from the first that I belonged to this land.

And now he is my great love, and my fondest wish for the future is that I be able to keep him close always. So when he tells me I never elicit anything but good thoughts in him, it warms me all the way through and I think that anything is possible.

We walk into the gardens and through the vast array of flower beds and blooming vines on our way to the waterfall. He reaches for my hand and I give it to him willingly. I would give him anything, and I know this will always be so. I squeeze his hand to suggest what I am thinking. For a few moments, at least, the past and its harsh moments fade and there is only Harrow and me. I take a moment to revel in how special I feel. I don't dress up often, so this feels like I have given myself a gift. I still don't see myself as anything special, but I like knowing that Harrow sees something more. This is how he makes me feel all the time—beautiful and precious to him.

How good it feels to be able to think this way. How lovely to imagine it might be true.

"Let's walk down there," Harrow suggests, indicating the small flat-stone viewing platform on the lake directly across from Promise Falls.

I let him lead me down and stand with him on the uneven layer of stones, looking over at the towering falls as water spills from several hundred feet up. The way the sunlight reflects against the sheen of the tumbling water forms a rainbow of dazzling, clearly identifiable colors. Harrow looks at it with a strange mix of disbelief and pleasure, then exhales sharply. I end up staring at him in confusion.

He turns to me. "You know how some things are just too perfect to be true?"

I cock an eyebrow. "I know that it doesn't happen often."

"Well, you just saw it right there." He takes my hands and stands squarely in front me. "I have a great favor to ask of you. I have reason to think you might grant it, but I will understand if you choose not to. I am deeply, hopelessly in love with you—and I have been since the first time I saw you. I am so in love with you that I cannot imagine not having you with me always. Auris Afton Grieg, I wish to partner with you. I want us to be together for the rest of our lives. I am already yours; now I am begging for you to be mine."

I stare at him. All the air goes out of me, and at the same time I flush with the heat of what his words make me feel. I keep my eyes on his, imagining myself falling into them as I have done so many times before. My answer is right there in my heart, waiting for me to deliver it. But my mind knows it is not this simple.

"How many of the Sylvan people will accept this union, Harrow?" I ask. "I don't look like a Sylvan. And my background is different from theirs. Up until I found you, I lived my life as a Human. How hard will things be for you once you ally yourself this firmly with me?"

He shrugs, his expression stubborn and set. "Does it matter?"

"You know it does."

"Nothing that others think makes any difference to me. Not having you with me every minute of every day is what matters— which is exactly why I am asking you to partner with me."

"You can be with me anyway," I point out. "You can have me with you as much and as often as you want. We don't need to partner."

"I think we do," he disagrees. "Commitment matters, and I want everyone to know that I have chosen you."

I shake my head. "Even if it costs you Viridian Deep? I might not be Fae enough for the Sylvan community to allow us to remain here."

His patience is slipping. "Is this conversation really necessary? Must we consider all the possible obstacles to partnering before we do so?" He pauses, squeezing my hands hard. "What does your heart tell you? Forget everything else. What does your heart say?"

I stare at him, measuring the extent of his determination, and melt. "It tells me to stop talking and say yes. It says I will never find anyone to love the way I love you. It says to kiss you right now."

So I kiss him, and he kisses me back. I close my eyes as we hold the kiss, and I feel something shift inside me—a mix of heat and movement and deep release that I cannot understand and don't care to. I don't want to do anything but kiss Harrow. I want to kiss him forever. I want this kiss to never end.

But when we do end it and I open my eyes to look into his, I see sudden disbelief mirrored there. "Auris!" he whispers, a sense of surprise and wonder in his voice. He reaches out to stroke my hair, then takes a few strands and lifts them in front of me. "Look!"

I glance down, discovering what he already has. Tiny leaves, pale as jade, are budding out all over, unfurling in the sunlight.

My Changeling identity has finally awakened. I no longer look entirely Human. I am beginning to look a little like one of the Fae.

Like I am supposed to look.

Like Ronden, my sister.

I can feel the smile as it forms on my lips, knowing I am one step closer to home.

If you loved *Child of Light*,
be sure not to miss Auris's continuing story in

DAUGHTER
OF DARKNESS

TERRY BROOKS

Coming in Fall 2022

Here is a special preview.

T HE GOBLINS COME FOR US IN THE EARLY MORNING HOURS, the heavy cloud cover blocking both moon and stars, rendering them all but invisible. The Ertl warns us, its piercing chirp waking us instantly. Harrow and I, lying next to each other in bed, roll out and stand silently facing each other.

Goblins, again. At first it was a surprise; now it is business as usual. You would think we would be done with Goblin intrusions. We thought we had sent the last of them packing almost two years ago—just before the Human invasion led by my father. The invasion that my mother put an end to. Yet here they are, returned once more. Five times in two months.

It was frightening in my early days in Viridian Deep; now it is mostly an annoyance. We don't even know what they are trying to do or what they want. It was me they wanted in the old days. They came for me twice then—sent once by my mother and once by my father. But that is the distant past. My birth parents are both dead, and there have been no Goblin threats since.

Until now, when suddenly they've started up again.

But why? What is the point of coming after us now? Who is responsible for these most recent intrusions?

The front door creaks slightly as it opens—something Harrow engineered to give us warning after the first two nighttime visits. The Ertl is a further safeguard, and a more reliable one. You can sleep through the creaking of a door, but you cannot sleep through the chirp of an Ertl.

The Ertl is a forest bird, but it can be domesticated and trained to perform simple functions. This, as it happens, is one of Harrow's specialties. It took him less than two weeks to turn the Ertl into an early warning system, and it has paid off. We now keep the bird caged in the house each night—and three times it has alerted us to these Goblin attacks—including tonight's. Goblins have been enemies of the Sylvans since forever, and Harrow and I know them well.

Though perhaps I know them better, for I did spend five years in a Goblin prison.

We creep over to our closed bedroom door and stand waiting patiently. We have trained rigorously for moments like these. We know without any communication what we need to do. The front door closes, and soft, cautious footsteps approach our hiding place. They must believe we are sleeping. You would think they might have learned better by now.

I look over at Harrow. His deep green skin is striped with shadows, and the tiny leaves that grow in his hair are rumpled as if knocked about by a strong wind. *Rats nest.* I mouth the word so he can read it on my lips, remembering the term from my time in the Goblin prison. He touches his hair in response and then points to my head. I reach up to find my leafy locks as tousled as his. The momentary look he gives me is one of irritation. His patience with these invasions is at an end. I nod my understanding. Another day, another infestation of Goblins.

We considered moving to a different residence to discourage these incursions, but this has been my home since the first day Harrow found me in the wastelands—a nineteen-year-old girl who had managed to survive for twelve days with almost no food or water. It was Harrow who first told me of the existence of the Fae and suggested that I might be one of them—even though I did not look it. It was Harrow who later took me back to the Human world and the city of Harbor's End to find out the truth—a truth so horrendous that it nearly destroyed any hopes we harbored for a life together.

But love endures. We loved each other then and we do so now, and we remain committed to the promise we made when we partnered: that this would never change.

Still, so much of my past remains a mystery, so much of who I was before my time in the prisons a dark vacancy in my mind. No amount of effort to discover the truth has uncovered my past; the long stretch between what little I remember of my childhood and my incarceration is a deep empty hole in my life. I have promised myself I will find all that is missing from my memory, but to date I have discovered so little.

And that will not change today.

I focus on Harrow as the footsteps stop at our doorway, and he smiles in quick reassurance. We have been here before. We have survived worse.

The door bursts open, practically ripped from its hinges, and the Goblins surge in. The foremost pair carry nets with which to snare and bind us so we cannot use our weapons, should we have one or two close at hand. Five times they have come at us this way, and they *still* don't get it. Regular weapons are unnecessary. We have our *inish* and we carry that inside us—always at the ready, always just a second's thought away from surfacing. In this case, it doesn't even take that long, since we already hold it at our fingertips.

The two that follow the net bearers wield blades and axes. They are so certain of themselves, these Goblin intruders, that they exercise little caution. They look neither left nor right, but straight toward the empty bed before they realize the truth. And by then it is too late. Harrow and I have used our *inish* to propel the rear Goblins violently ahead into their companions, so that all four are knocked off balance. By that time, Harrow and I are out the bedroom door behind them and charging down the hallway. The front door stands open, and we rush through into the open air.

Here, atop the second level of the treelane on which our cottage sits—not much more than fifty feet from Ancrow's house where Ronden now lives with her sisters Ramey and Char—we turn to fight.

It is a deliberate choice, made shortly after the last bunch of Goblins tried to catch us off guard. Why wreck our bedroom when we can deal with the matter outside? Plus, there is more space to maneuver out here, with less chance of being cornered by cottage walls. Not to mention the possibility of someone from the nearby houses coming to our aid. Not that we can't handle four Goblins easily enough, but with hand-to-hand combat, there is always the risk of something going wrong.

It doesn't seem likely to now. The furious Goblins burst back out through the front door and come for us, a disorganized melee armed with nets and blades, but they never get close. Using a combined web of *inish* we have practiced assembling and casting, Harrow and I scoop the Goblins up and throw them screaming off the elevated walkway. They continue to scream as they tumble away. It is almost a hundred feet to the ground below. When they land, the screams stop.

Maybe I should care about the damage I've inflicted—maybe I should feel remorse or regret—but I don't. I am sick and tired of being hunted, and of the Goblins, both.

But when I turn to Harrow, I find his attention fixed on something else, and I regret my earlier confidence.

Not a dozen feet away stands an armored giant.

This is no exaggeration. The giant is eight feet tall and broad across the shoulders and chest, with huge arms and tree-trunk legs. It is encased in metal—and I'm not talking just armor-plating. No, what covers this beast is more on the order of a second skin— a form-fitting, flexible coating that I can tell would shimmer and reflect in the light. I have never seen anything like it. If this being has a face, I can't tell. A helmet encases its entire head, hiding its features entirely. Black light flickers from behind an opaque face-plate, as if something liquid is contained within.

Strangely, it carries no weapons. Its arms hang loose; its hands are empty. There are no blades strapped to its body. But its size alone is intimidating, so I suppose that makes some sense. What does something this large need with weapons?

Harrow and I exchange a look. The giant has squared off with him, meaning Harrow is the one it thinks the most dangerous. Little does it know. If we have to fight, I will change its mind quickly enough.

We wait for its attack, but it just stands there. Where did it come from? I don't remember seeing it when we rushed from the cottage. Is it allied with the Goblins? I think it must be, yet it seems not to know what it should do next.

I watch its head move slightly as its gaze travels from Harrow to me, and now I can sense it looking at me more closely. As it does, something odd happens. Almost as if it is startled, it takes a step back. I read all this from one small movement, and yet I am certain I am not mistaken.

"What do we do now?" I ask Harrow quietly.

He shakes his head, then takes a step away from me. As he does, the giant moves with him—a clear indication it will not allow us to get past. Well, at least we know one reason it is standing there. I take a step in the other direction, but the giant doesn't respond. It has indeed chosen to focus on Harrow rather than me. I should be grateful—and I am. But I am also oddly irritated to be seen as less of a threat.

A burst of activity from Ancrow's house catches our attention. The front door flies open and Char appears, rushing to the rescue once more. Her thick mane of leafy hair is flying out behind her as she pelts toward us with a stout cudgel in hand. I admire my little sister's pluck, but despair at her lack of caution. Once before, when I first came to Viridian Deep, she charged to my rescue in a foolish display of bravado and love. That time, I was able to save her. This time, I don't know if I can.

When she sees the giant, she skids to a stop at once, the cudgel lowering as she realizes what confronts us. Then, "You get away!" she shouts, raising the cudgel once more, demonstrating her determination to take action. "Get away right now!"

Where in the world, I wonder, are Ronden and Ramey? How are they managing to sleep through all this? As I glance about, I wonder the same about all the residents bedded down in the darkened homes surrounding the square. No one has appeared. Are they all such sound sleepers? Or do they simply think it unwise to interfere?

"Char," Harrow says in his calm, measured way, "go back inside, please. Let us handle this."

The giant seems content to let that happen. It has barely glanced at Char since her emergence and doesn't bother to do so now as she slowly backs away toward her house. I glance again at the other houses for some indication of help but find nothing. It seems that Harrow and I will need to manage this threat alone.

If there even is a threat. Thus far, the giant hasn't approached us; it just seems intent on blocking our path. I take a moment to consider why. The elevated treelane continues to wind through the old growth toward the west end of the city, past a scattering of houses that sit mostly to one side.

One of which is Ancrow's, into which Char has just disappeared.

Suddenly I realize what is happening.

"Char!" I scream, and rush forward.

Harrow is a step behind me, and it is he that the giant continues to evaluate, ignoring me completely. My *inish* is already gathered, so I send every bit of power I can summon hammering into the giant, but the creature barely reacts, as if my strike was no more than a bothersome breeze. I scream at Harrow to run, to find help, but he ignores me and advances on the giant. When the two collide, the sound is audible. Harrow gives his best, but the giant is too much for him, breaking his grip and shoving him aside. Then it comes for me. For something this huge, it is amazingly quick. It is on me before I can reach Ancrow's house, its huge arms drawing me into its grasp. But Ronden's lessons on overpowering a stronger foe have stayed with me and I use my *inish* to spray the planking in a wide slick that takes its giant's feet out from under it the moment it touches me. It topples and skids away in a thrashing heap—though it does not follow the first Goblins off the treelane.

Still, this gives me enough time to reach Ancrow's house and rush inside. Ronden lies unconscious in the hallway and Ramey pounds on the closet door from inside. Goblins have hold of Char and are hauling her toward the doorway in which I stand. I am debating how to stop them when huge hands grab me from behind and lift me off the floor. The giant has me, and the Goblins rush past us with Char in their grip. I see the fear in her eyes.

Then all three are out the door and gone.

I try to use my *inish* to break free, but the giant has been paying attention. One hand holds both of mine locked together, while the other covers my mouth. It looks into my eyes, studying me. No, not just studying me. Identifying me.

This creature *knows* me!

I stare back. "Who are you?" I snap.

But the giant simply sets me aside—almost gently—and goes out the door after the Goblins, swiftly disappearing over the side of the treelane. I scramble up and rush after it, almost colliding with Harrow as he arrives in the door. Without speaking, he points to where the giant leaped off the pathway, and we charge over to look down. We catch just a glimpse of it disappearing into the darkness, accelerating so quickly it is gone almost instantly.

"Char!" I scream and start in the direction I think the Goblins have taken. Harrow starts to follow, but I shout over my shoulder, "No! Go back! Ronden needs you! Don't worry about me!"

He hesitates, but then turns around and I tear down the nearest stairs after Char's captors. The giant must have been with them; there is no other explanation for its behavior. It will follow them, so I must go after it. I do this without stopping to consider what I am risking. How can I not? This is Char we are talking about. Char, for whom I would do anything.

Once at ground level, I turn into the darkness where the giant disappeared. It is so quick; I am not sure I can catch it. But if it is with the Goblins, it will have to slow down. Goblins are strong but slow-moving. What I will do once I catch them remains to be seen, but I will have to come up with something—especially if the giant is with them.

As I run, I remember how the creature looked at me as if it knew me. But I have never encountered anything like it—or at least, not that I recall. Which might be the crux of the issue. Though I have learned a lot about myself in the past two years, I still don't recall more than fragments of my past before I entered the Goblin prison. Still, it doesn't look to be Fae, and it is certainly not Human. I can think of no one and nothing I have encountered that might fit the description.

Yet it seems to know me. It doesn't make sense.

I push on through the network of buildings and shops that is Viridian Deep, further into darkness until no artificial lights are visible and the only illumination that guides me comes from the moon and stars, now revealed as the cloud cover lifts. I have not yet caught sight of those I track, but my instincts—which I have come to trust implicitly—tell me they are not far ahead. I skirt a series of small ponds and head toward a broad stretch of heavily wooded hills. There are Goblin settlements north of where the Sylvan territory ends, but all of them are miles off, and I doubt that Char's kidnappers intend to travel all night. More likely, they will stop to rest a little farther on—perhaps no more than another few miles.

It grows more isolated and lonelier, and I find myself wishing Harrow had accompanied me after all. But I couldn't let him leave an unconscious Ronden behind, with Ramey locked in a closet.

I reflect briefly on my family, and how close we have all become. We were kindred spirits from the start—even before we knew we were related by blood or adoption. Ronden and I are half-sisters, and the only blood children of Ancrow, while the younger girls are adopted—and Harrow, too, although he didn't know it until my arrival turned his world upside down. But even in the midst of that chaos, Harrow was my rock, and the girls were my champions. When Ancrow died, we bonded even more tightly. Ronden moved home to stay with Ramey and Char while Harrow and I, now partnered, remained in the cottage down the lane.

But still, there was one thing that kept me separated from them, and that was my physical appearance—for I looked completely Human. Or I did, until right after Harrow and I pledged at Promise Falls. Then my hair, sleek and dark, began to take on a greenish tint, little leaves blossomed among the strands, and my feeling of alienation lessened. Since then, I have begun to assume further Sylvan characteristics. Now, my skin is changing from Human olive to Sylvan pine. My hair has begun to sprout more of those soft tiny leaves that always make me want to run my fingers through Harrow's locks, and the undersides of my arms and the insides of my legs have exhibited a steady growth of short fringe from shoulders to wrists and thighs to feet.

I am not entirely altered; further change will take more time. Or maybe I am already as Sylvan as my body will allow—whether that be from my half-Human heritage, or because of whatever my adoptive father's medicines might have messed with in his efforts to keep me looking Human and safe in a world hostile to the Fae.

One day, I tell myself, I will know. One day, I will know everything.

I have reached the boundary of the city, and I pause to see if there is any indication of where to go next, but I have lost the trail. I stand rooted in place as the darkness looms ahead, trying to figure out what to do next. I should go back. I should find Harrow and return in daylight to track the Goblins and the giant when I can see evidence of their passing. But I dislike the idea of giving up.

Just a little farther, I think. Char is depending on me. I will walk another mile and then turn back and begin again when the night fades.

I set out once more, searching out anything that will confirm I am on the right track. I work my way deeper into the trees, catching a glimpse of an owl as it flies past and listening to the distant sounds of night birds hunting. But I can see no traces of the Goblin trail. Either I have missed a sign or I have misinterpreted what my instincts told me earlier. I have to give up for tonight. I have to turn back.

Yet when I attempt to do so, I find myself face-to-face with the giant.

It blocks my way like a wall, staring down at me. My heart is in my throat. How did it manage to get so close without me knowing?

I consider running, but know I won't make it past the first two steps. And as I hesitate, the giant picks me up like a toy and holds me in front of its concealed face.

Again, I am being studied, examined in a way that suggests familiarity. Its head cocks one way and then the other, and it moves me close to its faceplate. I cannot see inside, but I can feel its eyes on me.

A deep rumbling rises up from within. "Auris?"

I stare in shock. It *does* recognize me. It knows me.

"Auris?" it asks again.

And suddenly, I know that voice. Something about it . . . Something is familiar . . .

But it can't be.

"Malik?"

The shock is profound. His voice is not the same, yet the inflection and the tone both attest to the same truth. Malik is alive.

"Malik?" I say again. "Is it really you?"

The giant shifts me in its grip, just enough to confirm what I already know. "It's me."

"But I thought you were dead!"

"As I thought you were."

"No. I was just roughed up and knocked unconscious when I was thrown from the ATV. But you were inside, with the others, when it crashed."

"And they died—everyone but me and Khoury. We ran. Got split up. She was caught first; I could hear it happening. They took her back. Is she dead?"

"She is. She was shot."

"At least it was quick. What happened to you? Why do you look like one of the Fae now? You've got greenish skin and leaves in your hair!"

"I am a Forest Sylvan—or at least half Sylvan. It's a long story. What about you? You look different, too. How did you get to be so big? And why do you look like a robot?"

His laugh is deep and unpleasant. "Yes, my new look. An example of what technology and a twisted imagination can create. Is anyone with you?"

"Can you put me down so we can talk?"

Malik shakes his massive head. "Can't do that, Auris."

Vintage Malik. Straight to the point. He never used more words than he had to when we were imprisoned together, and his tone of voice says that he means what he is saying. "Can't or won't?"

"Does it make a difference? I let you go once already when I realized who you might be. I hoped you wouldn't follow. But you disappointed me."

He let me go deliberately. What is going on? "If you let me go once, why won't you let me go again now?"

"If I do, will you turn back and stop following me?"

I consider lying. Decide not to. "I can't. That little girl? That's my sister, and I want her back."

"We all want something we can't have."

I can hear the regret in his voice, but I am not sure if it is directed toward me or him or both. "Will you take me to her?" I ask.

He makes a snorting sound. "The Goblins took her to get to you. They couldn't find another way. I didn't know who you were or maybe I could have stopped them. I didn't realize you were the one they were after."

"Would it have made a difference? Are we still friends?"

"Difference? Probably not. Friends? Always."

"Then help me get her back to her family."

He sighs inside his helmet, an odd wheezing sound. A shrug. "I can't do as much as you think."

Again, regret is evident in his words. I frown at him. "I would think you could do almost anything you wanted."

"I could say the same about you. You've got that Fae magic, don't you? That way you hit me, trying to get past? I felt that. Where does your magic come from? You didn't have it in the prison. How did they make you like them?"

"I was always like them," I answer. "If you put me down, I will tell you everything. And you can tell me everything, too. We owe it to each other. We're all that's left of our friends, and I have so many questions. How did you get so big? I mean, you were always big, but not . . . like this." I pause. "Can you take that helmet off and show me your face? I want to see what you look like now."

His laugh is harsh. "No, you don't. No time, anyway; I have to catch up to the others. But I'll take you with me. At least you can be with your sister."

"Goblin prisoners, the both of us? Sounds delightful. Are we to be hung and dismembered?"

Malik's posture changes—a suggestion of discomfort. "The Goblins won't touch you. They want you for someone else—for my creator." His voice changes as he says this. Whoever did this to him is someone he hates. "But Chorech—that's the Goblin leader—was clear: no one is to hurt you or your sister. I promise, Auris. I won't let anything happen."

"And is that a promise you'll be able to keep?"

He doesn't answer. "I need your promise that you won't use your magic. Not for anything. Not in the littlest way. And I need you to promise you won't run off. You wouldn't get far, anyway."

I nod my agreement. "I've seen how fast you are. I promise not to use magic or to try to run. You know my word is good."

"I do, or I wouldn't have bothered asking for it."

He sets me down carefully, surveys me for a moment, then nods.

It seems he knows about my *inish*, and how it works. Nevertheless, I will not do anything to endanger Char.

Our pact made, we start walking, with Malik leading the way and me following. Whatever else happens, I have to get Char back before I can think about freeing myself. I cannot bear for anything to happen to her, no matter what happens to me as a result. . . .

TERRY BROOKS has thrilled readers for decades with his powers of imagination and storytelling. He is the author of more than forty books, most of which have been *New York Times* bestsellers. He lives with his wife, Judine, in the Pacific Northwest.

terrybrooks.net
Facebook.com/authorterrybrooks
Twitter: @TerryBrooks
Instagram: @officialterrybrooks

ABOUT THE TYPE

This book was set in Goudy Old Style, a typeface designed by Frederic William Goudy (1865–1947). Goudy began his career as a bookkeeper, but devoted the rest of his life to the pursuit of "recognized quality" in a printing type.

Goudy Old Style was produced in 1914 and was an instant bestseller for the foundry. It has generous curves and smooth, even color. It is regarded as one of Goudy's finest achievements.

EXPLORE THE WORLDS OF DEL REY BOOKS

READ EXCERPTS
from hot new titles.

STAY UP-TO-DATE
on your favorite authors.

FIND OUT about exclusive
giveaways and sweepstakes.

CONNECT WITH US ONLINE!
⊙ ⨍ 🐦 @DelReyBooks